Toward the Gleam

TOWARD THE GLEAM

·A NOVEL·
BY T·M·DORAN

IGNATIUS PRESS · SAN FRANCISCO

Cover and title page illustrated by Daniel Mitsui

Cover design by John Herreid

© 2011 Ignatius Press, San Francisco
All rights reserved
ISBN 978-1-58617-633-4
Library of Congress Control Number 2010931311
Printed in the United States of America ∞

CONTENTS

Come my friends,
'Tis not too late to seek a newer world.
Push off, and sitting well in order smite
The sounding furrows; for my purpose holds
To sail beyond the sunset, and the baths
Of all the western stars, until I die.

Alfred, Lord Tennyson

PART I

Discooperire

November 8, 1972

Saint Hugh's Charterhouse, Sussex

Porter broke silence. That was no little thing, but the breaking of his silence was as nothing in comparison with the breaking of that other silence.

Abbot was surprised to see Porter at his door, as the time for Compline was near. A visitor at this hour was out of the ordinary, so he wondered if something was troubling the young man. Abbot decided after his election that he must be available to the brothers, day and night, whenever they needed him. For a contemplative man, it had not been an easy transition. It was still not easy.

"A Mr. Hill would like to see you, Abbot", Porter said.

Abbot gave him a look that Porter immediately understood.

"He understands our Rule, but he insists."

Abbot said, "What is his business?"

"He didn't say."

Would Porter have asked him? That would depend, Abbot concluded. If the visitor seemed unscrupulous, or desperate, Porter would have seen to it himself; he had the authority to do so. Porter's presence here meant that the visitor was another sort of person, someone who would not be pressed for an explanation, someone with gravity, someone who warranted disturbing Abbot, and maybe Compline.

Abbot said, "You may show him in." He experienced a momentary self-incrimination for the anticipation he felt in awaiting the visitor, an anticipation superior to that which he had felt for Compline. Not that this realization bothered Abbot too much. Examination of conscience was a way of life for him, as natural as breathing.

It was cool in the bare room and colder outside than early November ought to be. Frost was on the ground that morning. Fortunately, everything needed for winter was in the stores, and it had been a good season, thank God. He could hear stirring in the corridor; he knew it to be the brothers going to chapel. They would wonder where he and Porter were; they were prayerful men, yes, men of God, but still men. They would wonder what kept their abbot from night prayer.

When Porter showed the visitor into the room, Abbot saw before him an old man, in his seventies, at least, with thinning hair. His features could be described as craggy but not unjovial. He cradled under one arm, carefully it seemed to Abbot—as if it contained a baby, or was filled with eggs—a large wooden box. The visitor was tentative, fingering the weather-beaten hat he held in the other hand.

"Welcome", Abbot said, with more formality than he intended. Porter started to leave, but Abbot motioned him back.

"Sit, please", said Abbot to the visitor, who sat in a wooden chair before an age-darkened table that functioned as Abbot's desk, tea table, and workbench. Porter stepped to one side and stood there, awkwardly it seemed to Abbot, who wondered if Porter was worried that admitting the old man would reflect poorly on his judgment. Abbot concluded that it would be even more awkward to dismiss the young man now. Besides, Porter was observant; he might be helpful. If this matter turned out to be altogether mundane, Abbot said to himself, he would make it a point to put Porter at his ease.

Had he seen this fellow before? Those features, the wry smile on the old man's face, seemed familiar. Hill ... that didn't ring a bell. The visitor looked comfortable enough—that was a good sign—with the box on his lap and the battered hat on top of the box.

On those rare occasions when Abbot met someone from outside the community, he was invariably struck by the other person's need to move, to talk. Not everyone exhibited this behavior to the same degree, but Abbot observed that constant engagement with the world had a way of producing it. He already suspected that this man was different, for he was at peace, or so it seemed.

The man spoke in a soft voice, so that one had to pay careful attention to comprehend what he was saying. "I am terribly sorry to disturb you."

Abbot was tempted to wave this apology off but decided to wait.

"My name is Hill ..."

"May I get you a cup of tea, or a glass of ale, Mr. Hill?" Abbot said in reply.

The visitor's eyes lit up. "I haven't had ale for some time, if it isn't too much trouble."

"No trouble at all", Abbot said. "We brew our own." He didn't have to say a word to Porter, who silently exited the room.

"I know this is irregular", Hill said. "The decision was not taken carelessly, I assure you."

The man's English was impeccable, though not his oratorical skills, Abbot thought. His guest had a tendency to be less audible, to mumble, as he progressed with an idea. Fortunately, the room was quiet, and Abbot was a patient listener. He wondered what the visitor wanted. It had to be connected to the box—a donation to the Order? The box was about eighteen inches long, more than twelve inches wide, and perhaps six inches in depth—unwieldy. The wood was nothing special: pine, sanded but unvarnished and unpainted, soiled.

Abbot noticed how dark the room had become. The time of year brought with it troubling sensations, even to him, the father of the community. The deficit of light in the house as autumn waned had become a physical challenge as Abbot aged, but the spiritual darkness that accompanied the season was the harder part.

Porter had returned unnoticed, like a ghost, with a glass of ale and a small cake on a tray. Spectral movement was more commonly a trait of the older brothers, who had, in a sense, practiced this skill for years. To discover this aptitude in one so young was disconcerting to Abbot.

"Thank you", the old man said, with genuine warmth. His smile, incongruous amidst those cracked and creased features, was childlike. "You may set it on the box."

The visitor sat like a circus performer, with his cumbersome box, the hat, and now the tray with the ale and cake all balanced on his spindly legs. Without being asked, Porter lit another lamp. Now there was more light, and more shadows. The old man leisurely nibbled at the cake; he seemed to be in no hurry, and neither was Abbot, who could hear—faintly—the chanting of the brothers down the hall.

"Your cake is excellent", the visitor said.

"It's honey cake. We keep bees."

The visitor grinned. "I don't suppose you have to worry about bears."

"Not for some hundreds of years."

"Too bad", the old man observed.

If Abbot was as good a judge of character as he believed himself to be, then this statement by Hill contained not a trace of irony; that is, the man honestly believed that it was too bad bears didn't frequent these parts.

He set down the cake and put the glass to his lips, muttering something that sounded like "furthering" or "fathering". "First-class ale", he said.

"Thank you", Abbot said, more perfunctorily than he ought to have done, but when he was pondering something he could not help being abrupt. "Is your car in the yard?" The best parking was on the south side, where the ale was stored and sold. It had rained earlier, and the visitor's car wouldn't be the first to mire in the mud.

"I do not drive", the man answered with some enthusiasm. "I hired a car to take me to town and made a hike from there."

Could this be true? Abbot wondered. The old man was not an invalid, but he did not seem to be in robust health either. From what he'd observed, Abbot would have said he was rickety. That "hike" was every bit of three miles, and it was cold, dark, and damp outside. The box was not massive, but it wasn't a trifle either. Porter nodded discreetly; he would check to see if a car was in the yard.

Remarkable. Was the man mad? Abbot had known men who made a convincing pretense of sanity but were hopelessly—Abbot tried not to use that word—insane. He resolved to accept this "diagnosis", if proven accurate, with equanimity and goodwill. Would the ale reveal the man's true state of mind sooner?

"It was hillier than I imagined it would be." The visitor grinned again. Was the pun intentional? Abbot thought so but then cautioned himself; some madmen possess a keen sense of humor.

The visitor examined the room while he was eating and drinking. Several times, his eyes locked on Abbot's as if probing or seeking something. Abbot wasn't in the least distressed by this. By the time the old man finished his ale and cake, Porter had silently returned. With a shake of his head, he confirmed the absence of a car. He removed the tray and set it on a small corner table. As if a magnet had drawn them, the visitor's hands went to the sides of the box, so that he presented the image of a supplicant, or one of the Magi.

Without looking at Porter, Hill said, "I mean no offense— none whatsoever—but I would speak with the abbot alone, if I may."

No offense would be taken by Porter, Abbot reflected, but was it wise to dismiss him, to be alone with this old man who pricked his memory, who had come from nowhere, on foot no less? Porter inclined his head, and Abbot did likewise. He watched Porter leave the room and close the door; he wasn't going to allow that pup to amaze him with another vanishing act.

"What is your Christian name?" Abbot asked Hill.

Was there hesitation? There was, but very few would have detected it.

"John."

Abbot said, "It's late in the day and late in the year, John Hill, to be wandering the hills of Sussex."

The old man's face split into a wide smile, a delighted smile, it seemed. "I suppose it will be my last adventure", he said.

"Who can say?" said Abbot mechanically, though something told him that the old man had not made this statement frivolously.

"I have a story to tell, if you will indulge me. It is quite a fantastic story, and only one other living person knows it."

Abbot decided to let the man speak. One could learn much by allowing the other person to speak, by listening without thinking about what one would say next.

"You will not be inclined to believe me, but I know something of your Order and something about its abbot. I made a judgment that I will get a better hearing from you, and a greater probability of a favorable ending, than with anyone else."

A better hearing? A favorable ending? What could be in that box? Abbot was prepared for anything, even for a heap of sand the old man would claim—no doubt passionately—he could turn into gold.

"You are pondering whether I'm mad", Hill continued. "I imagine the temptation to dismiss me as a lunatic will grow stronger as I proceed with my story. I'm resigned to that, and am even prepared for it. I said I expected to get a better hearing, but I do not hope for a sympathetic one. You see, my dear Abbot, I am old and desperate; I could not delay. I had to take the risk. Time is short."

Abbot was tempted to feel flattered, but the old man could also be trying to manipulate him. Or was his visitor so deluded that the reality he had created for himself was girded with something like logical consistency?

"Regardless," the man continued, "thank you for your courtesy. It was a more difficult journey to your charterhouse than I had expected. This starling no longer follows the flock south and back again. A little exertion and I must rest. The cake and ale were indeed welcome, more so than you can imagine."

"How may I serve you?" Abbot said with genuine conviction. Mad or no, he liked the old man.

The visitor's eyes gazed into his. "I appeal—that is not a strong enough word—I entreat you to abandon yourself to Mystery."

Without an explanation or further embellishment, Abbot knew that the word had been capitalized in the old man's meaning.

The visitor continued, "It is important that no one knows I am here. That is the reason I traveled after dusk."

Abbot's mind was racing. Paranoia? What was in that box? Who was he?

"This is a beautiful place", Hill said. "Peace pervades it. Perhaps I have not erred in coming." Abbot could tell that the comment was more self-directed than intended for him. "I have with me an antiquity", Hill continued. His left hand caressed the box with affection, or maybe the gesture was meant to direct Abbot's attention to the box, but what did Abbot, or the Charterhouse for that matter, have to do with antiquities? True, there were objects within these walls that might be considered valuable artifacts, but this was not so much a matter of collection or acquisition as it was of ordinary items simply becoming old. The monastery was not a museum, though some outside the premises so considered it. Abbot could feel his emotional heels digging in, as they often did when he sensed that someone considered the Order irrelevant. Was this stranger just seeking a museum for his so-called treasure?

Did the visitor anticipate Abbot's objection? Whether he did or did not, his next words addressed Abbot's apprehensions. "If this were an ordinary antiquity, I would not have come here. I daresay the British Museum could find space for it. You may come to agree that this is a priceless antiquity, but I am here for an altogether different reason: this Mystery must remain a secret."

Abbot chewed on this pronouncement. He was interested now and would be disappointed if the old man turned out to be a lunatic. He said, "Mr. Hill, you traveled by car from"—Abbot gave him time to speak, but the visitor did not offer his place of origin—"and then walked three miles over hills in the cold and wet darkness, carrying this ... antiquity. Why do this, unless you intend to reveal the secret that will reveal this Mystery?"

The old man extended both hands. "Just that. Why would I reveal the secret that I so desire to remain a secret?"

Abbot could hear the brothers returning from Compline. Porter would not have said a word, not only for the sake of discretion but also for the sake of the Great Silence that descended upon the abbey after night prayer. Abbot had missed the calming effect of the prayer that closes the day, and now the Rule required that brothers and guests alike quietly turn in for the night.

"Will you stay with us tonight?" Abbot asked.

For the first time, the old man looked genuinely troubled. "I never intended to. My car arrived late, and the walk from town took longer than I expected; but I must not impose upon you. I'll walk back."

"Nonsense," Abbot said. "It's much too late for that. We have a room prepared for guests, and you can't leave without another glass of ale", he said cordially, hoping the man was less stubborn than he seemed and calculating that another round of ale would settle the matter. For a moment, distress was displayed on the visitor's features. Then he bowed to Abbot, who was already making for the door.

Abbot's long strides took him down three corridors. His sandals made hardly a sound against the worn stone floor. The alehouse was quiet and practically dark, with only a small night lamp burning. After so many years, Abbot could have navigated the place with his eyes closed. He was weary, for his day had begun very early, but the fresh, crisp scent of fermenting hops invigorated him as he filled two glasses with the golden brown liquid.

When he returned to the room, the old man sat as if he hadn't moved a muscle, as if both box and visitor were inanimate objects. Abbot gave him his glass and then tapped it with his own before taking a drink. People came from Ireland,

Scotland, and the Continent to sample Charterhouse ale, and Abbot never tired of its refreshing bittersweetness.

John Hill said, "The cake and this ale have made a feast."

"A meager one, I'm afraid", Abbot rejoined.

But the old man said, "I have reached an age when I would trade ten more-than-ample meals for one morsel or sip of something delightful. Do you understand?"

Abbot nodded and then wondered if this man were so much different from the brothers, in spite of his jacket and hat and town life, but not even he, a man who often looked into hearts, could be certain—not yet.

"Did you bring an overnight bag?" Abbot asked. He had almost forgotten the box in his solicitude for the visitor.

"I'm afraid I came with just what you see. I can manage."

"Let us see what can be arranged", Abbot said.

"I'm in your debt."

"Hardly", Abbot protested. "You are a guest."

The old man's eyes moistened. "Perhaps I have made a wise choice after all."

Abbot wondered if the old man was referring to the overland hike, or the absence of a night bag, or something else.

"Are you happy here?" the visitor asked him.

Abbot was taken aback, not because he did not know the answer to the question, but because the question was so unexpected. He had not seriously pondered his decision to join the Order for twenty years. What he had missed in the world had been more than compensated for by the life he had chosen.

"Yes, I am happy."

The old man nodded. His eyes were still moist. "I believe it. I sense it", he said. "You see, I could never confide this secret to a man who was not happy, a man discontented with his lot in life. Never."

What a strange man, Abbot thought. What did his happiness have to do with the visitor's secret, with whether this secret would be revealed? There were many forms of madness, he reminded himself, and some were insidiously subtle. He must not lower his guard completely for all this man's appreciation for honey cake, ale, and a room for the night.

"Now that it is established that I'm happy," Abbot said, "what about this antiquity?" He was not in a hurry, in spite of the Rule, and the ale had revived him rather than made him drowsy, but he was concerned that the old man, after so long a walk, was fatigued. Let him open the box and speak his piece. Then the man could retire for the night.

"Are there good lies?" John Hill asked.

There was, apparently, no end to the old man's surprises.

"I'm not a philosopher", Abbot answered him, annoyed despite himself. Did the old man's visit have any purpose at all? Was the box just a prop for the man's fantasies? He could tell that the visitor was distressed at his answer, so he said, "Some make a distinction between telling a known falsehood and withholding the truth, when the consequences of withholding the truth are less grave than revealing it; it is generally accepted that this mental reservation is not the same thing as a lie. One might call it a good lie, though I've never liked that definition."

"Yes, I see that", the old man said.

Abbot could not resist. "Why do you ask?"

"It is relevant to this"—the man patted the box. "I have been tortured by this matter of a good lie. I wonder about what has been expressed as 'They lie, and they worship their lying.'"

"About whom do you speak?"

"Myself", the old man said.

Had the old man come to make a confession? Abbot was about to ask him but suspected that if that were what his visitor wanted, he would ask forthrightly.

"Has it been a good lie?" the man mumbled. "I hope so." Abbot could see that this conversation was between the man and his conscience, so he left him alone with it for a moment. The visitor's eyes rested on the box, and his mumbling became unintelligible.

At what seemed to be a propitious moment, Abbot said, "It is not often that a lie rises to the level of malevolence, but it is possible when it does grave harm to another person. Most lies fall short of malevolence, but there is such a thing as evil." Immediately, Abbot wondered why he'd said it. What did this tired old man have to do with evil? Perhaps the odd lie—yes—and then a stricken conscience, but Abbot could not imagine that the person across the table from him had known willful wickedness. Even he, who had heard thousands of confessions, and not just those of the brothers, had rarely encountered it.

The visitor took his time answering. He fingered the box and looked toward the window. He seemed afraid of being overheard.

"There is such a thing", the visitor repeated.

"And where do you think evil comes from?" Abbot felt compelled to ask.

"It comes from desiring to be served rather than serving, from lusting after power; it is a choice."

A choice, Abbot pondered, how true and how terrifying. Where did the old man come by all this? At that moment, Abbot realized something else: the substance and duration of the conversation had made him giddy. He could not remember when he had conversed for so long. He even wondered if he weren't taking excessive delight in it. This

internal debate produced a pang of anxiety. Should he push the old man off to bed and then out the door with the dawn? Hadn't he given him ample time to tell his story?

These deliberations could not have taken more than a few seconds, but when he looked up he saw that the old man was asleep—not a deep sleep by any means, but his eyes were closed and his head dipped toward his chest.

Of course the visitor was tired. He had endured a fatiguing journey, and the hour was late. He'd had little to eat and had imbibed two glasses of the house's potent ale. Abbot debated whether to wake him or let him rest for a while. He took the opportunity to observe the man further and was reinforced in his opinion that his visitor possessed kindly features to complement a kindly bearing. He judged the man to be shy by nature, intellectually formidable, without pretension, perhaps tending toward scrupulosity, and probably ascetically disposed; a most remarkable old gentleman, Abbot concluded.

In the distance, he heard the anguished call of an owl—Philomena, he had named her. This bird's call was so different from that made by other owls as to be readily distinguishable, at least to Abbot's practiced ear. He could not hear her cry without experiencing a pang of emotion. He imagined it was a sort of antiphonal call, though he hadn't heard a prompting one. Was she barren, or isolated from others of her kind; was she infected with an avian pathology?

"I'm so sorry", the man said, his eyes now open and a smile wrinkling his lips. He wiped his lips again with his sleeve and blinked.

"Would you like your bed now?" Abbot asked him.

"No, that wouldn't do", the man answered, mumbling something, and then, "... work to do." He sat up straight

and took a deep breath. "This box"—he tapped it with both hands—"contains an antiquity of some ... of great significance."

Abbot smiled and said, "Tonight I'm admitting to so many things I am not—philosopher, antiquarian, a tolerable host—that it may be hard to fathom what I am. The truth is I am a simple monk, Mr. Hill. I don't understand how I can help you except for a simple meal and a bed." There was Philomena again, louder than before. The old man started; he heard her too.

"You have a magnificent owl on the grounds."

"Philomena." Abbot had not revealed to anyone else the name he had given her.

The old man laughed out loud. There was a sip of ale left in his cup, and he emptied it.

"The pathos in her cry reminds me of someone—Agnes was her name. But we have business to conduct. I will show you, as I seem to be stumbling badly in explaining", the visitor said.

Abbot leaned forward. He could not help feeling excited, like a young boy on his birthday, though reason suggested that the contents of the box would be less than remarkable. Still, he could enjoy the anticipation, couldn't he? Was there harm in that simple human pleasure?

The old man undid a latch on each end of the pine box. Abbot concluded that it must contain something of senti-mental attachment, but who was he to crush his visitor's hopes? Wasn't this evening, after all, about compassion for the man sitting across from him?

The lid came up toward the old man's chest, revealing a silver box, which, allowing for a piece of felt around its perimeter, fit snugly in the larger wooden container. This smaller box was another matter altogether. Even in the dim

lamplight, it gleamed like nothing Abbot had ever seen before. Its visible surface had been etched with unfamiliar runes and a beautiful abstract pattern. John Hill lifted it gently, even reverently, from its wooden cradle, and Abbot could not help being reminded again of one of the Magi preparing to present his gift to the Infant. The old man's face, suffused with something like wonder, reinforced this image.

"Would you kindly move the container?" the old man said.

Abbot stood, slid the wooden box from the old man's lap, and placed it on the floor. "Thank you", the man said, setting the silver—if that was what it was—box on the table.

"It is beautiful", Abbot could not help saying.

"I suppose so", John Hill said, enigmatically.

Abbot could not take his eyes off it. The glow of the metal seemed otherworldly, though this idea struck him as ridiculous at that moment.

"May I?" John Hill said.

Abbot realized that the visitor desired to open the metallic box. He was seeking Abbot's permission, so as not to startle him.

"By all means", Abbot whispered, as if in a trance.

The old man placed a thumb on each side of the box, near the top and toward the rear, the side closest to him. Abbot could detect no seam where a cover or lid would be; to his eyes the box seemed to be of a single piece. Before John Hill's thumbs made contact with the metal, Abbot thought he saw something like the image of a thumbprint on one side of the silver box—or was this something suggested to his imagination by the old man's actions?

The lid rose slowly to a vertical position. Abbot could see no mechanism inside the box that would account for this movement. He could not have been more absorbed in what was transpiring: the beauty, the wonder, all colored with a sense of drama, even menace. Was this man a magician? Was this a performance?

The box was lined with fabric that shimmered like silk and displayed different colors depending on how the light touched it; one moment green, then red, then a different green, now sky blue ...

"It is a book", the old man said needlessly as he lifted the bound pages from the box.

Once Abbot pried his attention from the box, he observed a large volume with a blood-red exterior, absent any markings or defects. He experienced a powerful urge to touch it; only years of discipline prevented him from acting on this impulse.

"I want to leave this with you", John Hill said matter-of-factly.

Abbot could not look at the man, so astounded was he by his declaration. This object—he considered both box and book all one piece—was the most wondrous thing he had ever seen. "Why?" he said, as calmly as he could.

"It is necessary", was the answer.

Abbot sat down again. He invited the visitor to sit too. There they were, looking at each other, and perfectly comfortable doing so. Abbot would not have been surprised to learn that they understood each other better than many who had spent a lifetime living or working together. Suddenly it struck him that he had seen that face before ... Good heavens, he thought, could it be?

"A story must be connected to this", Abbot said.

The old man's eyes positively shone. For an instant, one could almost believe that he was fifty years younger. "Actually, there are two stories, one old and one new. Which would you like to hear first?"

August 16, 1916

Region of the Somme, France

Another long, painful, terrifying night awaited the young lieutenant—and that was if he was fortunate. The lice were everywhere, perhaps in places he dared not imagine. The fever came and went, and when it came he felt like he was on fire. He hadn't slept in more than fits and starts for weeks, but the thing that troubled him the most was the trembling; he could not stop his left hand from shaking. Considering his other ailments, it was next to nothing, but it drove him to distraction.

With "stand-to" over and the last of the day's light vanishing in the west, there was little for the lieutenant to do but wait for the darkness, and the terrors it brought. He and his comrades found themselves that night, as they had found themselves for the past seven days, in dugouts and trenches captured from the German army. The German soldiers who had lately occupied these holes were not far off—less than a mile, he'd been told. He could expect people—mostly soldiers—to move in and out of the dugout and along the trench line all night long. He rarely recognized anyone at night. At times he longed for a familiar face. Just as often he sought a thoughtless anonymity.

"Kill the little devil", he heard someone say, and he knew what the man was speaking about, knew it as well as if he were at the man's side. The "little devil" was a rat, and not one of the men had mercy on the rats, not even those who'd balk at killing an attacking Hun.

"Did you get him, mate?"

"I should hope so."

"No—there it is, the plaguey bugger."

"Give me that club, you clumsy fool," a third voice interjected.

"I guess I can kill it myself!" the first voice asserted.

"You've made a bleeding mess of it."

"Screw off, then."

The lieutenant could listen in on conversations like this half the night if he had a mind to, which he didn't. The rats would have to vie for his attention with the lice and the other vermin. He reached into his bag for some salt. Then he rolled up his coat sleeve and exposed his forearm. There were marks on the flesh like small red boils. He rubbed salt into them, expecting little relief. The salt provided, he suspected, more salve for mind than body.

The oppression of this place must be something like drowning, he told himself. His chest always felt heavy. The muscle pain and the ache in his legs seemed to get worse every day. Yesterday, he had gotten a headache that hadn't gone away. When he looked in a handheld mirror, he was astonished to see how emaciated he was. His high forehead reminded him of a skull. His nose was a spear protruding from his gaunt face. His already thinning hair pitched to both sides of his head, like a beggar's or a fool's. His eyes were pits in his face, out of which something, or someone, looked, but not the man he remembered. Only his thick moustache retained some semblance of normalcy. If he was gradually losing his mind, who could blame him? No one, not one of them, was unscathed by this desperate existence.

He must remember to get more salt, he told himself. Whenever his imagination threatened to run wild, he tried to concentrate on the practical exigencies of survival. Where had they put the stores? That's where they kept the chloride of lime he so counted on to keep the vermin at bay.

Could it be that his fever had worsened? The sun had gone down, and it had not been a particularly warm day—so why was he so hot? It was fever, he told himself. A pang of terror gripped him. He fought it off, knowing there was nothing to be done until morning. He had a blanket and he was safe; that would have to suffice.

"No rain, please, God", he heard himself say. He might have added a litany of other woes to his plea but gave it up as useless. They had not had any rain the previous night, but for three nights prior it had come down in buckets. The few working pumps they possessed were powerless to keep up with the torrent. The water—fetid from the moment it struck the ground—was still ankle-deep in the lower areas. He thought he knew the places to avoid, but at night it was hard to keep one's bearings. Of course, it was best if he could stay still, sleep even, but such hopes were fantasy in this place.

He heard a rumbling in the distance; was it thunder, or cannon fire, or something else? Would it sound a little nearer next time? Would he hear it again? He crouched in a corner, hot and flushed, aching all over, tired but unable to sleep. It was then—it was always then—that he thought of her, or about the stories he loved, or about ideas. Sometimes, these thoughts would occupy him for hours. Sometimes, they even put him to sleep for a while. Tonight, he had the sense that there would be no sleep.

The thunder ceased, and he heard the ubiquitous cries and moans. He lamented that they were background noise for the most part. One did not have the capacity to sympathize with every sufferer. He had to be selective or risk losing his mind. He was beginning to recount to himself the story of Beowulf when he heard the husky voice.

"Sorry to disturb you, sir, but I got something."

Was the voice speaking to him, or had he fallen asleep already? Was this a character in a dream?

"Sir, I say I got something."

He opened his eyes and peered into the darkness. It was a clear night with a half moon, so he was able to recognize the smudged face.

"Yes, Corporal?" the lieutenant said.

"I brung quinine", the man said, timidly, holding out an oversized hand. "How's the fever coming, sir?"

He was hot, that he knew, and to be honest, he was frightened of dying in this seared landscape.

"It's quinine, sir", the corporal repeated, as if he were speaking to a child.

The lieutenant raised his head. The corporal wasn't his corporal, but for some reason the young man had attached himself to him. They knew next to nothing about each other. The lieutenant had learned that Corporal Miller—he did not know the man's Christian name—was from Sussex. He was in his early twenties and had been at or near the front longer than the lieutenant.

"It'll help that fever, I'm guessing."

The lieutenant stretched out his hand and took the small blue bottle. He was ashamed that his hand trembled so noticeably. After uncorking the bottle and sipping, he asked, "Where did you get it?"

"Stores", was the answer.

"I should have said, how did you get it?"

"Better not ask, sir. Ask me no secrets and I'll"—he hesitated—"as my mum would say." The corporal said this as if the saying had been original to his mother.

The lieutenant took another sip and handed the corporal the bottle.

"You keep that, sir. I don't have any use for it. Strong as a bull, I am." Then the corporal said, self-consciously, "I won't be bothering you any more tonight, sir."

"Please stay," the lieutenant said, suddenly, "unless you want to sleep."

"I don't sleep much. My dad always says a man needs to keep a step ahead of the vermin. Now I know what that means." He sat next to the lieutenant. "Do you want a smoke, sir?"

Where had this remarkable man come by tobacco? the lieutenant wondered. He decided not to ask.

"I would, Corporal, if you can spare it."

"I can, sir." He reached into his coat, and out came a leather bag and a pipe. The lieutenant found his own pipe. Perhaps it was his imagination, but the quinine and the prospect of a pipe made him feel more alert and less feverish. They smoked together in silence. For a while, the fragrance of the tobacco smoke masked, or at least sweetened, the terrible odors in that place.

"This is the best pipe I've ever smoked", the lieutenant observed.

"Them brownies don't like it so much. It sends 'em scurryin', which is all right by me. It's medicine, then, isn't it, like the quinine. That's how I see it."

That's how the man must have "seen it" when he acquired the tobacco, the lieutenant thought. He had been on a medical mission. How reasonable it all sounded as the corporal explained it.

The big man had been scratching behind his right ear. That was not so remarkable. It was a rare man who wasn't infested with lice. Even the major was afflicted.

"Would you like some salt to rub behind that ear?" the lieutenant asked.

"It won't help, sir. Not a bit. It's scrapnel got in there from a shell. It was before your time", he said, as if he were a veteran of years of campaigning. "There was this big boom, and then I couldn't hear nothin' for a long time. I was all in one piece, which was a good thing, but Davis, he notices blood on my neck and then we finds the scrapnel. Some of it he picks out, but some is in too deep. Maybe a doc can pull it out when I'm home again. It tickles sometimes."

The lieutenant doubted that it tickled. The smoke from their pipes mingled in the corner of the dugout. Someone shouted down the line, but the lieutenant couldn't make it out. The corporal hadn't paid any attention; his sole occupation was the pipe.

"Tell me about your family, Corporal."

The corporal emitted a cloud of smoke. He seemed to be wreathed in it. Big as he was, he might have passed for Vulcan at his forge. "My dad and mum are farmers. Our farm is at the bottom of a hill near Maidstone. I'm the eldest. I've two brothers and two sisters—a perfect little den, as Mum says."

"Do you have a girl back home?'

"That I do, sir, name of Jenny. Her dad and mum farm down by Heathfield. We expect to marry when I'm home. Here she is, sir, and you may see yourself what a bright girl she is." The corporal handed him a photograph.

The lieutenant could barely see it in the moonlight. The most beautiful woman in the world would hardly have looked "bright" in that place. She was a robust girl with a generous head of hair and a broad, lively mouth. "She's handsome", he said—and dependable, he thought.

"Indeed she is, sir, my Jenny." The photograph vanished into the recesses of the corporal's coat. Then his hand sought out the area behind his ear.

"And what about you, sir?" the man asked timidly. "Have you heard from your lady?"

His lady. How had the corporal known about her? He supposed that all the men had to do was listen, as he talked about her often with the junior officers. He was constantly torn between the desire to think about E. M. and the terrible longing that accompanied it. When would he see her again? Would he ever?

"She's well, Corporal", he said, puffing more enthusiastically.

"They have no easy job of it, worryin' about their men and waitin'. Could you use a fill, sir?" The bag emerged again from the corporal's coat.

The lieutenant wondered if they ought to conserve the tobacco. He looked around the dugout, considered the desperateness of their lot, and rejected the idea. Now is the acceptable time, he quoted to himself.

"Thanks." He refilled his pipe, and the corporal's match illuminated the little space between their faces.

After a while, the corporal made a move as if to rise and said, "I suppose I'll be getting on, or the vermin'll be finding me."

Before the corporal could get to his feet, the lieutenant said, "What do you think of all this?" Why he asked, he couldn't say, but he felt at ease with this man.

The corporal sat again and laid the hand with the pipe on his knee. He was looking straight ahead, not at the lieutenant. "I don't mostly. I do what I'm told, within reason. When I can't help myself, I wonder if this is the best our great and smart gentlemen can do, if you know what I mean. No disrespect to you, sir", he added timidly. "I'll do my duty, I guess, but I don't have to like it, and I don't guess I'll ever understand it."

"Are you frightened?" the lieutenant asked.

"You can count on it, sir. I'm not an officer, just an ordinary fellow."

"I'll tell you a secret, Corporal. We're all frightened— anyone with a brain, anyway", the lieutenant admitted. "It was kind of you to bring me the quinine and the tobacco."

"Don't mention it, sir. You're a good egg—there I go spoutin' without thinking. Begging your pardon, sir."

The lieutenant laughed. "I'll consider it a compliment."

The corporal stood again, rubbed himself from head to toe, knocked out his pipe. "When I get back—*if* I get back being a more proper way to put it—Jenny and me will take up a small farm ourselves. We talked it over. Of course, we'll have to marry first. We don't crave a big place, neither Jenny nor me, just somewhere we can make our way. Jenny wrote that she found a few acres near the river belonging to Mr. Price. He might sell, she said. My dad did a favor for Mr. Price once, and that gentryman is a big one for obligations. Of course, we'll pay him a fair price." He laughed out loud as if he'd practiced the line. "Well, that's far off, or so it seems in these straits we're in, sir. One has to look the facts in the face, as my ..." His voice trailed off to a whisper. He took half a step toward the trench line, then turned and stopped. "Sir, maybe I could ask you a question that's been bothering me."

"Go ahead, Corporal", the lieutenant said. He'd already pulled his blanket up. He was chilled again.

"People killin' other people, folks they don't know. Where does that come from?"

The lieutenant was tempted to offer the stock answers: leaders divorced from the common man, lust for power and riches, national pride, blood feuds. Instead, he sat there puffing. The corporal waited expectantly, as if the young officer had wisdom to dispense. Actually, the lieutenant had made this question an intellectual pastime at university. He had learned enough to realize that the roots of war and brutality far outstripped his knowledge and wisdom.

Something moved next to him, causing him to start. Once, after a bombardment, he had been terrified to see a moving hand at his side. It had still been attached to a mangled body, but the hand had been the only thing that retained life. It had opened and closed; in his horror he had counted the number of times. Then the hand had gone still.

It was just a frog this time. They were abundant in the trenches, especially after heavy rains, wallowing in low places and feasting on lice, he supposed. He watched it hop toward him, then up and over one outstretched leg, then over the other leg. Finally the darkness took it.

The corporal had not left the dugout.

"I suppose it is the evil that seeks to master us, that desires to feast on us—like the lice. Some utterly succumb to it, or seem to."

"That's a terrible thought, sir", the corporal said. "It don't seem quite so bad when the other fellow's to blame. I never considered it that way, and I thank you, sir."

"Are you sure you want to thank me?" the lieutenant asked.

The corporal saluted and trudged into the darkness. The lieutenant heard him say, "Thank you, sir. Don't forget the quinine." If it weren't for the pain and the fever and the ceaseless anxiety, this might have been a play, with the corporal having exited by a stage door. For all intents and purposes, Miller had utterly vanished.

35

So the quinine and the pipe tobacco came to the lieutenant, and he was grateful. Later, he wondered if the medicine hadn't saved his life. The corporal, he decided, was a
bedrock man, a term he applied to those people, practically
invisible, who do things so that others can survive. In good
times, they're ignored, even ridiculed. In bad times, though,
they're indispensable.

He pulled the blanket tighter around him and closed his
eyes. He might have slept. He could no longer distinguish
between sleep and a state where his conscious and unconscious thoughts commingled. An explosion woke him. It
was loud, and the earth shook. Dirt from the dugout walls
cascaded down and dusted his head and shoulders. He heard
men shout. This went on for a while, and then all was
silent, as it had been before. At one point—who could tell
what time it was—he woke with a start. Perhaps he'd been
dreaming. The first thing he thought of was the horned
beetle he had seen, before darkness had descended, making
its way to the rear of the dugout. His eyes had marked the
creature's slow but determined progress. It had plodded on
until it had come to an unidentifiable object in its path.
Undaunted, up it had gone and down it had come on the
other side, but the lieutenant's eyes had fixed on the object.
He had crawled the short distance and lifted it from the
ground.

The object was a small leather case. When he had opened
it, thinking it belonged to one of his comrades, three German notes of small denomination fell out. This case had
belonged to the enemy, had been lost by someone in his
retreat to the east. Tucked in a flap was a two-page letter,
beginning with "Lieber Gunther". Though he read German, he had folded the letter again and returned it to the
flap. Behind another, larger flap was a photograph.

A young soldier—a boy, really—with his arm around the waist of his young bride.

How different was this man in the photograph from Corporal Miller? If this soldier and he were to face one another, surely each would try to kill the other. "An evil that seeks to master us", he remembered telling the corporal, but who was he to expound on evil? Was there such a thing, or was what man called evil just a matter of conditioned response, phobias and other mental pathologies, or even self-interest? Was there a difference between the routine ill done in the pursuit of one's interests and willful wickedness? In this desperate place, such questions could not be avoided by any thinking man.

He wanted to believe there was meaning to be found in these dire circumstances. He'd once believed it. Meaning; truth; even beauty. All that seemed so remote from what he experienced here. Was this interminable brutality and misery, in fact, reality, and all the rest illusion, or even delusion? Were the materialists right after all?

In the dark, his fingers sought the leather case. In a fictional story, he would meet Gunther, and something profound would happen. There would be choices between evil and good, ugliness and beauty, deceit and truth. Consequences would proceed from these choices, and lessons would be learned. Instead, on this battlefield, evil had ceased being evil. Choices had been reduced to survival.

The frog returned briefly, landing on his knee before disappearing into the darkness. The creature had no concept of evil; it did what it must. He reckoned that with each passing day, he and his comrades were becoming more froglike. Perhaps, someday, they would no longer have a word for evil.

The lieutenant felt like weeping. He had not wept in as long as he could remember. Dehumanization pervaded everything, had crept into his own heart, ossifying his sensibilities and making him into something new, but not better. Still, he reminded himself, hadn't he and the corporal met and spoken as two human beings, notwithstanding their inequality in this army? They had, he admitted, and they had talked about love and friendship and hope—and evil. What would become of the boy, he wondered, a "boy" scarcely younger than the lieutenant? He imagined himself walking down a country path to a small house near the river. It was a neat little home, prosperous for its type. He knocked at the door, and a big yeoman answered. They shook hands, and the yeoman introduced him to his wife and children. He saw that she was indeed bright. He and the yeoman drank a pint of ale at the kitchen table and, later, another at the public house down the way. Then, he told himself, and only then, would this myth make sense, when order was restored and there were ordinary things again.

He was not a man of abstract ideas, a philosopher. He had to relate ideas to something concrete. So why not start close to home? he told himself. As a signal officer, he hadn't had occasion to kill. But in directing the attacks of others, hadn't he participated in killing? While this was not willful wickedness, it could be said that he was doing evil out of self-interest, from the need to obey orders or face the consequences, or from the need to kill the enemy before they had a chance to kill him.

He was frightened by the vermin, the bombs, the disease, but especially by the notion that he'd placed his soul in jeopardy. He could feel the fever taking hold again, and he wondered how much it was affecting his thinking. He removed the blue bottle from his coat and took another sip.

The lieutenant closed his eyes and imagined he was sitting under a tree in an English forest. He frequently retreated to a place like this at night. He tried to be there and nowhere else, to smell the pungent soil, to feel the wind cool his face, to see the tiny shade flowers that survived beneath the canopy, to hear the intermittent patter of objects striking the forest floor, to taste a piece of dried bark he'd placed in his mouth, to caress the skin of a fallen leaf and trace its ribs. He tried so hard to be there, and in spite of the oppressive reality of the dugout, he almost succeeded. Amidst these thoughts and imaginings, he realized that he was still holding the leather case. He put it back where he had found it, as if the young German were returning for it. Then he reached inside his jacket and removed the yellow envelope, the envelope containing the letter E. M. had sent him. How he treasured that letter. How many times he had read it. Some days, it was only the thought of her, of her love and patient waiting, that kept him going. When he closed his eyes, he could see her clearly. How that heartened him, as he'd overheard one of the men saying he couldn't remember his sweetheart's face. What a hell that must be, he thought.

Maybe it was the quinine and maybe it was thinking about her, but he began to feel stronger. He dozed on and off, rested better than he'd hoped to. He woke from one of these naps to find another officer seated on the ground, facing him but too timid to disturb a man's sleep. It took him a minute to recognize him. Martin—that was his name, a brother lieutenant but not a close friend.

"Didn't wake you, I hope", the man said. He was handsome. One might say dashing: clean-shaven, with gray eyes, thin brows, and a wide, expressive mouth.

"Not at all", the lieutenant replied. In fact, he was glad for the company. Waking up alone in this place was never pleasant.

"I've been nosing about—worried about you", the man said.

"No need", the lieutenant said, though he knew he looked a wreck.

"Glad to hear it. Been here all night?"

"Yes."

"Not bad lodgings." The man looked around.

It occurred to the lieutenant that there was something on this fellow's mind. "Plenty of room and plenty of company of the furtive variety", he said.

The man laughed. "Has your fever broken?"

"Comes and goes."

The man said, "I've been lucky, but good luck doesn't last forever. Do you have a cigarette?"

"Sorry." The lieutenant didn't bother to tell him about the corporal's tobacco. He'd smoked the last of it anyway. "What time is it?"

"After four", the officer said.

"Almost morning."

Still the man sat there.

"Is something on your mind, Martin?"

"Everyone in this godforsaken place has something on his mind", Martin said. Then he added, "Got a note from my parents. Brother George killed in action."

"I'm sorry", the lieutenant said. He had said it often enough.

"George was the better of the two of us; that's the shame of it", Martin said dispassionately, but the lieutenant could tell that he was straining to keep his emotions in check.

"The war plays no favorites. I'm truly sorry." How incredibly didactic that was.

"I knew you would be; that's why I came. The others say the proper things. I wanted someone who means it."

A roach the size of a birch leaf scuttled beneath the lieutenant's hand. He cried out in spite of himself, as if the creature were an angel of destruction. He wanted to find a stone or a hammer and crush it, but it had already vanished. He looked at Martin, embarrassed at the outburst.

"I was the best sportsman, but George had the best heart. When Father lost his position and we had to take quarters, George left everything behind, no regrets. The rest of us fumed and ranted—not George. He said we'd find our way, and we did. That boy could sing, everything from Bach to pub songs. We'd sit at night, and he'd sing whatever we requested; he never refused. I don't remember him ever refusing." Martin stopped speaking, choked with emotion. "As for me, I wouldn't lift a little finger unless there was something in it for yours truly."

"Don't be so hard on yourself."

"I'm being honest. George came over first. I read his letters. He never complained, wouldn't worry us. Where do people like that come from?"

Where indeed, the lieutenant wondered. He couldn't guess.

"Not a political bone in the poor boy." The officer started sobbing. He put his hands over his face.

The lieutenant said nothing. He knew he was unable to bring solace out of his own emptiness. Furthermore, he doubted that Martin wanted him to say anything.

"This will be a hard blow for the *pater* and *mater*", Martin said, composing himself.

"You will have to help them through it." The lieutenant was on unfamiliar ground. He had never known his own father, and his mother had died when he was a boy.

Martin laughed sardonically. "Me? I don't have it in me. I mean to say, I've never done it. I wouldn't know where to start."

"One can learn these things."

"So I've been told. Listen, I'm grateful you let me bend your ear at this ungodly hour." He stretched out his hand, and the lieutenant took it.

"I hope you don't mind shaking hands with a red socialist", Martin said.

The lieutenant smiled.

"It's something I keep to myself. You've heard all the rest, so you might as well hear that too."

The lieutenant hesitated before saying, "Does that make you an atheist too?"

"I'm afraid it does. It's part of the creed. We may not believe in the Deity, but we have our stern men."

The lieutenant said, "Your secret is safe with me. Come by whenever you have a mind to. I'm here most nights, and I don't sleep much—the accommodations are rather wanting."

They both laughed.

"I'll pray for your brother", the lieutenant said, wondering whether it was impolitic of him to say so.

"One of us ought to." Martin got up slowly and thought to wipe his eyes, though his tears had already dried. He walked away with his head bent and his hands at his sides.

The lieutenant stood up and stretched. It was almost time to move down the trenches to the officers' assembly dugout for morning stand-to. The fever had abated. Two rats, out of sight, started fighting over something; he knew the sounds well enough. "Hasn't anyone taught you boys to share?" he said out loud. It made him feel better to try on humor. It didn't seem quite so desperate if one could still laugh; but by no means was it easy.

This night had been quiet, almost peaceful. He seemed to recall an earlier disturbance, but it was all muddled with months of nights just like this one. He removed a small brush from his pocket, a brush she'd given him before he shipped out, and carefully dusted his coat and trousers. When he finished, he combed his hair with it. The grotesque thought came to him that the monkeys at the British Zoo, picking fleas off each other, were better groomed than he was. Well, he told himself, they didn't fight bloody wars, and they weren't led by bloody idiots.

He made his way out of the dugout and down a trench that led to the southwest. He began to hear bird songs and thought the grayness was brightening. What would this new day bring?

He didn't encounter too many men on his way, and those he met were lost in their own thoughts and cares. By the time he reached the assembly dugout, most of the officers were already there. Martin, leaning against a dirt wall and smoking a cigarette, didn't acknowledge him. The others looked much alike: bedraggled, weary, and preoccupied. Several were conversing, but most were standing still, like weather-beaten statues.

Later than he expected, Sergeant Major Booker entered the dugout. The sergeant major, unlike the rest of them, was a career soldier. Somehow, he managed to project competence and order, even under these hellish conditions. The lieutenant respected him, even held him in awe. But what was he doing here alone? Where was the major?

"Good morning, sirs", he began. Though the lieutenants and captains in the dugout were ostensibly his superiors, they had no illusions they were superior to him in this business. In a pinch, they would all have deferred to him.

"The major is indisposed this morning", the sergeant major said matter-of-factly; he spoke not a word more about it. "Are we all present?"

Each officer confirmed his presence.

"Very good." While to the officers he was a grizzled veteran, and even something of an oracle, the sergeant major was not yet thirty-five. He was stout, had long since shaved his head and face, and possessed the strength of a prize fighter. He seemed to make no concessions to the hell they resided in. Perhaps, as some suggested, he preferred it.

He reviewed the duty roster with the nonchalance of the caretaker at the Cliveden gardens on a tranquil summer morning. When he finished, he looked up from his notes and peered intently at the officers. "Sirs", he began, but he sounded as if he were speaking to a room of schoolboys. "We must see to it that those in our charge do not take advantage of the stores." The lieutenant, at that moment, felt that the sergeant major was addressing him as his school-master had once chastised him in front of his classmates. "The stores are restricted for a reason. The major asked that I make particular note of this." The lieutenant would not have been surprised if the major had asked no such thing and if this had been the sergeant major's idea. "Discipline, sirs, is what we need. I—that is, the major counts on your cooperation."

The officers shuffled and coughed, and the fortunate ones puffed on cigarettes.

"We had a quiet time of it last night", the sergeant major continued. "A bomb struck the D trench and Corporal Miller was killed, but that was the extent of the casualties."

It took several seconds before he comprehended what the sergeant major had said. Then a sensation of utter ruin struck the lieutenant like a bolt of lightning. He felt as if all the poison of those months had been distilled into a concentrate and injected into his soul. The idea of an idyllic visit to a man and his wife in Sussex had become myth—rather, a numbing tragedy—in a matter of hours. Like a penitent, he fell to his knees, not out of reverence but because his strength had evaporated.

Is there any justice to be found on the earth? he asked silently, repeating the plea of countless prophets—and madmen. Where was Divine Providence in this despicable business? His eyes were screwed shut. What a spectacle he must be making. Now he had fallen on his hands like a dumb beast. He didn't care that this combination of afflictions had paralyzed him. Why was it that the only thing he could think about was the pipe and the drifts of smoke he and the corporal had produced together?

Her name was Jenny. Jenny ... Jenny ... Jenny ... Jenny. He must not forget. But who cared if he knew her name? His last conscious thought was that the tobacco must have been Turkish. It must have been. Such a memorable aroma.

When he woke, he was lying on a cot in the infirmary miles behind the lines. Martin was sitting in a camp chair next to his bed.

"You put on quite a performance. People aren't supposed to survive with fevers that high. Three medicos have been in. I've been picking leeches off you ever since."

The lieutenant tried to answer but could not. He managed a wan smile. Jenny, her name is Jenny, he thought.

"The doctor said they're sending you farther back—trench fever. You're very sick."

Hadn't there been something about a brother? Or was it a corporal? He couldn't remember. Martin was smoking a cigarette.

"They sent me to keep you company. I'm not complaining. This is the promised utopia." Martin took a deep drag on the cigarette.

The smoke made him feel sleepy. He closed his eyes, heard the sound of motors and voices, smelled something sweet. Now what he really needed was his pipe.

July 8, 1917

Northwest England

The day that irrevocably changed his life could not have begun with less pretension. True, the crisp early air was inebriating, and the winding, tree-shaded path irresistibly beckoned him, but, in spite of the invigorating environment, it was an otherwise ordinary morning.

E. M. had encouraged him to make this journey, despite expecting their firstborn in November. After leave had been arranged by his superior officer, the lieutenant found himself on a train to northwest England. With great anticipation, he had awakened this morning in the little inn in the little town, eagerly put on his army-issue boots—the same he had worn in the trenches—breakfasted, drank two cups of black tea, and made off down the road. Barely a mile from the inn, he had arrived at this dirt path. He gripped his ash walking stick and abandoned the macadam road for the forest trail.

He wanted to savor everything. His nights, and especially his dreams, were still plagued by images of the war. Sometimes he woke with the certainty that he was still in the trenches. In those dreams, he could see Miller and Martin and the rest as clearly as if they were beside him. One time, he was talking to Miller, knowing that the boy would be killed, yet struck dumb as the corporal was preparing to leave the dugout. Another time, he was facing three German soldiers, and all three soldiers were the man in the photograph he'd found in the leather case. In these dreams, there was always a sense of helplessness, even of doom. Too often, he woke more tired than when he went to sleep.

Though he couldn't control these dreams, he owed it to E. M., who was bearing their child and who was so worried about him, to do all he could to return to health. He needed to be outside, walking, breathing fresh air. Both E. M. and his superior had been apprehensive about this solo journey, but the lieutenant had been insistent. He had to purge the demons, and he was convinced this sojourn was a means to that end. There had been no recurrences of the fever and joint pain for months. Despite occasional bouts of weakness and melancholy, he believed he was on the mend.

The first stretch of the path was heavily wooded. Birds were everywhere: on the wing, high in the surrounding trees, pecking at the ground. He saw squirrels, a badger, and a hedgehog in the first hour. Then the woods opened up to meadowlands. The grasses, knee high, swayed in the light breeze. At this point, the trail turned north, paralleling a line of tall hills to the east. As he emerged from the woods, he was almost a mile from these hills. There was nothing between but grass and small shrubs.

Before going on, he surveyed the area and picked out the tallest tree he could find. It was an ancient oak, black and gnarly. He took off his bag and boots and sat against it. He'd promised himself in the trenches that if he survived, he would fulfill that half dream of his. Sitting there in the morning sunshine, he willed his senses to experience everything. He broke a piece of bark from the trunk and chewed it with relish. He picked up a fallen leaf and traced every rib with his finger. He breathed deeply, many times, banishing every urge to get up and move. After some time had passed, he removed his pipe from the bag and smoked. He could almost sense the demons fleeing. He couldn't remember when he'd felt more relieved, more at peace.

He could hardly make himself rise, but the town where he intended to spend the night was almost ten miles to the north, and he didn't relish the thought of a night outdoors.

One arm at a time into the shoulder straps, the bag in place, the stick in hand, and he began walking again. He was almost happy, he told himself, and he'd never expected to be happy again. The western face of the hill was rocky, but there were plenty of trees and shrubs all the way up the slope to the ridgeline. He had half a mind to scale it, but laughed at himself. As it was, the path veered ever closer to the base of the hill until it was right up against the incline, and the meadow that once separated the hill and the forest was entirely to his left.

He hadn't expected to meet anyone, and he didn't. There was clover in the field, and as the day warmed, there were bees aplenty to be seen and heard. His mind wandered: E. M.; the monotony of his duty here at home; comrades from the front, especially Miller. A month earlier, he'd visited Miller's girl in Sussex. He'd almost hoped that he wouldn't be able to find her, that he would make the effort, fail, and go home with a clear conscience. But he did find Jenny, and when he entered her house, Miller's last night and their conversation erupted afresh from his memory. He could see everything in her eyes, everything she must have experienced when she heard the news. How dare he resurrect that horror, he told himself— but it was too late for incriminations of that sort. When he had arrived at the small farmhouse in Heathfield, she had greeted him, reverently, as if something he did or said could take away the pain.

He had felt utterly helpless in the presence of her grief. Miller had not been interred yet; the wheels of the army moved agonizingly slowly when it came to matters of compassion.

She took his hand. "Thank you for coming, sir."

"You need not call me sir. I'm John", he replied.

"I'd like to, sir", she said. "*He* did."

"Very well", he conceded. Why couldn't he speak her name? Hadn't it been seared in his memory?

"Sit, please."

He sat, put the hat he had removed upon entering the house on his lap, coughed.

"Are you well?" she said, with concern.

"Yes. Thank you."

"I'm glad."

Her parents were gone. Perhaps they'd decided to give the girl some privacy with her lover's friend. He could not guess, and he would not stay long enough to learn the reason.

"I'll brew tea. Do you take milk and sugar?"

"Yes."

She returned with one cup.

"What ..." she began, after he'd taken a sip.

He waited, but she never finished the question. She was wringing her hands. Not as stocky as he expected, young, bright eyes when she smiled. She wore a plain dress. Her shoes were made for work.

"He spoke about you", the lieutenant said. "You made him very happy."

She started crying.

And so it went. He didn't rush, but he didn't stay over-long. They had nothing in common, except the memory of a young man who wasn't coming home. They were both young; life must go on.

"You were very kind to come, sir", she said, taking his hand at the door.

He smiled at her and squeezed her hand. "He saved my life. He loved you. He was a fine man."

She nodded and closed the door. He would never forget Jenny, any more than he would forget Miller.

This journey was a welcome respite from life as a shelved army officer. He was of little use to the army but not yet discharged, so he was unable to get on with his career. He was mired in the past and anxious for the future, bored beyond description from lack of mental stimulation and awash in an emotional malaise that sapped his strength and heart. Only E. M. and the life she carried gladdened him.

How he had dreamed of a small house with E. M. and children, and a university career. Before the war, that dream seemed so far off, beyond reach. In the trenches, the dream kept him from utterly losing heart. His career was important, but at the center of his hopes was E. M. He was not the sort of man who considered a wife his property, nor the breed that idolized her and set her on a pedestal like a museum piece. E. M. was his friend, his dear friend, his best friend. And not because they were much alike. She was beautiful—surely that—generous, steadfast, and more perceptive than most suspected. She could also be, he reminded himself, proud and dismissive of those she suspected of being disingenuous. Even he, at times, came in for a dose of her caustic tongue. She would do anything for him—he knew that—even as she was castigating him for putting on airs. Their conversations were a blend of banter, kindness, and disputation. What would he do without her? he wondered.

And how would the baby change their relationship? He eagerly anticipated fatherhood, even though it occasionally frightened him. She knew he was apprehensive, though neither had spoken about it. His emotional lethargy had prevented him from being candid. He often reminded himself that he must whip these spells of melancholy before the baby arrived. E. M. would need help, and he could not allow himself to be a burden. That was why he was here, on this path, under this July sky—to restore himself.

He stopped for lunch. There was plenty of summer daylight left for him to reach the inn, but he cut short his meal when he saw threatening clouds approaching from the north. It was going to rain, he told himself, though the morning would not have portended it. The lieutenant was invigorated by the sensation of cooler air on his face, and he picked up the pace. He didn't mind getting wet, especially when a warm, dry inn awaited him.

The wind picked up, gusting so that he had to hold his cap to keep it on his head. The grass on his left rippled like waves on water, and he noticed that all the bees had gone. No cover, he observed, unless he wanted to leave the path and make for the woods. Then what? It would be harder going. He had marched through woods and knew that one could get plenty wet there too. Head bowed, he plowed ahead.

Within minutes, a bolt of light flashed from the base of the clouds to the ground. He counted the seconds until he heard the thunder and mentally calculated that the heart of the storm was still a few miles distant. When he felt the first drops of rain on his hands, the sky was a black blanket. He'd seen plenty of rainstorms, but this was shaping up to be one of those rare summer tempests. Was he foolish to march into the storm when the worst of it was still ahead of him? As he scanned the hills, he saw clumps of smaller trees interspersed with rocky projections; there were gravel washes too. Flash floods had occurred in this region before, he reminded himself; he needed to get to higher ground and cover. Several hundred feet up, almost due east of where he stood, there appeared to be a stone outcropping, and he wondered if he could wait out the storm beneath it.

While he was deliberating, his hat blew away. It was raining harder, and the lightning was more frequent. He realized that he was the tallest object between the forest and the hills, a disconcerting thought. At the edge of the forest, a dead tree came crashing down, uprooted by the wind or struck by lightning.

Stick in hand, up he went. It wasn't easy, especially with water cascading down the slope. Even more unnerving were the lightning flashes and thunderclaps. His heart pounded and his breathing quickened as if he were back in the trenches.

When halfway to the outcrop, he pushed harder and slipped. The next thing he knew he was lying on his face in a pile of rocks. His head hurt. He touched the place where the pain was centered and saw that his hand was stained with blood—a lot of it. He knew that even minor head wounds bled effusively, so it was not necessarily serious; anyway, he had no time to worry about it. He must get to the outcrop. Where was his stick? For a moment, the panicked thought came that he had lost it, that it had rolled down the face of the hill, but there it was, not far from where he'd fallen. When he stood up, pain darted through his right ankle. He must have sprained it. He leaned on the stick and kept resolutely on.

Heavy rain continued to fall, and the wind threatened to unbalance him. Though he knew his need for shelter was urgent, he was equally aware that the footing was perilous. Just when he thought he might have veered off course, he looked up and saw the outcrop a few steps in front of him. With a lunge he flung himself beneath its stony roof.

For many minutes he didn't move, or even think. He was conscious of little except the pain, exhaustion, and the power of the storm. The show was so spectacular—wind, rain, and lightning; streams flowing down the hillside; even rocks tumbling down—that he couldn't focus on anything else. Finally, he removed a soggy handkerchief and swabbed his head. He had an egg-sized lump, painful to the touch, but he was glad to see that the bleeding had almost stopped. It was no use removing his boot and examining his ankle. He would have to walk on it no matter how badly it was damaged, and he couldn't risk being unable to get the sodden boot back on his foot again.

As he sat, he realized that he might have to overnight in this semiexposed place. At first, he told himself that when the storm finally subsided, even if it was dark, he'd push on, but how wise was limping in the dark on a freshly sprained ankle? Better to rest it for a while. His clothes laden with water, he began to shiver with cold. Fortunately, he had brought a small fuel lantern, though he'd been tempted to leave it behind. Now he lit it—not an easy operation—and tried to warm himself a little.

The floor, back wall, and side walls of the alcove, as well as the outcrop itself, were hard stone. Fortunately, the direction of the storm was such that he was protected from the brunt of the weather. Could he recline next to the rear wall and dry out a little? He moved in that direction and discovered that the ceiling and walls narrowed until they ended at the mouth of a cave. He took a deep breath, thrust the lantern forward, and stooped to enter the chamber. Once inside, it was large enough that he could stand erect, and in the dim light he saw a fissure in the back wall. He moved toward it and saw that, indeed, there was a narrow opening in the stone.

"That would be foolish", he said out loud. And could he squeeze through the opening, even if he wanted to? He could still feel intermittent bursts of cool, moist air. It might be drier and warmer in there, he reasoned—and filled with bats, or worse things, he argued with himself. He was shaking now, and he didn't have any warmer clothing. Who could have expected this deluge after such a benign start?

He extended the hand with the lamp into the fissure. The light illuminated little and revealed nothing. He might take a step into that darkness and fall a hundred yards before he struck something. He didn't ponder the choice long. For a man of mind, he could be impulsive, even stubborn. He pulled off his rucksack, and holding his stick in one hand and the lantern in the other, he turned sideways and went through.

It was warmer and drier behind the fissure, though he could see nothing except the small spheroid illuminated by the lantern. He tapped the floor with his stick; it was stone. Then he waved the stick with an outstretched arm, like a wand; it didn't come in contact with anything. He reached outside the fissure and pulled the bag inside, complimenting himself on a well-executed maneuver.

The ordeal had exhausted him. He hadn't recovered his prewar stamina, and this business had spent him. His forehead still throbbed and his ankle hurt, even without any weight on it. He was sure his knees were rubbed raw; his hands and chin were tender too. A summer walk indeed. He turned off the lantern, and using the bag as a pillow, he lay on his back and closed his eyes. One fortunate consequence of his time in the trenches was that the prospect of sleeping in these conditions held no terror for him. He felt safe enough, and except for the pain in his head and ankle, he was reasonably comfortable.

He slept, though he didn't know for how long. When he woke up he was hungry and thirsty. It was dark and quiet outside the crevice. He turned the lantern on and removed some bread and cheese from his bag, washing it down with cold tea from his canteen. As soon as he finished eating he was ready to sleep again, but first he had to relieve himself.

He stood, and his ankle hurt like the devil. Leaving the lantern and stick behind, he took a few tentative steps, stopping when he came to a stone wall. When he finished, he turned to retrace his steps. He shuffled toward the light in exactly, or so he thought, the way he had come. But suddenly, he felt himself hurtling downward. Pain overwhelmed him and his heart pounded like a jackhammer. Almost immediately, he struck water, cold and utterly black. Down he went, flailing, twisting. His left foot made contact with a rock, and he pushed against it with all his strength, kicking both legs and stroking the water with his arms above his head. Soon, his hands struck stone; there was a rock roof above him. Feeling his way along this surface, he desperately sought the opening he had fallen into. In the total darkness, he was completely disoriented, not knowing whether he was moving in a fortuitous or fatal direction. His lungs felt as if they would burst, and he thought of E. M. If he prayed, it was an insensate prayer, and not in words. The feeling of panic gave way to light-headedness, and his limbs became slow and heavy. Just then, he broke the surface of the water and gasped for air. His hands, and then arms, found the ledge, and he heaved his body out of the water. There he lay breathing laboriously, and sobbing with relief, exhaustion, gratitude. He crawled along on his belly toward the lantern. His only thought was to get out of the cave as quickly as possible.

If he hadn't been wet and chilled, the experience might have been a nightmare, so quickly had everything transpired. He thrust his rucksack, lantern, and then his body through the fissure by which he had entered—or so he thought—but before he could lift his lantern, it went out. He realized then that he had not gone through the right fissure, for he would have seen the mouth of the cave in front of him. Instead, before him was utter darkness. He could not even see his own hand in front of his face. Instinctively, he reached out his arms in front of him, and his hand touched something. How it was possible, he couldn't guess, but he was sure the object he touched had been fashioned by human hands. It was boxlike, with smooth surfaces and straight lines for edges, and it had been fitted into some kind of alcove.

He drew out the object and held it in both hands. Fumbling in the dark, he put the lantern into the rucksack and pushed it back through the opening. Then, hugging the object to his chest, he squeezed himself out. Back in the chamber, he hugged the wall and tentatively felt his way to the fissure by which he had entered. He recognized the opening by the gray morning light illuminating the mouth of the cave.

The ordeal had occupied the entire night. He could hardly believe he'd survived. There had been a moment when he had been sure he was dying. His ankle was no worse— maybe slightly improved—and the pain in his head had lessened. Still, he didn't know the extent of his injuries, he was exhausted, he was out of food and water, and he could not—dared not—spend another night out-of-doors. He told himself that he must set off and get to the inn as soon as he was able. Then he could decide what to do next.

He scrambled out into the open air. Except for the pools of water that dotted the landscape below, one would never know that such a fierce storm had passed. The sky was turning pink, and birds were singing; there was no wind—not even a light breeze, though it was cooler than it had been the previous morning.

Beneath the overhang, he sat on a rock and placed the object in front of him. It was a box, but that description didn't begin to do the object justice. In size, it was something like a banker's or accountant's strong box. It was made of metal, but one that was unfamiliar to him. The color suggested silver, but the luster and lack of tarnish made him think of gold. There were markings on the surface, but this was not the time or place for detailed examination. With effort, he managed to cram the box into the sack, but because of its bulk, almost half of the object protruded from the bag. As best he could, he covered it with a spare shirt, wet but better than leaving it exposed.

As the lieutenant hobbled down the hill, the thought came to him that after all the anxiety E. M. had suffered while he was France, she need not know the degree of peril he'd experienced here, at least not right away. Considering what he'd been through, his heart was light. True, he was famished, and walking was difficult, but he didn't lose heart as he made his way down the path. He supposed he was experiencing the giddiness of those who knew they'd escaped death.

As the sun rose above the ridgeline, he basked in its drying warmth. He was making acceptable time on the path, considering his lame ankle, and he grew more tranquil as he progressed, imagining the comfortable inn, a plate of food, and a pint of ale.

As the hiking path turned onto the road, he saw a mule-drawn cart coming toward him. The driver of the cart was small. He wore a wide-brimmed straw hat that hid much of his face, and he held a switch in his left hand. A large and menacing dog trotted alongside the cart.

The lieutenant was instantly on his guard, even as he told himself that this sense of danger was irrational on an English country road in the twentieth century. It occurred to him that he must look awful. His clothing was dirty and torn, his trousers still wet, his face battered, and he was limping. The dog growled, and the man did nothing to silence it.

Just a peddler, the lieutenant surmised. As the cart came closer, he noticed that the man wore red boots. Something with a red handle protruded from one of them. The man switched the mule on the face, and it came to a stop.

"Bad weather", the man said. The hat, and the shadow it produced, made it difficult to see the man's face.

"Yes", the lieutenant said.

"Are you alone?" the man asked.

Should he answer? He did not.

"Better weather", the man said when the lieutenant failed to reply, even as the dog moved off the road and cantered to the lieutenant's right. It had stopped growling, but its silence was more unsettling than belligerence.

"Yes", the lieutenant answered, keeping an eye on the dog.

"The village was battered", the peddler said. The lieutenant had a suspicion that the man was using this repartee to decide something. He tried to see more of the man's face, without success. It was a weathered face; that much he could tell. Where was that cursed dog?

"What do you have in the bag?"

"Clothes."

"What else?"

"Nothing", he lied. A good lie?

The man chortled, making a sound that was, at once, hearty and sinister.

"I'm late", the lieutenant said, stepping forward.

"I'm a curious man", the peddler said. "Show me what's in the bag." The man reached down and grasped the red handle that protruded from his boot. With it came a long knife.

"Put the bag on the ground", the man said, stepping down from the cart. He still held the switch in his left hand.

Where was the dog? The mule stood as if at attention. The lieutenant heard a snuffling from behind him; he was flanked.

He pulled the bag from his shoulders, exposing some of the gleaming box. The peddler must have seen it. The lieutenant knew what he must do; he would have one chance. From the flap in his bag, he removed his service revolver, turned, and put a bullet in the dog's head. It did not even whimper. Then he whirled to face the man, who was closing on him with knife and rod.

The peddler took another step. The lieutenant could see his face now, greed and desperation competing for ascendancy. The gun was pointed at the man's heart. After an instant of indecision, the peddler dropped the knife and fell to his knees, transformed from an agent of menace to a supplicant. Now the lieutenant could see nothing of his face or guess what was going on in the man's mind.

"Stay still", the lieutenant ordered. Wouldn't it be ironic, he thought, if after never having fired his revolver in battle, he killed this man on an English road? His blood was up. This treacherous man seemed to the lieutenant to represent every adversary he'd faced in that terrible war. This was the man who had killed Miller, the man who had nearly shot his head off that day when he peered out of the trench, the man who had driven Baker mad with incessant shelling. He felt an almost diabolical urge to pull the trigger and obliterate him.

It was evident that a demonstration of resistance was the last thing the peddler expected from this bedraggled hiker. The lieutenant picked up the knife and slid it into the bag. The revolver remained pointed at the peddler's head.

"On your face", the lieutenant ordered, and the man immediately complied. Was the peddler still calculating? Was he frightened? Was he resigned to death? Was he even capable of rational thought, or did he act only on dark instincts? The lieutenant lowered the weapon; the bloodlust receded. He slung the pack over one shoulder and limped down the path in the direction of the town, not comfortable taking his eyes off his adversary.

So much for convalescence, the lieutenant told himself as he rounded the bend. He stopped for a few minutes to conceal the box with the shirt as best as he was able. He tried to pick up the pace. If he didn't reach the town soon he would have to rest, even sleep, and he didn't relish the thought with that malevolent peddler nearby. He guessed that the knife and switch weren't the only weapons the man kept in his cart.

Never had he been so happy to enter a town. The innkeeper was surprised to see him and even more surprised to learn that he'd survived the storm in the open. Did he need to see a doctor? No, he told him. He was well enough. He enjoyed a hearty meal—he indulged himself with two pints of ale—and struggled up the stairs to his room. He was tempted to undress and fall on the bed; he desperately needed sleep. He looked into the dresser mirror and saw that the left side of his face was badly bruised. His hands and arms were striped with cuts and contusions. His ankle was blue and swollen, but it looked better than he had anticipated.

The bundle was on the floor, still sodden and looking like a heap of trash. The lieutenant uncovered the box, withdrew it from the sack, and for a second time, it took his breath away.

It must be silver, he told himself—but such a warm sheen. It positively gleamed. There were no visible seams. Patterns had been etched on its surface, and there were runelike figures on the top and sides. It must be very old, he thought. Perhaps it was of Norman, or even Saxon, craftsmanship; he doubted that a modern metalsmith could replicate such workmanship. No wonder the peddler lusted after it, though the man had only glimpsed it.

The lieutenant wiped his eyes, which had misted over. He had nearly lost his life finding and keeping this object. Now, on seeing it, he felt exhilarated; it was magnificent.

Was there something inside? There was nothing to suggest that the box opened. To the eye, it appeared to be of one piece. He had an idea, however, that it wasn't empty. He turned it around and upside down but could find no apparent way in. So tired that he could barely stay awake, he was on the verge of giving up when he saw a strange swirling pattern on each side. He could read and interpret nothing, of course—the runes were meaningless—but these patterns reminded him of fingerprints, thumbprints. He set the box on the bed and applied gentle pressure with both thumbs against the swirl on each side.

As if by magic a seam appeared near the top of the box, and the lid rose, slowly and silently. A horde of trench rats could have scurried into the room and he wouldn't have noticed. The interior was lined with a fabric that cradled an object. It was a book with a red cover. What was he to do with it? Dare he even touch it?

For a long time, the lieutenant was paralyzed; even his fatigue was forgotten, or repressed. Only his trembling hand signified that he was alive. Should he close the box—if he could—and convey it to the British Museum? He took a deep breath ... another ... another ... and lifted the book from its couch. Then he opened it—and saw.

July 12, 1917

Southeast England

It was an unassuming room, a small office adjoining an equally small kitchen, that housed the objects the lieutenant had discovered and brought home at the risk of his life. Three days had passed since his ordeal, and he was rested and healing agreeably, this according to E. M., who was playing the piano in the front room.

After a good night's rest, he'd had two cups of tea and a big breakfast. Though it was late morning, he still wore his tattered robe. Three days from now he would be on the train, returning to active duty, though not to the front; that was unlikely given his still-precarious health. But who could say with certainty? Another advance by the Germans might compel the Allies to throw every man who could bear a weapon into the battle. And what would be the impact of the American colossus that had just declared war on Germany? For now, he would remain in England with little to do. Guilt gnawed at him whenever he thought of Martin and the others in the trenches.

He walked to the trunk against the wall and opened it. Toward the rear, beneath a small blanket, was the box. He lifted it as if it were a living thing and carried it to the desk. A window looked out on the backyard and the alley. He was careful to make sure that no one was about. Not another soul had seen the box. At the inn, he'd wrapped it in a sheet, and it never left his possession all the way home. E. M. had been in town when he arrived home.

E. M. was playing Chopin, a melodic, hypnotic piece. The music relaxed and refreshed him. He had every intention of revealing the box to her before he returned to active duty. Indeed, he intended to leave it in her care.

He had measured the box; it was exactly nineteen and one-eighth inches by fifteen and one-sixteenth inches by five and three-sixteenths inches deep. Irregular dimensions, but perhaps significant using the units of measurement of its maker.

It was not silver. He had brought a well-polished silver serving tray into the room, and its color compared to the box like a pencil drawing to an oil painting. Perhaps it was an alloy; he didn't know enough about metallurgy to say. All he knew was that the box shone with indescribable radiance, as if it absorbed the light around it and then emitted it with new qualities or, as impossible as it seemed, generated its own light.

He had contemplated the craftsman who made it, tried to imagine the man. He could not have been Norman or Anglo-Saxon because he must have lived and worked in an advanced civilization, a society rich in artisans and metalsmiths. Greece? Rome? China? Egypt? Babylon? The Americas? He had surely been a master of his craft—how else could the seamless lid be explained, and the elegant patterns on the surface? Could it be that the box was one of a kind? Could a genius have built this box as a prototype and then perished without revealing its secrets, like an Archimedes or a Leonardo?

He'd inspected it with a magnifying glass and had come away even more impressed with the fineness of the detail. There wasn't a visible flaw in the workmanship.

The lieutenant placed his thumbs in the proper places and opened the box, the first time he had done so since his stay at the inn. Again, he marveled that he could see no mechanism, no hinges, nothing to explain the opening and closing.

Inside, the book was nestled in the fabric. This fine material too was outside his experience. The fabric was silky, but he was certain it wasn't silk. Though its surface appeared smooth, it was velvety to the touch. At the inn, when a drop of water had fallen on the fabric, it had been wicked away. Not unlike the metal box, the fabric seemed luminous, shimmering with hues of green and blue. The combination of box and fabric made him wonder if they were even of this world, a fantastic, disconcerting, and ridiculous thought.

Still, there was the book, a more familiar object. The cover was clean, in excellent condition, blood red with what seemed to be tiny flecks of gold. The material was like leather but more supple. He removed the book, set the box on the floor—even in the shadows it seemed to glow—and began turning the pages. The craftsmanship of the binding was itself noteworthy. There was no resistance or stiffness when he turned the pages. Everything was perfectly aligned. The pages were finer than the best parchment he had ever seen— thin, translucent, and without a trace of yellowing. There had to be at least several thousand pages, he guessed. The absence of yellowing suggested something else: that the box, when closed, must be absolutely airtight and watertight. The pages were tightly packed with runelike letters. As he turned the pages he noticed demarcations that suggested chapters, or books within a book. At each of these demarcations, the subsequent page began with an oversized rune colored red, green, or blue. At the top of the pages with the larger runes was an image something like a crown, though it was more pictographic than literal.

The pages were remarkably sturdy considering their thinness. He could not help turning one after another. What story did they tell? Was it a log of accounts, a listing of assets, a record of transactions? He refused to believe that a thing of such beauty was nothing more than a ledger. He'd rather believe it was a chronicle or a compilation of myths.

As a philologist, he'd studied many alphabets, but he didn't recognize this one. It was neither Latin nor Greek, nor was it any of the Germanic or Celtic languages with which he was familiar, though stylistically it was closer to those than to the Oriental alphabets with which he was acquainted. He decided that the objects must be thousands of years old; otherwise, the alphabet would be familiar, even if he couldn't read it. Were the book and its box, he wondered, products of a long-lost civilization?

There was another explanation, and he could not dismiss it out of hand. Perhaps these objects were modern fabrications. Perhaps the box was airtight and the pages weren't yellowed because they had been recently produced. But if that was the case, why had the box been residing in a practically inaccessible location?

Seated at the desk, with the box on the floor and the book opened in front of him, the lieutenant noticed that the music had stopped.

"Is that for me?" she asked from the doorway.

He stood and faced her. No matter that he had known her for years; every time E. M. entered the room his heart raced. She was dark, stately in bearing, possessing ethereal beauty. Her cheekbones were pronounced, her nose small but distinctive, her lips thin, expressive. She was twenty-eight, three years his senior.

"As a matter of fact, it is."

"It's quite beautiful, John", she said, hovering over it.

"There's a story attached to it."

"I'd love to hear it, but only if it's true." Vintage E. M., never predictable or agreeable for the sake of agreeability. She lifted the box and was inspecting it. "What is it?"

"You won't like the tale", John said.

"I've already guessed that much." She sat in a cushioned chair in the corner of the room, still holding the box. "There is the matter of the red-handled knife I found in your bag. I don't think you own such a weapon." Then she said, "It's not silver, you know."

He had forgotten about the peddler's knife. "So I suspect", he said, and he told her the whole story, omitting nothing.

"You're a fool, John", she said when he finished. She was visibly shaken. "You should have shot that villain first. The dog was just following orders."

That was E. M., practical, protective when his well-being was threatened.

"There wasn't a great deal of time to think things out. And I wasn't quite myself."

"You were able to pull the trigger. You might have managed a second pull. I'm not bloodthirsty, but I don't like highwaymen. Well, it's finished, and you're here. You say these runes or characters are unfamiliar?" she said.

"Completely. I'm at a loss."

"John, it frightens me to know you suffered such misery, as if the war weren't bad enough. What am I to do with you?"

He shrugged. "I'm leaving these things with you when I return to duty. They won't be safe with me." He bowed his head. It was a familiar signal that a melancholic mood was coming on. In spite of months of convalescence, he still looked gaunt. Truth be told, he felt gaunt inside—bursts of energy followed by despondency.

"I've been thinking about Miller", he said.

"You can't help him—or the girl", she said. "And it does you no good either."

"Who can say?" he said, absorbed in thought.

"I can, John. A year from now you may be capable of thinking about your corporal. Today and tomorrow you are mending."

"Those memories are hard to dismiss", John said.

"Of course they are when you compound it by visiting bereaved lovers. You aren't up to the job, in spite of what your heart tells you. You need time, and it's my job—my responsibility—to help you. Before you leave we must go to our tea room."

He smiled, remembering their practice of casting sugar cubes at the passersby on the street below. And when they ran out of sugar they'd move to a new table and a fresh bowl.

"I love you", he said.

"I want you to be happy again, John."

He said, "It hurts to leave you alone with our baby."

"I'll be too busy to think about it. And if I know you're mending, I'll be happy. I might sell this box and earn us a fortune. Perhaps I'll buy you a baronetcy."

She lifted the box from the floor. "You must have ideas about this box and book. Four days is plenty of time for you to have spun theories. I know that fertile and devious mind. A knock on that turtle-shell head won't signify." She was turning the box around in her hands. "I can't remember when I've seen anything this beautiful."

"I suspect it has resided in that cavern a long time." He chose his words carefully so as not to rekindle E. M.'s anxiety. "I don't see how it could be native to England. It must have been brought here by someone."

"How old do you think it is? The designs are spectacular. What is this metal, John?"

He was happy to see her interested in the artifact. "I'd be surprised if it was less than three thousand years old. It must be an alloy of silver, but I can't guess the composition. E. M., we must keep this an absolute secret, at least for a while. That peddler, in a sense, did me a favor by confirming that spectacular objects provoke avarice. No one else must know."

"Then I can't make a candy server out of it?"

"No candy server or planter or curio on the shelf", he said, with feigned seriousness.

"And the book?" she asked.

"It is so closely matched in size to the box that it's hard to believe they don't belong together. The runes, or characters, are strange. You will not be surprised to hear that I intend to translate it."

She'd expected it from the moment she first looked at an open page. How many hours would they spend apart as a result of this discovery? She looked at him. "Don't let this project consume you."

Of course she would go to the heart of the matter.

"What would you have me do with it?"

"I'd have you follow your heart, but not at the expense of obsession and isolation."

He felt a surge of resentment. Did she give him so little credit? She was still examining him. She saw—she knew him. "You will have to help me", he said.

She said, "We ought to make something—simple and solid—to conceal the box. Something so ordinary that it won't attract attention."

"Yes", he agreed.

"It's too bad", she said, fingering the lining. "This would make a lovely scarf."

"How do you feel?" he asked her.

"I'm well, and the baby is well. We may have a foot-baller, John." She got up and carried the box to the desk. Then she turned several pages in the book. "The calligraphy is stunning. Whoever wrote, or copied, this was a master. Will you be able to make sense of it?"

"I hope to", he answered. "It will be arduous work."

"Yes", she said. "If it's a boy, we shall name him John." They had not said a word about this before.

John said, "I want you and the baby to be well. That's all that matters."

She was looking at him. Her wide gray eyes were bright, even cheerful. There was an expression on her face he couldn't interpret. He took her hand.

"John", she said.

He waited for more, then realized that she wasn't speaking to him or about him.

"And if it's a girl?"

"What names do you like?" she said.

"Mary, Eleanor, Priscilla ..."

"Priscilla, that's it. There, not so difficult a decision, is it?"

"Remember, E.M., not a word to anyone about the box. I have an intuition of danger. Probably my imagination running wild—indulge me."

She reached into the box and ran her fingers over the fabric again. "It's selfish, John, but I wish you hadn't found it. There—I've said it."

"I may come to agree with you", he said. "But there's no turning back now."

"No", she agreed. "I suppose not. Our lives will change because of it."

"It needn't be so, E.M." But he couldn't help glancing out the window into the alley as he said it.

"You aren't the only one with intuitions. I'll do my part. Don't worry about that. Get better. That's enough for me."

She looked at the box and book one more time before she exited the room. Soon he heard the melody again. Just when E. M. needed him most and just when this fascinating project beckoned, he was ordered to occupy a desk at a nondescript outpost. There was nothing to be done about it, he told himself, but he need not like it.

To translate the manuscript was a linguist's dream, and the vast content told him that the probability of some success was reasonably good. It was the isolated parchment or stone with meager content that presented the greatest obstacles. E. M. had suggested that the magnitude of this project would consume him, dramatically alter his life—*their* lives. She had gotten to the marrow sooner than he had; not all that surprising, he admitted to himself. Once he embarked on this project, unless it turned out to be a fraud— something he hadn't dismissed as a possibility—he knew it would become a task of long duration and intensity. What effect would this have on their relationship and family?

The music suddenly ceased. He heard E. M. clearly from the other room. "Wouldn't it look smashing in Johnny's room? You may keep the book, of course. He won't be able to read for years. Think of the things we could store in it: toy soldiers and sweets, even socks and shoes. What do you say, John?"

"I'll teach him to read the book instead", John said.

"One professor per household is plenty," E. M. said, and added, "if not one too many."

The music drowned out his reply.

PART II

Idioma

October 6, 1923

University of Leeds

The professor's office was a riot of incongruity. Books were everywhere: on permanent shelves, on makeshift stands, on top of the lone desk in the room, even stacked in corners. There was no thematic consistency to the art on the walls. There was a devotional picture of the Virgin and Child, a pastoral landscape, and a depiction of a medieval battle. There was a pile of unopened mail on the desk. There was a vase of cut hollyhocks on the floor, presumably because the desk itself was too cluttered to accommodate them.

Often, he forgot where he was—the work, the secret work, that consuming work was to blame. So vivid were these mental transports that it was jarring to return to his proper time and place.

The young man had already entered the room when the professor looked up.

"I'm sorry, Professor. I knocked."

The visitor was tall and too ascetic looking for one so young. His straight dark hair was at odds with his angular features. He had a Roman nose and long, mobile fingers. Jacob Basile—that was the student's name.

"May I come in?"

He was already in. The professor had been looking forward to spending the morning with the book. "Sit. Please", the professor said, reminding himself of the proper order of his responsibilities.

The student seemed to anticipate John's request. He was already seated on the other side of the desk. He looked around the room, then fastened his eyes on the professor.

"You were in the war, weren't you, sir?"

"Yes", the professor said. "I was in France."

"Was it as bad as they say?"

"Yes. Worse."

"Most men don't want to talk about it", Basile said.

"It wasn't pleasant." The professor opened the desk drawer and put the page he'd been working on inside. What did this man want? What could Jacob Basile have to do with the war? Surely he was too young to have fought. Furthermore, he lacked a certain furtiveness that was common among men who'd once been so desperate. The professor had come to recognize that look, and often observed it in the mirror.

"I respect you", Basile said.

"Thank you." Basile was obviously on some sort of mission. Best, the professor concluded, to let the young man reveal it at his own pace.

"I want to talk to someone—someone I respect—outside the movement I've adopted."

The professor detected more resolve than confusion in this young man, but he was prepared to suspend judgment. "Have you adopted it, Jacob, or has it adopted you?"

"Does it matter?" Basile said.

"It matters a great deal."

The visitor ignored the professor's comment and said, "The world is changing."

"How so?" The professor sensed a reservoir of energy within this young man.

Basile's eyes shifted to the devotional picture. "Is that picture art, or more than art?"

"You said you respect me. That implies you know something about me. What do you think?"

"You aren't an easy man to label. That's the reason I'm here."

The professor folded his hands. He could see that his project would have to wait. Though he hadn't had much contact with Basile, he had found him to be alert and inquisitive. The young man might have missed out on the war but he had been splattered with its psychic mud. The result, a common result in the professor's experience, was an excess of earnestness but without the experiential framework to give it perspective. Careful, he cautioned himself. Experience didn't necessarily point one toward true north.

"Go on", the professor said.

"The world is changing", the young man repeated. "We have progressed beyond good and evil as certain categories."

"To what new end?" the professor said.

"Will, action, science, progress ... Yes, progress."

The professor said, "There was once a common understanding of good and evil. I wonder if the same can be said of these new ideas."

"There needn't be a common understanding. Outcomes are what matter. The utility of an action defines whether it is good or not."

"Jacob, your statement is logically inconsistent because one then needs a common understanding of utility. Who defines it?"

"Those who know better", Basile said. "I mean, those few who are better prepared—equipped, one could say—to define it."

"The Raskolnikovs of the world, the supermen?"

Basile shook his head. "Dostoyevsky is a relic of the past, Professor. He had a mistaken view of the priority of will.

He lacked the sophistication to understand the nuances that separate will and hubris."

"I don't want to be rude, but your argument is incoherent, logically speaking", the professor said. "How have you reasoned this out?"

"Reason ought to be at the service of will", Basile said.

The professor smiled. "Aha. So there it is. I chose the wrong literary allusion. This is Mad Hatter business. Why did you want to see me, Jacob?"

"I've said I respect you", Basile said, obviously stung by the professor's comment.

"Then you know enough about me to realize that I would consider this utilitarian mantra rubbish. It's nothing more than a formula for the advantaged and powerful to do what they please. Don't deceive yourself into thinking these are new ideas. Furthermore, they lead to worse than medieval serfdom because their advocates want to assume all the power but none of the responsibility. Lastly, it's devoid of grace and beauty."

"You do the movement an injustice", Basile said.

"Hear me, Jacob. Once an idea becomes a movement, rational discourse goes out the window."

"You were in the war. You know how senseless it is. You've experienced the consequences of the decisions of incompetent dreamers and schemers. You ought to be an ally of the movement." The student's voice betrayed emotion. "We would do away with war."

Basile hadn't come to consult. Why was he here? "Who sent you?" the professor said.

"No one. I'm here on my own initiative. What this world desperately needs is order."

"And people to order it, I daresay", the professor interjected.

"That stands to reason, but for the right motives."

"So it is always claimed."

"These are new ideas. You talk as if they've been tried."

"Often enough, Jacob, under different names and banners and social prophets."

"Would you rather war with bigger and better weapons?" Basile countered.

"You know what I believe. Are you trying to convert me—or yourself?"

The visitor shook his head and grimaced. "I don't know. That's why I'm here, I suppose. The old ideas are dead. They've failed. We need a new way."

"We need to find our way", the professor said.

"So we're not so far apart", Basile said, eagerly.

"Your idea is a new nihilism, a scientific take on materialism. It is a very old idea, older than you know." The professor's eyes inadvertently moved to the wooden container on the top shelf of the bookcase that housed the box. He could not get the Traitor—that immensely talented and powerful being—out of his mind. The book spoke to him even when he put it aside.

"Can we agree that some men are more capable of guiding civilizations than others? Can we agree that strife among nations is destructive? Good and evil, right and wrong, virtue and vice do not suffice in the modern world. Science has debunked them."

"And God?"

Basile hesitated, then said, "If we are honest with ourselves we will admit that theism is anachronistic, an opiate, as Marx put it."

"Yes," the professor said, "Marx has said so."

"We have the opportunity to form the future—a more efficient and ordered future."

"Does that excite you, Jacob?"

"Yes", Basile admitted. "It's a superior way. There are many great men who agree with me." That reservoir of energy was spilling over; the professor felt it.

"What can I do for you?" the professor said. He was sure there was something Basile hadn't said, and he was getting frustrated by this circuitous conversation.

Basile glanced again at the devotional picture. "We'd like you to join us."

"We—or you?"

"I have influence in the movement."

"I am known to be a disciple of reason, even too scrupulous a reasoner", the professor said with enforced patience. "I fear that reason isn't highly valued in this new order."

"Reason has its uses," Basile said, "and its limits."

"I'd expect a movement grounded in science to impose no limits on reasoning."

Basile's hands came together, and his fingers laced to form something that had the appearance of a beehive. "There is practical reasoning and impractical reasoning."

"Sentence first, verdict afterward", the professor said. "More Mad Hatter stuff, Jacob. There is muddled reasoning, but there is no 'practical' and 'impractical' reasoning."

"The movement wants bright men, experienced men. If you learned more about us, you would come to recognize that it's a superior way", Basile insisted.

The professor shook his head determinedly. "You have potential, if you don't limit yourself to so-called practical reasoning. One of the problems with grand movements is there's no place for humility. Even if you dismiss me as someone unworthy of respect, I hope you don't forget that." He winced as soon as he finished. It all sounded so sententious. E. M., could she have heard him, would have laughed out loud.

Basile looked confused, unsure if he had been complimented or admonished. He opened his mouth as if to speak but didn't. He unwound his tightly woven fingers and extended his hand. The professor took it. Without another word he left the room.

The professor sat still for a long time. The interview had upset him. A bright young man, inquisitive, and so susceptible to the Voice; that was how the professor had come to see it. He had made a mess of the interview. He glanced again at the top shelf. He was several men in one body: the husband and father, the teacher, and a kind of amanuensis for the author of the book, his voice in this time and place; last but not least, there was the lieutenant, who wandered in and out of his dreams at night. Where did one man begin and the other end? Could all be contained in one skin?

Basile was right about one thing. There was a wave of something washing over Britain. The war had dispirited so many, had made them question what they believed to be true. He himself had fought that metaphysical battle. How could he hope to counsel Basile, and others like him, when he was still spiritually bruised?

The room now quiet, he could hear bustling outside and voices in the courtyard. He admitted that the ethos that had prevailed in Britain, in Europe, for so long was coming undone. It had been under assault for over a century, and the terrible war had tipped the scales. Would Basile's new way—will, action, progress, utility—replace the social order of Christian Europe? What would that mean for the ordinary man, the Corporal Millers of the world?

The professor recognized that he'd adopted a mission antithetical to Basile's. He was not just translating a manuscript; he was being instructed by it, even formed by it. Yet this project was a secret from everyone except E. M. He yearned to share what he'd learned, but he dared not, would not—not yet.

He pushed thinning hair back from his forehead and lit his pipe. There was a lecture to be delivered later that day. He had been dilatory in preparing for it, and he was annoyed at himself. His need to publish, to advance at the university, was suffering as a result of his work on the manuscript. He told himself—he had told himself before—that he must put the book aside and attend to more conventional research, but every time he tried to do this he found himself distracted by this mesmerizing project. He had to remind himself again and again that this book would not put bread on their table, at least not in the foreseeable future.

The professor had inadvertently locked the drawer when he put the page inside. This was habitual; he never left the drawer unlocked, even for a minute, when he was not seated there. He removed the key from his pocket and opened the drawer, removed the paper, and, before closing the drawer, looked at the material he'd translated in the six years since he had found the book.

The professor had discovered that the runes were related to the family of old northern European languages with which he was already familiar, but the translation could never have been accomplished, even initiated, without the picture pages that the author, or editors contemporary with the author, had included in the book. Each of these picture pages contained small images that had been drawn by a skilled hand, along with their corresponding runes or "rune phrases". While most of these images were objects—sword, horse, axe—not a few depicted action, or even what the professor interpreted to be ideas. Using these images and his linguistic comparative tools, he had translated a significant amount of material. In doing so, he had stepped into another world, a world he was just beginning to plumb. He had taken to calling these chronicles the *legendarium*.

He vividly remembered the day he'd unlocked the first word, the sense that he was communicating with someone across centuries. Other words followed. There were still many gaps in the text he had already decoded, and he found himself filling them in with his own informed and fruitful imagination. For years, he had studied the oldest extant stories of northern Europe, and many of these he had read in their original languages. In many respects, the world he discovered in the book did not differ greatly from those stories, or even from his own world. There were trees and hills and water, cottages and farms, but also grand cities and creatures he could barely imagine, as well as wondrous and terrible events.

The presence of sentient creatures distinct from human beings in these chronicles seemingly proved that they were a work of fiction. It was possible that the events, or something resembling the events, had actually occurred and had been memorialized and embroidered; there was ample precedence for this in the legends from many cultures. All in all, it was so fascinating an enterprise that it was hard to attend to anything else. In short, it absorbed him, and he knew it.

The book exacted an emotional toll, and not only on him. E. M. had been stretched by his preoccupation with it. For the most part, she indulged him, knowing his determination to translate it, but lately, E. M. had pushed back, demanded his attention, objected when he suggested he had work to do. The tension frustrated both of them. He knew he'd been selfish and resented her for recognizing it. He told himself, as he had so many times before, that no project, no matter how intellectually satisfying, was as important as E. M. or young John, Michael, and Christopher. They were his North Star. His family had led him out of the spiritual miasma that had burdened him during and after the war.

The time for lecture approached. He put the paper in the drawer and locked it, realizing he had become compulsive, but unable to act otherwise. He took one deep breath after another to bring himself back to the present, to connect him to the topic of his presentation: philology. The previous week, he had—unwisely in retrospect—brought linguistic elements of the book into the classroom. Afterward, he admitted to himself that this violated his proscription against revealing anything about the book. Nothing he'd said could have raised the least suspicion, but he had diminished his own integrity by breaking the promise he'd made to himself. Now where would he draw the new line?

Why did that incident in the classroom remind him of the peddler on the road, and Miller? Miller was the easier matter. He imagined the corporal would have been pleased that the man whose life he had saved was a father and a teacher. Miller would call that success. If that humble man were still alive, the professor knew he could tell him anything and trust him to keep it secret. He sometimes wondered what had happened to Jenny. He had not seen or talked to her since the day of their awkward meeting. As for the peddler, that memory took him down a darker path. He knew that his reticence to reveal anything relating to the book hearkened back, in part, to that encounter. The book was more than story. It was artifact, icon, and treasure. To reveal it was to subject himself and his family to risks he couldn't define.

The locked drawer reminded him of the one in his mother's desk. At the time, it had seemed such a grand desk, but it was smaller than this one, and more worn. He remembered the chipped corner, the legs bare of varnish, and the scratches. He was very young when his mother died. The memories he retained were few but vivid. What long-lost treasures had she kept in her desk drawer?

He took a long walk after the lecture, circling the park until he began to tire. It was a summerlike day, but he barely noticed. He'd seen Jacob Basile in the front row, listening and writing like all the rest. One must test well, he reckoned, even in this new age. The professor was annoyed with Basile and, he admitted, with himself, because he was attracted to many of the student's ideas: an end to wars and strife between nations, an end to poverty, an increase in order and efficiency. In contrast to the heroic ideals depicted in the book, Basile's objectives seemed eminently practical. The professor yearned to discuss the book with others. What did the myth's ideals have to say to modern man? And who was the author? That remained a riddle. Was truth a human construction, or did it have transcendent value? Was there someone he could consult without revealing too much? He had broached this idea with E.M., who was receptive to whatever moved this project to a conclusion. Like the Pilgrim in the book, he might have to travel from place to place, seeking and hoping that something more could be learned. Where these travels would take him, he could not guess—not yet, but he had an idea where he would begin, the person he would see first. He knew the man by reputation: a large man in every sense of the word, a man who admitted reason and imagination, fact and possibility.

Shortly after he returned to his office, he heard a knock on the door and, this time, called out in a voice uncommonly loud, "Come in, please."

Basile walked into the room, unnerving the professor more than the latter cared to admit. Would the young man not leave him alone? The professor knew the type: inflamed with religious zeal for some cause.

"I'm sorry to bother you again", Basile said.

The professor wondered if he really was sorry. He asked the student to sit. Perhaps something he'd said to Basile had resonated with him. Then, he saw the look in the student's eyes and dismissed the idea that Basile was going to retreat from anything he'd said.

Basile laid a newspaper on the professor's desk, the small area that wasn't cluttered with papers and books. "Have you seen this?" he said, in a tone of suppressed superiority.

It was today's *Times*, and the professor had not yet read it. He often missed a week of news. He shook his head.

"Here", Basile said, perfunctorily.

The headlines concerned the European situation. The war to end all wars did not seem to have settled things. The situation in Europe was not so dire yet, but everyone sensed something building again, especially in those countries that had been defeated and with the peoples who were disappointed with postwar borders. The professor could almost believe that there was a "Voice" instigating this new strife.

"Not that", Basile said. "Settling big things will come when the movement succeeds. *This* article."

The professor could not help wondering what "settling" would entail. The young man's finger pointed at a piece below the fold.

Sir Richard Hope Missing; Murdered Woman Discovered

The professor knew Hope by reputation; all of Britain did. Though details were vague, it was widely believed that he'd been a hero in the last war. He hadn't led charges or rallied

86

peoples. Rather, it was said, Hope had labored in Germany and Russia at great personal risk to support democratic movements. If the stories were accurate, he had barely escaped capture by the Leninists and German militarists. He was also known as a man of integrity, a man with a rigid personal code, even a selfless man in a willful age. The professor recalled reading an article about Hope's humble lifestyle that contrasted with the man's notoriety.

Basile said, "You may find this interesting."

What Basile thought the professor would find interesting would probably be tedious, and the heading portended this.

The professor read:

> The dead body of an unidentified young woman has been found in the London townhouse of Sir Richard Hope, the British patriot and philanthropist. Few details have been made available by Scotland Yard, which is investigating the matter, but the woman, who was well dressed, appears to have been strangled.
>
> Sir Richard has not been found for questioning, and his valet told the *Times* that all was as usual when he left the flat yesterday evening for his club. Sir Richard, he said, exhibited no signs of distress or anxiety.
>
> A maid found the victim in the cellar early this morning.
>
> As to Sir Richard's whereabouts, there is speculation that he may have gone, or is attempting to go, abroad, as the circumstantial evidence is highly suspicious.

"It's a sad story", the professor said.

"Surely more than that", Basile said. His eyes were boring into the professor's. Those menacing hands were clasped together again.

The professor sat back and lit his pipe. "Instruct me."

"Don't you see?" Basile said. "This business is a ribbon on our conversation this morning."

The professor felt cornered and angry. He wondered if his features betrayed his disquiet.

"This man Hope is an icon of the old world: virtue on the surface and rottenness underneath."

"You're certain of that?" the professor said, but without conviction.

"It's quite evident. The article fairly screams what happened."

"It looks damning", the professor conceded.

"Thank you", Basile said, condescendingly.

"We don't know everything yet", the professor said. "Hope is one man, not a canonized saint as far as I know."

Basile stood and said, "May I suggest—I do not mean to be disrespectful—that your statement is disingenuous. You yourself warned me against muddled reasoning. Hope has been held up by the old order as an exemplar of its particular ethos."

The professor bristled but remained outwardly calm. "Even when we look up to people, we recognize that no man is without flaws—sin, some call it. Each makes his own choices, and there are always consequences, for good or ill."

Basile said, "I contend that Hope represents the bankruptcy of a society that produces civil strife and war and misery in the world, a veneer of goodness masking bad fruit. I say, let's be done with it, let's replace it with order and efficiency."

Didn't the Necromancer desire this sort of world, the professor asked himself? Wasn't the book rife with beings that believed what Basile believed?

"You've extracted much from this sad tragedy", the professor said.

"Tragedy?" Basile laughed robustly.

"A woman is dead", the professor said.

"One woman. What is that in comparison to the millions who suffer from wars and poverty? That's what ought to concern us."

"Isn't there any room for compassion in your movement?"

"Of course there is, but compassion must be subordinate to principle."

"I'll ask again, Jacob, how can I assist you?"

"I felt compelled to bring this matter to your attention", Basile said. "If you will indulge me, it is an allegorical rebuke to your ideas."

The professor leaned forward, head wreathed in smoke. He looked up at Basile and said, "What do you think happened to the woman?"

"It's obvious", Basile said. "Saint Richard knew the woman in the biblical sense, something went wrong, and he killed her. Then he fled."

"They haven't identified her."

"Not yet. They will. A society piece of fluff—probably the daughter or sister or wife of a peer."

"It would seem so", the professor said. "Still, one expects something more concrete before it's made an anthem for a movement." He smiled and emitted a cloud of smoke. He only wished he felt as confident as he portrayed.

Basile shook his head and coughed. "If I said any more you would think me intemperate." With that, he turned and left the room.

The professor was perturbed, in part because he had failed to refute the young man's assertions. Also, he was more troubled than he'd let on about Sir Richard. He respected the man, had put him on a pedestal. Incidents like this made him wonder whether a life of virtue was possible or whether the best one could do was avoid Sir Richard's notoriety. All men were flawed, he said to himself, but this ...

He lifted the newspaper from his desk and dropped it on the floor. It opened to the usual minutiae that characterized a great metropolis: the interminable Irish question, uprisings, bitter arguments in Parliament; the problem of the automobile in the city; a new statue unveiled in Hyde Park; a series of lectures at the University of London by a professor of paleohistory from the Sorbonne ...

This last piece captured the professor's attention, and he read it in its entirety. The visiting professor, Adler Alembert, was speaking on the relationship between myth and ancient history, even prehistory. It made him wonder. Could he accelerate the unlocking of the manuscript by consulting a scholar like Alembert? Could he get to London and schedule an audience with the lecturer before Alembert returned to Paris? The piece said the man would be in Britain for three more days, but the professor had lectures of his own to deliver, and an outing with E. M. and the boys that E. M. was eagerly anticipating.

Now that the idea had come to him, he was frustrated that he couldn't pursue it. A man like Alembert could provide helpful suggestions. Should he try to correspond with him? No, it was too sensitive and too subtle a matter for correspondence between strangers. If he wanted to see Alembert, he would have to seek him out.

It was almost time for supper. E. M. would be expecting him soon. Later, he would put young John on his knee and tell him stories, sometimes his own and sometimes episodes from the book. These stories were starting to come together, he realized, as he groped in the dark for the missing words and phrases in his translation.

The book. Everything seemed to orbit it. He unlocked the drawer and removed the copied pages he had been working on. Now, this rune in combination with these others—what could that mean? After experimenting with the word order, he refilled his pipe. The passage described a hard and radiant material forged by a strange race. Could it be the metal from which the box was fabricated? If so, he might conclusively link the box with the author's own culture. Now, where had he put that infernal pipe?

June 15, 1925

Royal Standard Pub, Beaconsfield

Entering that place was like stepping back in time. Not that there was anything contrived about the Royal Standard. It had the look and feel of having been transported intact from Her Victorian Majesty's empire and not having been built to replicate it. The pub was dark and smoky, and the wood—there was much of it—was redolent with age. It wasn't crowded, but those present, animated and cheerful, seemed to fill the room. Plates heaped with beef and bread and tankards of ale or porter were everywhere. It made John thirsty.

He didn't take long to identify the person he was seeking. The man was alone at a table in a broad alcove that seemed to fit him; even from across the room, it could be seen that he was a large man. A wide-brimmed hat hung on a peg to the right of his bench, and a cane rested against the side of the table. The man had not removed the gray cloak that covered his shoulders but left his arms free. He possessed a mobile mouth that greeted John with a broad smile; it was crowned with a thick gray-brown moustache. His spectacles were secured by a ribbon attached to his vest. Most noteworthy were the man's penetrating black eyes, which threatened to observe more than might be comfortable. In spite of this disquieting feature, these were not unfriendly eyes. Before him was a tankard of ale.

When the man rose, he was seen to be tall as well as broad, a mountain of a man. He gripped John's hand with vigor. "You may call me Gilbert", the man said.

"John. Thank you for seeing me."

"Your letter piqued my curiosity. Sit. Ale?"

"Thank you."

In less than a minute, a big pewter mug was set in front of John by a middle-aged woman.

"Thank you, Molly", Gilbert said.

"Are you well, sir?" she asked.

"Very well."

"And your good wife?"

"She is well too."

"We haven't seen so much of you, sir." She made a figure eight on the tabletop with her washrag.

"I'm slowing down, Molly. There is too much of me in pounds and years."

"Nonsense", Molly said with affection.

"It's good sense, not nonsense", the man said, grinning. "I hope you are well."

"Well enough. None of us is getting younger", she said as she bustled away.

After a sip of ale, John felt more at ease. He'd removed his hat. Now he took his coat off and filled his pipe. The big man lit a cigar. They drank ale and smoked together as if they had known each other for years instead of minutes.

John had come to this place to learn something, but as he sat opposite this man, he began to sense another purpose, hard to describe and impossible to hurry. Whatever it was, it required his cooperation.

A tall, thin man with a hooked nose and a pipe that looked foreign in origin approached their table. He extended a hand to Gilbert, who took it eagerly, then introduced the man to John: Colonel Banner. The man's clothes were of good quality but old and fraying at the sleeves and collar. The tobacco he smoked emitted a strange fragrance. He wasn't exactly furtive—distracted, perhaps. He put his hands and threadbare sleeves behind his back.

"It's good to see you again, Gilbert", the man said.

"And you, William."

"Are you still contributing to the *Times*?"

"Yes, but not so faithfully."

Banner shook his head. "How do you manage it? Takes me a week to write a letter. Wouldn't want to see it in print."

"It's akin to hunting foxes", Gilbert answered. "One gets accustomed."

"If you say so. Dogs and foxes I understand." Banner looked at John, as if noticing him for the first time. John already suspected that encounters with Gilbert had the effect of rendering others all but invisible. "What is your business, sir?" Banner said to John.

"I'm a teacher. At Oxford."

Banner snorted. "Another wordsmith. I'm outnumbered. Gilbert collects 'em."

"We're all ale drinkers", Gilbert said. "That makes us comrades in cups."

"Hah. I'll drink to that", Banner said. "I won't disturb you. Couldn't resist saying hello."

"How is Betsy?" Gilbert asked before the man could leave.

Banner's eyes dropped. "Lost her last winter." His hands emerged again.

Gilbert ran a hand through his mop of hair and frowned. "I hadn't heard, William. She shall have my prayers."

Banner said, "I miss her."

"God knows", Gilbert said reflectively. He stood and shook Banner's hand with enthusiasm. "Let's have dinner next week."

John saw that Banner was touched. John stood and shook the colonel's hand too, imagining a world without E. M. He hoped it would never come to that. When John sat down, he noticed Gilbert's somber expression.

"Betsy was a good woman. I ought to have known. Too many distractions. Too many so-called important things to do." Then those dark eyes bored into John's. "Were you in the war?"

"The Somme."

Gilbert nodded. "That business changed the world, and not for the better." He took a sip of ale. "You wanted to speak to me about a discovery you've made."

John said, "Yes. I'm grateful you agreed to see me."

"We shall see. Perhaps I will be the more grateful." Two tankards of ale descended in front of them. "Thank you, Molly", Gilbert muttered. "Satisfy my curiosity", he said to John after sampling the fresh ale.

"I've come into possession of an old epic", John said, tentatively.

"Are there any new epics? Forgive the interruption. Pray, continue."

John said, "It's an old work but altogether new. I mean, it's unknown. It's not a modern fabrication; I've ruled that out. I'm a linguist, and I'm convinced that I'm reading an unknown language, though an ancestor to ancient northern European tongues."

"Stop, sir. Reading? You've been translating it?"

"Yes."

"You have my undivided attention. How old do you judge this document to be?"

John hesitated. "I can't say. The book—"

"A book—ah!"

"—describes a remarkable culture, but it's not the content alone that indicates a high culture; the container that houses the book is ... *sui generis*. No description can do it justice. I'm convinced it's made of an altogether new metal, or alloy. When closed, the container is entirely secure and protected from the elements, and after eight years of having it in my possession, I still cannot comprehend how the opening mechanism works."

"Is the book a mythology, an *Iliad* or a *Gilgamesh*?" Gilbert asked. He had recommenced smoking his cigar.

"I'm not sure", John said. "On one hand, it seems to be a chronicle of events; on the other hand, the story is too fantastic to be true."

"That doesn't make it untrue, or false for that matter. Many fantastic things are true, and the mundane is often false."

So often, John mused, when one met a man of reputation or notoriety, he turned out to be a disappointment. Not so with Gilbert. This man possessed depth. He subjected statements to reason, but not the stilted reason that proceeded from untested premises.

"How can I help you?" Gilbert said.

"Is that you, G. K.?" A face descended between John and Gilbert. It was a lined and pock-marked face, with not a hair on it or on top of it.

"Is that you, Burt?" Gilbert said. "Good heavens."

"It's me."

Gilbert rose and shook hands with Burt. The way Gilbert greeted his friends struck John as something like Old King Cole holding court. His greetings were heartfelt too, rather than perfunctory.

"Been an age", the newcomer said.

"Meet my friend—John."

Burt turned his gaze to John. "Burt the dustman. Pleased to make your acquaintance."

John took his hand.

"G. K. and I are old friends. He's an extremely good egg", Burt said to John, as if Gilbert weren't present. Miller had called John a good egg. "Helped me out of a jam more than once. Tells a good story too, for a learned gentleman."

Gilbert laughed out loud. "Don't let him fool you, John. Burt makes this place tick. He brews a tolerable porter too."

"Not so much anymore. I'm semiretired these days. Rheumatism in the digits." He wiggled his fingers.

"Burt can grow roses on pavement. Ask my good wife. Will you have an ale with us?"

"Thanks all the same, but I'm sure there's too much thinking going on here. I said to myself, Burt, this business is way above your head, but you'll not miss shaking hands with an old friend. Now that that's finished, I'll be on my way."

"You are always welcome at my table, Burt", Gilbert said.

"Likewise; goes without saying. Good to meet you, John. Don't let this fellow tie your brain in knots, and don't try to match him pint for pint neither." Burt touched the top of his head and wandered away.

Gilbert waved his cigar and said, "Burt is quite a fellow, and an artist in the garden. Now, where were we?"

John scanned the room to make sure their conversation was as private as possible. Satisfied, he took a sip of ale and said, "I have suspicions about the manuscript. I need to speak to an authority. That may require travel, but I dare not reveal too much."

"To whom do you propose to speak?"

"A historian—ancient history, paleohistory. Then a biologist and a geologist."

"Well now", Gilbert said. "What leads you to believe that the book is that old?"

Here was the crux of it, and Gilbert had put his finger on it. John said, "How could a civilization with a written language, a history that spanned thousands of years, and amazingly skilled artisans be unknown to the modern world unless it predated recorded history?"

"You are certain that it is history and not mythology?"

"I'm not certain. That's the reason I asked to speak with you", John said.

"I'm not an oracle, sir"—Gilbert lifted his spectacles and let them rest on the crown of his head—"but I can tell you that literary history is replete with vivid representations of lost places: Atlantis, Camelot. Even the civilizations we know about were as old as the hills before they built their towers, temples, and tombs. And, of course, there are the human artifacts, thousands of years old, that we know very little about; for instance, the White Horse of Uffington, or Stonehenge. I'm thinking out loud. This idea of yours takes getting used to." Gilbert lifted the tankard to his lips. "Thinking is far from passive, and hard thinking is positively Olympian. It demands exertion. You will have another? Good."

Molly appeared with two more tankards and scooped up the empties. She snapped her towel at the big man before departing.

"Bring another to Burt", Gilbert instructed her.

"That'll just encourage him", she said.

Gilbert laughed. "I'll run that risk, Molly." Then he turned to John. "This was our favorite table, Belloc and I. Burt joined us from time to time. He's a natural philosopher at heart. What he lacks in vocabulary he makes up for in originality. You might say his vocation trails his intellect, but he won't fall for sloppy reasoning. He's a thirsty devil too. Back to your story—you have only told me the half of it, if that much."

"I'm sorry. You've heard more than anyone, except my wife", John said.

"Tell me how long you've been at it."

"Eight years."

"And you are still trying to determine if it's a chronicle or a fable", Gilbert said.

"I must know if it's a true story", John said, knocking the ash from his pipe.

"A story that reveals truth is a true story, whether it actually happened or not", Gilbert said.

"Yes, but I hope to learn if this story has any basis in historical fact. At times, I'm convinced it has, but it's so fantastic."

"The most wondrous truths happen to be fantastic. Let's do an experiment in reason. Lord Russell has referred to me as a superstitious, though witty, fool. I will try to manage this experiment in spite of those intellectual limitations."

John restarted his pipe. He sensed that his companion was building a head of steam. John was determined to hear him out. That was why he had so looked forward to this meeting. The din around them effectively afforded them the privacy of a locked room. John was finding it hard to hear his companion without careful attention.

Gilbert said, "You have discovered something mysterious, and I see only five possibilities."

John's pipe was smoking. He waited.

"The possibilities are these. First, the document is of medieval European authorship, but the author is obscure. This doesn't explain the language, so we are compelled to imagine a genius who created a language, along with a mythology. If this is true, who made the box? It strains credulity to believe that one man living in England in the Middle Ages, or even a few such men, were responsible for the manuscript and the box, if that container is as prodigiously ingenious as you suggest.

"Second possibility: the chronicle is a modern fabrication, but expertly executed. Perhaps it is the product of an organization working over many years. Many good minds might have authored the book, and built the box you've described. But why? You have not told me how or where you discovered these objects, but they must have been well concealed.

"Third possibility: it is the product of an obscure culture, coincident perhaps with medieval Europe, perhaps predating it, but within the span of recorded history. But why then have we no other artifacts from this culture, if it was so proximate to us in time?

"Fourth possibility: it is a prehistoric manuscript. Recorded history extends back in time about seven thousand years. Agreed?"

"Agreed."

"If this book—you called it a book—is older than recorded history, it signifies something important." He looked at John, who nodded.

Gilbert said, "It signifies that an advanced northern civilization predated recorded European history."

John knocked his pipe against the side of the table. "You said there are five possibilities."

"I did. There is another possibility, though I am loath to produce it."

"You must produce it", John said. "We have undertaken a reasoning exercise."

"So be it", Gilbert said, swallowing a mouthful of ale. "There is another possibility. It's personal."

"In other words, it involves me", John said.

"The story might have been fabricated by you, for reasons unknown. I may be a test case. I'm known to be a skeptic. If I can be convinced ..."

"It's a more credible explanation than all the rest", John observed.

"Except that I am a keen judge of character, and I do not believe you are being deceitful. Furthermore, your reputation is impeccable. I conclude that if this is the true explanation, you would have brought pages of this fabrication with you, knowing that my competency is not linguistics. It would not have been difficult to dupe me."

"I don't agree that duping you, in any matter, is easy, but I take your point", John said.

"Shall we assess these possibilities?" Gilbert said.

John grinned. "It may say as much about our predispositions and competencies as the truth."

"We will get to know each other better, then", Gilbert said. "What is your opinion?"

"Prehistoric in origin", John said. "Not a certainty by any means, but it fits better than the other explanations. I make this suggestion humbly, as such an answer, if it is true, would present a colossal quandary for historians and scientists alike. And your opinion?"

"This exercise was never about my opinion, as you know. I have drawn you out; that is enough."

John's fresh tankard of ale slid down the table and stopped in front of him. At a moment when fuzziness was a distinct impediment, he was beginning to feel a little bit fuzzy. The big man opposite him seemed unaffected by the ale. The pub was now filled with people, and the conversation amounted to a low roar. Barely a minute passed when John's companion was not waving or otherwise acknowledging someone in the room. He did this while drinking, speaking, and even while engaged in deep thought.

"If I understand you, you are asking me if it makes sense to consult experts about this chronicle", Gilbert said.

"That's part of it", John said.

"I prefer to consider matters in toto", Gilbert rejoined.

John screwed up his courage and said, "Will you accompany me on these interviews?"

The giant man churned with laughter. "I'm flattered, as close to the vest as you're keeping your secrets. You tempt me. Alas, my body is too large to travel, and my imagination is too large to be still. It's a predicament."

"Travel is more congenial these days", John said.

"It's faster. Congeniality is another matter." Gilbert wagged a finger. "An omnibus, trains, ships—they are all instruments of torture. They are engines of danger, doubt, discomfort, and drudgery. I must decline your offer, which is not to say that I refuse to help you. I prefer this bench. It is unlikely to pitch, jerk, start, or throw me to the floor."

John packed another pipe and lit it.

"You expected that answer", Gilbert said. Then he looked past John and raised his voice: "And to you, Burt", he said, lifting his tankard. "Tell me, John, what you can about this story."

John took his time answering. "It's as vivid as the history of England. It's as relevant as if it happened yesterday. It's subtle and heroic and tragic. Everything I discover makes me eager to learn more."

"How close are you to a complete translation?"

"A complete translation will never be accomplished, by me at least, and I must admit that I am filling in the gaps with my own imagination. Unwittingly, I've become a co-author, a participant in the transmission of a message, like—dare I say it—a mystic entrusted with a private revelation."

"I envy you", Gilbert said. "And, in a certain sense, I pity you. You must be careful. Such an artifact would be swallowed up by those who move the world. When it comes to treasure hunting, you cannot slide a playing card between the government colossus and the corporate colossus. They will take your treasure without blinking."

"There are laws protecting private property", John protested.

"Ha!" Gilbert shouted so loudly that half the room looked at them. "Don't count on laws when there are millions to be made. Laws are all right for a pound and sixpence, but not when real money is at stake. You have done well for eight years, but the path you're suggesting is a dangerous one. Plan well, what you will say and what you will not, what you will reveal and what you will not, which questions you will answer and which you will not. The people who can help you can also do you harm; sad but true. But no omnibuses for me, my friend." Gilbert's tankard met the table with a crash. His face was beaming with a sort of mischievous delight.

John could not help smiling, in spite of his disappointment. "It's worth the effort and the sacrifice, this timeless story", he said.

"More evidence that it is true. Every true story is timeless", Gilbert said. "I judge that it has done more than entertain you. It's teaching you something, isn't it?"

John lowered his voice to little more than a whisper. Gilbert had to lean forward to hear him. He said, "There are powers that would grind man to dust."

The big man frowned and coughed a cloud of smoke.

"Then, and now", John added.

"Especially now." said Gilbert, nodding.

John could not help but recall his encounter with Jacob Basile. After that day, the young man hadn't said a word to him apart from academic matters, though John had tried to engage him in conversation on several occasions. He wondered where Jacob was now, if he was actively pursuing his new order. John said, "A student tried to recruit me into his movement at Leeds. Great men ordering life for the rest, no more war, order and efficiency. He was persuasive—"

"They all are", Gilbert interjected.

"In his new order, everything is valued according to its utility."

Gilbert shook his head. He smiled and said, "The world so turns. I regret to say that I am not large enough to impede it."

"Basile disarmed me with the story of Sir Richard Hope's perfidy."

"Hold on", Gilbert said, raising a hand. "Next you will tell me that honor and goodness are consigned to the dustbin because Sir Richard has fallen from heaven."

"Something like that." John said, smiling in spite of himself.

"And that story is supposed to confirm that young man's materialist credo."

"Basile said so. I botched the rebuttal."

"Of course you did!" Gilbert boomed. An old man at a nearby table shouted, "Give 'em hell, G. K.!" which, ironically, had the effect of subduing the big man. "Listen, these Leninists and fascists are shameless. They use falls from grace to buttress their cause but dismiss their own butchers as aberrations. They're bloodthirsty rascals in lamb's clothing; if that's modern science, you can have it.

"Let's consider Sir Richard with more light and less heat. At the onset of that business, it looked bleak for Sir Richard. I admit to knowing and liking the man. People would say that prejudices me. I contend it enlightens me, but let's set that fine point aside. The early reports suggested that the dead woman would soon be identified and that Sir Richard would soon be located. The notoriety of that business has long since receded, but the facts are these: the woman has never been identified, and Sir Richard has never been located. What does this suggest to you?"

John felt like he was in a classroom rather than a pub. He took a minute to ponder Gilbert's question. "I recall that the news reports identified her as a woman of pedigree. That she wasn't identified suggests her family didn't want her identified. Perhaps they had an aversion to scandal."

Gilbert raised a finger. It was as still as an obelisk. "That's one explanation, but it is not the simplest explanation. I have pondered this business. There is another explanation. No, sir—do not ask. You have your secrets, and I have mine. I'm not being capricious. My ideas are best kept under wraps for the time being.

"As for your debate with Mr. Basile, let me say that it is easy to be led along the smooth and wide path. Mr. Wells, Mr. Shaw, and Lord Russell, my adversaries in print and public debate, have tried to take me there often enough. The materialists are compelling because they give the illusion that intellect and reason are in their camp. They are scientists in the age of science, or so they claim, but behind the sluice of their science is a tide of irrationality and passion."

"Can I eke out anything more about Sir Richard?" John said.

Gilbert pursed his lips and smiled. "I suppose I can tell you this. I posed two questions, and the police generously obliged me with answers. The commissioner and I have supped at this table on more than one occasion, though we have yet to talk shop over dinner. He is a devotee of Raphael, and I happen to have an attachment to that master too. Where was I? Two questions: Did the dead peeress have calluses, and who in London died from other-than-natural causes on the night Sir Richard vanished? I'll save you the trouble of asking: the young woman had calluses on her hands and feet. Five men died in London that night: a young and an old vagabond died of alcoholism and a crushed skull, respectively. Lord Huppy's son walked in front of an omnibus, apparently because his lover threw him into the street. A stock trader in Bloomsbury fell off a balcony after consuming a bottle of single malt scotch. A university student ingested opium and suffered heart failure."

"Did these answers suggest something?" John said.

"They not only suggest something—they explain everything", Gilbert said with some emotion. "There is little doubt what happened. I don't know who was responsible. My suspicions will be hard to test with my aversion to modern transportation. I'm consigned to speculation."

"These clues are opiates; they excite but don't satisfy", John said. "Still, I can't guard my secrets and expect you to empty your trove."

"As to your mission", Gilbert said, abruptly changing the subject and pushing the tankard away. "No more ale. My sense of direction is impaired under the best of circumstances, and I am expected home in less than an hour. As to your mission, may I ask whom you propose to consult?"

John had thought about this question and his answer. He had come to receive as much guidance as possible from this man, someone he judged to be trustworthy. The more information he shared, the more the man across the table might help him. "I'm considering a professor of paleohistory at the Sorbonne by the name of Adler Alembert."

"Alembert", Gilbert said. "I know a little about the man. He is a connoisseur."

"I'm interested in his academic credentials", John said. Didn't Gilbert realize that this was the only reason John would bother to consult Alembert?

"I am interested in everything about the man", Gilbert countered.

"Does he enjoy a good reputation?"

The large man tapped the table. "He has gained some notoriety. As to his academic credentials, I can't comment."

"He is said to be at the pinnacle of his discipline", John said.

"By whom?"

"Historians I have consulted."

"I won't try to dissuade you, but be careful."

"I intend to be very careful."

Gilbert sidled along the bench. His corporation pressed against the table. He stood up, removed his hat from the peg, dropped it on his head theatrically, and let the cloak fall over his arms. He surprised John by saying, "Your wife—what's her name?"

"E. M."

"An economical name. You mustn't forget her in this business. I suspect she is a good woman."

"Yes."

"The better they are, the easier it is to take them for granted. That sort of woman makes few demands. I have a suspicion that you will not be successful in this mission without her help."

"What makes you say it?" John asked.

"I have met her, in a sense, by meeting you. The character of a man informs one about the character of his wife, and vice versa."

"I'm far from a good husband", John said.

"Hush. You mistake admonition for criticism. You didn't ask me here to be entertained by witty epigrams. You must keep E. M. in your counsel, even when you're troubled. Especially then."

Out of the corner of his eye, John saw the wizened Burt approaching their table. "Hello, Burt. I'm going home now", Gilbert said to the dustman.

"Well, G. K., it was almost like the old days. I miss it. Thanks for the ale."

"Don't mention it. I trust you're taking care of yourself—and your soul."

"I'm working at it", Burt said. "Getting old makes a man mindful of his limitations."

"Age has nothing to do with it", Gilbert rejoined. "The old just happen to have different temptations. But if advancing years can start a man, so much the better. I hope to see you soon, Burt. And you too, John."

Burt walked away, and Gilbert chuckled. "The good Lord broke the mold with that one. Here now—I think you are on to something. I've been thinking about this plan of action you're contemplating. It's wise and dangerous, but I don't have a better idea. You need information, and to get it, you need to reveal certain things. That's a high-wire act. Is this thing in a safe place?"

John hesitated. "It's safe enough."

"I doubt it", Gilbert said. "Let E. M. be the judge of that. Go ahead and consult your experts, but pretend that you think this chronicle is nothing but a fairy story, and do a better job of it than you've done with me. If I'm a judge of anything, I reckon you've received a gift. You're right to conceal some of it and to trust your judgment when your suspicions are aroused. The world is bigger than modern men who try to engirdle it with psychology and economics.

"I say again: make your good woman a partner and confidante. Lord knows I couldn't have accomplished a whit without my Frances. I wish I could walk the road with you. No, sir, don't tempt me with a steed I cannot mount and a lance I cannot shoulder. That path is yours alone." Gilbert wiped his brow. "And now I have a letter to write to the *Times*. They are obsessed with deadlines, and I'm a scourge to them." He pulled the cloak closer and grasped the head of the cane. In that moment he looked old and unsteady. Then he smiled down at John, and the sense of age and debilitation evaporated.

"Godspeed, John. I'll do what I can. You may hear from me again."

The room was smaller when he left it.

August 10, 1925

Paris

The man who admitted John to the brick and stone building was almost seven feet tall and weighed over three hundred pounds. His ebony face was laced with scars, as if some mad painter had decorated it. His hands were like anvils. He was unforgettably attired in evening dress.

"I'm John Hill. Professor Alembert is expecting me."

"Come with me", the man said.

John's sense of surprise began when he discovered that the building where Alembert resided was one of the most exclusive addresses in Paris. Apparently, professors commanded more income at the Sorbonne than at Oxford.

They arrived at the suite via a lift. John's guide crouched like a troll inside the chamber as it ascended. John felt unnerved in that confined space with the silent giant. He was being irrational, he told himself. The man had not said or done anything threatening; it was only his size that was intimidating. When the lift door opened, John discovered that he had been transported to another, finer world. Tapestry and art adorned the walls. Alcoves and tables featured sculpture and artifacts that appeared to be of great age. No expense had been spared on the paneling and flooring.

John was pressed to keep up with the giant's long strides. When they came to a huge wooden door, not polished or painted or gilded in any way, the giant didn't wait to be acknowledged, or perhaps he had a means of communication with the person inside the room that John didn't perceive. He opened the door and stepped in. John followed.

"Thank you, Christopher", a pleasant voice said. The room was so bright that, initially, John couldn't see the man behind the desk. The ceiling was at least twelve feet high. Two of the walls were made of floor-to-ceiling glass. The transparency of this glass exceeded anything that John had ever seen, as if it was cleaned daily.

He heard the door close behind him.

Slowly, John's eyes adapted. The man coming toward him wore a sweater and trousers. He resembled many of John's academic colleagues in that there was nothing visually remarkable about him. Adler Alembert was slight but tending to portliness, with a bespectacled, cherubic face. He had an unruly shock of silver-white hair, which made a pronounced V on his high forehead. The smile on his face— John came to learn that it was characteristic—was in contrast with Alembert's deep-set, dark eyes. Except for the hair, he was a person one would scarcely notice.

"Come in, Mr. Hill."

"John", John said, taking the man's hand.

"And you may call me Adler. Come; sit."

John settled opposite his host, who stood behind an ornate and ancient desk. Much of what he saw as his eyes scanned the room spoke of privilege, even permanence.

"How long has your family resided in France?" John asked Alembert. It was part of his plan to learn as much as practical about Alembert before discussing the reason for this meeting. He would make that concession, at least, to Gilbert's admonition for caution.

"We have hung our hats here, as they say. We have never resided here."

"But your surname is certainly French," John protested.

"My family name was once a jumble of consonants. My grandfather adopted the name Alembert. It exudes a certain dignity, don't you think?"

The chair offered to John was a lacquered antique. The desk was massive, solid maple accented with natural golden veins.

"Most men wonder how I manage all this on a lecturer's salary", said Alembert with a wave of his hand. "I was fortunate; I inherited some wealth, and it affords me the freedom to pursue my interests and to live as if I were working hard at something. My grandfather didn't have any interests except making money. As you can see, he was good at it." The man's English was smoothly enunciated, with only a hint of an accent.

"They are lovely accommodations", John said, still somewhat tongue-tied.

"I own the top three floors of this building. My living quarters are in the penthouse. It provides a spectacular view of Paris. You might have seen the Seine through the east window when you entered the room."

"Yes", John observed. He was still trying to acclimate himself to these luxurious quarters. He'd expected a modest flat and a narrower man than Alembert seemed to be.

"Visitors invariably ask about the origin of this flat, so I won't keep you in suspense. This building was constructed by Louis XV. He kept his mistress on the penthouse floor. No expense was spared, for which I am grateful. The door you passed through was an addition of my own. It is said to have graced Charlemagne's royal chamber. When it came into my possession, it required restoration. The wood is indigenous to southeast France, and the cladding—before I removed it—was consistent with the Carolingian period. It seemed a fitting portal for a historian."

The windows contained few structural members, affording a two-sided view of the city. The wall containing the door through which he had entered was paneled in a dark wood. The ceiling was overlaid with beige leather, sewn into six-foot rectangles. There were two large Persian rugs on the polished parquet floor. In spite of the room's lavishness, it seemed sterile to John—beauty lacking life. Perhaps, he thought, it suited a man whose work took him to the distant past, when rocks and storm clouds defined the landscape.

Louis XV might have sat in the chair he was sitting in, might have looked out a smaller window over his Paris, might have sipped an eighteenth-century Bordeaux with his paramour. John's host would have made a poor king, he reflected, with his squat figure and nondescript features. But, he reminded himself, hadn't Louis XV inherited power and fortune from the Sun King, as Alembert had inherited all of this from his grandfather?

John said, "Your Christian name intrigues me. It's German, but I've never encountered it as a first name."

"Quite", Alembert said. "My father was an amateur mathematician; he named me for an Austrian mathematician who fascinated him. I disappointed him by pursuing history as my field of study. He was hoping I would be another Newton. That's often the case with fathers and sons, isn't it?"

"My father died when I was an infant. I didn't know him", John said.

"That might be a tragedy, or a blessing", Alembert said.

An odd thing to say to a person one just met, John thought. Already, Alembert impressed John as someone who said exactly what he meant to say. So what did he mean by that comment about fathers and sons?

His eyes were drawn to a glass case against the window wall. It was longer than it was tall, probably eight feet long by four feet wide, and at least four feet in height. There was foliage inside it.

John saw that Alembert was beaming. His host said, "You have noticed my terrarium. Come and see."

John followed Alembert to the window. It struck him that, though Alembert was an academic, there was not a single book visible in the room or a piece of paper, and except for the foliage in the terrarium there were no plants or flowers. He was reminded again of the past, of a practically barren landscape. Did it say something about Alembert, or was it simply a matter of taste?

"My specimens", Alembert said, hovering over the case.

The specimens that John could see amidst the flowers and greenery were magnificent. Butterflies were perched everywhere, displaying a riot of color and pattern.

"It's usual to see these specimens pinned", John remarked.

Alembert reddened. "A barbaric practice. Once life is extracted, they lose dimension—and color too. Research is one thing, but displaying these marvelous creatures as art—bah!"

John was surprised by the intensity of Alembert's response. It contrasted with the clinical, even emotionless, comment he'd made about fathers and sons. "I have no such displays, if that's any consolation," he said, by way of mollifying his host.

"Commendable. These creatures are rare and delicate, and they live only a short while. To kill such a creature is a crime against art, not to say science. It is no simple matter to sustain them in captivity. I own a greenhouse outside the city where these creatures are nurtured, from egg to caterpillar to butterfly. I keep a variety of host plants for the eggs and larvae. My curator is quite successful at tricking the animals into replicating on my schedule. The specimens with black and blue bands and red dots are *Rhetus periander*. They were found in Venezuela." He put his hand through a door in the glass cover and rubbed a leaf, removed his hand, and brought his fingers to his nose. "The others, with turquoise and brown rays, are extremely rare. They come from Paraguay."

"They are spectacular", John said, sincerely. He'd never seen such colorful animals.

"If all of this evokes an image of a man scurrying in the brush with a net and a wicker basket, you would not be far from the mark. Do you see anything else?"

John looked again. Nothing else was moving. He wondered if Alembert was referring to the plants. Those in bloom displayed purple and orange flowers.

"You must look closely", Alembert instructed him.

John was embarrassed that it took as long as it did before he finally saw it: a gray-brown walking stick, as still as a twig. He had read about such creatures but had never seen one. In a sense, the creature was more twiglike than the twigs it perched on.

"How many do you have?"

"There are three specimens in the terrarium. The most subtle creatures I have ever encountered. Nets and binoculars aren't much use in stalking these animals. Unless you are looking closely—in large part, it is a matter of knowing where to look—they are invisible. Even then, it is no easy matter to distinguish them from their habitat."

"I can attest to that", John said.

Alembert erupted with a hearty laugh. "Don't let it trouble you. They say a man needs a hobby. Thanks to the mercantile genius of my grandfather, I can afford expensive ones. But you didn't come here for butterflies or bugs of any stripe. Sit. What can I get you to drink? I have a superb wine collection—Bordeaux is another passion. Will you have a glass with me?"

John hesitated, then agreed.

"Good." Alembert pushed a button on the wall, and Christopher soon appeared. He was already in the room by the time John noticed him. How could such a huge man move so unobtrusively?

"We will have the eleven Bordeaux. Let it breathe for half an hour and then decant it."

"Anything else?" Christopher's voice was a rumbling baritone.

"Nothing", Alembert said, clearly dismissing Christopher, who exited the room as silently as he had entered. "Now, John, I was intrigued by our correspondence. You teach at a country school. I can only imagine the stamina that requires. Young people are brimming with energy and mischief. I salute you. But I've forgotten where you teach."

"West Sussex."

"Yes, I remember now."

Was it John's imagination, or was Alembert's intonation ironic? Maybe the man was second-guessing his offer to be interviewed by an ordinary teacher, an intellectual pedestrian in comparison with Alembert's colleagues at the Sorbonne. With every glance around the room, John was more impressed. The view of Paris from that vantage point was something few had ever experienced. It was enough to take one's emotional breath away. And then there was Alembert—an ordinary man by all appearances.

"You said that you are writing a literary history", Alembert said.

"That's right."

"I'm not sure how helpful I can be. I haven't much imagination. Historians are a dull lot."

"I want the history to be as accurate as possible. I'd be grateful for any advice you can give me", John said.

"I shall expect a credit in your foreword." Alembert emitted a barking laugh. These outbursts, John concluded, were his exclamation points.

"Your work has influenced other scholars", John said. "When I began researching early history, even prehistory, your name figured prominently."

"One hopes so, but as I grow older, I wonder. I'm a sedentary and reclusive sort of man. Influential? I wonder."

"If citations and footnotes are evidence, your influence is profound. I'm particularly interested in prehistory."

"The Atlantean empire?" Alembert suggested. "It is the common magnet for those with such interests."

"Something along those lines", John admitted.

"That represents, as my colleagues suggest, a pseudo-scholarly pursuit. They are attentive when I expound on Sumerian ritual and law, but Atlantis is another matter. They are skeptics to the man."

"Do you agree with your colleagues, Professor?"

He wagged a finger. "Adler. No, I don't agree, but they have scholarly *gravitas* in their corner. I don't mind being considered eccentric, but I draw the line at heresy. Heretics are burned at the stake, even in these enlightened times. The modern stake is a scholarly journal, and the consuming flames are critical reviews. Excuse me", he said, glancing at the terrarium. "The *Rhetus* has been sluggish. I fear some pest has infected it. I've been spraying it with a concoction an entomologist at the university made up for me."

Alembert walked to the terrarium. He opened the glass door in the top of the case and sprayed one of the creatures. "Henri instructed me not to overdo it, or the remedy will be more toxic than the pest. That's plenty, I guess."

Darker clouds were obscuring the blue sky. John wondered what it would be like to experience a bad storm in this place. Even though the two men were enclosed, the glass walls gave one the sense of being exposed to the elements.

Just as Alembert sat down again, Christopher appeared at John's shoulder with a serving tray, a decanter filled with wine, and two crystal wineglasses. Christopher set the tray on the desk and bowed.

"Anything else?" he said.

"Have you made your rounds?" Alembert asked.

"Yes."

Alembert and the giant looked into each other's eyes, and Alembert said, "Nothing else, then."

Alembert poured the wine from the decanter and dipped his nose into one of the glasses. "It will do", he said. "A very good year." He lifted his glass, and John touched it with his own.

"To scholarship", Alembert said.

The Bordeaux was luscious. John couldn't help recalling his interview with Gilbert, the tankards of ale, the earthiness and camaraderie in the pub. That memory also reminded him of Gilbert's cautions. E. M. had also urged restraint, but Alembert seemed less a stranger than an old friend, or at least a familiar colleague. Gilbert and E. M. had not met Alembert. Wasn't his own experience of the man more reliable than their apprehensions?

"The wine is excellent", John said.

"It will do", Alembert said again. "This story of yours— where did you get the idea?"

John was prepared for this question. "I studied Norse and Greek legends in school. It seemed a good idea to use them as a starting point. I decided to go further back, but

I didn't have anything historical to rely on. There was the Sumerian civilization, but I imagined a civilization that was older, more advanced than the Sumerians, Babylonians, and Egyptians."

"A period with no historical interferences", Alembert said.

"That was the idea."

The man behind the desk gently swirled his wine and took a sip. He was examining John in a way—penetrating, intense—that seemed at odds with his casual demeanor. Was he thinking about the project John described, or something else?

"How can I assist you with this literary project?" Alembert asked him.

The wine warmed and invigorated John. He hadn't eaten since that morning when he disembarked from the boat, and then just a baguette. He felt at ease with this voluble and fascinating historian. Would it do any harm to share a little more information than he had intended, now that he'd met Alembert and taken his measure? As to the menacing Christopher, why wouldn't a wealthy man take prudent precautions to protect his person and possessions?

"Where would you place Atlantis, historically speaking?" John said.

"I delight in that sort of question", Alembert replied. "My colleagues consider Atlantis and Asgard to be cut from the same bolt of cloth. I have a different view. Plato puts the Atlantean civilization in the eleventh century B.C. It is thought by many—not me, by the way—that other accounts of Atlantis are derivative of Plato, his *Critias* and *Timaeus*. These later accounts—those of Theopompus, Crantor, and Zoticus—supposedly mimic the philosopher's original works."

"Why don't you believe this?" John asked.

"My colleagues say it is because I don't want to believe."

"And you?"

"Ah", Alembert said, accompanied by more finger wagging. "I'm not a romantic man. The foundation for my beliefs may be thin, but it possesses academic integrity. There are differences in the works of these other chroniclers that suggest nonidentical source material. Even my critics grudgingly admit that there are such clues in the original texts."

"You have access to these original texts?" John said, with amazement.

Alembert took another sip and nodded. "The problem is, we have artifacts from Sumer and Egypt and Babylon but nothing from an earlier advanced civilization. That is the chief reason the Atlantean civilization is considered to be legend. As to where I would place the Atlantean civilization, if such a civilization existed, I would guess further back than Plato—more than fifteen thousand years B.C. As to location, somewhere in the Atlantic Ocean. I'm not inclined to the Mediterranean island or African hypotheses."

"Do you consider it legend?"

"What Alembert the scholar and Alembert the antiquarian believe aren't necessarily identical", was his oblique answer.

John wasn't deterred. "Do you think there might have been a sophisticated civilization that predates recorded history?"

"I think it's possible. I have been attempting to prove it, but without a great deal of success."

"Have you had *any* success?" John inquired. Alembert had already supplied more than he had expected, and more candor than a stranger had any reason to expect. Here was a kindred spirit, someone with whom he might speak about common interests, and perhaps more. He wondered if he could greatly accelerate progress toward the answers he sought by collaborating with this scholar.

Alembert finished his glass of wine. He got up and walked toward the window, then peered into the terrarium as a mother might peer into a crib. The sky outside had grown dark. There were drops of water on the glass. Alembert's hands were folded behind his back. Small of stature and straight-backed, rocking back and forth on the balls of his feet, he reminded John of descriptions of Napoleon. The image was amusing. The man he was conversing with could not have been less like the French emperor.

When Alembert turned, he said, "I'm going to show you something."

"You needn't", John said. He was feeling guilty that Alembert was so forthcoming, while he was guilty of brazen dissimulation.

Alembert walked to the paneled wall but not to the door. Rather, he went to a location near the corner where glass met wood at a ninety-degree angle. He did something— John couldn't see what—and a man-sized panel in the wall opened. Alembert went into the opening. While he was gone, John looked out the windows at the darkening sky and pondered what else he dared to reveal to his host. He kept coming back to Gilbert's and E. M.'s admonitions. But hadn't Alembert earned more consideration by virtue of his honesty? There was also the possibility that John could learn more by revealing more. Could he summarily dismiss this opportunity because of Gilbert's and E. M.'s timidity? He'd almost finished his glass of wine when his host emerged from the dark space.

Alembert was holding something in his hand. "Have another glass of Bordeaux", he said.

John was inclined to submit, but he heard himself say no.

"Are you quite sure? It's an excellent year and a good château."

John said that he was sure. He felt a little unsteady—not drowsy, but light-headed. He should not have gone all day without eating. Furthermore, in preparation for the boat trip, he'd eaten little yesterday. He had to keep his wits, notwithstanding the geniality of his host.

"There are few who have seen this", Alembert said. He placed the object he'd been holding on the desk in front of John.

John needed every ounce of self-control he possessed to disguise his emotions. His pulse pounded and his heart raced. The goblet was beautiful—gold of the best quality, and masterfully crafted. The design was simple and elegant, but it was the runes that dominated his attention. He recognized them immediately. They were his runes. He could read them: *The King's Cup—may it be a vessel of gladness.*

John looked up. Alembert was watching him, hungrily, it seemed to John.

"What do you think?" Alembert asked.

John knew he had to be careful. He was playing a part— the country teacher—and his words must be consistent with that role. "It's a beautiful cup. What is its origin?"

"I acquired it from a dealer in antiquities", Alembert said. "It's a strange piece, isn't it? I consulted linguists, who told me the runes don't easily compare with any known runes or glyphs."

"I must take your word for it", John said, swallowing the desire to display his knowledge. He lifted the cup. He couldn't resist. There was no doubt about the meaning of the runes.

"In my headier moments, I imagine it originated in Atlantis", Alembert said.

John forced himself to laugh. "You suggest that this artifact is prehistorical."

"I speculate. I have no proof, so I dare not suggest."

John returned the goblet to the table. His hands were tingling. "I'm grateful you allowed me to see it, even touch it."

Alembert said, "You are composing a story about a prehistorical civilization—a fictional story," he said with emphasis, "and I'm seeking proof for a prehistorical, not to say mythical, civilization. This goblet is an interesting artifact, but as my colleagues would remind me if they could see it, it proves nothing. In isolation from other artifacts or, say, a manuscript, these runes can't be interpreted. They might as well be blemishes. But we know they say something, don't we?"

"Yes", John said. "I mean, they must say something."

"You cannot imagine what I would do to unlock their meaning", Alembert said.

Suddenly, rain lashed against the windows. The storm had arrived, but Alembert didn't seem to notice. To Alembert, or so it seemed to John, there was only this cup and, to a lesser extent, his guest.

A peal of thunder brought back memories of the tempest in the hills. That was the day this adventure had begun, the day he made the discovery that had brought John to Paris and to Adler Alembert. Where else would the box and its book take him, he wondered, as he sat opposite this fascinating man.

Another peal of thunder, aligned with the harmonics of the silicon structure of the glass, vibrated the window. Turning toward the terrarium, Alembert chuckled. "The butterflies sense everything. The charged atmosphere tricks their cellular memories, I suppose."

"The weather is bad", John said.

"Is it?" Alembert was examining the goblet with such single-mindedness that he didn't seem to notice the storm or Christopher approaching from the entrance. Without looking up, Alembert said, "I said there was nothing else, Christopher."

"A matter has arisen", Christopher said, apparently undaunted by his employer's rebuke.

"Yes?"

"The trouble in Argentina—"

"Yes?"

"Fowler doesn't seem to be up to it", Christopher said, dispassionately.

"I'm not surprised. Where is Agnes?"

"At the monastery."

"Very well. Tell her to handle the matter."

"It will take her two days to reach Buenos Aires."

"As soon as possible", Alembert said. His eyes never left the goblet.

"What shall we do about Fowler?"

"Dismiss him; it can't be helped."

"Will you speak to him?"

"There's no need. Tell Agnes to handle it."

"Shall we send one of the Germans to assist her?"

"An intriguing idea. Let me ponder it."

Christopher departed. John wondered how a man could be so large and yet so shadowy. Christopher hadn't conversed with Alembert as an equal, but it was clear that he was more than a domestic servant and a bodyguard. Where had he been trained? He had the air of someone who'd been disciplined by experts. Finally, Alembert looked up and smiled at John. "Business. I inherited my grandfather's assets *and* his liabilities."

John said, "Has Christopher been with you a long time?"

"Years."

"I've never met anyone quite like him."

"He has a charm all his own", Alembert said.

John's fascination with the giant spilled over. He said, "Where is his home?"

"His home is with me—wherever I am."

"His birthplace, then."

Alembert waved a hand. "Somewhere in Africa, I imagine. We have never discussed it."

Such an enigmatic answer—was there more to it than this simple summation? John said, "His family—are they here?" He had no sooner asked this question than he regretted it, realizing that this degree of interest might be intemperate in a virtual stranger.

"I wouldn't know", Alembert said, almost as if he was speaking to a pesky youth. "They are not in this building, if that's what you mean. He never mentions them." Alembert lifted the goblet and rotated it slowly. "Don't these runes fascinate you? Do they remind you of anything? Have you seen anything resembling them?" He said this as if Christopher, not to mention the storm, was a distraction from what really mattered.

"No", John lied.

"How could they be familiar?" Alembert said. "If I'm correct, these glyphs represent an unknown language. But you didn't come to see a trinket, no matter how lovely. You are seeking help with your story. That's right, isn't it?"

"Yes", John said.

"I will do my best to answer your questions," Alembert said, "as I'm sure you would be equally honest with me."

John had the strange sensation that Alembert knew who he was and why he had come, a ridiculous idea that must have arisen from the guilt he felt for lying to his host. John said, "You've inspired me with this artifact. If it's prehistoric, it suggests an advanced culture that predates everything we know. Plato may be vindicated."

"Plato wrote about an island civilization that dominated its world. This cup, even if it hails from that lost civilization, doesn't imply great power."

"It implies an appreciation for beauty. That's an even better thing", John said.

"That's an opinion I haven't considered." Alembert looked at the cup and then at John, as if he was measuring one or the other, or both. "I'm sorry to say I have a dinner appointment. I'd like to prolong our conversation, but business is a demanding master. Please ask any other questions you may have."

An abrupt dismissal, or so it seemed to John. Had he done or said something to upset Alembert, or was it nothing more than an appointment that must be kept? He wondered if his keen interest in Christopher had soured Alembert. John still had so many questions. "Could the civilization Plato described have been older, maybe much older, than he recorded? That could explain the absence of artifacts", John said.

"Destroyed by ice ages or geological upheavals", Alembert said. "That's an interesting idea."

"Yes. It's a fantastic idea, but only a literary idea", John said.

"Yet, there is this." Alembert picked up and fondled the goblet.

"Where was it discovered?"

"Who knows?" Alembert said. "It might have been in the possession of a hundred men, or a thousand, before it came to me. The gods or fates saw to it that it wasn't melted down or coined. Perhaps there are other artifacts that adorn men's homes or secret rooms—artifacts that are not recognized for what they are or that men desire to conceal."

"It must have cost you a fortune", John said, feeling the need to steer the conversation away from "other artifacts" and concealment.

"Sacrifices were made. Look, the rain has ended. I may not need an umbrella. The streets of Paris are more pleasant bareheaded. I never wear a hat. I don't believe in them. I will summon Christopher to escort you out."

"Such a man must come in handy", John said.

Alembert laughed. "It is clear that he has impressed you. He is more than a large man; he is a resourceful one. That's a valuable attribute. I could tell you a story, but we will leave it for another time. Look at this goblet, John. Almost perfect, in spite of these senseless glyphs."

"They aren't senseless", John said, without thinking.

"Why do you say so?" Alembert said, so softly that John could barely hear him.

John wavered between believing that Alembert was something of a bloodhound that raced from scent—interest—to scent, and a fox whose every move was carefully planned. Alembert had been nothing but a gracious host. Wasn't this an opportune time to share more of what he knew? John said, "It's hard to believe that such a beautiful object contains anything meaningless."

Alembert smiled pleasantly. "For a moment I thought you wanted to tell me something."

"What could I say about the cup that would interest you?"

Alembert laughed yet again. "Don't be offended, but I suppose it stretches the imagination to think that a country teacher could interpret these characters."

"It does indeed", John said.

"Look, there's a glimpse of the sun. It promises to be a good evening. When do you return to England?"

"Tomorrow."

"You are welcome to reside here tonight", Alembert said.

"That's good of you, but I've imposed long enough. Perhaps we will meet again."

"Of course we will", Alembert said. "I'm eager to read your story."

"May I say that you impress me as a native Englander", John remarked.

"Thank you. I was raised in England. My father was an English curate. Does that surprise you? He didn't inherit my grandfather's passion for business. I spent my boyhood in the English countryside. In a certain sense, I consider it my home."

"Did you see much of your grandfather when you were in England?"

"Occasionally. Not so often when I was small. Later, when I was older, I saw a great deal of him."

John said, "It sounds like your grandfather lived a life much different from that of your parents."

"Oh yes", Alembert agreed, giving John the impression that there was more he could say.

"When did you leave England?"

"I went to live with my grandfather when I was fourteen."

"It must have been hard to leave your family at so young an age."

Alembert seemed to be looking past John. He said, "An opportunity presented itself. I took it."

"And your parents?"

"They accepted my decision. But we digress. My story is not very interesting. You have made a long trip to be here. You see me as I am, a lover of antiquities and a caretaker of these lovely creatures." He pointed at the terrarium. "I attend to business when I must—only when I must."

"With your resources and interests, you have surely made a difference in the lives of many", John said.

Alembert shook his head and said, "The many do not move the world; movements move the world."

John heard that sentiment all too often these days. The Jacob Basiles of the world were working their magic. He felt compelled to respond. "I can't say I take that view."

"Then we must not talk about it", Alembert said. "This conversation has been so agreeable, it would be a shame to tarnish it. May I be candid with you? For a moment, I imagined that you could read the inscription. It's an odd sense I have. I'm often right."

"Any reading I could offer would be in jest", John answered. Alembert's observation was more than unexpected; it was startling. "I'm sorry to say I'm limited to the English language. Thank you for your hospitality . . . Adler."

"There, that wasn't so hard. It cements our friendship— two honest men who share a passion for history."

John stood. "I wish you good fortune with your project", Alembert said.

"And you with yours", John said, gazing at the goblet.

Christopher appeared. John had not seen Alembert send any signal to the giant. He was beginning to believe that legerdemain—hidden corridors, invisible signals, mystery— was another of this man's passions.

"Please show our guest out."

John followed Christopher. For so large a man, his fluidity of movement and balance were remarkable. On more than one occasion, Christopher had to bend and twist to avoid obstructions, and he accomplished these maneuvers deftly. Other than tending doors and serving wine, what exactly did he do for Alembert, John wondered? Christopher said nothing as he led John to the exit. He waited for John to open the door and let himself out, then the laconic giant pushed the door closed behind him.

John pondered his meeting with Alembert all the way back to his room. The air was delightfully clear, and the late afternoon sun was drying the pavement, producing a visible mist. Proprietors were mopping their chairs and tables free of water. Motorcars were inching up and down the busy streets. Paris was making ready for the evening.

Of course, the goblet was an artifact from the same civilization that authored the book. He wondered if he'd revealed anything by his remarks or expressions but convinced himself that was an unfounded fear. Had he been overly sensitive to Alembert's words and expressions because he, John, had a guilty conscience? He wasn't a practiced liar, but that by itself was no reason to think that Alembert suspected him of duplicity. How could John Hill, a country teacher from Sussex, know anything about such things?

He feasted that evening on bread and cheese and escargots—and a lesser Bordeaux.

August 3, 1927

London

The white cube traced an arc as it exited the balcony and descended to the sidewalk. It glanced off the shoulder of a stout man in a gray suit, struck the shoe of another man, and rolled off the curb and into the street. It came to rest on the grate of a gutter, still reasonably white and still recognizably cubic.

"Your turn", she said.

Not too many years ago, John would have launched the next sugar cube with childlike gusto. There it was, in the palm of his hand. All he had to do was reach back and fling it over the balcony.

He looked through the doorway into the dining room. A waiter was watching them. Though they were alone on the balcony, he felt as if every eye on the sidewalk and in the dining room was observing him.

He dropped the cube into the bowl.

Calmly, deliberately, she lifted the cube and threw it high and far, saying, "An inauspicious start, John."

"Because of a sugar cube?" John said.

"You're a great one for discovering meaning. It's not the object, but the meaning."

He reached toward the bowl, but she grasped his wrist and prevented him. "If it's coerced, there's no meaning. You know that."

Once, this had been their restaurant, and this balcony overlooking the street, their balcony. Outwardly, not much had changed: the same tables and tablecloths, the busy street, even the same red bowls filled with sugar cubes. The balcony dining area seated four small parties. It had a cement floor and an ornamental railing—nothing that would recommend it to a discriminating diner, but it was a magical place to John and E. M. During their courtship, they'd often eaten on this balcony overlooking the street. They liked the coziness of the balcony and the frenetic activity in the street.

"You look lovely", he said.

She smiled at him. "Thanks. Shall we have a drink?"

He looked for the waiter, who approached him with a grim expression. He could see the man's eyes dart to the sugar bowl.

"Two ales, please."

As the waiter retreated into the building, a bird passed directly above them, casting a shadow on the tablecloth, and landed on the balcony rail. It was a falcon, at least eight inches tall, a magnificent bird. Not five feet away, it seemed to be observing them.

"It's confused", she said, quietly.

John said, "It's bold, fearless. It's eyeing something."

"Nonsense. Something's wrong with it." Her posture was so rigid, her profile so still, that she reminded him of a cameo.

"You'll change your mind when you see it fall on something."

"It isn't looking at the street. It's looking at us, or something near us."

"Can we agree that it's entertaining us?" he said, in an attempt to find consensus on something.

"Yes", she said. "It's a kind of entertainment. It will sound strange, but I sense its dismay."

"Can birds be dismayed?" John said.

"Why not? I think this one is."

As the ales were set on the table, a man in a brown suit darted from the building and rendered the bird a glancing blow with a cane. It lifted off and began flying, but erratically. For a moment, it seemed about to fall into the street, but it managed to land on the rooftop of a nearby building.

"Be off", the man said, slapping his hand with the cane before exiting the balcony.

"That was uncalled for", E. M. said, loudly enough for their waiter and the patrons to hear.

John said, "I imagine it menaced the patrons."

"If anyone felt menaced, it should have been me. The creature was confused. If it had been left alone, it would have flown away sooner rather than later. That man deserves a sugar cube in the eye."

"Let's not make too much of it, E. M."

"You don't decide what is and isn't important to me, John."

He sat back and took a mouthful of ale. They were often at odds these days, and he was convinced that the book was at the root of it. She resented the hours and days he spent researching and translating. For his part, he was torn between his family and the project. When he was working, hours passed like minutes. The project was a sort of opiate that he couldn't resist for long.

Since the time they had been escorted to the balcony, the sky had been reddening. The sun was riding near the horizon, and the air was still. Blue sky and white clouds, in combination with the sun's red cast, had turned the air an ethereal pink. Everything looked different in that light, as if they were swimming in rose-colored water or had been transported to another world. The phenomenon was noticed by more than John and E. M.; people stood still in the street and looked around in a state of wonder. John and E. M. said nothing as minutes passed. Then, in a matter of seconds, the sun fell, the sky darkened, and people resumed their activities.

"That was beautiful", E. M. said. "This world has good surprises too. Are you hungry?"

"Not terribly. You?" He'd been watching her watching the strange sky. She had looked so natural and untroubled in those few minutes.

"Not terribly."

"Then let's sit for a while."

Below them were fast walkers, deliberate striders, lingerers, and not a few who looked to be lost. John and E. M. used to make a game of guessing where people were coming from or going to. Sometimes they would pick out an attractive target and bombard him with sugar cubes. They hadn't been watching for long when E. M. gave John a look of concern and whispered, "That man—gray coat and hat—do you see him?"

The man was standing on the corner down the street from them. John wondered if she was going to take aim, but the man was too far away.

"I see him", he said.

"Does he look familiar?"

"No", John said.

"Are you sure?"

"I'm not sure, but I don't think so."

E. M. said, "I've seen him in Oxford."

"Is that strange? We reside in Oxford, and here we are. London is a popular place."

"This is a different matter."

"How is it different?"

"I have seen him before—often."

"What are you saying, E. M.?"

"I don't know. Let it be, then. I didn't intend to trouble you."

"How can I let it be when you are being so mysterious? Are you suggesting that this man is following us, that there is something nefarious about him?"

"Look at him again, John."

"I tell you, he isn't familiar, but I'm not the most observant of men. Shall I go down to the street and confront him?"

"Don't be ridiculous. Now that you've seen him, remember him."

"He looks like an ordinary chap. Nothing of note to distinguish him. How certain are you?"

"Certain enough", she said. She hadn't taken her eyes off the man. Her animosity toward him was plain enough.

Since they began discussing him, the man had moved farther down the street. John thought he'd glanced in their direction but couldn't be sure. John had feared for some time that the book had put E. M. on edge, but this—was it paranoia?—was a new development.

His consternation must have been evident because she said, "Don't look at me like that. I'm not imagining things. I'm not an Oxford professor, but I'm as rational as any of them, maybe more so, and I'm more observant. Am I speaking loudly enough?"

"Plenty loud", he said, as a couple was escorted to a table on the opposite side of the balcony. The woman gave them an odd look and whispered something to the man who accompanied her.

"Good," E. M. said. "Then I'm having the desired effect."

E. M. made no secret of her disdain for John's Oxford colleagues, asserting often enough that they were more pretentious than his fellows at Leeds had been. Normally,

John ignored these broadsides, but now he was angry about the remark and E. M.'s apparent obsession. His eyes were drawn to the sugar cubes in the bowl, and he mourned the days when he and E. M. were so unreservedly glad to be together.

"Are you ready to place an order, sir?" the waiter asked. Another glance at the sugar bowl, then at E. M.

John looked at E. M., who shook her head.

"Give us a moment", he told the waiter.

"Not our finest hour, I'm afraid", he said, when the waiter was out of earshot.

She grinned and put her hand over his. "I'm not your enemy, John. I am your true friend."

He realized that E. M. had upped the ante by suggesting that strangers might be interested in their business, that the problem might be more than a domestic disagreement. Having survived that terrible war, John harbored no illusions about men and their motives, but who could have found out, or suspected, that he possessed something of inestimable value? Since he brought the box to their home years ago, he'd revealed it to no one except E. M. and Gilbert. When he moved the objects to his office at Leeds, the box and manuscript had been concealed within the wooden container he'd made. From the first day that the artifacts resided in his office, they had remained hidden in the container on the top shelf, a container as nondescript as could be imagined. The day he'd moved the container from Leeds to Oxford, along with books and other academic paraphernalia, it had never left his sight. Only when working on the manuscript did he bring the book to his desk, and he always—obsessively, one might say—concealed it again when he finished working.

Could one of his students or colleagues have searched his office? And if yes, why hadn't they taken the artifacts? Fumbling for an explanation, he entertained the fantastic idea that the peddler on the trail had followed him to the town, then all the way home; that was the only other person to have seen the box. Impossible, he told himself. He'd been trained in the army to be on guard, and though he didn't consider himself to be an especially skilled observer, he didn't think he could be followed for days at a time without being aware of it. Or could he?

Yes, he'd consulted Gilbert and Alembert, but he had revealed next to nothing to Alembert. Gilbert's reputation was unblemished, and he trusted the man implicitly; but hadn't he once trusted Sir Richard? He had crossed paths with Alembert for one afternoon, and their conversation, though fascinating, had concerned an abstraction (Atlantis) that interested them both. How could Alembert have taken anything more from that innocent meeting?

"We ought to eat", he said to E.M. "I doubt they'll let us sit here and exhaust their stock of sugar." He caught the waiter's attention, and they placed their order. E.M. draped her sweater over her shoulders and arms. The air was cooling. John lit his pipe. The taste and fragrance calmed him.

"I wonder if the bird is all right", E.M. said. "I can't see anything moving on the roof. That man had better not show his face, or I'll put that cane of his to better use than he did."

E.M. had changed little in the time he'd known her, except that her beauty was more mature. Her dark eyes and often-animated features complemented that beauty. Her attractiveness and natural reserve made her easy to underestimate. She possessed a keen intelligence that usually cut to the heart of a matter. He'd learned that sloppy reasoning was her bane.

"The man on the corner", E. M. said. "I'm not finished with him either."

John knocked the ash out of his pipe and refilled it.

"Shall I tell you why, or have you already decided to dismiss whatever I say?"

John said, "You know better than that. Speak your piece."

"I will speak my piece. I fear that man may be more than just a familiar face. I have seen him walking in the neighborhood, and I am practically certain he doesn't live there. There have been two occasions, a month ago and earlier this week, when something in the house was moved."

"John or Michael, even Christopher, might have done it, E. M."

"An item in my bureau? An object on a closet shelf in our bedroom? The objects never moved more than inches, but they moved. As for the children, I asked them. They're good boys but poor liars. I'm convinced they aren't responsible."

"What are you suggesting?"

"I'm saying that I believe our home has been invaded. So far as possessions go—including your precious box—I couldn't care less. My family is another matter."

How seriously should he take this? he wondered. Perhaps he'd moved the objects himself, though he had no recollection of opening E. M.'s bureau. He was certain of something, and that was E. M.'s earnestness about the matter. Even if an "invasion" was improbable, he had to give it credence for her sake.

"I'm sorry for what I said about the box", she said to him. "I was making a point. I know it's important to you."

"I'm not dismissing your suspicions. Why haven't you said anything before?"

"I didn't want to worry you. And it's not a certain thing. But what other explanation is there?"

"Has anyone else been in the house?"

"Jesse comes Mondays, but she doesn't clean our room. John's friend William spent a day with him. I can't imagine they'd go into our bedroom."

"Still, it's possible", John said.

"If you put it like that, just about anything's possible. The constable might have jimmied the window and waltzed in."

"Do you have an explanation?"

"Just the obvious one", she said.

"No one except you and Gilbert knows anything about the box or the book."

"How sure are you of that?"

"Quite sure. Are you suggesting I've told someone else?"

"Have you?"

"I have not." He wanted to say more but dared not, as angry as her suggestion made him.

Both of them held their tongues while the meal was served. E. M.'s eyes were brightly defiant. John pulled on his pipe so hard it was fuming like a little volcano.

"Bring me another ale", he said to the waiter. "I have not", he said to her again when the man had gone.

"What did Alembert ask you? You told me he was inquisitive—and intuitive."

"He was all of that, but I didn't reveal a thing. He was the one who revealed things."

She closed her eyes, shook her head, and said, "I'm afraid he knows, John. There it is. There are people who learn things, who know things, without being told."

"Nonsense. Let's eat before the food gets cold."

"I'm not hungry", she said, laying down her fork.

"It won't do to go hungry."

She pushed her chair back from the table. John could not remember when he'd been more frustrated. This creeping separation from E. M. troubled him. Something was always coming between them. John, Michael, and Christopher were getting old enough to notice the tension, something John had vowed would never happen. He knew that E. M. was frustrated too, with him, his project, and now this perceived threat.

The food was unsatisfying. Even the ale had lost its taste.

As he ate, and he ate little, he weighed what she had said and the emotion that accompanied her words. Whether he agreed with her or not, she was in deadly earnest about her fears. His plate was still half full of food when he said, "All right, E. M., I'll take this seriously. We'll have the locks changed. If it's the box and book that someone is after, it's fortunate that they've never been kept in the house, not since those first days. I'll consult the police too."

"You must move it out of your office", she said.

"I'm afraid it's too late for that. If someone is watching us—has broken into our home—they will be watching the office too. The most foolish thing I could do is carry it out of there. I'll have to bluff it out, E. M."

"Perhaps you're right." She put a morsel into her mouth and ate it without enthusiasm.

"As for the culprit—if there is a culprit—I don't believe that Alembert is involved, and I will not believe it until there's evidence to incriminate him. It must be someone in the town or at the college."

"I can't dispute that, or support it", she said. "Where is it?"

John knew that "it" could only mean one thing. He said, "On the top bookshelf in my office."

"A bulkier version of Poe's *Purloined Letter*. Who'd believe you'd keep a priceless artifact in plain view, inside that ugly crate you made? Humor me, John. Don't keep anything on your desk when you aren't in the office."

"I'm careful."

"Promise me."

He nodded.

"Your word is still your bond, I presume", she said.

He puffed and fumed. E. M. had always been strong willed, but he hadn't known her to be subject to nerves. Still, if she suspected an invasion of their home, she must have had good reasons for it. She was frightened; that was plain enough.

"That's the best we can do, I suppose", she said resignedly. He could hardly stand to see her so distraught. "You're making progress, I hope," she said.

"What?"

"With the book, John. What else is there?" She stirred her potatoes with a fork.

"It would make me happy to see you eat something", he said, in spite of the fact that he'd barely touched his own food.

"Tell me how the translation is going."

"It's just a matter of time; in a year or two I will have done all I can. There are words and phrases, whole passages, in fact, I will never be able to translate. Informed guessing will have to do for these. The project is evolving from deciphering the content of the book to comprehending the history and culture of the civilization that produced it."

"Can these things be fathomed?"

"That's the question, E. M. Who can say? Alembert's goblet was an unhoped-for discovery—independent corroboration of the existence of this civilization. He was a reservoir of information, and I suspect he knows more than he's revealed."

"It's what you know that worries me. What aren't you telling me?"

Only the dregs of his second glass of ale remained. She had consumed just half a glass. The lamp on the wall was a necessity now. Moths fluttered around it. The street was still awash with people. The man and woman at the table across the balcony were preparing to depart.

He pushed the plate away and said, "I'm convinced it's a true story."

"Do you think that surprises me?"

"It ought to. It's a nonsensical idea."

E. M. said, "You've believed it for a long time. You believed it before you admitted it to yourself."

"That doesn't make it any less outlandish. There's nothing in the historical record to support such a notion. What's more, the condition of the box and book argue against them being one hundred, much less ten thousand, years old. The Americans would say three strikes and you're out."

"And the opposing evidence?" she asked.

"The box and the manuscript exist. Alembert's goblet exists; the runes are the same. The more I translate, the more credible the author, or authors, of the manuscript proves himself to be. The cohesiveness of the work is astounding. And there is a legend—Atlantis—that fits the manuscript, like a tailored glove fits its owner."

She said, "What else can be done?"

He looked at their plates, smiled, and said, "Do you think they will bring us pudding if we haven't eaten our dinner?"

It made him happy to hear her laugh.

"You didn't answer me", she said.

"You won't like my answer."

"Let me be the judge of that."

"Here are the things I've been considering. Can the geologic and geographic records identify prehistoric periods when an advanced civilization might have existed on the European continent? Can the biological record suggest periods that correspond to animals and plants that populate the story? Then there's Alembert's specialty, history. Are there any other historical clues? Can these clues be put together like puzzle pieces to locate this civilization in space and time? That's the golden goose I'm after now."

"The project grows," E. M. said, "and I am convinced that Alembert is a puzzle piece too."

"I can't ignore him. He might be the central piece. There may be more than the goblet in his treasure trove."

She made a move as if to take his hand, but then withdrew it and said, "What are you willing to risk, John?"

At that moment, the waiter returned. He was surprised to see that the meal was practically untouched. "Can I get you something else, sir?"

"You may take it. We'll have coffee."

The waiter looked at them. Then he removed the plates. John thought he remembered the man from long-ago visits. He could tell that E. M. would not allow him to avoid her question. What was he willing to risk? What did he have the right to risk?

"I'll be careful", was all he could think to say.

"I don't know what that means. Were you careful in the cave, where you almost drowned? Were you careful when you brought those objects into our home? Were you careful when you masqueraded as a country teacher in Paris?

143

Were you careful when you made no provisions to protect our family? I'm a practical person, John. I need to know what being careful means."

He was bristling inside, but he had to concede that her reasoning was sound. Though he knew that these artifacts were priceless, he'd been playing this game as if it were nothing more than an academic exercise.

"We'll discuss each step, E. M.—together. We'll decide together what action to take."

"In advance?"

"In advance."

"I'm frightened. What about Alembert?"

"Look at what he's already revealed."

"And what have you revealed to him?" she asked him, earnestly.

"Nothing. Well, next to nothing."

"That's a supposition, not a fact", she said.

The waiter heard her remark. He couldn't serve the coffee quickly enough.

John put his pipe on the table. "What makes you say so?"

"Your own characterization of the man and your meeting with him. Why would he produce the goblet at your first meeting? Why is he interested in an ordinary country teacher?"

"He's a teacher too."

She laughed, but it was a nervous laugh. "I doubt that he's at all like you. Do you have a Zulu bodyguard? Do you gambol all over the world? Do you keep a wine cellar with expensive Bordeaux? I would be curious to hear the true story of how that goblet came to him. I doubt that he found it on a hiking trip."

"You do violence to a man you don't even know", John protested.

"It sounds like you've made up your mind."

"I haven't made up my mind. I won't make up my mind without your advice."

She shook her head. "My advice—it isn't worth much anymore."

"How do I respond to an accusation like that?"

"I don't know. So what are you going to do?"

"You're bound and determined to convict me."

"You're not being honest with yourself. You want to see Alembert again, don't you?"

John hesitated. "I've considered it."

"You have certainly considered it. More than that, you've thought about how to convince me. Don't bother; it's not important."

"It's important to me, E. M."

"Then what is your interest in Alembert?"

"Am I being interrogated?"

"I'm sorry. What do you hope to accomplish?"

"Alembert has the cup. Perhaps he possesses other artifacts. I'll be better prepared next time."

"So will he."

"What is he preparing for? He couldn't have known why I asked to meet him. He's a teacher with enough money for expensive hobbies. His scholarship and his hobbies are of interest to me. Why shouldn't I see him?"

"No reason, when you put it like that. Didn't Gilbert caution you?"

"Gilbert never met him; neither have you."

"Does that matter? If he's dangerous, he's also devious enough to disguise it."

"What do you advise, E. M.?"

She took the last cube out of the bowl and cast it over the railing. "Here's my advice: stay away from that man. I have a feeling you've gotten everything you're going to get from him."

"You didn't see the goblet or the runes."

"You have my advice. Take it or leave it."

"What if Alembert has the key to unlocking the mystery but doesn't know it? That knowledge might save years of work."

"And meeting him again could be a waste of time—or worse", she said, holding the bowl in one hand as if it were the next projectile.

"Do you think he's a villain, E. M.?"

"I don't know; do you? You said you respect Gilbert. I'm just repeating what he said to you. If you don't want our opinions, why bother asking?"

"I'm considering every option."

"But you haven't changed your mind, have you?"

"I told you I haven't made up my mind."

"That's what you said. What you decide to do is your business, but I won't permit our family to be threatened. Do you understand that?"

There was a moment when their eyes met. More was said in that moment than in the words she'd uttered.

"I understand."

"Then we understand each other", she said, resolutely.

He knew her, and he understood her in spite of their conflict. Furthermore, there had been more contained in her questions and admonitions than the words alone suggested. She would take the boys away if she concluded that they were threatened. It stung him, but how could he dispute her logic, a mother's practical logic?

"I understand, E. M.", was all he could say.

"It's empty", she said.

"What?"

She lifted the bowl. There weren't any cubes left in it.

"I'll ask for more", John said.

"Don't bother. We don't need them."

"Are you sure?"

"I'm sure. That's finished."

John swept bread crumbs off the table. Two wrens swooped in and pecked them all away. His mind was a blank, and his heart was heavy.

"We ought to be going home", E. M. said, standing. "It's getting cold."

He tried to help her with her sweater, but he was too late. As he followed her out the door, he looked back at their table. There was no magic there anymore.

September 21, 1929

Paris

The larger man stared across the table at the smaller man and said, "It can be done."

The room was tiny. The lamp on the table produced very little illumination but lots of shadows. The sounds of traffic could be heard through a curtained window. The wallpaper, pale green with small blue flowers, was faded and peeling in more places than it was intact. The floor was strewn with ashes and paper. The only furniture consisted of the table and the chairs the two men sat upon.

The larger man hadn't bothered to remove his hat or dark glasses, while the smaller man appeared completely at ease, hatless, with an open collar and a tumbler of purple wine near his right hand.

"It might be done", the smaller man said, skeptically.

"We have done much the same before", the larger man said.

"This one is different. Must I enumerate the risks?"

"It is so outrageous it is bound to work", the larger man insisted. Despite the fact that they were alone, he spoke in little more than a whisper.

"Nothing is bound to work. We have been suspected in the past. This scheme will be harder to choreograph and control."

"Our patron is powerful. He will make it worth our while."

"There is that, yes", the smaller man said. His eyes were dark, like a doll's eyes.

"Think of the challenge."

"Challenges do not interest me. Challenges have a depressing way of shortening one's life. I like money, but I like living more." He brought the tumbler to his lips.

"You will consider it. Our patron desires it."

"Is that a threat?" the smaller man said, putting both elbows on the table and leaning toward the larger man.

"Don't be foolish", the larger man protested. "Your interests are my interests, aren't they?"

"Of course", the smaller man said, fixing unblinking eyes on his companion, whose own eyes descended to the tabletop. "This scheme hinges on one thing. Remember that."

"Hasn't it always hinged on that one thing?" the re-energized larger man said.

"You have seen fit to tell your patron our secret."

"I have not. I do not know how he learned. I urge you to ponder that."

"Bah."

The larger man, in what would have been a comic gesture if there had been any hint of levity in the conversation, pulled his hat lower, as if to cover his eyes. Then he stood and walked to the window. "This place is filthy", he said, without turning to face his companion.

The smaller man snorted. "I remember when you resided in a room much like this one. The money we have made has gone to your head."

The larger man turned and smiled. "I have tried to forget those lean times."

"And I have never forgotten", the smaller man said. "I can survive in places that would make this room seem luxurious."

"That is a pathological disposition", the larger man said. "You are a wealthy man."

"At the moment. Why should I take unnecessary risks?"

"Fifty thousand francs if we are successful", the larger man said.

"And if we are not successful, prison and poverty. I have never been a gambler", the smaller man said with vigor.

"It can be done. Our patron does not countenance failure. He has considered everything."

"You are such a fool. No one considers everything. By the way, have you considered the possibility that your patron might make sacrificial lambs of us if things go awry?"

The larger man waved dismissively.

The man at the table wagged a finger. "A propensity to take risks along with blind trust is dangerous, my friend; one might call it a pathological disposition. I am not inclined to tie my cart to that ox."

"I recommend caution in defying—"

"You are pathetic!" the smaller man said, so loudly that the larger man cringed and put a finger to his lips. "As usual, I must do the thinking for both of us. It isn't I who have the wooden head. Let me assure you of something. If this man were not involved, if this were your scheme, I would not even consider it." The smaller man waited until his companion returned to the table and sat again. Then he said, "You are profligate, my friend. That is why, with all the money we have made, you must take risks and I need not. Your penury will not enter into my deliberations, nor will appeals to tests of wit or courage. My calculations are purely a matter of risk and reward."

"Don't forget our patron", the larger man said, bitterly.

"There is that risk to consider too, my dear." He snorted and sipped from the tumbler.

"I'll expect your decision tomorrow."

"You will have my decision when it is made."

"You little devil. You will make me dance to your tune. All of the principals are in town. The stars are aligned. Our patron's patience is wearing thin."

"Tomorrow, then. Tell your patron tomorrow."

"Our patron."

"He is not my patron. I would rather have nothing to do with him."

"Think of the money, Mika."

"You are obsessed with money. Not me, my friend. How many times do I have to say it?"

The larger man removed his hat and turned it with his fingers. His hair was pitch black and full, a magnificent head of hair. Absent the hat, more disguise than headwear, he could be seen to be a handsome, even striking, man, tall and lean like an athlete. He stood, shook his head, replaced the hat on his head, and left the room. The smaller man remained in the chair, his features now lacking the self-assurance they'd displayed during the conversation with the other man.

Though almost half the glass remained, he consumed the rest of the wine in several determined gulps. "There is that risk to consider too, my dear", he said out loud, but he could not help shivering as he said it.

July 4, 1930

Scotland, Old Forest

John set out toward the hills. A quarter-mile meadow, rich
with heather, stretched before him; the upward ascent was
so gentle that he had no need to rely on his walking stick.
He had started a pipe before he left the cottage. It promised to be a fine day for a walk in the woods.

He was content because E. M. was content. She was more
at ease than she'd been in a long time. They were midway
through a two-week holiday in a tranquil, middle-Scotland
setting: hills everywhere, some rugged, some reminding him
of the English downs; the deep loch, with a handful of
cottages surrounding it; plenty of space for the boys to run;
fresh fish for dinner. E. M. was laughing again. He suspected that the baby, Priscilla, had something to do with
E. M.'s buoyancy. The reason didn't matter; seeing her happy
was enough.

As he made his way across the meadow, he recalled the
conversation they'd had at their restaurant in London three
years ago, E. M.'s fears and his frustrations. She was worried that someone was watching them, had even invaded
their home, but there had been no incidents since then. If
they were being watched, if they had ever been watched, it
no longer troubled them. That confrontation in the restaurant had acted as a kind of talisman, warding off a menace.

He looked behind him and saw E. M., now a tiny white
figure against the red background of the porch, setting up

her easel and laying out her watercolors. Michael was chasing John on the shore. The boys saw him looking back and waved. He raised his stick in reply.

Before he realized it, he was singing a childhood song, though he couldn't remember many of the words, and he was feeling that nothing could ever again go seriously amiss. Of course, he knew better. But as for today, all was well.

He entered a grove of tall oak and Wych elm, a spur from the hills that penetrated the meadow. In the shady stillness, he half expected the ancient oaks to extend branches and rumble greetings, or the craggy rocks that erupted from the earth to rise up and reveal themselves as monstrous trolls. Instead, he saw a badger scurry into a clutch of rocks. Flies began buzzing about him, tickling his ears and trying to bite his neck. His hope that the pipe smoke would ward them off was proving to be unfounded.

He was wearing a light coat and a hat in case of rain. He had the pistol in his pocket, more out of habit than apprehension. He moved a snake off of the path with his stick. He wound his way amidst the trees until the ascent steepened and the ground got rockier. After half an hour climbing the winding trail, he noticed the elm giving way to sessile oak and silver birch.

He couldn't help musing about the translation. The fly in the ointment, as opposed to the flies in his eyes and ears, was the realization that the translation hadn't advanced in a year. Furthermore, he had made no progress in identifying the people who had produced the manuscript. Who were they? When did they inhabit the world? What happened to them? Not a hint of an answer to any of these questions. He'd practically resigned himself to never knowing the truth.

As the trail straightened out on the crest of a foothill to a ridge of taller hills, John saw a large figure coming toward him, a long-haired bearded man with a dark coat that reached to his knees. He hadn't expected to meet anyone in these hills but he wasn't amazed either; the trail was well-worn. As John approached him, he could see that the man was bearing a bow.

John raised his hand in greeting. Out of habit, his other hand was close to the pocket with the gun.

"Who are you?" the man said cautiously. He stood on the path like a storybook sentinel.

"John ... Hill."

"Well, Mr. Hill, visitors aren't all that common in this forest."

"We're staying at a cottage on the loch", John said.

The man stepped toward him. "I'll save you the trouble of asking. I'm Gosdier Jones." He pronounced it Goss-dee-ay. "Mind if I walk with you?"

The man's long hair was tied behind his head like a pony's tail. His clothes were soiled but not tattered or patched. His boots were caked with dirt, but they were of good quality. Except for the bow, John couldn't see any other weapons, but the man's coat had pockets like John's. Anyway, a man this big was weapon enough if it came to a physical contest. "I don't mind", John said. What else could he say? Then he added, "Do you live in the village?"

"I live here—in the forest."

John imagined a stone cottage on a hill.

As if seeing the image in John's mind, the man said, "I don't have a home, as most reckon a home. I bed down in half a dozen places, mostly caves."

John supposed this could be true. The man looked like he was chiseled from a boulder. His beard and hair were rusty red. His face was lined. His eyes were hard to see for his squinting and shaggy brows.

"What would please you?" Jones asked him. "High hills? A pine forest? A waterfall? Rocky cliffs? Some peace and quiet too, I guess. That's why most city people come to the forest. Come along."

They went in the direction that Jones had come from. After following the trail for a while, Jones veered from the path onto what looked like a rabbit run. John had to be careful with his footing, and to avoid a twig in the eye. They were ascending again, which didn't slow Gosdier Jones but taxed John. The big man finally halted but only to see how John was faring.

"Have you lived in these hills your whole life?" John said. He'd been relying more and more on his stick.

Jones laughed. "I was born and raised in Glasgow."

"What brought you here?"

"In the beginning, Hume, Thoreau, and Whitman. I earned a philosophy degree at the University of Edinburgh. I decided these hills were a place a man could think and ponder without distractions. That's why I came. I brought a bag of books with me. They're scattered about in caves now, those I can still put my hands on—less thinking and pondering as time went by. Now it's mostly a matter of survival. I won't say I've abandoned the ideas, but food comes first."

"How long have you been here?"

"Five years, give or take. I slim down in winter, but I manage. We've almost reached the high pasture. Follow me and be as quiet as you can."

They continued their ascent. The flies were less abundant here. And the oak gave way to the pine. Needles carpeted the path, and more sunlight filtered through the canopy. Keeping up with Jones was not easy. Once John almost stumbled over his companion, so intent was he on the path. When he finally looked up, he saw it—the high pasture, not a spectacular place but nevertheless enchanting: ankle-high grass, pink and blue wildflowers.

"A pretty sight, isn't it?" Jones said.

"Yes."

"Something like a painting."

"Yes," John said, still trying to catch his breath.

"It's a fine place to think. I haven't given up thinking altogether." Jones leaned against his bow and turned to John. "Special places like this make me wonder—make the philosopher in me wonder, I should say. Even here, one can't abandon one's training. Let me pose a question if I may. A man who lives alone doesn't often have the opportunity. Do you think experiences like this are real?"

John was more surprised by the question than the vista. "That this meadow exists apart from our senses and consciousness? The answer is yes."

"How can you know that?"

"By using logic and my senses, and from the evidence of witnesses. You are such a witness, Jones."

Jones pushed against the bow until it bowed. "Your argument is not unknown to me. But, logic is a construct of man, the senses are less than trustworthy, and witnesses are just men, subject to these limitations of logic and the senses. That argument isn't entirely persuasive."

John finally caught his breath, physically and mentally. John had given a classic philosophical response, but Gosdier Jones knew the counterarguments.

Jones said, "I sensed that you are a man of ideas. I haven't met a man with a philosophical vocabulary in longer than I can remember, and a contrarian at that."

"These weren't always contrarian views", John said.

"Progress has left you in its wake."

"Something has left me in its wake, but I wonder if it's progress", John said, testily. There was a soft breeze on the high hill, creating something like colored waves in the grass. Jones was asking if all of this was illusion, just a sensory and intellectual construct, an extreme variation on the theme of beauty being in the eye of the beholder.

"I hope you don't mind this exploration of ideas with your walking", Jones said.

"I don't mind", John said, though he'd counted on this time alone for an altogether different reasoning exercise.

As they stood there, John leaning on his stick and Jones on his bow, a deer emerged from the trees on the opposite side of the clearing. With a kind of graceful artistry, Jones removed an arrow from his quiver and loaded the bow. As he raised the bow and drew the string, the shaft remained remarkably steady. The deer was at least fifty yards away, but its broadside presented a generous target. Jones drew the string farther back. John could hear the breath escaping from his lips.

Simultaneously, the deer leaped forward and the arrow struck a tree that the animal's flank had shielded an instant earlier. The sound of the impact was enough to drive the beast into the woods.

"A good shot nonetheless", John remarked, amazed at Jones' facility with the weapon.

Jones lowered the bow. "Practically speaking or philosophically speaking? That might have been my dinner."

John laughed.

The meadow was as it had been before the animal arrived. The woodsman raised his index finger in the air and said, "How often does reality parallel ideas? This experience—hunter, beast, bow and arrow—embodies everything we were discussing: morality, meaning, freedom." Jones laid the bow on the ground. He was the most unlikely philosopher John could imagine, more caveman than scholar. Jones said, "I'll tell you what I mean. Is what I did—attempting to kill the animal—a moral or immoral act regardless of my motives? Do my motives, whether I kill the animal for food or to inflict suffering, make the act moral or immoral? Is it moral because I decided it was expedient, or is there a true standard that makes the act moral or immoral regardless of my beliefs?"

"My view", John said, "is that the act is objectively moral or immoral but that one's motives and psychology affect culpability, degree of guilt if you will."

Jones said, "I'm afraid we differ again, friend. You may not be surprised to hear that. My view is that the measure of the act is man. That is the humanistic perspective."

John looked up at him and said, not without a tinge of apprehension, "One might also say it's the egoistic perspective."

"To the extent that humanity and ego are conjoined, you're right, but if your observation is judgmental, I can't agree. My humanism isn't bounded by convention or tradition. This existence in the wild won't permit it."

"Christian hermits have survived in the wild for millennia without adopting that egoistic philosophy."

"But did they eat well?" Jones said, laughing loudly. "Now, as to meaning. The arrival of the deer, the drawing of the bow, the flight of the arrow—are these things ephemeral? Gone forever, dissipated in time and space? Or are they cosmically captured and recorded? What do you think?"

It was the oddest of lecture halls, this space between a wall of trees. Flies darted, and the occasional bird swooped overhead. Jones looked more Pan than Panhellenic. How could John have imagined such an intellectual workout when he left the cottage that morning? His mind certainly hadn't had the focus he'd expected.

"It is retained", John said. "It isn't altogether gone."

Jones clapped John on the shoulder and said, "You are a perfect foil, friend. Let's cross the meadow. The event is gone. Where would it be recorded? Already the sounds are reduced to less than the faintest whisper. The light is diffracted into millions of rays. The residual vibration of the arrow is unmeasurable. Memory is imperfect."

"In a meaningful universe," John countered, "events aren't lost."

"There is the crux of our dispute. The mind of man is meaningful to the extent that his view of the world is coherent, but the inanimate universe cannot be said to have meaning."

"You've contradicted yourself", John said. "Coherence implies a norm or standard of coherency that exists independent of the mind. Without such a standard, these terms are meaningless and nothing that occurs in the mind of man could be said to have meaning."

Jones used his bow as something like a baton. "I have not had such a debate in years. Then, let us say these are imperfect conventions that reasoning men hold in common."

"That's a dodge, I'm afraid," John rejoined.

"Ha. You haven't convinced me. Now as to the freedom of the act: was it necessary—an act predetermined by a billion antecedent events—or was it a willful choice?"

John hesitated before answering, then he said, "It was certainly influenced by many things—your own disposition; the actions, or reactions, of the deer; the weather—but ultimately it was a choice. You weren't predestined to encounter that deer and send a dart at it."

They'd passed out of the meadow, and Jones had found a path winding down the back side of the hill into a forest of mountain ash and silver birch. He said, "I don't like to talk of predestination because it implies a directing intelligence.

Mechanistic processes brought that act into being, processes in my own mind, natural processes in the surrounding environment, the influence of your companionship—far too complex to be analyzed but, in the end, deterministic. Human freedom is an illusion."

"You describe a bleak world", John said, gripping his stick tightly as the trail became more rugged. He slapped at a fly that was especially persistent.

"I describe the world as it is, as it must be accommodated", Jones countered. "I might ask how you can embrace a world so at odds with experience."

"The world I embrace", John said, "is not contrary to logic but aligned with it."

"Logic itself", Jones said, "is a human construct. Better to talk about cause and effect, actions and outcomes, and their utility."

"Utility can produce horrifying outcomes", John insisted.

"Only when utility is poorly defined or poorly understood. That's not an ideological dart, John. Imagine one has produced a noble project, an enlightening and broadening project. Can one allow so-called ethical or human considerations to interfere with seeing it to completion? What do you say?"

John could not help thinking about the book. Hadn't John's pursuit of that project corresponded in a certain sense to Jones' definition of utility? Notwithstanding this prick of conscience, he said, "One cannot produce something worthy by unworthy acts."

"Then one must define worthy acts as those which produce worthy projects. See, the Gordian knot is cut."

"I always thought Alexander the Great a cheat", John remarked. "His was an inelegant way to unravel the knot."

Jones turned to John and said, "You are a persistent intellectual adversary. It's my good fortune to have met you. But listen, we're evolving from inhibitions and superstitions to pure science and social utility."

The unconscious cadence of John's steps and the stick striking the trail invigorated him. "I'm not sure that we aren't devolving."

"John, you are too intelligent to stand in the way of progress."

"You speak of progress as if it's natural, even inevitable. Was it progress when the democratic Greek states succumbed to dictators? Was it progress when republican Rome succumbed to the emperors? Is that the inevitable progress you're talking about? I see nothing but a Nero at the end of your inevitable progress, then and now."

"Imperfect outcomes do not mitigate progress", Jones protested.

John said, "They are the natural fruits of your ethos of utility and efficiency."

Jones planted his feet on the path like two tree trunks and rubbed his beard. "I can't match your wit, but wit is not proof. I'll put this to you. There are two young men who are standing conventional wisdom on its ear. You may not have heard of them, but they are shattering scientific and philosophical preconceptions: Einstein and Gödel. The former says that time itself is relative, and the latter goes further, suggesting that time may not even exist outside the human mind. Einstein demonstrated that if the physical laws of the universe are immutable, then dimensions like space and time must be relative. If the speed of a ray of light is constant, and if a man on the ground and a man on a train measure it traveling at the exact same speed, then distance and time must be relative—not fixed—because speed equals distance divided by time. To

Gödel, time is a human construct that speaks to the simultaneity or the sequencing of events. Thus, to Gödel, time has no absolute reality and may not be real at all. The point is that thinking about a fixed and irreversible time line with past and present events on sequential points is flawed. That thinking belongs in the past."

"What practical consequences come out of these theories?" John said. "I don't know these men, but I don't fear honest science."

"We finally agree on something", Jones said, striding down the path.

If not for Jones' booming voice, John would have been challenged to hear his companion. John said, "We also agreed that there was a deer in the clearing."

"In a manner of speaking", Jones equivocated. "I ask you, how can we assert universal morality, transcendental events rather than ephemeral events, and free will when nature is telling us that everything is relative, that nothing is fixed?"

"I say there's a difference between what honest science is saying and what nature is supposedly telling us, as you represent it."

Jones' voice had been getting louder as the debate progressed. "You're resorting to semantic gymnastics. Here's a thought experiment. If time is relative, as Einstein asserts, or nonexistent, as Gödel suggests, is the distant past any more distant than our encounter with the deer?"

"You've told me that events in the past are lost, so the question is irrelevant."

"But this is a thought experiment, not an assertion", Jones said. "What do you say?"

What John wanted to say was that it was as likely for a monster to emerge from the loch as for a philosopher-physicist to emerge from these hills. Again, he thought about the book and the events that had occurred so long ago, or so he believed. He said, "If you accept the premise, I suppose you must accept the conclusion that remoteness may be unrelated to separation in time."

"Good. Then something that happened ten thousand years ago—this is just a thought experiment—might, in some sense, by some device, be accessible to us here and now."

"I don't see how that connection can be made", John answered.

"It can be made if one doesn't think of time as fixed, as a straight line, but as a related or dependent variable, like a looped string, a moving looped string where events separated by thousands of conventional years can be brought side by side."

"That's a fantastic notion", John said. "There's no evidence of such a thing."

"Is it any more fantastic than Atlantis or Olympus or any of the great myths that might once have been fact?" Jones said.

"Those myths, as you call them, are more credible than this business of time strings."

"Explain yourself!" Jones thundered.

"In the case of those civilizations, one may discover artifacts, written sources, tangible proofs, or pointers, at least."

"You refer to Plato or the oral historians of Camelot?" Jones pressed.

John started mentally. He was talking about the book, with a stranger. Well, why not talk about it—something he'd been yearning to do for years—with a stranger, and such an insightful stranger?

"Plato and Homer and the other ancients", John said.

"You consider these myths credible on the testimony of those men? They were more soothsayers than scientists," Jones said.

The trail was not wide enough for them to walk side by side, so John walked half a step behind Gosdier Jones. He observed the woodsman with an eye trained by his laborious translation of the manuscript and his experience in the army signal corps. One never knew when observation would be rewarded. He examined Jones' heavy horsehair coat, robelike in its length and girth, his wide-brimmed leather hat, his denim trousers, and his boots—especially the boots, especially the heels of the boots. What he didn't see told him more than what he did see.

John said, "I consider these myths more credible than your theories about time."

"What is your own belief about Atlantis?" Jones asked.

Atlantis—how had this conversation converged on Atlantis, John wondered. And how easy it would be, he told himself, to debate Jones on this subject. So far, he'd been intellectually honest with Jones, which made it all the more difficult to lie. But it couldn't be helped. John said, "I'm a skeptic."

"Come, now. You impressed me as a reasoning romantic. Such a story must have something to recommend it."

John wondered if he could glean something more about the civilization described in the manuscript by better understanding the science of space and time. Maybe there was another path to the answers he was seeking. In this hermit he might have found a sage who could give him clues as to how to proceed. John wasn't a scientist. He admitted to himself that it was unclear how these scientific theories could help him advance the portrait of the civilization, no matter how intriguing those ideas might be. Could there be a link between these strange concepts of time and space and that civilization? Was this the moment to relax his guard, even if this idea-laden man was only a foil for the questions he yearned to ask?

A small rodent crept from beneath a clump of dead leaves and needles into a space where the path opened up to a little clearing. The sun's bright light bathed the space in a golden glow. In the animal's eagerness, it ignored the men's approach. The sight of the creature running in circles, stirring motes in the light, caused them to halt in their tracks.

A hawk swooped in and took the creature. It had come from nowhere and, in an instant, it vanished.

"*Delenda est Carthago.*" Jones' voice boomed like an orator's. "That event is a succinct summary of the meaning of life. We have come full circle, friend John. There's nothing to suggest the creature ever existed."

John took up the gauntlet again; he couldn't resist. "If you mean that all living creatures must die, there's no disputing that, but if you equate the meaning of this rodent's existence with the meaning of the existence of human beings, I could not disagree more. Still, I think you're right to find a sort of sign in that event." The destruction of the rodent had resolved John's questions and doubts about confiding in Jones.

Jones kept walking. There was a certain ironic tone in his hearty voice when he said, "Where was I before I was interrupted by a creature that no longer exists, or may never have existed? We were talking about the past, the distant past, and whether what happened then might be accessible to us now. John, you say that the past is not utterly lost. Give me an example."

John said, "I haven't any. I'm not a historian. I can't say anything about it." He was preoccupied with boots and rodents.

"You disappoint me. Are you sure you haven't anything to add?"

John said, "I am sure. I'm a professor of languages. That field of study is connected to the past, to history and peoples, but that's the extent of it. Atlantis and Asgard, if they ever existed, have not given us their languages; thus, their history—if they, or something like them, ever existed—exceeds my competency."

"I'm sorry to hear that you are so timid on this subject", Jones said as they topped a hill. "We've come round the circle. You are close to home, and I need to find my dinner. I should have asked you to shoot the deer with your pistol, but my vanity got in the way. Thank you for your company, John, and the contribution of your wit. I can't remember such an invigorating conversation. For a moment, I felt that we were close to something—a revelation? But I didn't mean to insult you; far from it. Keep an eye out for Einstein and Gödel. This is their century."

"Better it belong to them than to these supermen who are springing up like weeds", John said, looking down the hill at the loch and cottages. How had Jones known about the weapon he carried? Was it a guess, an intuition, or a practiced eye?

Gosdier Jones gave him a quizzical look. "If you come again, look for me." Bow in hand, the woodsman strode into the woods.

John stood on that hill overlooking the loch after Jones left him and wondered. What sort of life would it be in this wilderness? More important, how could someone so intellectually curious tolerate the incessant solitude? Then again, he reminded himself, immersion in the world brought drawbacks as well as advantages. The daily drumbeat of news from the Continent was often overwhelming. A shadow seemed to be descending over Europe so soon after he'd fought a war that was supposed to cure Europe's ills. Ominous economic developments plagued the world. In Russia, the communists were strengthening their grip on power. In Germany, the brownshirts were stirring people into a frenzy of resentment and hatred. In Italy, the fascists were imposing order at the expense of liberty. Even in Britain, constant labor strife was threatening to rend the social fabric.

There was also the letter to be considered. It had been forwarded from a post-office box he maintained in Sussex. He'd been both expecting and dreading this letter because it forced a decision he knew he must make and portended conflict with E. M. John removed the letter from his coat pocket and reread it.

Dear John:

Please pardon my failure to correspond with you in recent years. You will remember that I complained about the demands of business when we last met. I can only say that it has been an incessant preoccupation, involving much travel and less time for happier pursuits.

I hope this note finds your family well and enjoying country life in Sussex, and I trust that your young students are absorbing much useful information.

Recently, I have come into possession of astounding information that bears on our mutual interest in prehistory. I have not fully fathomed its meaning and would welcome the opportunity to discuss it with you. Needless to say, correspondence of this sort is inappropriate for discussing something of this nature. Thus, I would welcome another visit to Paris, where we can share a bottle of Bordeaux and continue our happy collaboration.

Please let me know if such a meeting is agreeable.

Most sincerely,
A. Alembert, Professor

He refolded and returned the letter to his pocket. It seemed to be his fate to encounter singular characters. Gosdier Jones also fit that description. Scanning the landscape, there was no sign that Jones had been more than a figment of his imagination, but the woodsman's words and ideas continued to trouble him.

Coming across the meadow, he met E. M. She must have seen him coming. She was carrying a wicker basket. As she drew closer, she opened the basket and removed a warm loaf of sweet bread and two bottles of ale. They sat in the meadow on side-by-side boulders and consumed both the food and drink.

"Be careful of the bees", she said. "They like bread better than heather."

"They're marvelous company compared to those infernal flies. The bread is delicious."

"I thought you'd be hungry and thirsty."

After his hard work on the hills, this bread was cake and the ale nectar. "I want to see the pictures", he said.

"Later."

"Your word is still your bond, I presume."

She smiled.

After dinner, all of them sat on the porch, even Priscilla. That evening, with a crimson sun on the horizon, the loch was on fire. The air was still, and the water lapped the shore in ripples instead of waves. Christopher and Michael were playing with toy boats as E. M. rocked Priscilla. Young John sat on the porch next to his father. The elder John never tired of observing E. M. and of basking in the sense of presence that surrounded her.

John was proud of the boy, of all his children.

"Next time, may I walk with you, Father?"

John puffed his pipe. There was tea on the table between him and E. M. "I'd like that, Master John."

"I can keep up."

"No doubt you can." John recalled his own effort to keep up with Gosdier Jones.

"How big was the snake, Father?"

John spread his arms, and his son emitted a sound of appreciation.

"Do you think we can find it?"

"That might be a tall order. I'm sure there's quite a clan of them in the hills; perhaps we'll come across one."

"When can we go?"

"We'll go before we return to town."

"Promise, Father?"

"Promise."

Young John extended his hand, and his father, smiling, took it. The boy was growing up so quickly, he reflected.

The surface of the loch was transformed from red to silver when the sun vanished and the moon rose in the sky. Now just John and E. M. were on the porch. The teacups were empty. He picked up a sugar cube and threw it into the loch.

She said, "What a bold husband I have."

"May I see your watercolors?"

"I'm not sure."

"Why not?"

"I'm afraid you won't be honest."

"Of course I won't. I'm prejudiced in your favor."

"That's what I'm afraid of."

"E. M., the day you aren't able to read my true feelings is the day you've lost your eyesight. Regardless of what I say, you'll know."

"Yes. I'm afraid of that too."

"Get them, please. You promised."

She left the porch and returned with a large portfolio. One by one she removed the pictures and set them against the porch railing. The moon and the two porch lamps added a spectral cast to the pictures. John examined them: animals in different environments, with features slightly exaggerated but not so much that one would think them caricatures; earthy colors; light and darkness.

"Delightful", John said.

She inspected him closely. "Do you mean it? You're trying your best to be inscrutable."

"Delightful", he said again. "I like the falcon best, but the badger is the most interesting."

"I'll ask again when you're sleeping. Then we'll see what you say."

"You must continue painting."

"It's such satisfying and frustrating work", she said.

"I know."

"You do know, John. And to have to keep your work secret, as you have had to do, must make it all the more frustrating."

"We're discussing your pictures", he said. "They're very good."

John got up and went inside. He read to the boys for nearly an hour. Young John was getting to the age where he preferred reading rather than being read to, but he sat patiently enough. Michael and Christopher hardly moved.

Now they were all in bed except E. M., who was attending to Priscilla, and John, who was seated on the shore of the loch, smoking his pipe and listening to the water. He was thinking—he was always thinking about something: his family inside the cottage, the book, Adler Alembert, and now Gosdier Jones.

The children were growing. As hard as it was to accept, they would be grown too soon. Was the project, his project, depriving him of the most important thing, the company of his family?

With the translation as complete as possible, had he accomplished everything that could be accomplished? Notwithstanding Gosdier Jones' bizarre ideas on time and space, was it time to close the book, so to speak? Was it time to turn the manuscript over to the professional historians and scientists and get on with his life?

And yet the letter from Alembert was tantalizing. He'd often thought about another meeting with that intriguing man, someone who shared his own passion for the mystery of a great prehistoric civilization. E. M. was opposed to another meeting with Alembert; what should he do?

The encounter with Gosdier Jones was the last thing he expected when he set off into the woods that morning. He'd read about rustic philosophers, and he was familiar with religious hermits of profound intellectual depth; but to meet such a man was an epiphany. Was Jones the hermit and hunter he portrayed himself to be? One arrow had proven he was adept with the bow. But the more John pondered, the more he questioned whether Jones was someone who moved from shelter to shelter, as he'd represented. The man's clothes weren't new, but where were the fraying, the tears, the patches? He had observed the heels of Jones' boots— not worn, almost as good as new. If John were to make inquiries, would he find any evidence that Gosdier Jones had attended the University of Edinburgh? Most mysteriously, how had he known about John's pistol? If that wasn't clairvoyance, it was a canny skill that could pass for it.

The rodent, running in circles in that splash of light, and its fate, had given him pause. Was his debate with Jones actually intended to put him off his guard? In short, was their meeting as innocent as it seemed?

But who was Jones if he wasn't who he claimed to be? Perhaps he was a weekend hiker who liked to impress those he encountered. John didn't expect to meet the man again, so he had little expectation of learning the truth, if it was different from what Jones had told him.

He looked at a sky crowded with stars. Long ago, or so he believed, these stars had looked down on the civilization that so absorbed his thoughts, on the personages of the Burglar, the Hero, and the Hero's faithful companion.

Tomorrow, he would tell E. M. that he was accepting Adler Alembert's invitation.

PART III

Contentio

December 12, 1930

Paris

Alembert sat across from him with the massive desk separating them. Only one glass of wine had been poured; John had declined to share the Bordeaux.

The Turkish rugs were missing, and even though the terrarium was in the same place, it was empty. A black telephone was close to Alembert's left hand. The room seemed colder.

Maybe it was the weather; Paris was gray and icy. Or maybe it was John. All the way from his hotel, he had felt more conflicted than enthusiastic. E. M. had grudgingly accepted his decision to meet with Adler Alembert again. John hadn't consulted Gilbert. He admitted to himself that he'd been apprehensive about what that indefatigable man would have said to him had he been consulted. Anyway, his mind had been made up. He had more information than either E. M. or Gilbert, and he was convinced there was more to be gained than risked in hearing what Alembert had discovered.

Christopher set fine-china plates with generous helpings of caviar in front of them, and a glass bottle of spring water next to John.

Alembert said, "The caviar is fresh. I have it brought in by air from Saint Petersburg. I cannot say Leningrad—the man was such an intellectual pygmy. Lenin couldn't finesse an acorn through a barn door. A spellbinder and an executioner—nothing more."

The cab driver had tried to engage John in conversation. Had he been in Paris before? Where would he be dining? Was he traveling alone, or with a *belle femme*? Was John a policeman? *Les gendarmes* were cautious too.

No, he wasn't a policeman, just a teacher.

Where did he teach?

It was so innocuous a conversation that he almost revealed he was an Oxford professor. Something prevented him. He was John Hill from Sussex. It wouldn't do to be careless, even in a cab.

"Have you had snow in Sussex?" Alembert said, bringing John back to the present.

"No. Not yet."

"In the streets of Paris, ice can be treacherous."

John agreed that ice was an unwelcome phenomenon in the age of motorcars. He looked out the windows, remembering his first visit, the sunshine and the storm.

Adler Alembert was a stretched version of his earlier self. He had visibly aged. John hadn't noticed it before, but Alembert might have had oriental ancestors. The changes in Alembert's appearance emphasized the slight elongation of his eyes.

Christopher still hovered over John's right shoulder.

"Excuse me for a moment, John. Business is a constant distraction. Christopher, what have you learned about Agnes?"

The giant had changed too. It had surprised John to see Christopher when John had been admitted to the building. Alembert's servant was still a dominant presence, but grayer and missing his left eye. John had tried to strike up a conversation with the man, but it was fruitless. Christopher didn't utter a word until he had conducted John into the office.

"She is still missing", Christopher said, in that characteristic bass monotone.

"That's unacceptable. I told you to find her."

"I have ordered Medina, Black, and Gesch to give the matter their full attention."

"Do we know if she left willingly, or was she removed?"

"No. Not yet."

"In other words, we don't know anything."

"Black said all was well the day before she vanished from the Monastery."

Alembert pounded his fist on the desktop. "Do you know how long I've been acquainted with Agnes?"

Alembert waited, but the giant didn't answer. "We were children together—in England."

"They understand the urgency", Christopher said. John found it hard to believe that anyone could intimidate this giant.

"I wonder if they do. Perhaps we should engage Krieger."

"He has joined the brownshirts."

"I know that. Isn't he still one of us?"

Christopher glanced at John.

"Isn't he still one of us?" Alembert said again.

"Yes."

"Very well. I want him on the job. Have him brought here immediately."

"Yes."

"That's all."

John could not help being disturbed by the tension in the room. He heard the door click closed. Alembert took a sip of wine. "I really must apologize for that, John."

Was Alembert associated with the German brownshirts? What did that say about his host's character and trustworthiness?

"I find that theatrics are sometimes effective in moving projects forward. I assure you, everything that was said and done was for effect." His host made a fist and tapped the desk with it, smiling all the while.

"Who is Krieger?" John asked.

Alembert seemed taken aback, as if the question was impertinent. He stopped smiling. "He's a useful man who has been in my employment for some years. You might say I trained him."

"Is he a brownshirt?"

"He's nominally associated with the brownshirts. I like to keep track of movements like that one, and I've found it helps when there is someone I trust inside the movement. Kindly keep that *entre nous*. Let me satisfy your curiosity. Aggressive political movements can be bad for business. Sometimes it makes sense to inhibit their growth, and sometimes it's prudent to influence them to enhance business. It's all a matter of calculation. Do you see?"

John said he saw.

"Good. We'll let Christopher attend to Krieger. Agnes is an old friend. One can't let old friends vanish without lifting a hand." Alembert's frown froze John's blood.

"At our last meeting, you mentioned that Agnes—I assume it is the same person—was stationed in Argentina. Are your interests in South America extensive?" John asked him.

"One could say so. You have a remarkable memory for extraneous information, John. I have people in a number of countries on that continent. I own a large institution in Argentina. My people call it the Monastery, but there is no religious affiliation whatsoever. Is the caviar agreeable?"

"Yes. Excellent."

"Are you certain you won't taste the Bordeaux?"

"No thank you."

"Maybe you are too ascetic. We live only once; that's the old saying."

"That's the reason I try to be prudent", John said.

"I like that. I don't imagine Bordeaux and caviar are plentiful in Surrey—I mean Sussex. What does your lovely wife do for New Year's Eve?"

There was no doubt that the room was cooler. Perhaps it was the month, or the glass conducting the cold city air, or maybe the absence of the butterflies and walking sticks. John was glad he'd worn a sweater.

"The New Year in Sussex is a practical matter. Our celebrations are muted."

"Of course they are", Alembert said. "John, I've often thought your talents are wasted in the country. Would you consider joining one of my businesses? Your salary would be doubled or tripled. What do you say?"

John set down the small silver fork and said, "I'm a country teacher. I don't suppose I'd be happy anywhere else."

"But think of the money."

"I appreciate your generous offer, but no." John took another taste of caviar. What was Alembert up to? he wondered.

"I suspected that would be your decision. I value men of integrity, truthful and honest men. They're rare. I'm certain you are such a man, John." Alembert's words were complimentary, but John could not dispel the sense of being in the presence of an actor on a stage.

"What was it that Shakespeare said? I have it", Alembert said.

> "The purest treasure mortal times afford
> Is spotless reputation; that away
> Men are but gilded loam or painted clay.
> . . . .

179

Mine honor is my life; both grow as one;
Take honor from me, and my life is done:
Then dear my liege, mine honor let me try;
In that I live and for that will I die."

"I couldn't help noticing the empty terrarium", John said. He felt compelled to redirect their conversation, in spite of his host's compliments—or rather, because of them.

Alembert glanced at it and shrugged.

"Are you no longer keeping butterflies?"

"On three separate occasions I had young butterflies brought from the greenhouse. By the following morning, they were dead, every one of them."

"Disease?" John asked.

"I think not."

"Then what happened?" John said.

"I'm afraid it was sabotage."

"Why would anyone kill those beautiful creatures?" John said.

"It had nothing to do with the butterflies. It was intended to cause me pain. Of course, I knew who was responsible. The matter is settled."

"I'm sorry", John said.

"Nothing of consequence—pardon me, you mean the butterflies. They are replaceable, but it is the principle of the thing."

"Did you know the guilty party personally?"

"It was my brother. An act of spite."

The fork was halfway to John's mouth. "I'm sorry", he said again.

"There's no need. But see here, when you visit we waste time talking about my affairs. You've come a long way because I suggested I possess something that would interest you. That's so, isn't it?"

"Yes", John admitted. Why had Alembert's brother destroyed the insects? Was the man deranged? Did he reside in this building? Was Alembert his caretaker?

"When we last met, I showed you the goblet with those maddening runes. This new discovery is something different, but no less fascinating."

John's heart began to race. Was it possible that Alembert had something that would bring him closer to the answers he sought?

Alembert said, "Are you familiar with Morley's *Early Civilizations*?"

"Yes, I'm familiar with it."

"Then you are a peripatetic man. I'd expect to find that work at, say, Oxford, but not Sussex. Do you go to Oxford often?"

John started. "Not often."

"It's an alluring town, isn't it?"

"Yes. I enjoy it."

"I've often thought it would be a pleasant place to live. Did I tell you I keep an office and flat in London? Sometimes, when business takes me to London, I go on to Oxford. I've never been disappointed."

John poured the spring water into the glass and drank. He would have preferred the Bordeaux at that moment.

"I've been anxious to tell you the story of my visit to Oxford last May. I saw someone who might have been your double. I was passing in a motorcar and wasn't able to stop. Was it you?"

He could lie and tell Alembert that he'd visited Oxford that month, but he suspected this would lead to more questions—and the need for more lies. "That wasn't me", John said.

"An amazing likeness, then, even down to the pipe and hat."

"I've been told there are others that closely resemble us."

"I've heard the same thing, but I've never been fooled like that before."

Alembert was slowly fraying his story, starting at the edges and working toward the center. Was there a purpose, or was he just a pathologically curious man?

"Do you have other residences?" John said, trying once more to redirect the conversation, which felt like fending off a persistent hornet.

This time Alembert seemed unbothered; he even smiled at John. "I keep a flat in Amsterdam. I have homes—you might call them estates—in Kent and Buenos Aires. You remember that my grandfather was a good businessman. Sometimes I think these lodgings poor compensation for the business demands. I have no permanent home—just lodgings, places to hang my hat."

John ate the last morsel of caviar and finished the water. Alembert had consumed the better part of the bottle of Bordeaux but seemed unaffected; he was neither exuberant nor morose. If anything, he seemed to become more calculating as he drank. John found him to be something of a hypnotist. Alembert's voice—that was it—reminded him of the Voice in the book: subtle, patient, and manipulating. If Alembert possessed a fraction of the psychological power, not to say malice, of the Traitor, then it would be wise to leave this place and never return.

"You are pensive", Alembert said.

John was determined that Alembert not unnerve him. Should he make an excuse and leave? Would Alembert allow it? He could not help thinking about the one-eyed giant, the brownshirt—Alembert had called him Krieger—who was in his host's employ, and the brother who had killed Alembert's butterflies.

"Let there be no further ado. I will retrieve the artifact", Alembert said. He rose from his chair, looking in that instant like an unremarkable middle-aged man, and walked briskly to the secret panel in the wall. John watched him go. Absent the sunlight, this room was a gloomy place, something, he imagined, like the bottom of a lake.

Alembert came back and placed a long metal cylinder on the desk. He used tweezers to open one end and extracted a scroll-like piece of paper. He unrolled it with the care, not to say the sense of awe, one might afford a newborn. When the scroll was opened, he removed four brass weights from the desk drawer and placed them at the corners. Then he put his hands in his lap, looked up, and said, "Presto."

The thing would not have impressed the man on the street, but it stirred John. The scroll itself wasn't old. It was the scraps—some as large as an inch square, and others so small they could have been mistaken for confetti—that captured his attention. These scraps were distributed on the scroll as if each had one and only one proper place. These brown and brittle pieces had been attached to the scroll by a practiced, if not masterful, hand.

Alembert said, "I call it the cuneiform scroll. The scroll is my invention. The scraps, if I am correct—and I think I am—were produced in ancient Sumer. The characters are early cuneiform."

"Prehistoric?" John said.

"No. Very early, but not so old as that."

John's features must have registered disappointment, because Alembert immediately added, "It isn't the period when the scraps were produced that interests me but what they reveal."

There was a disturbance in the street that made enough noise to annoy Alembert. He got up and walked to the window. "History is always happening. If I were to chronicle this event in the street—I see that someone may have perished—a historian a thousand years in the future might spend a lifetime unlocking its meaning, seeking to know something of 1930 Paris. To us, it's a meaningless event."

"You said a man may have died."

"Death is meaningless. As I was saying, to us a meaningless event; but to our future historian, purpose."

"When you put it like that, it seems so mundane", John said.

"Of course it is. Life itself is mundane. That's precisely why the enlightened man defines purpose for himself, which directs his every idea and action. In so doing—don't you see?—we become gods, in the sense of being different in kind from ordinary men, because there is nothing higher in life than that purpose we have prescribed."

"When we self-prescribe purpose, we must be aware that it's artificial, if not superficial", John said, still thinking about the condition of the victim in the street.

"Not artificial—personal. The purpose we define directs our ideas and actions for as long as we exist, which, in a certain sense, is forever, since time before and after our life has no meaning or reality."

"You don't believe in a spirit or a soul?"

"I believe in an animating spirit, the mind, with its myriad electrochemical connections and reactions, that comes into existence when we are conceived and ceases to exist when we die. In the interim, it strives to be and then to direct."

"That's an uninspiring image."

"Why do you say so? This animating spirit would live forever if it could. It believes it should. By defining a purpose and pursuing it unreservedly, this spirit finds a practical substitute for eternal life."

"You think so?" John said, incredulously.

"Of course. We cannot say a life is cramped because it exists in a finite period of time. Outside of that lifespan, time is irrelevant, if not meaningless."

John could not help thinking of his dialogue with Gosdier Jones. He said, "Have you heard of Einstein or Gödel?"

Alembert's eyes widened. He almost hopped from the window to the desk; it was not the playful hop of a rabbit—not to John anyway—so much as a feral hop. Perhaps Alembert had been sensibly amused by the Bordeaux, but John doubted it. As soon as he sat down, he poured the rest of the wine into his glass. "Are country teachers physicists and mathematicians? I've made it a point to be introduced to both Einstein and Gödel. I can't say how their work might be put to practical use—not yet—but I'm fascinated by their thinking."

John could not help noticing that Alembert seemed comfortable with the content of Einstein's and Gödel's theories, that their work did not seem to mystify his host as it mystified him. How could a historian grasp these complex concepts?

His host laughed and said, "Your confusion is palpable. How can Alembert, a professor of history, comprehend the work of these men of science? I cannot follow all of the technical developments that produced their conclusions; I'm not willing to invest the time to acquire that degree of understanding. But I have a gift for analysis. Once premises are laid out and the analytical process is identified, I'm able to follow the development. It is something like a map of Paris that one uses to get from one point to another. No matter how complex the grid, once one has the map—in this case a mental map of premises and processes—one can proceed to the conclusions, regardless of the subject matter. If this smacks of vanity, I can say only that it is truthful. I consider false humility a hindrance; it gets in the way of pursuing and achieving that purpose we prescribe for ourselves—our god-ness, if you will."

Alembert's explanation troubled John. "The divine Augustus, or Nero", he murmured.

Alembert sat ramrod straight in his chair and said, "You never cease to amaze me. If a country teacher can articulate so sublime an observation, then what might a teacher at, say, Oxford produce? You have said it better in a sentence than I did in a ream of sentences. I'm humbled. Augustus and Nero defined meaning and purpose in their age. We—those like you and I who are different in kind—can aspire to the same thing."

Had Alembert disguised ironic intent within that compliment? "Such men are hardly human, or they are mad", John suggested.

"Not mad; superhuman, perhaps. See how I digress? It's that way with friends. Back to the scroll. It reflects the labor of many, and for many years."

John's mind was a muddle. How could he assimilate all of this in so short a period of time: Alembert's association with the brownshirts, his host's fluency with Gödel's and Einstein's abstractions, his concepts of purpose and meaning, and especially the content of the scroll in which, John was certain, something remarkable was yet to be revealed? Alembert could not resist the dramatic flourish. He would open up the meaning of the scroll like Verdi an opera or Shakespeare a drama.

"It's a poem", Alembert said.

"A Sumerian saga?"

Alembert shook his head and said, "Sumerian authorship, but the saga is something older."

There, thought John, was the first clue.

"There are four stanzas in what was probably a lengthy epic or chant. Would you like to read the translation?"

John nodded. Alembert opened the drawer and removed a sheet of powder-blue paper. On top of it was an insignia, or crest, that was unfamiliar to John. It might have been a serpent or a dragon, but it was so intricate that it would have taken time to decipher it, and John's interest was the text that was typed on the page. There were spaces where words or phrases were missing, but what was translated read:

> Waves enormous
> Over waters
> Swarming mountains
> Lords far-flung
> North and south
> Shores seeking
> Cities rising
> All seeing
> Mighty in battle
> Conquering
> Sons of Lords
> To battle
>
> Lived all these
> Rock-hard plodders
> Sun shunning
> Maggoty creepers
> Night stabbers
> Deathless songsters
> Mighty in battle
> Mountain delvers
> Battle-axers

Lichen bearded
Men and Half Men

Lord over Lords
Sky sentinels
Scalish steeds
Eye and Voice
Half Men whole
The kingdom comes

Without looking at Alembert, John instinctively knew that his host was not paying an iota of attention to the scroll, just to him and his reactions. No expression or movement of eyes or lips would go undetected and unprocessed by his host. Inside, excitement surged like a pent-up volcano; on the outside, John was determined to display nothing but equanimity.

In these few verses he recognized the civilization of his manuscript. But Alembert's epic could not have been composed much earlier than 5,000 B.C. What source had provided information about a culture that he now believed to be far more ancient? Still, the words and phrases were consistent with everything he knew about the civilization in the book.

Was it possible that Alembert himself manufactured this artifact in order to extract something from John, something he suspected that John possessed? That would be E. M.'s take on all of this. For his part, John found that idea hard to accept. Even if it was true, where would Alembert have gotten such accurate information?

"Do you think the poet is writing about his own civilization, or another one?" Alembert said.

"Who can say?" John said. "We don't know anything about an advanced culture more ancient than the Sumerians."

"We have legends", Alembert said.

"Atlantis."

"Yes. That intriguing conversation the last time we met."

John said, "Do you think the poet refers to that lost civilization?"

"So I suspect. 'Waves enormous ... swarming mountains ... sons of Lords'. What do you think?"

"The last time we met, I said I wasn't competent to express an opinion. I find myself in the same position."

"And I said you were too modest. I still believe it. I'm curious as to how you interpret these stanzas."

"It's just a first impression, but they seem to suggest a tragedy, and a sort of restoration."

"What else?"

Would Alembert permit him to copy the translation and take it with him? He needed more time. He considered trying to memorize the verses, but his mind was too jumbled to attempt it.

"It seems to point to the past rather than to contemporaneous events", John said.

"What else?"

John felt like he was taking his exams all over again. "I don't know that I can say any more."

"Does it strike you as historic, or poetic?"

"Both, but that's just a first impression."

Alembert said, "I believe it is both. There are clues even in so spare a text, and there's an additional piece of compelling evidence. Isn't there something you want to ask me?"

Was it an honest question, or was Alembert trying to trip him up? Strange, how he'd assumed a defensive posture when his host had done nothing—overt, at least—to put him on his guard.

"I can't think of anything", John said.

"The text must have dazzled you. It can have that effect on one. Don't you remember I mentioned four stanzas?"

John remembered. The scroll contained three stanzas.

"The fourth stanza is quite lengthy and almost entirely intact", Alembert said. "That portion of the document, one could say, was almost miraculously preserved—"

John could not help thinking about the box. Was that where this was heading?

"—between stone 'sheets' in a high desert cave. It has been moved but can be viewed only with the greatest care. Can you guess what it reveals?"

It all must be in this fourth stanza, John reckoned: a description of the civilization, its history. Why else would Alembert value it so highly?

"I have no ideas."

"Of course you have ideas," Alembert said, smiling, "but you protect them."

Protect? Alembert was either a man of rare intuition or—far worse—he knew more than John credited him with knowing.

Alembert continued, "In this case, even the sage ideas you might offer could not presume to plumb the truth. The document contains a list of precisely eight hundred and seventy-three names."

John thought he'd heard Alembert incorrectly or that his host had lapsed into French or another language. Names? What could possibly be learned from a list of antiquarian names?

"I detect puzzlement", Alembert said. "You were expecting something ... dramatic?"

"Yes. I imagine I was."

"Let me suggest that the drama of the fourth stanza is precisely its genealogy. Imagine a caste of scribes, by birth or election, whose mission it was to pass on an oral tradition, the story of a culture. Perhaps these scribes, in the beginning at least, were actually descended from the great civilization. Thus, the story—the missing story—comes down, by word of mouth during retrograde periods, from master to acolyte, over eight hundred and seventy-three generations. Does that signify anything to you?"

"It signifies that the events occurred a very long time before the genealogical progression was committed to the cuneiform scroll."

"Precisely", Alembert said. "Yes, you have it, my friend. I calculate something on the order of twenty-six millennia. It also signifies the residual power or influence that the civilization was able to exert after it had fallen."

"Twenty-six thousand years plus five thousand to account for the age of the Sumerian author—that would place the events almost thirty-five thousand years ago", John said, as if he were doing a cipher.

"Yes."

"That's impossible", John said, disbelieving his own words but knowing that, in spite of Alembert's congenial pretenses, he was being interrogated like a captured enemy soldier. He knew it, and what was worse, he suspected that Alembert knew he knew it. E. M. had been right after all. Alembert knew or suspected something. John was here for a reason, and it was more than their shared interest in prehistory. He had to manufacture an exit that Alembert would accept as something other than a panicked retreat.

Alembert said, "May I ask if you are familiar with the Thule Society?"

"I am not", John said.

"In the main, they are mystics and fools, but they have unearthed some kernels of credible evidence that a mighty ancient civilization once existed. Their focus is on a land-mass in the extreme north that they call Hyperborea, but that might have been an outpost, a colony of this mighty civilization; that is, any glory this northern kingdom possessed was only a reflection of a greater light."

John said, "Can fools be trusted in anything?"

Alembert said, "Maybe—with caution and discernment. Some of my people are Thules. It does no harm to humor them." Alembert placed his left index finger over his pursed lips and said, "My puzzle has many missing pieces. The panorama it presumes to depict is mostly vacant. We have a piece, maybe several pieces, that comes down to us from Plato and the ancients, telling of a mighty civilization that preceded our historical civilizations and maybe mentored them into being. We have the goblet-shaped piece, exquisitely crafted and decorated with unknown characters. We have the tantalizing piece of the epic poem. We have a genealogical piece that identifies its storytellers so far back in time that the oldest historical events are recent history in comparison. Finally, we have a piece that has been called myth in which many cultures pass down the saga of a worldwide flood. It's a maddeningly incomplete puzzle, but not an empty one. It is my mission in life to fill in the pieces and to touch this mighty civilization in some fashion."

Then they had twin purposes—or did they? What did Alembert hope to achieve by "touching" that civilization? John knew there was an awful darkness in that age that vied with noble peoples for ascendancy in that world. Which of these competing forces would more interest Alembert?

"Now that you have seen the goblet and know the content of the scrolls and have my puzzle set out in front of you, I'm curious as to whether you've changed your mind about the credibility of a historical Atlantis. I have revealed everything to you, John. Do you have anything to tell me?"

How could anyone logically suspect that Alembert was not earnest and honest? Look at the knowledge, John told himself, that this man had shared with him. In spite of these facts, this logic, John sensed that he was being meticulously backed into a corner. He knew that an abrupt *no* would be a perilous response; it would raise the stakes rather than conclude the hand. Alembert was probably expecting it and would have devised his next move, a move that might be exceedingly uncomfortable. Something told him it was important that Alembert not remove the veil of hospitality and respectability he'd been affecting. John's only recourse was to introduce something new and hope it would see him through this interview.

"It's possible I can help you", he said.

For the first time in their association, his host expressed what John took to be genuine surprise. "I can't wait to hear what you have to say."

John's scheme was barely ahead of his words. He knew that delay would be recognized as dissimulation.

"Things I've seen—read. Sources. I need time to assemble them."

"How much time?"

"A matter of weeks."

"Excellent. I will be patient. I have suspected that you might possess things of mutual interest, and I am exceedingly grateful for this acknowledgment. Put things together, by all means, dear friend. I will eagerly await your notice. A very productive meeting, wouldn't you say so?"

"Yes. Indeed", John said.

"I'm certain you won't disappoint me", Alembert said.

"I will be hard pressed to deliver anything on par with the artifacts you've shown me."

"We shall see", Alembert said. "I'm glad we've reached an understanding. Christopher will show you out. May your journey to ... Sussex be a pleasant one."

Alembert stood. John sensed the man's eyes boring into his back as he took his leave, but he attributed it to emotional torpor rather than to anything psychic.

At the door to the street, after John had opened it, he said to Christopher, "Can we speak for a few minutes?" John had come to realize that Christopher was more than a useful factotum. The giant looked like he was ready to answer, then a clownish smile elongated his lips. He ushered John out and closed the door behind him.

Later that night John sat outside in a light rain, drinking the café's house Burgundy. The passersby stared at him, as if he were an inebriate or a lunatic. There were plenty of people inside the café; not a few of them peered out the window at the man in the rain. John used one hand to cover the wine glass; with the other, he wiped raindrops from his face.

He couldn't get this familiar verse out of his mind:

In the rash lustihead of my young powers
I shook the pillaring hours
And pulled my life upon me; grimed with smears,
I stand amidst the dust o' the mounded years—
My mangled youth lies dead beneath the heap.
My days have crackled and gone up in smoke.
I swung the earth a trinket at my wrist

Why did these verses so remind him of Alembert?

John could see all too clearly now that Alembert had shown him his artifacts because he had nothing to fear from

John and everything to gain if John disclosed his own secret. How Alembert knew about John's artifacts he couldn't guess, but every move had been orchestrated toward leading John to reveal them.

He had the feeling he'd barely escaped, though he had never been threatened or treated with anything but apparent respect. Perhaps, for now, he was more valuable held by a string than held over a fire, but the game was on, and John knew it. Furthermore, Alembert wanted him to know it. Why? To frighten him into doing something stupid? To break his will? To play with him like a cat plays with a beetle?

How had Christopher lost an eye? What business of Alembert's caused his friends to become maimed or to disappear as Agnes apparently had done?

The knowledge that the box and book were in a crate on the top shelf in his office made him frantic with worry. How had it gone undiscovered? There was only one answer: Alembert would never have kept something so valuable within easy reach of a thief or mischievous student, so he couldn't imagine anyone else being so careless. E. M. had once compared the crate on the shelf to Poe's *Purloined Letter*. She had hit the bull's-eye. Alembert would seek the artifact in an iron safe or a secret hiding place. Had not E. M. detected that their home had been invaded? Had it already been searched?

Alembert had made it plain that he was no stranger to England: the office and flat in London, the estate in Kent, his visit to Oxford. He'd also mentioned John's wife, though John had not revealed he was married. These hints surely had been intentional, to inform John that his ruse had been penetrated. They were a form of psychological warfare, warning John that his family was in danger if he did not cooperate, the most terrifying thought of all. John did not dare move the artifacts now.

A slender, dark man in evening dress passed the table. His eyes danced in his head, and his smile was mischievous. The man stopped, looked down at John with penetrating black eyes, and extended his umbrella to protect John from the now-pelting rain.

"You're wet, friend", the man said.

American, John concluded. "Quite", he admitted.

"You could do with a cigarette and a cocktail. My name's Porter, and I'm on my way home. There's a party in progress there. Linda won't mind one more. Come along, and let's dry you out."

"Thank you, but I must decline your gracious offer. I'm not in distress. I'm thinking."

"Thinking", the man said, in a musical, lilting voice. "How original. I shall not interrupt you. *Au revoir.*" And the man continued down the street.

The waiter was standing in the doorway with John's meal. "Please come inside, Monsieur, *s'il vous plaît.*"

"*Non. Merci*", John said.

He finished the watery wine and left five francs on the table. It was time to go home.

March 31, 1931

Oxford

The dog leading his man into the room was more or less white. If the animal had been human, one might have observed that while he may have come from a good, even noble, family, he had evidently declined in means, had been reduced to wearing last year's coat and boots. The terrier's bearing was majestic, but his coat was uncombed and spotted with burrs. The wagging of his tail suggested his appearance meant less to him than the company he kept.

The dog trotted unerringly to the corner table in the Eagle and Child—affectionately called the Bird and Baby—, an Oxford meeting place for the great and small. Evidently the terrier did not consider himself to be in that latter category. He boldly wound his way between tables, not pulling at the leash but making it clear who was leading whom. Hands dropped to pat his head, but he took little notice. When he came to his destination—a table already occupied by two men—he settled beneath it like Bucephalus in his royal stall. He had arrived.

"Hello, Mitchie", the balding man said. He was average sized and altogether inconspicuous. He wore a brown tweed coat and was smoking a pipe. John was seated to the man's right, also smoking. Two pints were on the table in front of them.

The newcomer at the other end of the leash was tall and thin, younger than the other two, and red faced, with a head of bushy dark hair. He removed his coat before he sat and undid the leash, which affected Mitchell not in the least; it might have been the man who was released instead of the terrier.

"Mitchie been hunting?" the man in the tweed said, pulling a burr from the dog's back.

"What else? What are you having, Jack?"

"Porter", the man called Jack said, raising the pint to his lips. "I was hungry."

Mitchell's companion removed a pipe from his jacket pocket and filled it with tobacco. It took him some time to find matches to light it. Then he sat back in his chair and closed his eyes.

"You look well enough, Owen", John said.

"Fine", Owen said, eyes still closed.

"Haven't seen much of you."

"Work consumes one."

Jack said, "You need a run in the woods like Mitchie. It does one a world of good."

"You're right, of course. It's the lack of motivation that gets in the way."

"Just pick up a stick and walk out the door", Jack rejoined. "Will follows action."

"So they say. It isn't that easy in practice."

"How is Warnie, Jack?" John said.

"Tolerably well, considering." Jack sucked his pipe, which had gone out.

"We all have devils to contend with", Owen said.

"We do indeed", Jack said. He relit his pipe.

"Bring him along next time", John said. "He's a good fellow."

"I'll consider it. Like inviting a fox to a henhouse." Jack set his pipe on the table and said matter-of-factly, "John, would you mind if I put you in a story?"

John said, "I'm not so interesting a fellow. It will be a dull story."

"So you say", Jack rejoined. "I'm not sure I agree."

"Jack's idea warrants more than an offhand remark. Ask him what he's up to", Owen said to John.

"Time will tell", Jack said.

"Time won't tell", Owen said. "Scrutiny tells. What the two of you need is more rigor."

Jack was refilling his pipe. "Too much rigor produces rigor mortis."

"Are you a Chestertonian now?" Owen exclaimed.

Jack shook his head and reached under the table to scratch Mitchell. "I'm still hungry. Shall we have sardines and crackers?"

"Not on my account", John said.

"I'll share a plate", Owen said. "Another instance of action absent willpower. What about your resident mouse, John? What's his name again?"

"Socrates."

"Are his lodgings still conjoined with yours?"

"It seems so. He's a surreptitious chap."

"You would be too if you shared quarters with a distracted giant."

"I hadn't considered that", John said. "Socrates isn't messy or loud. We are congenial enough roommates."

The Eagle and Child was half filled that night, and it was a quiet crowd by the pub's standards. Two men were engaged in an animated conversation at a table near the door, with one of them rapping his stick on the floor to punctuate his words; otherwise, it was a subdued gathering. The public house was comfortable, a homely place where friends gathered and familiar faces could be seen. John, Jack, and Owen made up a subset of a larger group of colleagues and friends.

They rarely met at one time, but this place served as a common bridge for them.

The plate with crackers and a tin of sardines arrived, along with a pint of porter and two pints of ale. The men, enjoying a comfortable alchemy, absentmindedly touched glasses, and Jack and Owen began consuming the food. Jack lifted a sardine and put his hand beneath the table. When it emerged, it was empty. "No truer friend than a grateful dog", he observed.

"Mitchie doesn't know he's a dog. He thinks he's a king, or at least an earl", Owen said.

"Why so quiet, John?" Jack said.

"Nothing at all", John said. But of course there was something weighing on his mind; he'd promised Alembert something of value. Since then, months ago, he had delivered nothing. He hadn't heard from Alembert, but he had no illusions that the matter was settled. Sometimes he woke in the night after dreaming about a confrontation with that complicated man, or he'd find himself distracted by apprehensions in the middle of a conversation or a lecture he was delivering.

Jack gave him a look that said he knew John's answer was false. The church bell tolled the half hour.

"John has four young children. That's enough to distract anyone", Owen said.

"E. M. has them well in hand", Jack said. "Too bad she doesn't like us. Her instincts are sound, I'd say. She knows we are too full of ourselves. To know it is one thing; to do something about it is another matter. I don't blame her."

John didn't try to talk Jack out of this view. They all knew how E. M. felt.

"Maybe it's the sardines", Owen said. "Not many women like sardines."

"That's an obtuse observation, even for you", Jack said.

"Women have been affected by stranger things than sardines", Owen replied.

Jack shook his head. "I don't send the little devils to her by post." He placed a sardine on top of a cracker and put it into his mouth. He followed it with a gulp of porter. "Will you give us a reading, John?" Jack said. "We wait on these installments."

John was taking a risk, and he knew it. For years he'd kept the contents of the book secret from everyone except E. M. and, to a lesser extent, Gilbert. Alembert might have guessed that he possessed an antiquity of some sort, but he hadn't known any details. One sleepless night an idea came to him—an idea he initially rejected but could not put away: could he present the story—his translation with his additions—as his own literary creation? He was reasonably sure it wasn't vanity that motivated this idea. He was convinced that the world needed, perhaps desperately needed, to hear the story, and to be inspired by it as he had been inspired.

When he discussed the idea with E. M., she had not immediately rejected it, as he expected she would. She listened and kept her counsel to herself for almost a week. When the subject came up again, it was she who introduced it.

"Tell the story", she said one morning at breakfast.

"Do you mean that? You understand the risk?"

"There may be less risk in telling the story, as a story, than keeping it secret. As it stands, if you and I are eliminated and the book stolen, there will be no clue as to motive. If more know the story, even as a story, it might be harder to threaten you, and harder to profit on the story in the future."

Her logic made sense. They agreed that he would be discriminating about who heard the story. He would present it as a work of fiction, his own creation.

"You ought to start with Jack and Owen", she said. "They're too brilliant to suspect the truth." Damning his colleagues with faint praise was an art form with E. M.

That evening, in the Bird and Baby, John read a part of the story where the Hero and his companions left their homes, pursued by a terrible menace and not knowing where their path would take them. The urgency of their journey moved him, as if he, Jack, and Owen were the principals in the drama, as if he could think the thoughts of those distant protagonists and feel their emotions. When he finished reading, he rolled up the typewritten translation that included his own creative insertions and stuffed it in his coat pocket.

"You must continue writing", Jack said. "It's a marvelous story."

"I agree", Owen said. "I presume you know where the story is going."

"I know. Jack, have you heard from Hugo?" John did not want them delving too deeply into the story's inspirations.

"He's been spending a great deal of time in London. We haven't spoken since January."

"I miss him", Owen said.

John nodded agreement. "And Charles—what do you fellows hear from him?"

Owen said, "He's preoccupied with a project. We had tea together last week. He thought about coming ahead tonight. Something must have come up."

"We aren't sparkling company", Jack said, trying to scratch Mitchie without looking under the table.

"Fie on you", Owen said. "I'll ring him up tomorrow."

John noticed that a man had taken a seat two tables away from them. He'd brought a pint from the bar, and a paper was tucked under one arm. He looked familiar, but John couldn't place him.

Jack said, "I knew that John was a thinker, but I never imagined he was a spinner of myths."

John was too busy examining the man to respond to Jack. The newcomer wasn't much older or younger than John; he was sandy haired and burly without being corpulent. He wore delicate wire-rimmed glasses.

A jumble began in the back of John's mind. Gradually this jumble began to assume a sense of order. Finally, everything was clear. "Remember him", E.M. had said. That memory took John by surprise. Could this be the man on the street below the restaurant, or did something else about the man or the pub remind him of that night in London?

"I think we've said enough about the story", John said, in little more than a whisper. "It's still something of a secret."

"Mum's the word", Jack said. "We're running short of crackers. Where's old Robert?" He turned back to John. "How could I have imagined that night when we discussed myth and the True Myth, the life of Christ, that this literary seed would sprout in you? I tell you, John, your story has the sense of being more than myth."

John looked nervously at the other table.

"Yes, I know. Mum's still the word," Jack said.

"And your work, how is it progressing?" John asked, thinking to steer the conversation away from the story.

"My ideas are moored," Jack said, "now that your wave has swamped them." He puffed and blinked.

"John's ideas are his, and ours are ours", Owen said. "There's no need for John's work to hinder us."

John's face reddened. If they knew the truth, would they understand his motives, or would they think him deceitful? Was this another good lie?

Jack said, "I suspect our ideas are more closely aligned than we think. Isn't much of what we write and discuss connected to truth, goodness, and beauty, man's understanding and search for these ideals in a fallen world?" The pub keeper set down another plate of crackers and another tin of sardines.

"The world is no longer inclined to think along those lines", John said.

Owen said, "I have my own ideas, but why do you say so?"

"Sin and its manifestations", Jack said.

"Sin has been with us awhile", Owen countered. "What is different here and now?"

John looked at his friends, then at the man at the other table, who seemed to be paying no attention to them. He was sipping from his pint and staring straight ahead. The paper was still under his arm. John said, "Something, or someone, is pushing the world."

"That's a fascinating idea", Jack said. "Do you mean that literally?"

"Yes."

"And where is the world being pushed?" Owen said.

"Where indeed?" John said. "Toward the material, toward utility, toward efficiency; there's no room for truth, goodness, and beauty in those equations."

Owen lifted the pint to his lips and took a long drink. Then he said, "*Agere contra*. It's nothing new; it's as old as man. Technology has advanced, but the Spartans adopted much the same model, philosophically speaking, two thousand years ago. What is the lure of utility and efficiency? Aren't those ends limpid, even banal? Why would one devote a life to efficiency for efficiency's sake? Those are old credos masquerading as new credos."

"I would hear more", Jack said.

Owen said, "I'm not trying to be obscure. The lure is pride disguised as stoicism, it's greed disguised as hedonism, and it's envy disguised as anarchism. Pride, greed, and envy are the ancient credos."

"Three deadly sins", Jack said.

"You suggest there's a connection between the modern stoics, hedonists, and anarchists and the movements that promote utility and efficiency?" John said.

"Yes", Owen said. "Stoicism, hedonism, and anarchism are, at their roots, urges for control, for the 'I' to dominate the other, if not the world. Dependency on any external authority is antithetical to these credos. The movement that promotes utility is a movement to make men, if not certain men, gods. Efficiency for the sake of efficiency, progress for the sake of progress, and advancement for the sake of advancement is a path to deification for these men. The stoic, the hedonist, and the anarchist have more in common than what separates them."

"Is that anything more than an impression?" John said. "It has oratorical energy, but that doesn't mean it's true."

"I can say that the contradictory evidence is meager. Whenever you find efficiency, order, and progress at the heart of a movement, you will find those ideas predominating. Gregory of Nyssa said, 'Ideas create idols; only wonder leads to knowing.'"

John pondered Owen's words. How closely his friend's analysis corresponded with the content of the book and with John's debates about progress and efficiency with Jacob Basile, with Alembert, and with Gosdier Jones.

"In their urge to resist 'slavery' to an external authority, the stoicist, hedonist, and anarchist embrace slavery to self. Worse still, they are infected with the emptiness at the root of this slavery." Owen pushed the pint to the corner of the table and said, "That's plenty."

"You can't eat sardines without beer", Jack said. "John suggests that someone is pushing the world. Isn't it the one who has been pushing the world since he fell from heaven?"

John's eyes were locked on the man with the newspaper.

"We can debate that point," Owen said, "but we need go no further than man to find the agent of these movements in our times."

"The brownshirts, the fascists, the communists, the Nipponese nationalists", John said.

"Precisely", Owen said. "There are less influential movements in South America and Africa. What do they share? The vague goals of progress, advancement, and efficiency, the deployment of human resources under the guidance of oligarchies or parties of elites."

It was the same man that was in that London street, John concluded. Their eyes met, and a wariness revealed itself in the other. John made up his mind, got up, and walked to the man's table.

"Have we met?" John said.

"I don't think so." The man placed his paper on the table, without looking up to meet John's eyes.

"I'm sure I've seen you before."

"I don't think so. I'm a visitor." The man's voice sounded more self-assured than he appeared.

The next thing John did was bold, and if he'd considered it, it was doubtful he would have proceeded. He didn't know what would be gained by this gambit, but he felt compelled to try it. "Why don't you join us?" he said.

The man looked at Jack and Owen, who were watching the exchange. John could almost see the gears tumbling in the man's head—wariness and indecision mixed with opportunity.

"Thanks, but I have to shove off." The man got up, clutched his paper, and walked to the bar. When he turned back to John, there was no expression whatsoever on his face. He left the paper on the bar and went to the door.

"Who is he?" Jack asked when John returned.

"I thought I recognized him. I must have been mistaken. I'm sorry for that interruption, Owen."

John's anxiety must have shown because Owen said, "Is there something you're not telling us?"

How could John begin to answer that question? "It's a complicated story—better leave it for another time."

"You are an onion begging to be peeled", Jack said.

John now knew it was the same man. The man wasn't a bad actor, but John's unexpected confrontation had unsettled him. How else could his excessive nervousness be explained? What had the man hoped to learn? He must have known John would be here, and probably with friends. Should he tell E. M.? Would anything be gained by troubling her? It was jarring to think that someone's interest in his affairs spanned years. What else could it be except the book? The critical question was, what did his adversaries know? Surely not the whereabouts of the book, or they could have it at any time. Mechanically, he took a sardine from the tin and reached beneath the table. Mitchell didn't waste any time consuming it.

The clock tolled a quarter hour. "I will tell you something", John said to his companions. "I'd like your advice."

"That's better", Jack said.

"Here's a hypothetical dilemma. There's a person who shares another person's interest in a subject. Furthermore, the first person may have information vital to the second person. But this first person is mysterious, possibly dangerous. What is your advice to the second person?"

"I need more information", Jack said. "For convenience, let's call the two men Mystery and Inquiry. How well does Inquiry know Mystery? Does Mystery have a history of threatening behavior? Does Mystery have the credibility to be trusted?"

Owen said, "I'd add, are there other resources, apart from Mystery, who might satisfy Inquiry's needs?"

John leaned toward his friends. He finished packing his pipe and lit it. "Inquiry doesn't know Mystery well. Mystery is not known to be dangerous, but his behavior and associations suggest it's possible. Mystery is eminently credible in Inquiry's area of interest. There are others who might be able to supply Inquiry with information, but their contribution is likely to be peripheral, while Mystery's information may be central to Inquiry's interests."

Jack said, "How important is it that Inquiry obtain this information?"

John hesitated, then said, "Very important."

"A thorny problem", Owen said. "My opinion is that Mystery should be engaged. At the same time, an investigation can be conducted to learn more about him. If investigation demonstrates that Mystery is untrustworthy or dangerous, then Inquiry can sever the relationship."

"My view is different", Jack said. "A person's credibility can't be separated from his character. If Inquiry is uneasy about Mystery's character, he ought to disengage and seek enlightenment, even if it's less promising, elsewhere."

"Let's say that Mystery is known to associate with the brownshirts", John said.

"We've come full circle," Owen said, "from philosophy to personality."

"What do you mean?" John said.

"Is Mystery a stoic, a hedonist, an anarchist?"

John said, "Let's imagine he keeps expensive quarters, his Bordeaux is superb, and he has caviar brought to Paris by air."

Jack made a disparaging sound. Owen said, "One need not be an inebriate or a satyr to qualify as a hedonist. Is he a stoic?"

"He has stoical tendencies", John said.

"Stoical in the sense of recognizing no authority but his own will?"

"I'd say so."

"An anarchist?"

"That's hard to say."

"It's usually the most difficult to detect", Owen said. "A few are wide-eyed bomb throwers, but most are quietly destructive. It's no wonder Mystery associates with brownshirts. That's what I meant by the connection between philosophy and personality."

Jack spoke as soon as Owen finished. "I said that a person's credibility can't be separated from his character. If Mystery's character is suspect, then Inquiry's continued association with him may make severing that relationship problematical, or even impossible, if Mystery becomes convinced that Inquiry has something he desires."

John nodded. It was time to change the subject. Jack and Owen wouldn't object. They'd respect John's decision to present this as a hypothetical matter; at least he hoped they would. Their analysis had been succinct and valuable. He said, "I forgot to bring the chocolates."

"I didn't know you liked sweets", Jack said.

"A student gave them to me. I couldn't refuse."

"So you foist them on your friends."

"That's the idea. I'll bring them next time."

"Sardines and chocolate", Owen said. "An interesting combination. What was the occasion?"

"Gratitude for the gift of knowledge I suppose", John said. "It's on a shelf in my office."

"I know your office. It's enlisted in an army of paraphernalia", Jack said.

John noticed that Mitchell had crossed the room and was lying at the feet of two old women in the opposite corner. "Your dog's abandoned us", he said to Owen.

Owen seemed surprised; the dog's exit had been furtive. "Mitchie!" he said loudly.

"That won't bring him back. He's found more interesting company," John said.

"Not uncommon", Owen said. "He isn't fond of philosophy. He likes his ears scratched."

"He needs training", Jack said.

"He thinks we're the ones who need training", Owen said. "He'll come back eventually—always does."

"Don't be too sure", John said. "Those women are scratching his ears."

"Who was that man, John?" Owen said. "You know you can rely on us."

"I know", John said.

"Two tins of sardines are ample", Owen said, when he realized that John had nothing else to say. "It's time to go."

"I'll follow", Jack said. "Good night."

Owen retrieved Mitchell and attached the leash. The dog got up, wobbled a little, and made for the door, with Owen trailing.

Jack put his pipe in his mouth and his hat on his head. He said, "Be careful, John."

John didn't get up right away. He finished his pint, gazed at the empty table where the man had been seated, heard the bell toll the hour. On the way out, he approached the pub keeper and said, "Robert, do you remember the chap who was sitting by himself?"

The man nodded. "I do, Professor."

"Do you know his name?"

"I know him as Jack."

"Then you've seen him before."

"Seen him before. Not often; not for some time. He made out of here right quick when he finished talking to you."

John leaned against the bar. There was still a small crowd in the place. "I'd like to learn more about Jack."

"I get your meaning, Professor. I'll do what I can, on the sly."

"That's appreciated. Good night to you."

John's walk home was quiet and uneventful. The streets were almost empty. There was no reason to suspect that he was being watched or followed. He pondered what Jack and Owen had said in response to his hypothetical question. It had been a brief conversation but packed with insight. He was most convinced by Jack's response. It was rational and straightforward, as Jack was rational and straightforward. Ironically, Jack's perspective corresponded to E. M.'s, and for the two of them to agree was noteworthy, if not conclusive.

He had a suspicion he'd learned all there was to learn from Alembert. It was time to sever the relationship, and if there were to be further correspondence, he would offer plausible excuses. Perhaps he would provide valueless information, leading Alembert to conclude that John was intellectually slothful. Perhaps—Alembert would not be an easy man to deceive.

E. M. was still awake when he returned. She was painting in the front room. She had an uncanny sense of his emotional temperature, and when she saw him, she put down the brush.

"What's wrong?"

"I've been talking to Jack and Owen about Alembert."

She rose from her chair and started to say something but didn't.

"Jack suggests terminating the relationship."

Her expression didn't change. He saw her hands clench and unclench. "How much did you tell them?"

"I posed a hypothetical situation."

"Which they knew to be a real situation."

"I imagine so."

"Was anything said about the book?"

"I read to them; otherwise, no. There are no suspicions, if that's what you mean."

"Don't be too sure. They annoy me, but they are gifted men."

"To learn, one must sometimes reveal."

"You've said that before. That cuts both ways. You know my feelings."

"I've concluded that you and Jack are right."

"You're done with Alembert?"

"Yes."

"I wonder if he's finished with you."

Why hadn't he brought the chocolates home? It would have been a nice gesture.

The skulker—Robert called him Jack. If he was going to say anything to E. M., now was the time. If the man was in Oxford, wouldn't it be best to put her on her guard? Still, there was the possibility—though he disbelieved it—that the man lived in town and had good reasons for being in the neighborhood when E. M. observed him, and in London the night they'd seen him from the balcony.

"That's a good picture", he said.

"Thanks. I'm dissatisfied with it. I may start over."

"Have you sold any more?"

"Clyde called today. The colt sold last weekend."

"That's five, isn't it?"

"Yes, I think so."

"You're developing a following", he said.

"Hardly that. I wish I knew what else is on your mind."

"Nothing."

"Something. I suppose you'll tell me when you're ready."

She looked at the painting and said, "I will start over."

"Too bad. I like it."

She walked over and kissed him. "Thanks for being so encouraging. And thanks for breaking with Alembert."

He shrugged. Then he walked toward the room where his children slept.

May 26, 1931

Heidelberg

Colleagues and students alike considered the professor to be a sedentary, cautious man, immersed in his work and devoted to his growing family.

The alter ego the professor had assumed in quest of information concerning the book's civilization, John Hill, was another matter. Two days, the Channel boat, and two trains later, he was seated in the small office of a medieval building at Heidelberg University. He was waiting for its occupant to arrive, waiting and observing.

The office was tidy, devoid of pictures or ornamentation. It had a tall ceiling and a stone floor weathered by centuries of Heidelberg dons. There was a small leaded glass window, more opaque than transparent, overlooking a courtyard. One wall contained books on shelves, mostly geology and paleontology texts; there was also a selection of philosophical and sociological works. He saw Darwin's *On the Origin of Species* and Nietzsche's *Der Wille zur Macht* (*The Will to Power*) and *Jenseits von Gut and Böse* (*Beyond Good and Evil*). Except for the empty ashtray, the desk was bare. Its richly grained wooden surface had been recently polished.

The man entered the room with a suddenness that made John start. He barely glanced at John, then circled the desk and sat. He set a book, a notebook, and several loose sheets of paper on the desktop and gazed at John over black-rimmed pince-nez.

"I'm Pepin Hermann", he said, without extending a hand.

"John Hill. Thank you for seeing me."

This was a Pepin of a different sort, John thought. Unlike his Frankish namesake, Pepin Hermann was a large man, well over six feet tall. He was blond with short hair, small ears, a prominent nose, and bright blue eyes. He wore a gray three-piece suit, white shirt, and gold tie, his only concession to color.

Hermann squared the sheets of loose paper on top of the notebook. "Your letter said you desired to consult me about a book you are writing—fiction", he said in heavily accented English. The man had been reticent about meeting John, rebuffing his first inquiry. John's second request had produced grudging agreement. John had no illusions that the interview would be amiable.

"A fictional story, yes", John said. "I want it to be as historically accurate as possible."

"I am not a historian", Hermann said curtly.

"Geologic and geographic history, then."

Hermann nodded, as he might have after a student corrected an ill-considered response. With Adler Alembert no longer a collaborator, John had scoured academic journals for people who might be able to supply useful information. Pepin Hermann had gained a reputation as one of the world's most renowned paleogeologists. He was one of two experts John had decided to consult.

"Heidelberg is a majestic town", John said.

"I have been told it is charming. I am not easily charmed." Hermann looked at his wristwatch. There was no mistaking the implication that his time was valuable and that John was imposing on it.

John had the sense that this room would always seem cold, no matter the time of year or temperature. The absence of color and art coupled with the person who resided here produced that effect. Still, he hadn't come to be entertained. "I'm interested in the period from 100,000 to 10,000 B.C. I'm aware that there were ice ages during that period. Were there also warmer periods on the European continent during that span of time?"

"Why does that interest a writer of fiction?" Hermann said, removing his glasses and setting them down. He might have said "collector of garbage" considering the condescension in his voice.

"The story I'm composing depicts a fictional civilization, a prehistoric culture, that existed during a warm interlude between ice ages."

Hermann emitted several snorts, suggesting a pig or a boar. John realized that the man was laughing. "Indeed. In that era, it is known that culture, as you call it, consisted of hunting and gathering and a very primitive domestication of animals. There was no civilization in that era, and there was no culture."

"Of course you're right", John said. "The story is pure fiction."

"If the story is pure fiction, there is no need to consult me. What you mean to say is that you want to give your story a historical veneer."

John sensed that Hermann had sized him up and found him uninteresting, even shallow. That didn't trouble John so long as he could get Hermann to answer his questions. He'd come a long way to leave empty handed.

"Can you identify the warmer periods in that span of time?" John said, ignoring Hermann's criticism.

The large man exhaled audibly. He reached toward the shelf to his right and removed a book. After opening it, he laid it down on the desk and said, as if lecturing to a class of first-year students, "There were two periods in that time frame when dramatically cooler temperatures prevailed in Europe. The first period extended from one hundred thousand to sixty thousand years ago. Much of Europe was deforested during this period; cold deserts and semideserts predominated. The coldest, driest point occurred during the Lower Pleniglacial about seventy thousand years ago. The second cold period occurred thirty thousand years ago and prevailed until ten thousand years ago. This Upper Pleniglacial period had similar characteristics to the earlier period: cold temperatures, aridity, and deforestation.

"In between, from sixty thousand to thirty thousand years ago, temperatures moderated, and Europe was blanketed with forests. The climate oscillated between warmer and cooler conditions. Such conditions might have supported advanced cultures if such cultures had existed. They did not."

"Would that period have been as temperate as the present age?"

"Similar. Less warm but not materially different."

"Were the mountain ranges in that period similar to those of modern Europe?"

"There were differences. We don't have time to discuss them in detail." He glanced at his watch and frowned. "The mountains extended further north prior to the last ice age."

If Hermann was barely engaged, John surely was. "During that period, were there any geologic or climatologic conditions that would have rendered the land uninhabitable to man—or to commerce?"

Hermann pondered the question, or his answer, as if an internal debate was raging between accuracy and being rid of his visitor. "Not that I am aware of; green plants and fresh water would have been abundant."

"The Mediterranean Sea?"

"In that period it was a bay, open to the ocean, rather than the interior sea that now exists."

"Is there anything more you can tell me about the mountain ranges?"

"In what sense?" Hermann said, with evident exasperation. He looked at his watch again. John expected the man to invite him to leave at any moment.

"Where would mountains have been located?" John said.

"There is evidence of an extensive north-to-south range whose remnants are the Alpine mountains."

"And the land bridge from the Continent to Britain?"

"The bridge, as you call it, existed until approximately 10,000 B.C. Prior to that time, one could walk from here to present-day Belfast."

There was nothing Hermann said that caused John to doubt the theory he'd developed. He had hoped, and here was validation of his theory. He would keep questioning as long as Hermann was willing to answer. "Isn't it true, considering the destructive force of the intruding ice, that if an advanced civilization once existed on the European continent, every trace of it might have been eradicated?"

"That is fiction, like your story", Hermann said.

"But is it possible?"

Hermann lit a cigarette and smoked it. "I do not like speculation."

"Your answer suggests it is possible", John said.

"I like inference less than speculation."

"I'm sorry."

Hermann waved his cigarette and reached for the ashtray.

"How deep was the ice at its zenith?" John said.

"You are annoyingly persistent", Hermann said ungraciously. "Hundreds of feet thick, I daresay."

"It's my understanding that the glaciers left lakes and massive deposits in their wake."

"Indeed."

"A glacier might have ground a city, even a great city, to dust", John said.

"It might have, if such a city existed. Accepting your wild premise, I would expect artifacts of this civilization to have survived."

Was that as innocent an observation as it appeared to be? "The period you described, from sixty to thirty thousand years ago—would the land have been fertile?"

"I suspect so. The geologic and climatologic conditions suggest it."

"Thirty thousand years is five times the span of recorded history, plenty of time for a civilization, or many civilizations, to rise and fall."

Hermann ground the cigarette in the tray and closed the book with a bang. "How old are you?" he asked.

"Thirty-nine."

"Did you fight in the war?"

The question surprised John. Was Hermann trying to distract him? The office was filled with smoke. Hermann, though he was only a few feet away, appeared as grainy and colorless as a motion picture.

"Yes, as a matter of fact, I did."

"Where?"

"The Somme, east and west as the tide turned."

Hermann sat back and lit his third cigarette. He snorted twice. "I was there also."

The men looked at each other across the desk as they might have looked across the killing ground. In spite of Hermann's arrogance and disdain, John felt an emotional connection to the man that he hadn't felt before. They'd both survived the misery of the trenches. They'd both served their nations and returned home. They shared a common sacrifice and experience.

But John detected an elevated rigidity in Hermann's bearing. His expression suggested he'd been insulted. The cigarette looked like a baton in his hand.

"The world is different now", John said.

"Is it? You would like to think so, I'm sure."

"We've learned our lesson, I hope." John regretted the words as soon as they were spoken.

"*We've* learned lessons", Hermann said. In spite of himself, he could not hide his anger. He put out his half-smoked cigarette. The tray was full. "Have you exhausted your questions?"

John said, "You were kind to see me."

"I found your letters interesting—as a geologist. I am intrigued by a writer of fiction who is interested in the minutiae of geologic epochs. May I ask if you are an adherent of Darwin?"

"In what respect?" John said.

"In every respect: the evolution of man, biologically, socially."

"Man may have evolved biologically, even intellectually. I suspect it's dangerous to apply Darwin's theories to social order and ethics."

Hermann seemed to relax. He sat back in his chair and pursed his lips. He might have been smiling, but it was hard to tell. His small ears were red. "I believe that Darwin's theories, survival of those most fit to survive, apply universally, especially in the social and ethical arenas."

"And do you believe that social and ethical Darwinism makes us more human?" John said.

"More human—what does that mean?" Hermann said.

"More sublime, more generous, more creative ..."

"Indeed", Hermann said cynically. "I do not count those essential qualities. It is the progress of the race that matters. I rely on science exclusively."

John could not help himself. "Then you must have high regard for the National Socialists."

Hermann snorted again. "You are wrong. Buffoons they are. Still, they can be useful in removing the refuse."

"Rats remove refuse, but they don't stop there."

Hermann snorted—this time ejecting something from his nose.

"Do you believe in God?" John said. He wasn't passive by nature, and he'd had enough. Boorishness was one thing, but rudeness was another matter. He intended to unsettle Hermann, and he was successful.

Hermann placed both hands, palms down, on the desktop. "I am an atheist. I have no use for religion. It muddles the mind. It prevents society from dealing with its ... refuse."

"The National Socialists and communists are atheists."

"What are you saying?" Hermann said.

"They are also social Darwinists. Do you consider their methods scientific?"

"They are useful fools, as I said."

"Are you sure they're the fools?" John said.

"What are you saying?" Hermann said, antagonistically.

"I'm asking if the most passionate adherents of social Darwinism, the most rabid antireligionists, are the most rational men. Following your reasoning, one would expect that to be so."

Hermann waved his hand dismissively. "I am not interested in word games, and I am late." He got up and took John's arm, escorting him to the door. "Do not attempt logic on the brownshirts. They are not so tolerant or patient.

And this is not England or 1920. You would be wise to remember that."

John did not waste time trying to decipher Hermann's warning. It was more of the same, superficiality masquerading as wisdom. How many, he wondered, could not, or did not, want to distinguish between what science actually demonstrated and the scientism they used to justify their visceral inclinations? The world was rushing headlong down that path, so much so that John felt like a stranger in the modern world. He was certain that his admiration of the cultures in the book contributed to this feeling.

Once John had crossed Hermann's threshold, the door banged shut, reverberating in the stone hall. He was glad to be rid of that fractious man. In spite of his short audience with Hermann, he'd learned enough to make the trip worthwhile. He passed beneath an ancient arch, left the grounds of the university, and took to the streets of the old city. Between buildings, he caught glimpses of the castle on the hill and the Neckar River well below the university. There seemed to be little rhyme or reason to the orientation of the streets that wound around and veered at odd angles. He was less concerned with reaching a destination than with walking and thinking about what he'd learned from Hermann. The late afternoon streets were percolating with activity, and the cafés were reopening for the coffee hour. Stores and open-air markets were peddling their wares to students, housewives, workmen, and professionals, as were adherents of the new movements vying for ascendancy in Germany. Many a street corner had a crowd gathering beneath either the hammer and sickle or the swastika. Loud, bombastic cries filled the air as one got closer to these assemblies, and around the edges men were shoving and shouting at each other. John remembered Hermann's parting words: "Do not attempt logic on the brownshirts. They are not so tolerant or patient."

To escape the tumult, John turned down a steep side street that led to the river. It was narrow but not dingy, with quaint, medieval facades on the buildings and flower boxes beneath the windows. He felt like he'd entered a picture-book Germany. Halfway to the river, he came upon an inviting café. There was an empty table at the curb, and as he approached it, two arguing men pushed past, tripping him. He fell against the table, knocking a coffee cup to the pavement.

"I'm so sorry", he said, staring into the face of the young woman who was sitting there. He bent down to pick up the remnants of the cup, but the waiter was already sweeping them into a tray.

The woman was startled but managed a smile, closing the book she'd been reading.

"I am terribly sorry. Please excuse me. I will pay for the cup and buy you another coffee."

"Don't bother", she said.

"I insist", John said.

"You are English."

"Yes—a clumsy Englishman. Waiter, I wish to pay for the broken cup and a fresh coffee for the Fräulein."

The waiter went into the café. John shook his head.

She gave him a long, even piercing, look, and then said, "Please sit."

"I've been enough of a nuisance", John said.

"Come; sit. You can watch me enjoy the coffee you purchased."

He pulled up a chair and sat. "I'm John Hill", he said.

"My name is Edith."

The coffee arrived. "What will you have, sir?" the waiter said. He was stout and middle-aged and wore a large apron.

He didn't appear to be perturbed about the cup John had broken.

John requested a stein of beer. He removed his pipe from his jacket.

"Do you mind if I smoke?"

"Suit yourself."

"I'm surprised to find so much turmoil in town", he said, when his pipe was smoking.

"It is a consequence of the intellectual poisons we consume."

He gave her a questioning look.

"Fascism and communism; they are twin madnesses. Now that they are unleashed, there is no restraining them. They will drain our culture of all its virtues before they are finished."

"You are a professional woman?" John said.

"A philosopher."

He could well believe it. "A teacher?"

She hesitated. "Yes."

"Do you teach at the university?"

"I am lecturing at the university."

He raised the stein to his lips. The woman appeared to be in her midthirties. Her dark hair was pulled back in a bun. The dimple in her chin contrasted with the intensity of her eyes, which were blue or gray; he couldn't tell.

"Are you a teacher too?" she said.

"Yes."

"Where do you teach?"

He started to repeat the lie he'd told to Alembert and Hermann but found that he couldn't. He took another drink of beer.

"I understand", she said. "Caution is prudence in these times." She drank her coffee black. She didn't seem to be a smoker. "So we are both visitors." She held the cup in both hands as does one who is chilled, though it was warm enough in the sun.

"Can you explain what's happening?" he said to her.

Edith put the cup down. "Speaking as a philosopher, we have succumbed to heresies, the heresies of materialism and positivism, the idea that empirical science is the only legitimate portal to knowledge, and material facts the only objects of knowledge. Now none are immune to the influence of these heresies. Hitler and Röhm are the worst, but they have competition. Stalin's surrogates are busy too. It is just a matter of which wolf will devour the rest."

He watched her until her eyes rose to meet his; then he said, "I've heard it's a perilous time to be a Jew."

"So true; animus toward the Jews has been unleashed. But all virtuous men and women have cause for distress."

"Have you considered leaving?"

"I have not said I am a Jew", she said, dispassionately.

He had no desire to press her. "Will you have something to eat?"

"If you wish, I will have a little something. I am rarely hungry when I lecture; later, I am famished."

John beckoned for the waiter and ordered meat, cheese, and bread. His travels had given him an appetite, and Hermann hadn't offered him so much as a cracker.

"Have you heard of Husserl—phenomenology?" she said when they were alone again.

John shook his head.

"Much of my training was in that school of thought. Phenomenologists believe that reality discloses important things about human nature and the moral duties that derive from it. Naturally, such thinking is antithetical to the National Socialists and communists."

John said, "From what I observed today, I'd be surprised if those ruffians could grasp the concept, much less debate it."

She shook her head and said, "One need not be able to grasp an idea to want to smash it. Their intellectual capacity may be limited, but their instincts are highly developed; they know whom to hate as soon as they meet them."

"I can't see how the idea you described could be a threat to them."

"Phenomenologists experience things as a whole, whereas the ideological movements place people in rigid categories of class or race. I have come to believe that phenomenology does not go far enough—there is an ingredient missing—but it is a good starting point."

"What is missing?" John said.

"The element of personalism, that is, the centrality of the human person and his capacity to get to the truth of things as he reflects upon his experiences."

"That is a phenomenal idea", John said. She smiled at him—patronizingly, he thought. He finished the slice of cheese on his plate. Then he swallowed some beer and broke off another piece of bread. There was much about her—he was certain of it—that she hadn't revealed, and wouldn't. In that sense, they were ciphers to each other. The tables were filling up. There were hardly any empty chairs.

"My friend Owen would enjoy talking to you", he said.

"Is he also a philosopher?" she said.

"He is a student of consciousness—how it has evolved, and how truth may be discovered."

"That line of thinking is not far from phenomenology. Both are anchored in truths that are not simply constructs of man."

John said, "I'm sure you would be welcomed in England."

"Get thee behind me", she said, but there was no animus in her voice. "My people are here. My work is here. I do not criticize those who have left. The brutality, barbarism, anti-intellectualism, paganism—I see them quite clearly. One man said that the greatest gift Divine Providence can give someone is to send him a trial he cannot bear with his own powers and then sustain him so he may endure to the end."

After witnessing the acrimony in the streets, he didn't like to imagine what the consequences of her decision would be. He heard a peal of thunder—or was it a gun? There were clouds in the sky, but it didn't look like rain. Several patrons started, but not Edith.

"May I sit?" a deep, melodious voice said.

John hadn't noticed the man. There was an empty chair at their table. The pavement was now crowded. Edith looked at the man. Her face was inscrutable, except that her eyes narrowed, as a cat's eyes narrow before a prodigious leap; it was a poor analogy because there was also sadness in her expression. Courtesy seemed to demand that they extend the man a place.

"Of course", John said.

The man was tall, lean, and dressed in a white shirt and tie. He had a long and prominent, but not unattractive, nose and a square, clean-shaven jaw. He immediately extended a hand to John. "I am Rudolph Kuiper. I hope I am not intruding. There were no empty tables."

John realized that the man was speaking English, though it was clear that he was German.

"I could not help hearing you talk. I am not so good with English, but I will try. You will be good practice."

"We were discussing phenomenology", Edith said, less than hospitably.

227

If Kuiper noticed her abruptness, he ignored it. He sat in the unoccupied chair and removed his hat, exposing a high forehead and golden hair. He seemed quite comfortable in the presence of these two strangers.

"What is your business?" John asked Kuiper.

"I am a street car conductor." Kuiper lit a cigarette and ordered beer and radishes. He tapped the table with his left hand as he spoke.

"Are there many fights in the cars?" Edith asked him.

He smiled at her. "Occasionally. Communists, anarchists." Then, nonchalantly, "May I ask your names?"

"John Hill."

"Edith."

"*Danke*, John Hill and ... Edith, for allowing me to share your table. What brings you to Heidelberg?" he asked John.

"I'm researching a book", John said. Kuiper seemed to be no ordinary man. This physically striking figure exuded ambition and charisma.

"What kind of book?"

"A work of fiction", John said.

"I do not read fiction", Kuiper said coyly. "Will you be in Heidelberg long?"

"Until tomorrow."

"I see. And you, Edith. I have not seen you in town before."

"I am visiting, lecturing at the university."

"On what topic?" Kuiper said.

"Feminism and personalism."

"Ah. Feminism. I hear about it often these days. But what is meant by personalism?"

John had the sense that he was watching a performance; Kuiper's and Edith's lines seemed scripted. But how was that possible? They were strangers, weren't they? The pavement was even more crowded. Many students seemed content to stand. One young man wore a swastika on his shirt sleeve. Another sported a beard that reached almost to his waist, an anomaly in the mostly clean-shaven crowd.

"Personalism", Edith said, "refers to the uniqueness, the specialness, of the individual—"

"Every individual?" Kuiper said, skeptically.

"Yes."

The young German tapped on the table. "Wouldn't you agree that those who contribute to society render more value to society than do those who take from society?"

"No, I would not agree", she said, firmly but passionlessly.

"Wouldn't you agree that society advances more rapidly if it removes those who use resources without producing anything that benefits society?"

"No, I do not agree. Isn't the bell ringer entitled to sanctuary somewhere?"

Kuiper nodded. John wasn't sure whether that signified he agreed with her. The man drew languidly on his cigarette and exhaled the smoke in something like exasperated bursts. Then he crushed the half-smoked cigarette in the ashtray. Finally, Kuiper said, "Bell ringing is without utility. Bell ringers are superfluous."

How did Kuiper's supposedly poor English encompass these nuanced words? John wondered.

"Sanctuary is contrary to an efficiently run state", Kuiper added, biting into a radish and turning toward John as if Edith had ceased to exist. "John, where is your home?"

"Sussex", he said, without hesitation.

"I have never been to England. Charming country, I am told. Who interests you in Heidelberg?"

"A scholar at the university."

"Perhaps I have heard of him", Kuiper said.

John was not inclined to say more. Edith sipped her coffee and broke off a small piece of the loaf.

"You must eat some meat with your bread", John said to Edith.

"Perhaps", she said, distantly.

"Lecturing is hard work."

"Are you a lecturer too?" Kuiper asked John.

"I'm a teacher", John said.

"I have chosen a stimulating table", Kuiper said, lighting another cigarette and starting on his third radish. "A philosopher and a creative writer."

"I am curious", Edith said to Kuiper. "What would you do with Russians or Poles or Jews who are capable of contributing to society?"

Kuiper's smile exposed bright white teeth. "I speak only for myself. No one cares what a conductor thinks. My view: there is apparent contribution and actual contribution. Some make a pretense of advancing society, but the fruit is rotten. As for the English," he said, leaning toward John and putting a hand on his shoulder, "they are an industrious people, natural allies of Germany, genetic brothers. You see, I have exposed myself as a poor speaker of English and a worse philosopher." He bit into the radish.

"On the contrary", Edith said. "A conductor's ideas may be suggestive of the ideas of a state. A conductor's beliefs may become the state's governing philosophy. It is possible, isn't it?"

"Perhaps", Kuiper admitted, dismissively. "John, are you stopping anywhere on the way back to England?"

"No," John said, "my family is waiting for me."

"I am a single man. I am envious of men with a family." Kuiper finished his beer. "I hope we meet again. It is not bad to hear different ideas, yes? I have learned something new—phenomenology, wasn't it? A pleasant journey to you, John." He got up without saying anything to Edith, made a half bow, and walked off.

Edith was still sipping her coffee, though it must have been cold. She hadn't eaten much. She looked this way and that, for the first time expressing something like anxiety.

"You must try the meat before the birds come for it", he said.

"The birds or the vultures?" she said. "I am sorry. Here, I am eating."

"Thank you, my dear", he said. "I will be able to sleep tonight."

"I sincerely hope so, John."

"Am I so obviously a fretful traveler?"

"Not that."

"Have another taste. Indulge me. I dislike wasting food."

"I have satisfied the demands of gratitude", she said.

"Kuiper is a man of his times, I suppose", John said.

"Yes. A prescient observation."

"How long are you staying in Heidelberg?" he asked her. They were awash in a sea of humanity, but this felt like an intimate conversation.

"I am leaving for Münster tomorrow."

"Your ideas are stimulating. I will ponder them, and I won't forget you", John said.

"We have had a short time together, but I sense that our sympathies are similar."

"I suppose I must be going", John said. "Please stay—and eat if you can."

"Good-bye, John Hill", she said, extending a hand.

"Good-bye, Edith."

He had already taken a step toward the street when he heard her voice. "What is your real business here?"

"I dare not say", he said, turning around, before realizing he'd been speaking too loudly. He moved back toward the table, and she put a finger to her lips with one hand and gestured he move closer with the other. "So I imagined", she whispered. "I will not probe any further. But listen to me, John. Take the night train to Paris. Do not return to your hotel. Leave behind whatever is in your room."

"What are you suggesting?" he whispered.

She took his hand. "This so-called Kuiper is a dangerous man. His real name is Reinhard Krieger, and he is no street car conductor. Anyone that interests Krieger should be on his guard."

Krieger ... he tried to remember the details of the conversation between Alembert and Christopher. He had heard that name on his previous visit to Alembert's office.

"Thank you, Edith", he said, releasing her hand and walking down the street toward the river. His mind was spinning. Krieger. They would expect him to return to the hotel. Whoever was tracking his movements would probably pick him up there. Perhaps they'd decided they couldn't allow him to leave the city, and so they sent Krieger to deal with him here, or remove him to Paris. Once night had fallen and he was safely ensconced in his room, they would be free to act. By coming to Heidelberg, he had put himself at their mercy. Now he must accept his peril and make the wisest decisions he could make.

He walked along the river until he was reasonably confident he wasn't being followed. There were hills on both sides. The river was gray and languid. A barge passed. There was a light on its bow and the word HERMANN. He could hear the hum of the motor. It reminded him why he had taken the risk to come to Heidelberg. It was the hope that he would learn something to corroborate or contradict his theory about the civilization in the book. In spite of himself, Hermann had confirmed there was a thirty-thousand-year temperate period in Europe between two great ice ages, and during that period what was known about that "Europe" corresponded to the geology and geography in the book. That, he told himself, notwithstanding the risk, made this adventure worthwhile—that is, if he survived. He discovered a narrow alley and by a stroke of luck, or a good sense of direction, found the street that led to the train station.

John was the last man to board the train. He had hidden in alleys and shadows for hours, afraid that someone was watching the station. Did he dare to hope that the train would embark before those watching the hotel grew suspicious? He shuffled to a nearly unoccupied car at the rear and found an empty compartment. The train lurched ahead. He felt gritty; he was tired and hungry. He especially regretted having to leave behind the new shirt E. M. had given him for his birthday. He entertained the idea that Edith had been wrong about Krieger, but reflecting on that woman's perspicacity, he dismissed it.

In his current state of dread, he doubted if he could sleep on the train, but more worrisome was the transfer in Paris, Alembert's base of operations. He had an irrational fear that Alembert was a superman and that John's every move was being watched and mapped. He was frightened, but he'd learned from men like Gilbert and women like E. M. and Edith. He wouldn't surrender to Alembert or anyone else.

June 2, 1931

Algiers

"Are you a doctor, ma'am?"

She was often asked that question because of the black leather bag she always carried.

"*Non.* No", she said, automatically.

The man looked at the bag wistfully and melted into the crowded bazaar.

The bag contained remedies only in the sense that potions may heal at one dose and kill at another. The toxins, poisons, and venoms she carried in the bag might be medicinal in very low doses, but these had been distilled and concentrated into substances so lethal that knowledge of their deadliness would have cleared the bazaar had the market-goers suspected.

The work of a lifetime.

She encouraged herself by remembering that there was something else in the bag: a book, words across time that would prevent her from employing, or deploying, these lethal liquors. Still, she hadn't been able to part with them. Ravens horde shiny things, don't they?

She couldn't ignore the strain of bearing the extra weight she'd gained, intentionally gained, especially in this infernal climate. She consoled herself with the fact that if she wanted to survive, she had to become another person. To that end, she had forced herself to add forty kilograms; she had had surgery on her face too. She used to be told she was pretty.

Though she was too proud to acknowledge compliments, they had delighted her. Striking a blow to her vanity was not a bad thing, but how she cringed when she saw her new image in a mirror.

Suddenly, the bag was wrenched from her arm with such force that it might have carried her arm with it. A stinging pain radiated up her arm and into her neck. They were street urchins, two of them, as quick as the little lizards that basked upon the walls of the city. She made a desultory attempt to pursue them, but she knew it was futile before she took the first step. No one would help her, a Westerner, and she could not hope to catch them; not now.

She experienced a momentary sense of loss, but it passed quickly. She was relieved to be rid of the toxins, something she'd not been able to accomplish on her own, and the book could be replaced. Perhaps it would find its way to another lost soul, sting him as it had stung her. But there was the animal to be considered; the creature would make mischief if it got loose. Innocent people were sure to die; she couldn't help fretting about that. There was a time when the fate of an army of urchins didn't matter. No longer.

Her arm ached, but the pain had subsided. She doubted there was any lasting damage. She returned to her room on the canal, a poor, even desperate, refuge, but off the beaten track. The room was as she'd left it—bed unmade, clothes everywhere, coins on the nightstand—except for the white envelope on top of the rumpled sheets.

Her chest felt constricted, and she found it difficult to breathe. Someone had entered her room and left this envelope. She had no illusions that she could escape his long arm forever, but she'd convinced herself she was safe here—for a while. She knew that her adversary possessed genius in copious amounts, but he wasn't a seer; she'd been so careful. Standing there, with the envelope on the bed, wondering if there weren't a dozen men outside her door, she remembered. She supposed the vivid memory was prompted by her surprise at being discovered in this hiding place on the edge of the world.

There was a windowless anteroom to her adversary's bedroom in Paris. When the door was closed, the room was so dark that a person couldn't see his hand in front of his face. The only piece of furniture in this room was a large table. On that table, in absolute darkness, he assembled one-thousand-piece puzzles. He told her he once succeeded in completing a puzzle in three nights, in less than three hours, as he never allowed himself more than one hour at a sitting. How difficult, how maddening that would be for a normal person. For him, it was nothing more than a honing of his analytical skills. She should have expected him to find her, when finding her was logically impossible for any other man.

There was nothing else to do but open the envelope. It contained a telegram that read:

Gregory taken away. Mortal peril. Help him, Agnes.
Charlotte

Charlotte was Gregory's lover, and housemaid, but Agnes doubted the message had been sent by her. How could that poor girl have found her here? No, it was unlikely that Charlotte sent the message. Would her adversary reckon that she would reason to this conclusion? Probably. Then why send it? Why not storm in and take her? With his resources, it could be accomplished easily enough.

One thing was certain. She must vanish—attempt it, at least—immediately. She stuffed everything she could into a large purse and buckled it. As she was preparing to leave the room, she saw the matchbox on the dresser. She'd forgotten all about removing it from the black bag that was stolen, removing it to feed the animal, which could be accomplished without opening the matchbox. The box seemed intact; it would be hard to imagine that if someone had opened it they would have had the aplomb to close it again. If the creature was loose, the sooner she got out of here the better. She shuddered, picked up the box, and stowed it in a corner of the purse.

Could she ever have imagined this when they were children, the three of them? As a boy, her adversary had been tedious but not wanton or malevolent. He'd changed when the grandfather arrived. She'd met that man only once, but she'd never forgotten him. That old man's face reminded her of an owl—the seemingly lidless eyes, protruding nose, and small, pinched mouth—a thoroughly hypnotic face. She'd been only a girl, but she'd been convinced that this man instantaneously categorized people as useful or useless, worthy or unworthy. She'd been rejected. Without him ever speaking to her, she knew this. She could not say how she knew it, but she did. Her adversary changed after that man entered his life. After putative attempts to separate herself from him, she was inexorably drawn into his orbit—until she encountered the book.

She slipped from the room and took an alley to the canal. The edge of the world had not been far enough.

June 13, 1931

Oxford

"Dorothy wants to know how long sharks can survive in freshwater", Owen said.

"What's that?" Jack said, frowning.

"How long sharks are able—"

"Yes, I understand. Why in creation would that interest her?"

"Seems she's entertaining the idea of a detecting story where one fellow murders another by introducing sharks into the victim's pond. The man takes his morning swim and is devoured. The sharks perish for want of brine and decompose—no evidence. That sort of thing."

"She has a fertile imagination", John said. "But that's a rather thin plot. It wants *gravitas*."

"Dorothy is talented in that line", Owen said. "So?"

"So what?" Jack rejoined.

"How keen is your knowledge of sharks?"

"Don't fish float when they die?"

"A shark isn't—"

"Of course it isn't", Jack said dismissively. "Fish as generally understood, then."

"In my experience, dead fish come to the surface", Owen said.

"Then wouldn't dead sharks be conspicuous in a freshwater pond?" Jack said.

"One would think so. I'll send her a note", Owen said.

There were plenty of vacant tables at the Bird and Baby. Almost all of the midday patrons had departed for jobs or errands in town. The weather was warm and sunny, conducive to being outside, so there were few stragglers in the pub. From the table by the window, the trio could hear the street noise and feel the warmth radiating from the glass.

Jack's chair was far from the table, and his legs were extended. He looked very much like a stretched frog. He was smoking his pipe. Owen could not have gotten closer to the table. His pipe stem was between his lips, but the pipe had gone out. John's head was bowed. Prior to Owen's digression into fictional murder—a nervous digression, as it seemed—they had been sitting there in silence, pondering John's astounding revelation.

Mitchell was sprawled beneath the table. There were no crackers or sardines on the table, just three cups with the dregs of tea, the remnants of a loaf of bread, and a block of cheese. The pub keeper was mopping the bar. Patrons at two other tables were preparing to leave.

Jack removed the pipe from his mouth and said, "John has proposed a dazzling anomaly. The literary norm is for the author to be fact and the work fiction. Here we seem to have a fictional author and a factual work."

"We have a factual but unknown author", John corrected him.

"I'm referring to the fictional author here present."

"It couldn't be helped. It still can't be helped", John said.

Owen said, "John is every bit the author of that work. He is a translator and thus a cocreator. And he has admitted adding quite a bit of his own material, even if it was suggested by the work itself."

"The humble clam bearing the mother-of-pearl", Jack said.

"I'm relieved to tell you the truth", John said. "It's been an awful burden."

"But can you trust us?" Jack said.

John sensed there was a lot packed into that question: chiding for having kept the secret for so long, and the rhetorical question.

"I can trust you", John said. "You could have abandoned honor long ago, but you haven't. You're serious about the quest for truth. If I can't trust you, I can trust no one. Even if our friendship were sundered, you couldn't break trust; your sense of honor wouldn't permit it. Not to mention that the world would think you fools if you told such a preposterous story."

"I'm not sure that was a compliment, though it was packaged like one", Jack said.

Jack pulled his chair closer to the table and sat up straight. He relit his pipe and snatched the last piece of cheese. "Necromancers and burglars and kings and demons and delvers and shepherds—"

"Don't forget the goblins", Owen said.

"I've been living with all of them", John said. "I'm convinced that many of these people and creatures and events are historical. Unbelievable things happened in that age and are lost to memory, except for myth."

"Don't disparage myth", Jack said.

"I don't mean to. I've seen myth come alive, not only in the book but in artifacts from that era."

"What do you mean?" Owen said.

"That's the other thing I haven't told you. The search I've undertaken to learn more about that civilization has borne fruit—and some thorns."

Now it was only the three of them and the pub keeper, who didn't seem to mind their tarrying. He was straightening the tables and whistling to himself.

"More tea, gents?" he said loudly, without looking up.

"We're finished, Robert", Owen said for the trio.

"What have you been up to?" Jack said to John.

"I met a man who showed me things I'm convinced are connected to the civilization in the book."

"A dealer in antiquities?" Owen said.

"A personage too complex to categorize: a historian, an antiquarian, an industrialist, a naturalist."

"An Englishman?" Jack said.

"He's the sort of man who makes himself at home wherever he is. His academic post is at the Sorbonne. He lived in England as a child."

"Mystery and Inquiry", Jack said. "What's the chap's name?"

"Alembert—Adler."

"A German name", Jack said, his pipe belching smoke. "Doesn't Adler mean eagle?"

"You haven't heard its genesis. It seems Alembert's father had a passion for mathematics and named him for a mathematician. In that sense, the son hasn't fallen far from the tree. Alembert is at home with abstract mathematics and physics."

"And what has he revealed?" Owen said. He was dourer than Jack, and had been since John disclosed his secret.

In some detail, John related his meetings with Alembert. He told them about Christopher and that man's conversations with his superior; about Alembert's brother and the butterflies; and about Krieger.

"This Alembert may be dangerous," Jack said, "or he may be nothing more than a martinet."

"I think you're right to avoid him", Owen said. "Too many coincidences suggest a guiding hand. Is there anything else?"

He told them about his trip to Heidelberg.

"Good heavens, man", Jack said. "You are becoming another T. E. Lawrence. I don't like it. I agree with Owen. Don't answer the man's letters, and keep your eyes wide open."

"Edith never revealed her family name?" Owen said.

"No."

"I am familiar with this woman, if I'm not mistaken. Her work is known to me."

"She was cautious in our conversation", John said.

"And yet she goaded Krieger", Owen said, smiling.

"I admit she was an enigma", John said.

"A riddle that may have an answer, based on my understanding of her philosophy", Owen said. "The waters of our age are treacherous, especially these currents. When she talked about National Socialism and communism, she might have included naturalism. They're different philosophical systems, but they have more in common than what separates them. All of these systems of thought repudiate the view that there is anything that's beyond the scope of scientific—in other words, material—explanation. Matter is given a primary position, and mind, or spirit, is considered a dependent reality, if it has any reality at all.

"Those who hold these philosophies are almost always relativists and determinists.

"In our age, there are Nazis, fascists, and communists. Though they profess to be different, and even antagonistic to each other, they share a common foundation: the rejection of the transcendence of the human person as a creature different in kind, not just in development, from every other creature. They reject moral absolutes because, for them, morality is a subjective bias, or the construct of man for convenience or social order.

"That is not to say that all adherents of naturalism are Nazis, any more than every carnivore is a tiger. But a carnivore has to hunt, and adherents of materialism are obliged to choose progress, as they define it, over the welfare of any one individual."

"If we deny Owen his lecture stand, then where will we stand when our own ideas boil over?" Jack said. "Go on."

"I'm grateful", said Owen, "to be able to debate ideas with people who think ideas are important. As to these particular ideas, they are seductive. There's something within man that resents dependency. A philosophy that purports to put man in control is attractive, seductive. No wonder so many succumb to it."

Jack said, "Control is illusory."

"But an addictive illusion", Owen said. "The more talented and intelligent one is, the more attractive is the lure to control. If one could harness science, if one could redesign humanity, if one could order society properly, a new world could be ushered in."

"As in Russia?" John said.

"It isn't the immediate outcome that's appealing", Owen said. "What appeals is the sense of control and the act of controlling, coupled with the promise of a future utopia."

"There are antidotes", Jack said.

"The antidotes have been drowned out by political and academic barkers. These ideas have been entertained and debated for centuries; they're not new. What's different are the forces that are brought to bear in this age, giving these ideas real momentum, making them more dangerous than they ever were. In systems where there are no absolutes or moral norms, the end truly justifies the means, any means."

John said, "We were so battered in the war, that we'd rather ignore the advance of these ideologies and hope for the best. I can't say I haven't ever succumbed to that temptation."

"But the small cadre of true believers is more committed to advancing themselves than we are to stopping them", Owen said. "Most of us are passive."

"We will be *passé* if we aren't careful", Jack observed. "John, you are moving in risky company. If I were your mouse—that Socrates fellow—I'd consider new lodgings. Then again, perhaps he's a bold rodent, or there's nowhere else for him to go."

"There are the tunnels."

"The ancient tunnels beneath our fair university, the realm of the greasers, those subterranean handymen who keep the school going", Jack said. "There's plenty of space for Socrates and a rodent empire down there."

"I imagine he's grown attached to me", John said. "Owen has Mitchie, and I have a mouse."

Owen said, "What will you do next, John? Can't you be satisfied with what you've learned?"

"I won't abandon the project. Hermann was helpful, in spite of himself. There's one other person I intend to visit."

"Where is he located?" Jack asked.

"She's at Lund University."

"What do you expect her to contribute?" Owen said, skeptically.

"She's a paleobiologist."

"I begin to grasp your method", Jack said. "Do the geology, geography, and biology of that era, as depicted in the story, correspond to what's known by modern science about a particular era?"

"I'm not expecting corroboration", John said. "I'm trying to assess whether there's anything we know about that era, or think we know, that contradicts the story: ice a hundred feet thick covering Europe during the period when these events might have occurred, that sort of thing. Hermann confirmed that there was a temperate and fertile period in Europe between two great ice ages. His description of the physical characteristics of Europe during that temperate period didn't contradict anything that was revealed in the book. I've prepared maps with as much detail as could be extracted from the story; the correspondence between these maps and what Hermann told me is encouraging."

"Does that correspondence go beyond general observations about geography and climate?" Jack said.

"It does. The north-south mountain range in the story, then more massive in the south and extending further north, may have been the forerunner of our Alpine mountain range. There was a large bay on the western shore of that landmass that might have been the precursor of our Mediterranean Sea. The land bridge between Britain and the Continent also corresponds to the geography in the story."

"Not conclusive," Jack said, "but suggestive. You didn't return empty-handed—or end up in a Parisian dungeon."

"I thought the latter more than possible", John said.

"Are there any obvious contradictions?" Jack said.

"No."

"Flying dinosaurs were extinct millions of years before the arrival of man", Jack said. "What explanation is there for the flying creatures in the story?"

"Jack, you must find the weak links. I have no explanation. The Necromancer had powers we can't even imagine. Perhaps the flying creatures were his creations."

"Be careful you don't use that as an explanation for every anomaly. The 'abracadabra' explanation, if you will. Otherwise, why consult experts?" Jack said.

"I intend to broach the subject with Dr. Erickson."

"How can we help you?" Owen said.

"E. M. says you are already helping me."

"If her compliment was meant for me," Jack said, "it might be a Trojan horse. What aren't you telling us?"

"She believes that sharing the story makes it less likely Alembert will belligerently intervene."

"I can't dispute her logic," Jack said, "but her motives are less pure than I'd hoped."

Owen said, "I'm intrigued by Alembert's theory, if not the man himself. If I understand it, he believes Atlantis was a historical civilization, the bringer of wisdom to the rest of the world. He believes the island was destroyed but that some Atlanteans escaped and settled among lesser civilizations, becoming their lords and mentors. Eventually, everything except the story—the myth—was lost to mankind."

"That seems to describe his beliefs", John said.

"What is he after?" Owen said.

"He told me he wants to touch that civilization."

"Touch it? If your theory is correct, that civilization was destroyed over thirty thousand years ago", Jack said.

Owen said, "Does he impress you as someone who'd be satisfied with knowledge for knowledge's sake, as you are?"

It was a troubling but pertinent question. John hadn't asked it himself, but he had little difficulty answering. "Alembert would desire more than knowledge for its own sake."

"Might one go so far as to suggest that he's seeking something useful from that civilization?" Owen asked.

"Like the tools of the Necromancer, or the Traitor", John said.

"Like them", Owen said. "Could his aim be power?"

"What could such an ancient civilization teach modern man about power?" Jack said.

"We've been listening to John tell the story for months. Have those supernatural powers vanished from the earth, or can they still be tapped?" Owen said.

"Might the storyteller have related a true story but added mythological elements: magic and nonhumans? That sort of thing's been done in many legends", Jack said.

John said, "I've been immersed in the story for years, and I am convinced that some of these beings possessed what we would call super-natural power."

"But sorcery? In this world, on this planet?" Jack said.

"I can tell you only what I've concluded."

"How much do you think Alembert knows?" Owen said.

"He probably suspects more than he actually knows. He seems to have remarkable intuition. He believes I have something in my possession that will advance his quest. He can't know what it is, or where it is, or he could easily have acquired it."

"Where have you hidden it?" Jack said.

"I won't tell you that", John said. "That knowledge would put you at risk."

"Can you move it if need be?" Jack said.

"I dare not. The man I confronted the last time we met here—E. M. is convinced he's been watching the house, and may have been inside."

"The scoundrel", Owen said. "I wish you'd told us sooner, John. We can be more than passive friends."

"I suspect Alembert is watching me too. I told you how he suggested that he'd seen my double in Oxford. I don't think he cares if I know. The two of you better keep your eyes open. You're associating, as they are wont to say, with a person of interest."

Mitchell had gotten up and gone to the bar. The pub keeper went below and came up with a sardine, which he dropped into Mitchell's open mouth.

"A tithe for an old friend", he said loudly. "I ain't seen you fer a bit, Mitchie. Behavin' yerself, old boy?"

"You know he doesn't have a behavin' bone in his body, Robert", Owen said.

"He's a good fellow all the same", the man said. "It's nice to have some company between hours. You gentlemen stay as long as you care to."

"Thanks", Jack said. Then he said to John, "You're sure this Krieger was interested in you and not the woman?"

"I'm not sure. She thought so. I had to take her advice. If you had met her, you'd understand."

"There were no incidents in Paris, I presume", Owen said.

"It was uneventful. I changed trains and went on to Le Havre."

"Krieger may not have discovered your *ruse de guerre* until late that night. You would have been on your way to Paris by then. Even this Alembert has his limitations. How long did you wait for the Channel boat?"

"It departed in the early afternoon."

"If you'd delayed until evening, they might have caught up with you", Owen said. "We'll never know."

Jack said, "*De inimico non loquaris male, sed cogites.* You are right to be concerned about such a man, someone with an obsession and the talent to indulge it."

Mitchell came back, tail wagging. Jack showed him his empty hands—no treats—and scratched his ears.

"I'm not sure it's wise to leave the country", Jack said.

"I've considered that. I plan to go to Stockholm. It isn't Paris or Germany."

"Alembert doesn't sound like someone who'd be deterred by borders", Owen said.

"I won't live like a scared rabbit. If I've learned anything from the story, it's that temerity in the presence of evil is not prudence."

"We may all learn that lesson soon enough", Jack said.

"When will we hear more of the story?" Owen said.

"Perhaps we can meet next week."

"When you finish with the Stockholm interview, what comes next?" Owen said.

John looked at his wristwatch. He reached down and patted Mitchell. He swept crumbs off the table. "There are no more avenues of inquiry, I'm afraid. I won't return to Alembert. There may be morsels of information buried in the text, but I've been over it many times. I haven't made up my mind."

"You're considering something", Jack said.

"I'm considering publishing the story."

"Heigh-ho", Jack said. "There's a bold one." His pipe had gone out, but he didn't seem to care. "Let Monsieur Alembert counter that move."

"It will get the story and its message out but in a manner the world might accept", John said.

"It's an interesting idea", Jack said. "You've given it more thought than we have. Why do you suggest the world won't accept the truth?"

"Look around. Heidelberg reinforced my conviction that the world isn't receptive to the truth. Look at the Russians who've spoken out, who've dared to tell the truth about that proletariat paradise. They've been shouted down, and worse. A story is altogether different, but the message is the same."

"Even a story isn't without risk. These radicals know that the imagination must be controlled", Owen said.

John said, "It will be a long time before the manuscript, the fictional story, is ready."

"It's a rousing story. I've no doubt it will stir the popular imagination", Jack said.

"Perhaps I'll send Mitchie along to watch over John's clan", Owen said. The dog was sound asleep under the table.

"There's not much in that suggestion except an increase in the grocer's bill", Jack said, looking down at his feet.

"Don't mind them, Mitchie", Owen said to the dog, who didn't appear to be minding anything.

"I guess I'll rely on Socrates", John said. "He's got a good nose for trouble."

"We ought to be moving", Jack said.

"We've been moving—intellectually speaking", Owen said.

"You are especially alert today, Owen", John said sardonically. "A right rousing lecture for sure."

"John, keep your eyes wide open. Do you understand? Wide open. You're too precious a friend."

"I'm careful enough", John said.

"Ha. Paris, Heidelberg, Stockholm. Is Mars next?" Jack said.

"You are a pair of scolds. Confirmed contrarians."

"You seek approbation. We aren't sycophants, nor shall we ever be", Jack said. "Do whatever you will, but don't expect our obeisance if we think you're being foolish."

The three of them got up as one man. Robert waved his rag as they passed and would have opened a tin of sardines—Mitchell gave him a pitiful look—if Owen had allowed it. As John passed, Robert whispered, "No visits by that particular fellow, Professor." The three shook hands outside the door and walked off in three different directions.

The sun was shining, and the streets were filled with people enjoying the mild weather. John barely noticed. In his mind, he'd crossed that threshold again. He was tumbling through time.

August 6–7, 1931

Paris and Southwestern France

"You considered that one hair fluttering at my neck; you gazed at it upon my neck, and it captivated you."

She said this as she looked into the dresser mirror in a squalid hotel room in Paris, pronouncing each word with conviction. The verse made her laugh. There was little in the image before her to captivate anyone. She was more than stout and her short stature exaggerated her bulk. Her nose zigged and zagged as it descended from bridge to nostrils. Her black hair hung limp, lapping her shoulders. The thin bangs covered her eyebrows. Her skin was a grainy olive hue. Her green blouse was at least one size too large; the loose-fitting sleeves hid much of her hands, making less noticeable the missing left-hand finger. She was ugly, she admitted to herself.

She remembered her portrayal of Peter Pan when she was away at school, a happy memory of a happy time. They were all girls, except for Hook, the headmistress' brother. Every rehearsal, every performance had been a joy.

The believability of her acting had nothing to do with any boyish attributes she possessed but came from her total immersion in the character, to the extent that every thought and action was rooted in that persona. At an early age she realized—sensed, rather—that she possessed this chameleon-like quality. She could even change the tone and timbre of her voice, like a myna bird. At one family gathering, she pretended she was her cousin Charles so convincingly that even the boy's mother was deceived.

Pretending. Now that she had abandoned all that or, at least, was striving to abandon it, could she still be a convincing deceiver? She'd put the skill to good use in managing to survive thus far, a not inconsiderable accomplishment. Still, she couldn't help recognizing the irony that when she desperately needed this skill, or aptitude, or whatever it was, she had the least confidence that she was still capable of it.

Her stomach turned, and there was nothing she could do to dispel the feeling except for emptying the little bit that was inside. That didn't relieve the anxiety; it might have magnified it. She rinsed her mouth of the mess and tried to get on with what she had to do.

Sadly, for most of her life she had been Captain Hook's obsequious servant, Smee, rather than a bold and courageous Peter Pan. Now, she ruminated, she even looked the part of that gross little sailor. Was Pan's courage to tweak a powerful enemy too much to hope for? She needed more than courage for the gambit she had been planning. She knew it was a long shot, and what her adversary would do to her if she failed.

The previous year was a blur: South America, Panama, a brief stay in Miami, Algiers, Spain, and now Paris. Movement had been the chief imperative, movement and transformation. For most of that year she retained the photograph of a slender and attractive woman with auburn hair and fair skin. But she knew it was foolish to keep it after she had taken so many pains to alter her appearance. She finally destroyed the photograph in Algiers, irrevocably destroying the woman it replicated.

Her inner transformation was more profound than her external one. Ever since she discovered that book in the

Monastery, her life had changed. She began reading it in order to ridicule it; wasn't it just a vestige of unenlightened times and rigid dogmatism? But the more she read, the more she found herself absorbed in the writer's mystical vision, a vision that didn't defy reason but transcended it, a vision that was a frog to reason's tadpole, or a butterfly to reason's caterpillar.

In spite of her adversary's brutality, there must have been something in her past, or psyche, that had been moving inside her invisibly, some smoldering ember that was enkindled into flame by the mystic's words and images. The experience had been like a reunion with a dear friend who'd been absent for a long time rather than like a meeting with someone altogether new.

She looked in the mirror again. The disguise had brought her safely to Paris, but only boldness and execution would see her through. Was she being followed? That apprehension was never absent from consideration. There was the telegram in Algiers, a sort of summons, but from whom? No doubt it was the work of her former employer, now her enemy. But even he, with all his talent and resources, could scarcely comprehend her motives, so much had she changed since she opened that book.

Out of the one traveling bag that she allowed herself, she removed an envelope, a matchbox, and a handgun. She placed these disparate items on the dresser, next to her hat and a small yellow rose she had purchased in the street that morning.

She returned the gun to her handbag. The bag was large enough to accommodate a folded shirt, wire cutters, scissors, and items whose only purpose was to distract an enemy, if such a need arose: a change purse with a few francs, a map of Paris, lipstick, and cheese in waxed paper. She handled the matchbox gingerly, placing it with care in the handbag's side pocket. An elastic band prevented it from opening. She had been concerned about keeping the resident of the matchbox alive but the device she used to introduce food without opening the box had been effective. When she placed the box close to her ear and shook it gently, she could hear the resident's faint scurrying movements. There was a single piece of paper in the envelope. She reread the words of the letter, as she had many times since she composed it. The crest at the top of the page, the red dragon and two black swords, invariably attracted attention. She knew it to be an ancient insignia, first associated with Attila the Hun, or so it was said. Now it was used by that rampaging chieftain's purported descendant, but today it would serve her. Satisfied with the letter, she returned it to her bag.

She was as prepared as possible. She looked around the room. It was a dirty room in a mean establishment, like many she'd inhabited since she left Buenos Aires. Prior to that momentous decision, she'd had her own chef and, when in town, dined in the best restaurants and stayed in the finest hotels. That was another person, she told herself, an almost unrecognizable person. She debated whether to wear the hat. It hadn't traveled well. She left it behind.

She exited the hotel and walked briskly down the narrow street. The hour was early and few were out, just old women with their bread baskets. Her left hand gripped the bag as if it contained a million francs. The Métro station was just two blocks away, one of the reasons she'd selected the hotel. Soon she was seated in an unoccupied car and was moving beneath the streets of Paris.

In Algiers, she might have lived in anonymity, if not comfort. In just a few months, she'd grown accustomed to the streets and bazaars, and the people had been friendly enough.

Why was she in Paris, and why had she pursued this ridiculous idea? It was the telegram, of course, the one that had been left on her bed. There was no ignoring it.

She remembered the day she had enticed Sally, Gregory, and his brother to climb Horn's Hill. It was a tall hill, not a mountain, but a challenging ascent for children. She and Gregory had been enthusiastic. Gregory's brother and Sally had only grudgingly agreed to go. About halfway to the top, Gregory's brother tired, and he argued that they should turn back. Sally immediately agreed, and eventually Gregory submitted too. She had mustered all the strength she had to resist and went to the top alone. Gregory's brother didn't speak to her for nearly a month. This was the first, but hardly the last, time he made her suffer for crossing him.

She was sure he never forgot that incident. She often wondered if he kept her in his company because she was the only person who maintained some psychological independence from him. He both loathed and was fascinated by her independent spirit. Now he'd come to grief over it, and his wrath would be all the more terrible.

The stations passed one by one, bright light and then darkness. Gregory deserved one friend, she thought as she gazed at her hideous reflection in the window. He hadn't had a true friend in twenty years. By now, he must have forgotten what friendship is. His situation—the isolation, brutality, and apprehension, if she knew the man who'd imprisoned him—was worse than death. If she didn't do something about it, nothing would be done. Gregory would eventually die, but not until every ounce of life and spirit had been sucked from him, and all because he had challenged his brother.

When she thought of that brother, she compared him to a spider. She and her adversary, once her employer, had long collaborated on a study of poisons that had produced scholarly and practical benefits, if such a word could be used to describe the fruits of their labors. Most likely no one else in the world knew more about biologically derived poisons than the two of them. From snakes, lizards, frogs, stinging insects, spiders, and other creatures, they had extracted agents that attacked nerves, muscles, or blood or that dissolved tissue. Financed by her employer's wealth, they had made exotic expeditions in search of the most lethal toxins. After discovering the poisons, they used them to eliminate his enemies. He had often referred to their discoveries as the "weapons of the gods" because they didn't need to be formulated by man. And now—wearing little better than a pauper's clothing and presenting a dismal appearance—she was en route to contend with this man who had once been her lodestar.

He'd taught her well. Her attack would be a lightning strike, after which she would—must—find a hiding place that would be invisible to him, if such a place existed anywhere in the world.

She was not without resources and had learned that Gregory was being held in a certain institution in Paris. The reason for his incarceration was harder to discern. Familiarity with Gregory's petulant temperament along with word of entomological expeditions to Asia and South America suggested an answer that terrified her, as she knew how much Gregory's brother valued his exotic butterflies.

The subway stopped at a station. An old man exited, and another old man boarded. She wasn't far now. Could she ever have imagined herself that man's adversary? Once, the thought would have paralyzed her with fear. Now there was a sense of liberation from that overwhelming personality. She recalled the day she left the Monastery. Despite her relationship with him—the closest thing to friendship he would allow—she knew there were only two choices: remain in his circle or disappear. He would never permit someone that close, someone who knew his secrets, to abandon him; the choice was between lifelong service or death. He would kill her when he caught her.

Her destination was at the end of the line, Porte d'Ivry. Then it was a few blocks' walk to the institution. She exited the train and mounted the stairs to the platform. She was glad it was a cloudy, rainy day because all were intent on staying dry and getting to their destinations. That left little time or opportunity to observe. Beneath the platform roof, after everyone had exited or boarded the train, she practiced the sleight of hand with the matchbox that the juggler had taught her in Algiers. She was now so adept that she could execute the action with one hand, though the knowledge of what was in the matchbox sent shivers up and down her spine. Yes, the elastic was still in place. It wouldn't do to have an accident.

As the raindrops struck her head, she reflected that she could have used that hat, though not because her appearance would have been improved by it. When she arrived at the institution—it was a walled enclosure—she surveyed the building and grounds. It did not take her long to locate the telephone line; it was attached to a pole immediately outside the enclosure.

She recalled finding a den of vipers in French West Africa. After assembling the necessary equipment, she had approached the pit and opened it up. As it turned out, she captured three of the creatures and killed the other two. The venom was a delightful discovery; her employer had been pleasantly surprised. One of the men they killed with the toxin was a would-be rival in Lima. What was the man's name

... Guillermo something ... it was German ... Hinkel or Heinkle. This institution was just another den of vipers. Careful planning and speed of execution would win the field, as they always had.

For a woman her size, she scaled the pole with amazing agility. To an observer—hopefully there were none in this remote place—she would have been a clownish spectacle, like a bear after a beehive. When she reached the top, some ten feet above the ground, she severed the wire with the cutters from her bag. The long-sleeved blouse she wore wasn't ideal for this work. It had been chosen for a different purpose. The locked gate presented little difficulty; she was skilled at breaching doors. She could have scaled the wall, but she needed an unlocked gate when she exited the grounds.

No one was about—good. The building was in the shape of a T; the wing at the rear was more elongated than the entry area. She had learned that the inmates were housed in that rear wing. The front door was unlocked, and she stepped inside. The foyer was in the shape of a semicircle, with a station facing the door, a hallway behind the desk leading to the long arm of the T, and an empty side room to the left of the receiving station, behind which sat a young man in a white uniform.

"How did you get in?" he said, curtly.

The room was bare and cold, dimly lit, and devoid of any color or ornamentation. She detected an unfamiliar and unpleasant odor.

"The gate was unlocked."

He scrutinized her before speaking. "It's normally locked. What do you want?"

"I have an urgent message for the director."

"He's not available."

"I said it's urgent. It's an order from Alembert."

The man's demeanor immediately changed. He lifted the telephone receiver and said, "An emissary from Professor Alembert to see you, sir."

She mentally registered the fact that the internal phones were separate from the external line that she had disabled. If she'd been dealing with anyone other than Alembert, this would have been a routine operation: breaching security, misrepresentation with bravado and forged documentation, with deadly force as a contingency. But she could take nothing for granted when that man was her opponent. What must be done must be done quickly and expertly.

The director was a stout, beleaguered-looking man. He wore a jacket but no tie, and he seemed acutely aware of the deficiency, buttoning his collar as he approached the station. "How can I assist you?" he said.

She'd been mentally timing the entire sequence of events since she scaled the pole. So far, nothing had gone awry. She expected Alembert's name to be an open sesame, and it was. The exigency of an outgoing telephone call to confirm her story had been accounted for by the cutter.

She handed the director the letter. "The request is urgent; read it for yourself. You are to deliver Gregory Zin immediately, and I will escort him to the professor."

"Yes, Mademoiselle," the director said, "immediately. Guy," he said to the man at the desk, "bring the patient here without delay."

The way events were proceeding, she expected to be outside the gate in five minutes. The letter was so convincing— the insignia even more so—that the director hadn't bothered to telephone to confirm it. She told herself that it was no time to relax her guard. When she'd attacked the viper den, she'd overlooked a serpent in the back of the pit. It had come at her, and she'd barely avoided being bitten. She'd killed it in the end but learned a lesson: beware of silent, invisible predators.

The attendant returned, followed by something that barely resembled a man. She was reminded of Edmond Dantès emerging from the Château d'If. The man was hunched over, his bare arms and hands were ivory white, and his matted hair had grown shaggy. He hadn't been shaved in at least a week. He was dirty, and a stench hung about him. She couldn't imagine where his clothes had come from. They were ridiculously small, probably relics from another inmate. She needed tremendous self-control to prevent a wrathful outburst. Was this the bright and happy boy she had once known, had played and laughed with? And how could any man, even her adversary, do this to his own brother?

She could not resist saying, "What have you been doing with Alembert's money? It's obvious you've spent nothing on this man. Come, Gregory. Move smartly now."

The director gave her a strange look and said, "This was the care the professor specified."

She should have known better than to make an intemperate remark, she told herself. If the director tried to telephone he would be unsuccessful, but there had been no need to put the least doubt in his mind. She took Gregory's arm and turned toward the door. The director and assistant were already halfway down the corridor that led to the patients' quarters. The gate was unlocked.

She was already considering the train schedule when the booming voice said, "Hello, Agnes".

It seemed to her a disembodied voice, as the foyer was empty. Then she saw the cyclops seated in the alcove room, his scarred face familiar except for the missing eye. He was hatless and wearing something like a military uniform but without decorations—not quite fighter's fatigues but definitely not parade dress. And how much grayer he was.

"Come in", he said.

"I'm afraid I don't know you. My name is Jane—"

"You are little Agnes CurLio. Come in. Leave that wretch in the foyer."

"Wait for me", she said to the man on her arm. Gregory didn't want to release her—he was shaking—but she lifted his chin, looked into that dirty, hopeless face, and smiled at him. "Wait for me."

There were three chairs in the room and a small table. Christopher was sitting in the chair closest to a door that was invisible from the foyer, a door that must open to the outside. There was a lamp on the table. There wasn't much light in the room, as there were no windows. Good, she thought.

Was it coincidence that he was here, or did Alembert know everything? She'd never believed that Charlotte sent the telegram, but had Alembert been able to follow her every move since Algiers?

"I am surprised to see you here", the man said. "Alembert will also be surprised. He wonders what has become of you."

"I've been searching", she said.

"It appears that you found someone, or something", the man said, looking past her at the man in the foyer. "But what you found is none of your business."

"He's my friend."

"He's no one's friend. He's a ghost. Do you know why that worm is here?" How much more malevolent he looked with that hole where an eye ought to be, and no less threatening.

"No."

"And still you came for him. You used to be so reliably practical. I will tell you, since that knowledge cannot harm us or help you: the fool introduced a brown recluse into the terrarium."

In spite of herself she said, "Why?"

"He left a note suggesting he'd produced in miniature what his brother produced in the world at large."

"I see."

"What do you see? It was an absurd act, signifying nothing, and costing the fool his freedom, not to mention other indignities." He gazed at the slumped figure in the foyer.

"Gregory always had a gift for the dramatic."

"And where has it brought him?" Christopher said.

"Integrity cannot be pacified."

"Of course it can; look at him. Look at you. When was the last time you bathed?"

"I'm dirty, but I'm cleaner than I've been in a long time."

"You are a filthy, ugly pig. Let's be candid."

"Candid? You don't know the meaning of the word. Power, that's all you understand."

"Now you are a philosopher. Is that what all this is about? You disappoint me, Agnes. Let's settle this business."

"We'll settle nothing, Christopher. We're just compounding something that started a long time ago."

"Give me your bag. You would not attempt this adventure without a weapon."

"If I do, you will kill me", she said.

"You made that decision when you betrayed us."

"I left Alembert's employment. I haven't betrayed anyone."

"Yet you attempt to spirit away a man we want punished. The bag. If you are prompt, I will do it quickly, for old time's sake."

He had always been a liar, and he was lying now. He and Alembert would make sure her death was miserable. She handed him the bag.

After removing the gun and pointing it at Agnes, Christopher emptied the contents of the bag onto the floor. The objects came out in a jumble, even the matchbox from the side pocket. He felt the inside of the bag with his free hand.

"A clean shirt for that worm. How considerate. I will take the wire cutters and scissors. I don't want you to be tempted to do something desperate." He picked up the matchbox, shook it, and stared at it pensively.

"I wouldn't open that if I were you", Agnes said, dramatically.

He smiled at her. "You open it, then. You will notice, dear Agnes, that my finger is on the trigger." Then he slid the matchbox along the floor.

"Open it."

She bent over and picked it up. She had always obsessively choreographed her assassinations, but now, this desperate situation demanded a desperate act. In those meager seconds that she had to decide, she tried to clear her mind of peril, and focus instead on the one thing that was necessary. The matchbox exercise she had so diligently practiced would help, but good fortune—something she had never relied on—would count far more.

Curiosity getting the better of him, Christopher leaned forward, and in an instant, Agnes flicked open the matchbox and threw it in his face.

Reflexively, Christopher pulled the trigger.

"It's not loaded, Christopher", she said.

He lunged at her while swatting his face and neck. Just as suddenly, the giant shivered and staggered back into his chair. There was a series of spasms, more and more violent, and he fell to the floor. She knew he was already dead.

She didn't know where the centipede—she had discovered it in the heart of a cactus in southwestern Mexico and had named it *Scolopendra letalis*—had gone, and she didn't have time to find out. She replaced the spare shirt—she shook it to make sure the creature hadn't hidden there—and scissors in the bag and led Gregory out of the compound as quickly as she could without arousing suspicion. They hid behind a large bush while she changed his shirt. The subway was five minutes late; they caught it just in time. When they arrived at the Paris train station, they quickly boarded. Before the conductor came for the tickets, Agnes had cut Gregory's hair. Shaving him would have been useful too. She regretted not bringing a razor. She made a bad job of it, but he submitted to her ministrations passively. He was drugged or something worse, she concluded.

"Having quite a day, aren't we?" she said to him as they settled on the bench. Gregory looked at her with a spark of what she thought was understanding.

As the train rumbled through the countryside, Agnes reflected that she'd added another man to her long list of victims. She had intended to leave all that behind when she fled the Monastery. She regretted killing Christopher, but there had been no choice, not if she wanted to save Gregory. Christopher would have killed her, and Gregory would have been returned to his prison. She had always known that even if she succeeded in this mad venture, she failed. Alembert would interrogate the director. By now, he probably knew everything there was to know about her disguise. She must change what she could as quickly as she could, but how could she hope to deceive Alembert and his human bloodhounds, especially now when she'd upped the ante by murdering his most trusted lieutenant?

Gregory's head rested against the glass. When they were children, he wanted the window seat on their trips to London, his brother being too immersed in some scheme to care where he sat or with whom. The twin in the window seat examined every farm and home and person they passed. How dramatically different were these two men now, so much so that the difference then seemed superficial by comparison. She took hold of his hand. Did anything remain of the Gregory Alembert she'd once known? It occurred to her that the same question could be asked of her, though something seemed to inform him that this caricature of Agnes CurLio on the bench next to him was familiar.

They traveled all night. With the sun came a view of the foothills of the Pyrenees. She'd managed to get them this far. Something told her she was just delaying the inevitable. No one ever challenged Alembert and survived.

An hour later they disembarked. She wouldn't have been surprised to meet a horde of Alembert's associates, but the arrival was uneventful. Her destination was a kilometer outside of this small town, and she judged that Gregory could manage the hike. He was more alert than he'd been the day before, which confirmed her suspicion that they had kept him drugged, but he still wasn't talking.

The town, Olorin, had been built on a north–south line with three spur roads: one west toward the mountains, one northeast into farms and orchards, and one southeast into a forest. Most of the buildings were two stories; a few were three stories; and all were fieldstone construction with wood trim. There was a well with a fountain in the center of town that featured a statue of a mounted Napoleon, hat in hand.

The path out of town to the southeast was bordered by blue wildflowers on both sides. For most of the journey, Gregory held her hand. Though he remained silent, she talked and sang to him.

Their destination would be, in a manner of speaking, where she had started, but as different as if she'd traveled to another world. All was quiet on the forest path. They must look an odd pair, she thought, storybook characters to match the storybook setting; but such a bizarre story, she reminded herself.

The abbot himself met them at the entrance. He was a younger man than she expected, fair with a high forehead and big, round eyes. The monastery observed a strict rule, but they made an exception for these guests. One of the brothers collected Gregory. Though Gregory was reticent, he allowed the brother to lead him into the labyrinthine building. The abbot escorted Agnes to his office and offered her a seat.

Inside, the room was cool and silent, and the air smelled fresh, with just a hint of wood varnish and bread dough.

"Your journey has been difficult. Would you care for a glass of wine?"

"Thank you."

He disappeared and returned with a glass and a bottle. "It's our own grape; not a *grande maison* vintage, but serviceable. Here." He handed her the glass, generously filled. "I didn't think you'd succeed. I heard enough about your mission to suspect we would not have the pleasure of meeting you."

"Here I am." The wine warmed and relaxed her. With her first drink she emptied half the glass.

"You are welcome, Agnes."

"I killed a man yesterday." She was shaking.

He brought his hands together. "Was it intentional?"

"Yes."

"Was it done in defense of another—was it necessary?"

"Yes."

"We'll talk more about that later. Do you think you were followed here? We are more practical than you think."

"I don't think so. If they had, they would have taken us at the station. But I'm sure they are searching for us now."

"Brother Jean vouches for you."

"He did me a great kindness in Algiers."

"How can we help you?"

"I would like you to keep Gregory until I can make permanent arrangements for him, and I would like to stay here until he is comfortable without me."

"That can be managed. What else?"

"I don't know."

"We specialize in that", the abbot said.

"If I stay here he will find me."

"Who will?" the abbot said, and she knew that he understood her perfectly. "I'm sure you're tired. I'll show you the guest quarters. Be not afraid. When you're ready, there will be food."

In the cell they provided for her, Agnes undressed and crawled beneath the blankets until even her head was covered. She hadn't experienced such profound peace since she was a girl in her father's house. Thus, she slept.

August 6, 1931

Stockholm

"You must try the herring. George's marinade is delicious. I insist you taste it."

His protestations were useless. She put a generous helping on the corner of his plate.

"Eat. Enjoy. You are in Stockholm. See, it is quite tasty."

"It's very good", John said.

"Of course it is. I said so, didn't I?" This self-flattery was represented as a statement of fact rather than as vanity.

"You certainly did."

"Are you making fun with me? Is that the correct idiom?"

"It's close enough."

"What should I have said?"

" 'Are you making fun of me?' "

"Are you making fun of me?" she said.

"Of course not. Making fun of you would be a dangerous occupation. Anyway, until I can execute an idiom in Swedish, I won't criticize your English."

"That is very kind of you", she said. He had no idea if this expression was genuine or contrived. Though he'd just met her, he judged that she was capable of both.

He hadn't expected to be dining in such elegant surroundings and eating delicacies when he arrived at the Museum of Natural History, where Greta Erickson had requested they meet. In fact, he'd resigned himself to doing without lunch. Instead, there were linen, candelabra, fine china and silver, and waiters in black tie. Greta Erickson had met him in the Grand Hall beneath the reconstructed skeleton of a twenty-foot allosaur and escorted him to this private dining room reserved for the museum's directors and their guests. John felt overwhelmed and underdressed, but she put him at ease with her lively description of the museum and city.

Greta Erickson was a professor of paleohistory at Lund University in the south of Sweden. After reading a paper she'd written on European mammalian evolution, he hoped she could advance his project.

Perhaps it was the high ceilings or the tile or the paneled walls, but it seemed cooler inside the museum than it had been on his walk from the hotel. Immediately upon John's being seated, a second waiter brought them iced teas with mint, as well as crackers and a plate of caviar.

All had happened so quickly that he'd had little time to appraise his host. Now, sitting across the table from her, he couldn't help being impressed. She was stunning, with short blond hair and mesmerizing violet eyes. He reckoned she must be nearly six feet tall; she was several inches taller than he. Her skin was like ivory. Her thin eyebrows were slightly darker than her hair. Her large eyes were oval rather than round, and her small ears seemed to hug the sides of her head. The white canvas of her face was marred in one place; there was a tiny scar on her left cheek. He couldn't be certain, but he thought this was the only place where makeup had been applied. She wore a purple dress and a small black beret. She didn't wear any jewelry, not even earrings. After barely speaking, he was convinced that she was a self-possessed and confident woman.

"You are comfortable?" she said, when he'd finished the herring.

"If I'd known we were dining so formally, I would have brought more suitable clothes." He was acutely aware that his jacket and trousers were plebian in these surroundings.

"Please do not worry yourself. As a director of the museum, I find this room convenient for conversation, and the food is quite good. Here we can speak without being disturbed, and I despise disturbances when I dine."

By the time they finished the caviar, the waiter had uncorked a bottle of Chardonnay and poured two glasses. He brought something else: a tray with petite towels, which he placed next to Greta. She lifted one of the towels and massaged, or washed her hands. After she finished, the waiter removed the tray. Oddly, a towel hadn't been offered to John.

"The veal shall arrive soon. The chef is masterful with veal. Your letter captured my imagination, John; the story you are writing, your interest in biology, the way you express ideas. I appreciate rigor in any endeavor. I wanted to meet and speak to the man behind our correspondence. Now that I have met him, I am not disappointed."

"Nor am I, Dr. Erickson. Thank you for the gracious reception."

"Greta. We shall be Greta and John. You describe yourself as a country teacher, but that seems too modest an occupation for such a Renaissance man."

"It suits me", he said.

"You are how old?"

An odd question, he thought. "Thirty-nine."

"I am thirty-five, and I am not married", she said. "My career is my preoccupation. There is so little time to accomplish what must be accomplished. Do you feel that way too?"

"Often. I struggle with what ought to be accomplished and what I desire to accomplish."

"But there is no difference", she said. "They are one and the same. Is that the correct way to say it?"

"Precisely, as to the idiom, but I differ with the conclusion."

"I like a man who differs", she said. "Here is the veal. I hope you enjoy it."

With the entrée, the waiter brought another towel. This time the man waited for her to complete her ablutions.

"You're right about the veal", John said.

"George is a culinary wizard. Is the wine to your liking?"

"It's very good. You are too generous." Those striking eyes and features—he couldn't deny that he was attracted to Greta Erickson. There was chemistry between them, sensible for his part. He suspected she felt the same way. He'd never experienced such a powerful, not to say bedeviling, attraction before, and the wine, the veal, and the surroundings enhanced the magnetism she exuded.

"I could tell by your correspondence that you are keen on science", she said. "Of course, I know many scientists, but few possess the artistic, creative spark. That which makes a successful scientist, disinterested rationalism, often excludes an artistic disposition."

John said, "I've immersed myself in branches of science that are pertinent to the book: biology, history, geography, climatology, and geology. I'm also interested in the relationship between science and philosophy."

"My," she said, "you continue to amaze me. There is more to you than I had hoped." Seeing his bemusement, she added, "I have a conceit that I can tell almost everything about a man by his correspondence. Perhaps it is not a conceit, as I have never been wrong. You are a bold but humble man, introverted and sensitive, with a gentle heart but with a will of iron. That is my conclusion."

"It's too flattering an appraisal", he said, but he told himself that the ability to infer "everything" about him from correspondence alone that she asserted was indeed a conceit, considering everything he'd withheld from her.

"We shall see about that. How do you imagine that science and philosophy are connected?"

"Science ought to be at the service of humanity", he said. "That's a philosophical notion."

She waved a long white finger at him. "Would you shackle science with nonscientific agendas?"

"Only when the product of science is destructive to human dignity."

"And what does human dignity consist of?"

"A concept of liberty that is grounded in responsibility to one's fellow man, especially the weakest."

"That strikes me as anachronistic. In biology, the herd is at risk when it is constrained by the slowest, the weakest. Perhaps in making the new, stronger man, we must leave the weakest behind. Science is pushing ahead. Every day there are new discoveries, new inventions, new medicines. How can scientific inquiry be restricted without impeding progress?"

"I prefer to frame the question thus: How can scientific inquiry serve man?"

"That will sort itself out", she said.

The waiter removed their plates, and another towel appeared. Though she performed the routine as unobtrusively as one could in a public place, John wondered what was behind this ritualistic practice.

"How distant is Lund University from Stockholm?" he asked her. He was not one to avoid confrontation when debating principle, so why had he changed the subject?

"About five hundred kilometers—a day's travel by train."

"You were right about the veal. It's the best I've ever eaten. I hope my visit hasn't inconvenienced you", he said as the waiter served flavored ice and refilled their wineglasses.

"I have a directors' meeting this afternoon. I visit the city often. My schedule at the university is flexible, and traveling to Stockholm is easier for you than a journey from England to the university."

"I'm grateful for your generosity", he said, looking into those lovely eyes. He found not a hint of reticence or self-consciousness.

She put the spoon with the flavored ice in her mouth. Even so mundane an act contained a suggestion of sensuality. "When you spoke of science at the service of man, it reminded me of my own philosophy. Shall I tell you what I mean?"

"You mustn't feel obliged to", he said, "but I would be happy to hear it."

"You fascinate me; you should know that. I am not easily fascinated."

Her words thrilled him.

"I consider myself a rational Epicurean", she said. "I believe in gratifying every inclination that is not harmful. I am opposed to ethical and moral inhibitions, except those necessary for social order. I indulge my appetites in moderation. I rarely succumb to indecision. Delay in the pursuit of one's desires is a characteristic of the weak-minded. I consider this a scientific approach to philosophy."

"I can tell that you have considered it carefully", John said. As a shapeless, faceless philosophy, it was repellent to him, but personified in Greta Erickson it was altogether different, even thrilling.

"You do not agree. It is plain to see."

He lifted his wineglass and sipped. He said, "Do you think Europe would be improved by adopting this philosophy?"

"Fewer inhibitions produce more happiness, and fewer inhibitions make it more difficult for the dogmatists to control us. That is why they resent this way of life."

"More pleasure perhaps, but more happiness?"

"Scientifically speaking, I do not distinguish between what is pleasurable and what makes one happy."

"They are sometimes one and the same," he said, "but they aren't identical. By the way, I'm not a Manichean. The wine and the meal—and the company—are delightful." He could look into those eyes for hours, he thought.

"Europe is deeply troubled", she said. "The antiscience parties have stirred the masses."

"But those parties profess to apply science to social progress", John said. "How do you explain that?"

He could tell she was surprised to hear him say this. "Come", she said. Greta Erickson rose from her chair, and he followed her to a large window. It looked out over an atrium with a pond and a stand of white birch trees. There were benches scattered about that tranquil space, but they were unoccupied. As he stood next to her, he felt her warmth and smelled her scent—lilacs, that was it. She took his hand in hers, so naturally that it might have been the hundredth and not the first time. He hadn't told her he was married, and he wondered if it would have mattered to her.

"Stockholm is more cosmopolitan than Lund. I delight in coming here", she said. "Our winters are hard, but we have beautiful summers."

He knew that he ought to have released her hand, but he could not make himself do it. All of the theoretical morality he'd espoused had been compromised by this woman in the space of an hour.

275

She led him back to the table, massaging her hands with a fresh towel that had been delivered in their absence. They sat again. Coffee had been served in delicate china demitasse cups and the wine removed. What had happened at the window? he asked himself. He felt as if he'd crossed a sort of metaphysical Rubicon, and he wondered if he could ever go back. Most of his colleagues would have laughed at the idea that this simple act constituted a moral transformation, but he knew better. He'd had too much formation to take this path without intellectual interrogation.

"I see a pipe in your jacket", she said. "Though I do not smoke, feel free to do so."

"Thank you", he said. He packed the pipe and lit it.

"I have occupied your time with everything but what you came here for. Please, let us discuss what interests you", she said.

"I've found our conversation very enjoyable", he said, realizing that if he was not careful, his reason for coming to Stockholm would recede into the background. He forced himself to concentrate and added, "But I'll pose my questions if it's convenient."

"It is", she said, so clinically that there might never have been any personal contact between them.

"How far advanced was *Homo sapiens* one hundred thousand years ago?"

She grinned and bit her lip. "I am happy the coffee has been served. I can say that the mental capacity and physical characteristics of man at that time were almost identical to those of modern man. The differences are superficial. Cro-Magnon and Neanderthal were contesting territories. Eventually, Neanderthal vanished."

"Biologically speaking, how long ago might an advanced civilization have arisen?"

"Biologically speaking, such a civilization might have developed one hundred thousand years ago, but there is no historical evidence that such an event occurred."

"In a biological sense, a highly advanced civilization thirty thousand years ago wouldn't violate anything we know to be true?" he said.

"That is correct."

"Giant elephants—mammoths and mastodons—were present until when?"

She took a sip of coffee. "Those large animals roamed Europe and Asia until ten thousand years ago. Strictly speaking, the mammoth and the mastodon were not elephants, though they were closely related to them."

"These animals coexisted with man?"

"Yes."

"And the horse?" he said. Even as he posed this question, he realized he was still contemplating her hand in his; it was impossible to dismiss that memory.

"*Equus* has remained virtually unchanged—except for relatively recent breeding for war and speed—for over one hundred thousand years."

The music was so unobtrusive that he couldn't have said when it began. A small ensemble consisting of wind instruments and violins was playing near the entrance. The musicians were young. Greta Erickson noticed his interest in the musicians and said, "Saint-Saëns; that's another benefit of this dining room."

"Culture along with a gourmet meal?" he said.

"We are not barbarians in Scandinavia", she said, flashing a smile.

"I said that poorly. I beg your pardon."

She laughed, and it was an infective laugh. "Have I exhausted your questions?"

"You'll think me foolish to ask, but is it possible that the flying reptile *Pteranodon* survived somewhere until one hundred thousand years ago?"

"No."

"Without question?"

"Without question", she said. "*Pteranodon* has been extinct for tens of millions of years. You seem dismayed. Had you intended to populate your story with men and dinosaurs?"

"Was there another creature in that period that resembled *Pteranodon*?" John said.

"If you are talking about another dinosaur, the answer is still no. There were large reptiles—crocodiles, alligators, lizards, and turtles—but by then dinosaurs were long extinct. There was a large flying creature, *Teratornis*, that superficially resembled *Pteranodon*. One can think of *Teratornis* as a large condor with a wingspan of over twenty feet. If I recall, that animal has been extinct for one hundred thousand years, but that's near enough to your period of interest."

"Could there have been a clutch of preserved *Pteranodon* eggs, buried somewhere, that were discovered, incubated, and hatched?"

"That is not possible either", she said. "Incubation is a delicate process. The organic material inside the egg would inevitably have been compromised, even if it were preserved."

She must have noticed his disappointment because she smiled at him and said, "Surely the success of your literary project does not hinge on these dinosaurs. As it is a fictional story, you can bring the creature alive with a frozen egg. There will not be one in a thousand who will understand these biological facts."

"Perhaps", he said. He was thinking about Jack's comment, that the story might be a combination of history and mythology. Maybe Jack was right. Still, John's analysis of the text revealed no evidence of this. Furthermore, the word image of the flying monster in the story was so vivid and so resembled *Pteranodon*—where had the idea come from if the creature had been extinct for millions of years when the story was written?

"I am reticent to tell you this because it is not so much science as speculation," she said, "but there are biologists—a few—who believe that the tiniest remnant of tissue may someday be enough to recreate the complete organism. This theory says that the entire blueprint for an organism is contained in each of its cells. If this is true, the discovery of tissue from a member of the genus *Pteranodon* could be used to reintroduce the animal to this world.

"Do not let this theory be too encouraging. We have never discovered intact tissue from creatures so ancient. It is invariably fossilized; that is, minerals have replaced the organic matter. And we can hardly imagine the technology that would be necessary to accomplish so complex a replication."

From what he'd learned about the Necromancer, it would not have surprised John to discover that something similar to what Greta described had once been accomplished. Had she inadvertently given him the answer, or was he grasping at any straw to justify his beliefs?

"That's a helpful idea, Greta", he said, noticing that she was pleased to hear him say her name. "A question concerning flowers and deciduous trees. How far back are they found?"

"In this case, we need not resort to fantastic theories. The deciduous trees and flowers we are familiar with were present well over one hundred thousand years ago. You may comfortably insert them into your story."

"That's much easier than creating new flora", he said.

She rose from her chair and said, "Will you excuse me for a moment? There is something I must discuss with the curator." As she walked toward the door, he could not take his eyes off her. Even an inanimate adornment like the beret was attractive. He knew that he was behaving irrationally, even irresponsibly, but he couldn't help himself. Greta was beautiful, elegant, brilliant, vigorous, mentally stimulating— all the things that attracted him. He was loath to admit it to himself, but she also radiated a sexual energy he couldn't ignore. He was stung to realize that he had already betrayed E. M., in his heart if not in fact. He defended himself with the notion that he had fallen under some kind of spell, which had commandeered his will. He remembered the object in the story that seduced those who gazed into it. Until this moment, he'd been unable to comprehend such absolute beguilement. Now he understood.

She was an egoist, he judged, not in the sense of one who disregards or disparages others but in the sense of a person whose actions are calculated to bring self-satisfaction, pleasure. Yes, this egoism might prove detrimental to another person if that other person's interests conflicted with her interests, but he was convinced that she wasn't predisposed to desire another's harm.

She and this egoistic ethos seemed so bound together that she would be an entirely different person if she didn't hold these beliefs, a lesser person—a lesser presence, at least. Her philosophy wasn't a coat she could cast off; it was more like her very skin. He admitted that this idea both fascinated and repelled him, and he wondered if he wasn't being unjust to this woman who had been such a generous host.

John had been in Stockholm less than a day, and so much had happened—was happening. Anxiety accompanied the recollection that the portfolio in his hotel room had been

moved ever so slightly when he'd dined the previous evening. He was sure of this because he'd measured its exact
location and left it, as bait, so to speak. There was another
explanation—the maid or another hotel employee—but he
no longer believed it. "Too many coincidences make intention", Owen had said. John was being followed wherever
he went. He had to accept that unsavory fact, as he accepted
the weather.

E. M. was alone with the children—their children, his
children. His absences were difficult for her, but she accepted
his trips because she knew they were important to him,
not because she had any love for the project. She was not
as pretty or vivacious as she once was; the demands of life
with four children and a mortgage had seen to that. He
recognized that he often took her for granted.

"John?" Greta said, sitting down again. "You are lost in
thought. I think that is the expression."

"That's the expression", he said. "I'm lost."

"The curator is a competent man but unimaginative. I
have found that a few words prior to the directors' meeting
are helpful. Now—your story. Please tell me about it."

"How could I refuse? You've been so helpful."

"I have done nothing but answer questions, and I have
had the pleasure of meeting you."

Everything he'd been pondering—the portfolio that was
moved, E. M.—dissolved as he attended to her question.
"The story concerns an advanced civilization that existed
tens of thousands of years ago."

"Is your civilization Atlantis?" she said presciently.

"For all intents and purposes, my civilization is descended
from that civilization."

"That's an idea that will interest many. May I ask what
inspired this story?"

It was a natural question, but he hadn't expected it. She must have seen his consternation; her reading of emotional temperature was uncanny. She said, "Perhaps there is a mysterious secret connected with the story."

Or had she been coached? He resisted that idea, perhaps because it suggested another motive for her interest in him. In spite of her allure, he was too well trained to abandon reason altogether and tell her too much.

"I will not press you. I am annoyed when others press me. I rarely tell them the truth, and I do not want you to think me a pest."

"I wouldn't think you a pest—ever", John said.

"I will read your story when it is published, and then I will have the answer—or will I? I seem to recall hearing someone speak about Atlantis not so long ago", she said. "Yes, I remember. At a conference in Berlin on human development, June of last year, I met a man who talked about Atlantis as if it were a historical civilization. Come to think of it, he asked some of the same questions you have asked."

"Was this man, by any chance, Alembert of the Sorbonne?" John said.

"Yes, that was his name. He was a memorable person—so intense. Do you know him?"

"I know him."

"Are you collaborating on this project?"

"No", John said.

"I much prefer your company to his. He was so persistent—one might say obsessive—though I do not know him well enough to make that judgment."

"He can have that effect", John said. "Did he express interest in anything else?"

"Yes—spiders."

"Not butterflies, or stick insects?"

"I have a good memory. He wanted to know about spiders, especially—"

There were three loud sounds in succession, like a motorcar backfiring. Greta looked toward the atrium window. Then they heard sirens. Greta motioned to the waiter. "Find out what is happening", she said.

"Were those gunshots?" she asked John.

He thought so, but he didn't answer her and pensively turned the cup around on its saucer.

"You should be proud of your accomplishments, of everything you've achieved", John said, trying to divert his attention, and hers, from whatever might be happening in the street.

"You are kind to say so", she said, reaching across the table and grasping his hand. "If you extend your stay in Stockholm ..."

He could hardly believe what he was hearing. Was this woman, who might have any man in Stockholm, trying to seduce him? She was looking into his eyes; there was no doubt of her intentions.

"Excuse me, Dr. Erickson", the waiter said. "Excuse me", he said again, when he saw the look on their faces. "You asked me about the incident in the street."

"Yes?" she said, breaking eye contact with John.

"A man was killed exiting the Larsen House. It was Harri Albertsen, the journalist."

"He was killed—on the street?"

"The police have just removed the body."

"Has someone been arrested?"

"I do not think so."

"Thank you", she said. There was fear on the man's features as he left the table.

"What is it all about?" John said.

"Who can say? Personal, political? Albertsen is well known in Scandinavia. He has written in opposition to the communists."

"I didn't expect this in Sweden", John said.

"Nor do we expect it, but the political temperature has been raised. Unrest has crept in from the east." She raised beautifully manicured hands and said, "Well, these things must sort themselves out. Reason will prevail. We live in the age of science."

The event in the street had been so startling, he'd almost forgotten about her invitation. The musicians were still playing. There was nothing on the table except for two cups and saucers.

"What have you decided? Will you stay with me?"

That was straightforward enough. To accept would be so easy. No one would ever know. For all intents and purposes, Stockholm was another world. He felt like all the strictures imposed on him by his society and his religion had robbed him of the joie de vivre that was his due. If he declined, he told himself amidst a haze of emotions, he might regret it for the rest of his life.

"Yes", he said, exhaling the word.

"I am staying at the Scandinavian Hotel. You may join me later. The directors' meeting will not be lengthy. You see, Epicureans are not as shallow as you imagined." She rose from her chair, bent over him, and kissed him. "Au revoir, John. I will expect you." The waiter approached the table with a towel, and she washed her hands more assiduously than she had previously. She looked down at the towel she deposited, and sighed. The gesture was the nearest she'd come to acknowledging this therapy or ritual or whatever it was. Was it his imagination, or were her features less than flawless at that moment—her mouth a bit too wide, her eyes pinched and weary? If so, this impression dissipated in response to her dazzling smile.

Her invitation, his acceptance, her kiss had all happened so suddenly that his equilibrium was shattered. He sat at the table a long time after she had left the room. He supposed that he had finally and truly become John Hill, no longer John the professor, father, and husband. *Falsus in uno, falsus in omnibus.*

When he reached the street, all evidence of violence was gone other than a police car parked near the place where the act had presumably occurred. The somberness of the people could easily have been attributed to the rain that had arrived with a bank of dark clouds. The sooner he checked out of his hotel and moved to the Scandinavian, the better, he told himself.

He hadn't come to Sweden for anything like this liaison with Greta. The information he'd sought, she'd provided. As in Paris and Heidelberg, he'd learned nothing that contradicted the theory he had formulated. Even the obstacle Jack had identified—the flying monsters—had been given a possible explanation by Greta. Why couldn't a scientific process have been employed to recreate these beasts? Everything else fit like pieces in a puzzle; now even this recalcitrant piece might be made to fit with some imaginative license.

She admitted meeting Alembert. Everything in her words and attitude suggested it had been a casual encounter, and perhaps it was, but at the very least it revealed the breadth of Alembert's quest. John and Alembert were on parallel tracks, and Alembert had arrived at Greta Erickson before he had; but Alembert didn't have the manuscript.

Could Albertsen's murder have anything to do with John's presence in Stockholm? He suspected that someone had been in his room. John had no connection to the journalist—no connection that he knew of, at least. The shooting was most likely another manifestation of the spirit of the times, he concluded, a spirit that was moving ever more swiftly and relentlessly.

He asked himself what Greta's need for the towels might mean. She didn't try to hide it or explain it. She had been so composed that the action seemed natural. Was she obsessed with cleanliness? Could it be a medical condition, with the towels having been infused with something other than warm water?

He pictured her in his imagination—the sculpted cheekbones, the fathomless violet eyes, the melodious voice, and most of all, the elemental energy she radiated. One could not be in the presence of that Circe for long without being affected. She'd been honest with him; she hadn't said a word about love, or even friendship. Instead, she had described a "rational Epicureanism" that sought pleasure where it could be found. How many other men, he wondered, had met her criteria for single-minded pursuit of pleasure? What would her attitude be toward him if, not to say when, he no longer interested her or gave her pleasure? Would he then witness *la belle dame sans merci*? In spite of the excitement he felt when he thought about Greta, an emotional pall descended on him.

The sun broke through the clouds, and umbrellas closed. The streets were bustling with walkers and motorcars. His hat was soaking wet, but it didn't matter; the image of him and Greta together monopolized his thoughts. His will had already been led down a path by a psychological, even spiritual, force he hadn't experienced to this degree before. To reconsider his decision would be like scaling a mountain he had just descended.

A bell rang, rich, sonorous. Two children skipped in front of him. The air was warm, but not cloyingly warm. The bell was still pealing as he came to the entrance of his hotel. An hour later, John had packed and removed his bags from the room. He learned that the Scandinavian Hotel was only five blocks away. He could be there in a matter of minutes.

He hailed a cab. The day had turned bright and sunny.

"Stockholm railway station", he said. "I have a train to catch."

September 14, 1931

Oxford

Socrates had been gamboling in front of John's desk for the better part of an hour, running in circles and burrowing beneath the rug. Speculation as to the rodent's motives had given way to appreciation of the creature's acrobatics. Abruptly, Socrates made a beeline for the wall hole and vanished.

The man came into the office without knocking. The umbrella in his hand was in token of the rain that was pelting the town. He wore a brown suit and a pale yellow bow tie. He wore no hat, as was his custom.

The man closed the office door and sat in the chair opposite John, as if he'd done it dozens of times before.

"John", the man said. "I decided it was time I visited you."

John dropped his pen on the desk and pushed his chair back.

"It is a miserable day", Alembert said.

John realized that Alembert went nowhere and did nothing without calculation. His presence here proved that he knew John had been lying to him. Until now, Alembert had made a pretense of believing that John was a country teacher.

"I understand you have no classes today."

"That's right."

"Then we will have time to converse."

"As you wish."

"I do wish. It is an opportunity for frank conversation."

John said, "May I get you a cup of tea?"

"I prefer that our conversation proceed without interruption. The time for tea, wine, and caviar has passed."

"Then be so kind as to tell me what you want", John said.

"I want what I have wanted from the moment we met. Do you think I would devote so much time to a country teacher's literary project? I knew exactly who you were before you set foot in my building. I knew you had something I wanted, and our conversations confirmed it. There were psychological moments when I observed your reaction to an object or a word. When you first saw the runes on the goblet, you could not prevent an expression of recognition. When we spoke about Atlantis, you could not sustain the fiction that the purpose of your visit was simply literary research. And when you read the translation of the cuneiform scroll, you betrayed an emotional attachment to it. To Alembert, it was as if your thoughts were written on your forehead."

"I'm not much of an actor", John said.

"On the contrary, you are an adequate actor, but you were attempting to deceive the wrong person. Now it has come to this."

"And what is this?" John said.

Alembert looked around the room. It struck John that everything his gaze encompassed was placed under the man's intellectual microscope.

"I had to travel to Oxford. The weather has been beastly ever since I crossed the Channel, but I needed to endure it in order to impress upon you that further recalcitrance is perilous. It is rare, some would say unprecedented, for

Alembert to attend to a matter like this himself. I have an army—I do not exaggerate—that does my bidding."

"What do you want?" John said. Out of the corner of his eye he saw Socrates' head protruding from his hole. Better not emerge, he thought. If only he could do the same.

"I want you to produce the artifact without further delay."

"You're convinced I have something."

"I pride myself on being ... thorough. I do not leave things to chance. You are a philologist. As such, given enough source material and enough time, you might be able to translate an ancient text. You have gone to considerable bother and incurred considerable expense by visiting the bombastic Hermann and the beguiling Greta Erickson, both experts in disciplines related to ancient history. Literary verisimilitude is one thing, but that level of research for a fictional novel defies credibility. Then there is Erzo."

"I'm not familiar with Erzo. Is that a person?"

"Some have said so. He has exceptional eyes and ears."

John's pulse was racing. Had someone discovered his hiding place?

"You met him, John, years ago, after a night of violent weather. He still bears you a grudge over the dog."

"I don't know what you are talking about."

"You are too intelligent to attempt such childish dissimulation. Erzo is a man with knowledge of my interest in certain artifacts. He often scours the countryside in the region where the chalice was discovered. I make it worth his while."

"What did he tell you?" John said.

"That's better", Alembert sighed. "However, I am always answering your questions, and you never answer mine. Erzo told me that you were conveying a box made of a metal he had never seen before, and he is something of an expert when it comes to precious metals. He told me you defended the object as if your life depended on it. By the way, you may not have missed it, but Erzo was delighted to recover his knife."

"I dislike intimidation and theft", John said. He had not thought of the knife for years, nor did he know that it had been stolen. But the knife was incidental. Alembert was telling him they'd been in his home.

"That doesn't surprise me. You fought in the war. That experience has affected you."

The man knew everything about him. John berated himself silently for not better preparing for this encounter. Surely he knew that Alembert would come to him when John decided to sunder the relationship. Still, this was England, not Heidelberg or Paris. But did that make a difference to a man of Alembert's reach?

"You are an interesting man, John. I admit it. But you are no match for me, and if you persist in this charade you and your clan will be destroyed."

"Why do you want this thing?" John said.

"An excellent question. I will not insult your intelligence by mincing words. The civilization I now know to have existed thousands of years before recorded history must have possessed powers that were unfamiliar to their primitive contemporaries. Where did those people and that power come from? I want to understand, to plumb those powers. I do not care about goblets as goblets, or scrolls as scrolls. I want to understand. I believe you have the key to that understanding, and I will not allow you to withhold it from me."

"So I suspected."

"Good. Misunderstanding at this stage of our negotiations will be fatal. When will you deliver the artifact?"

"I met your associate Krieger. Is an army of Kriegers what you want to create with these powers?"

"He underestimated you. That displeased me. Perhaps my conversation with Christopher in your presence was intemperate after all, but who would have guessed that you would connect the Krieger in that conversation with the man at the café? That incident confirmed that you should not be underestimated.

"Krieger and others in my employ are formidable personalities. Krieger, in particular, does not like to be humiliated. Let me tell you a story. It is a rainy day, and I have come a long distance. You have no immediate commitments; I confirmed that. I will take you back in time hundreds of years to the reign of your own King Henry II. There was a public feud between that king and the archbishop he appointed. A rapprochement ensued, but relations remained frayed, and one night as the king supped in his feudal castle he was said to have remarked: 'Will no one rid me of this troublesome priest?' Several of his knights made for England and killed the archbishop in the sanctuary of his cathedral church. Do you understand the meaning of this story?"

John said, "Do you remember what happened to the king?"

"He kept his head, which is more than can be said for the priest."

"I'm not afraid of Krieger."

"He is one of many", Alembert said. "Not a few are strong willed."

"If you kill me, you will never find what you're seeking."

"I will not kill you first. I respect your courage. Instead, I will kill those you value most. You need to understand that."

John had no doubt that Alembert meant exactly what he said. He would have to turn over the book. Nothing was as important as E. M. and his children. And he cherished his friends—Jack, Owen, Hugo, and Charles.

"Alembert", he said, as his mind raced from possibility to possibility. "You and I will die someday, someday soon as the world measures time. Are power and ambition all that matter?"

"Casuistry will not deter me. We have been over these matters in Paris. Listen to me. I know about your beliefs, what you hold sacred. The followers of that Nazarene were right about one thing, and one thing only: to allow the senses to govern one's will is a path to dissolution. You have asked what motivates me, and I will tell you plainly. Dorian Gray experienced what motivates me, that is, setting one's self, the ambition to master one's world, above everything else. Unfortunately for Gray, he made the mistake of allowing his senses to govern his ambitions instead of making sure his ambitions governed his senses."

"It's an old story—nihilism", John said.

"You will not move me from the views I have adopted. I do not desire to bore you with repetitive threats, but either you will give me the artifact or I will annihilate your friends, and then your clan, and then you."

"That will not deliver this thing into your possession", John said, wondering where the strength had come to pronounce those words.

He could tell that this statement surprised Alembert too, a man not accustomed to meeting resistance. John commanded himself to resist this man, as he'd commanded himself to lift himself out of the trenches. "You've said that ambition ought to govern the senses. You may kill my loved ones, and me, and achieve momentary satisfaction, but your ambition will be thwarted. You will never discover it on your own." What an outlandish bluff that was, knowing that the book was within reach of both of them. He dared not look at it. Socrates had fully emerged from his hole, nose twitching.

"I wonder if you are as strong as you pretend. I do not believe you."

The man was slowly backing him into a corner. Where could he go, what could he do, to dissuade such an indomitable adversary?

"I have applied some thought to where this artifact is hidden", Alembert said. "Given enough time, I will be able to find it without your assistance, but that is too tedious. I am impatient, and I suspect the actions I described will deliver it sooner. Still, here is my logic. It is not in your home. It is not hidden in one of the buildings at the college because you do not frequent any other building with regularity. It is not in a bank vault. It is not with friends; you do not spend enough time in their homes. Where could it be?"

"It doesn't exist. That is consistent with your logic too."

"Do not insult my intelligence; of course it exists. I have concluded that it is hidden in a natural vault, probably a cave. It is not uncommon for you to take walking trips in the country, and it is hard to follow someone in the wilderness. You know that. Henceforth, we will not disguise our surveillance. You will be followed wherever you go."

"Have you forgotten the police?"

"The police", he said, disparagingly. "Spare me that threat. You will not be the first person in England I have eliminated."

John knew he was matched against a mental superior and a man who would stop at nothing to get what he wanted. Alembert could and would crush him like a bug. He said, "I don't have what you think I have."

"Then what do you have? Reveal it, and if it is nothing, there is nothing to fear. That is the most salubrious action you can take. As it stands, I can conclude only that you are impeding my ambition. I am here to demand delivery; nothing else will suffice, surely not the artifice you attempted the last time we met."

If anything, it was raining harder. He noticed water seeping through the window casement and dripping onto the floor, as it often did in a hard rain. He'd always believed there was strength in knowledge, even if that knowledge couldn't be applied at the moment. If Alembert had learned a lot about him, John had learned something about Alembert too. The man had an ambitious grandfather. His brother had betrayed his trust. Someone who had once been close to Alembert had left him. Alembert had people—like Krieger—embedded in the violent and anarchic movements of the times. Were they really his men, as he suggested? As long as Alembert would answer his questions, John would continue to ask them. Maybe something he learned would suggest a means for survival. "Are you a Nazi, like Krieger?" he said.

"I am not, as you well know. The Nazis are pests but useful, like wasps in a garden. They eliminate vermin. Krieger is my man. He is on a short leash. Are you familiar with Nietzsche's *Will to Power*?"

"Yes."

"Then we understand one another. You disdain it; I embrace it. We shall see who prevails, the king or the priest."

"Becket's end may be my end too", John said. "I've considered it."

"I sincerely hope not, but it is possible. You fence with a master. You have a twig, and I have a rapier. Resign, and you and your clan will live. You have lied and inconvenienced me, but I am willing to look past it. I am rarely that magnanimous."

John stood. Socrates hadn't moved. He allowed himself a glance at the top shelf where the book and box resided in the rustic container he'd made with his own hands. He had to give it up, didn't he? And if he did turn it over to Alembert, hadn't he experienced the enjoyment of holding it in his hands, of translating the manuscript and learning so much from it? Yet he knew that it wasn't losing possession of the book that mattered but what Alembert intended to do with it. There were passages he'd translated but didn't understand, passages that required specialized scientific knowledge. He was convinced that wisdom, if not power, could be unlocked by someone who understood them.

John hadn't learned anything new by mentioning the nefarious Krieger, but he wouldn't give in. What was her name ... the woman Alembert and Christopher had discussed so passionately in Paris? Alembert was watching him, like a lion watching a wounded antelope.

"Have you found Agnes?" John said.

He suspected that he'd inflicted a scratch, if not a wound, with his twig. It was evident in Alembert's angry eyes. What was there about Agnes that so troubled his adversary? Who was she?

"What do you know about Agnes?"

"More than you do", John lied.

"Will you never cease to surprise me? I want to know what you know about Agnes. This is a dangerous game you are playing."

"You'll have to be patient."

Alembert laughed. "I wonder if you know anything, but why else would you mention that name? You have raised the stakes, John. If I find that you are more than a liar, that you are a committed adversary, it will go badly for you."

"You can kill me only once."

"If I find that you are plotting against me, death will be the least of your worries. You keep looking past me, as if you are expecting a deliverer. Is E. M. coming to rescue you, or your son John? Perhaps you are expecting Jack, or Owen."

"I'm looking for Socrates", John said.

Alembert squinted and said, "You are too intelligent to think I would believe you are mentally ill."

"He exists."

"I suppose you will tell me he has the artifact."

"No," John said, "but the truth is like that."

"The truth—what is it, anyway? I am not pressed for time. Play all your cards, John. The outcome will be the same."

"Socrates told me the story. He said he'd come into possession of a manuscript and had spent a lifetime translating it—"

"He was a philologist too; how convenient."

"Over a period of months, he told me a fantastic story."

Alembert said, "Who is this man? Did he teach you to be such an artful liar? How do you explain what Erzo saw on the trail? How do you explain your astonishment at seeing the runes on the goblet?"

"Erzo saw a silver-plated box illuminated by light diffracted by moisture from the storm. He was hardly in a position to appraise the item, practiced eye or no. I was conveying it to a friend. Ever since the war, I've had an aversion to being attacked; the contents of the box did not matter. As for the goblet, what antiquarian and philologist wouldn't be astonished at seeing those runes?"

"Bravo. You are indeed a respectable liar."

John said, "Do you have any proof that what I've told you isn't the truth?"

"You know that proving the negative is next to impossible. Nonetheless, you are a liar, John. That was stipulated when you told me you were a country teacher."

He had put Alembert off his guard with the question about Agnes. Hadn't Alembert given Christopher the mission to locate her? "What's become of Christopher?" John said.

Alembert started. He smiled—it wasn't a friendly smile—and said, "Is it possible that you have learned what transpired between Christopher and Agnes? Has she sought you out? She has always been bold, but this would be reckless. So that is how things stand. I see that you are not merely an impediment, but an adversary. You had better sharpen your twig."

An incident involving Agnes and Christopher must have occurred, John concluded. Something must have gone wrong. Something had happened to Christopher.

"He shouldn't have pursued her", John said, grasping at the few morsels of information he had.

Alembert ran his hand through his thinning hair and said, "Who told you? Was it Agnes?"

"You aren't the only person with eyes and ears."

"When eyes and ears intrude on my business, I amputate them."

"Perhaps Socrates told me", John said, more blithely than he felt.

"I am beginning to believe in this Socrates. Does he reside in the Foreign Office?"

"I have my secrets too. You're far from home. If someone wanted to take you, this would be a good place to do it."

"Do you think I came here alone? If the police or your Foreign Office friends arrive, fifty men will storm this building. You will be surprised at their weaponry and vigor."

"Do you think my friends will come alone?" said John. He was playing a high-stakes card game, and he'd put all his markers in. "The Foreign Office may not have an army at its disposal, but it can muster force when needed."

There was a knock on the door. It startled John as much as it did Alembert. If this had been a game of bridge, he was playing for a grand slam and needing to finesse every trick. He was terrified and exhilarated, like he had been when his company climbed out of the trenches, expecting death but moving forward.

"Come in", John said, as authoritatively as he could manage.

The door opened, and the portal was filled by that large man he never expected to see again.

"Hello, John." Gilbert removed his hat and leaned his cane against the wall. He took off his cloak and wrung it out, spilling water on the floor. He too was dripping copious amounts of water from his enormous frame. "I hope I'm not intruding. I welcome shelter from this drenching rain."

"You are most welcome", John said.

"Then I'll pull up a chair. What's this? Do you know you have a mouse on the premises? I see you do." After recognizing the mouse, he acknowledged Alembert. "Are you going to introduce us, John?" Gilbert was still holding the sodden cloak.

For an instant, John thought Gilbert was referring to the mouse. The big man's eyes were twinkling.

"This is Adler Alembert. He's a historian at the Sorbonne."

"I know you", Alembert said to Gilbert, examining him but not offering a hand.

"I know you too, sir", Gilbert said solemnly, draping the cloak over the back of the chair.

"Is this your lethal force?" Alembert said to John. "Is the Foreign Office now manned by hippopotami?"

"I am indeed a horse of a different order, and the only thing about me that's lethal, according to Mr. Wells, is my tongue", Gilbert said, with a piratical gleam in his eye. "I seem to have intruded on a sensitive matter."

"Sensitive and urgent", Alembert said.

"There are few things in life that are urgent, and those few things are mostly ignored."

"Your reputation for paradox—some would call it puffery without substance—precedes you", Alembert said. "As you suggested, this is a private conversation. It would not be wise to interfere."

"I am hardly wise, Professor. I happened to be in Oxford, and I happened to have an idea."

"May we hear your idea?" John said.

Alembert's eyes were fixed on Gilbert.

"Did you ever have a hobby turn into a cause célèbre? Mine happens to be detective stories. One thing led to another, and next thing I know, I'm on a detecting treadmill."

"I do not have time for fiction", Alembert said.

"No doubt a necessary concession in your line of work", Gilbert said. "As for me, I can't help applying things I see, hear, and read to my detective stories. It's the most natural thing in the world, I suppose."

"Is this the idea that brought you here?" Alembert said.

"In a manner of speaking. The idea that brought me here is a notorious event, a murder and a disappearance that occurred years ago in London. In my judgment, it makes for a delicious detective story."

Immediately, John thought of Sir Richard Hope. What was Gilbert up to? He remembered how Gilbert had chastised him for accepting the conventional wisdom that Sir Richard had murdered the young woman and then made a dash for it.

"It seems I'm dripping on your floor, John", Gilbert said, looking down. "As for Sir Richard, everyone accepted the explanation suggested by the police: a sexual liaison gone bad. Presumably, Sir Richard found himself in an untenable position. What would be more natural for a man of Sir Richard's exceptional talents than to vanish forever? Being a humble writer of detective stories, I couldn't stop there. John, if you remember, I informed you that one of the other men who died of other-than-natural causes in London that evening was an elderly vagabond; he was found dead in the streets with his head caved in. The young woman found murdered in Sir Richard's house was believed to be from a good family, a family too scandalized to acknowledge her, a not unprecedented reaction.

"I pondered what a detective story writer could do with such a run-of-the-mill murder and flight. I said to myself, What if that young woman didn't hail from a well-to-do family but, instead, was a woman of the streets with no family, no one at all who cared about her? What if someone gave her money to clean herself up and dress elegantly—then killed her and planted her in Sir Richard's house? Do you remember, John, when I informed you that the police told me she had calluses on her hands and feet? My writer's brain made that a residue of her working days. Money can't erase everything.

"What if Sir Richard didn't run off at all, or even vanish? What if he was murdered, his head caved in to make identification that much more difficult, and then redressed in shabby clothes and left on the street? That would be something like a play where the beggar woman becomes a princess and the prince becomes a beggar, with the unfortunate ending that both beggar and princess are killed.

"Professor Alembert, weren't you lecturing in London when that incident occurred?" Gilbert said.

Alembert's features were expressionless. "How can I say? It was so long ago."

"Yes, memory is a treacherous thing", Gilbert said. "Sir Richard was known to be a bold and fearless man. If he encountered an organization he considered a threat to England, he would have challenged it. Such an organization might have taken steps to see that he was eliminated. That would be how the detective story would develop. I'm sure that the real explanation is exactly as the police suggest."

"They are the experts", Alembert said.

"Oh yes!" Gilbert exclaimed. "They are procedural and logical. Logic is useful, but I prefer truth—when I can get it."

"If you are finished conjecturing, perhaps you will excuse us and let us conclude our business", Alembert said to Gilbert.

"You have made yourself clear, sir, but I am a man on a mission—undoubtedly dangerous—and I'm not finished."

"You're welcome to remain for as long as you like", John said to Gilbert. "Professor Alembert and I are at a standstill."

"There are no standstills where I am concerned", Alembert said. Then he said to Gilbert, "And you have walked into a lion's den. You may not be able to exit as easily as you entered. You were a fool to reveal those ideas about Hope, even if they are unprovable. You have associated me with murder. I cannot allow it."

"Because it is untruthful?" Gilbert said.

"Because it is adversarial", Alembert rejoined.

Gilbert gave every appearance of ignoring Alembert and the threat. "I met a well-known personage in 1920. He has recently died. We will call him Arthur. Arthur related the story of a trustworthy friend concerning one Gorgo Alembert, a man of humble origin, advanced intellect, and moral ambiguity who had been wreaking havoc in eastern Europe. This Alembert was not your typical criminal. Rather, he was a sort of pope of crime, the maestro of an underground army. This Alembert intended to carve out an empire without conventional borders. He was urbane when it suited his purposes, and bloodthirsty when necessary; he employed both the velvet glove and the hammer. As you may have surmised, Arthur used Alembert as a type for his own famous literary villain.

"This story did not enter the realm of the practical until I happened upon two articles that appeared on the same day: one described the discovery of a body in the home of Sir Richard Hope, who himself had disappeared. The other announced that a professor of history, Adler Alembert, was lecturing in London. I learned that Adler Alembert was the grandson of Gorgo Alembert, deceased by that time."

Remarkably, Gilbert said this as if Adler Alembert were a thousand miles away instead of sitting next to him. John could not recall a situation when the emotional temperature was so high.

"Let us pretend your fictional story about Hope's fate is true", Alembert said. "Would it be wise to contend with the person who prescribed Hope's demise?"

"It would be perilous, I imagine", Gilbert said.

"Wouldn't such a person be suicidal, or a fool?"

"You do not account for those of us who value some things more than life", Gilbert said.

"I have read about them—literary inventions—but I have never met one."

"A shame. I have met more than a few. Their example has the effect of improving one more often than not", Gilbert said.

Alembert turned to John. "You have frustrated me once again. If you are connected in any way to Agnes, I will find out. You will consider what I said and contact me soon. You know where to reach me. As for you," he said to Gilbert, "you have picked the wrong fight and the wrong man." He rose, lunged for his umbrella, and left the room as abruptly as he'd entered.

The storm hadn't abated. John opened a drawer in his desk, removed a towel, and proceeded to mop the puddle below the window and the pool Gilbert had created. When he returned to the desk, he said, "How did you learn he was here?"

"It was mostly good fortune, if one can use that term, that I learned he was in England—Oxford. My police acquaintance knows of my interest in Alembert. I requested that he advise me if the man entered England. I recalled our earlier meeting and your interest in the man; then I connected the dots, as they say."

"He's a dangerous man", John said. He told Gilbert about his two prior meetings with Alembert and about his encounter with Krieger in Heidelberg. John suspected Gilbert had deciphered more than John revealed.

Gilbert shifted his bulk, and the chair creaked. "He is indeed dangerous. The probability is high we will be dead in the near future. I don't say this to frighten you but because I know you value honesty. That fellow may be a villain, but I suspect he's a man of his word when it comes to making good on threats."

"What do you advise?" John said.

"I advise sending Alembert a very direct letter—immediately."

"Capitulation?"

"That wasn't what I had in mind, but if that is your choice, far be it from me to criticize it."

"What more can be said that hasn't been said?"

"You might tell him, as directly as possible, that if you are killed, he will never acquire what he's after, and if any of your family or friends are harmed—I do not presume to count myself in that company—you will immediately destroy this thing, on your word."

"I don't think it will deter him."

"You may be surprised. In spite of your deception, he knows you to be a man of principle. I don't think he will risk it, if he prizes this object. While you live, there is always the possibility that you will make a mistake and reveal this thing's whereabouts. There is also this consideration: you and your loved ones may be safer if you retain this thing than if you turn it over to him. Once he has it, he may assume that you confided in your wife and close friends and he may conclude that it is inconvenient to keep any of you alive. He could, and most likely would, kill all of you with impunity. Who can say how that fiendishly brilliant man's mind works? I lack the sangfroid to fathom it.

"And now I must board the train to Beaconsfield and my Frances." The big man ascended from the chair, reminding John, except for the jacket and tie, of an ancient chieftain. He pulled the wet cloak around his shoulders and put the hat on his head. He gripped the handle of the cane and rapped on the floor three times. "Pardon my puddle", he said, stepping gingerly to the door.

"And the story you told about Alembert's grandfather?" John said.

"As reliable as it can be. Arthur was a reliable man, and a talented writer. Fare thee well, John."

"You arrived in the nick of time."

Gilbert bowed, filling the doorway.

Socrates was already out of his hole. "We have a letter to write", he said to the mouse.

September 18, 1931

Oxford

"Mornin', Guv", said the stout man in the doorway. "Says here I'm to fix a bangy radiator."

The man could have been any middle-aged tradesman with his grimy overalls, calf-high boots, and blue cap. He held a piece of paper in one hand and a half-smoked cigar in the other. A sooty handkerchief protruded from his pocket.

John hadn't noticed any bangy-ness, but by then the man was inside the office and had already closed the door behind him. It was then that John noticed that the man had no tools. John couldn't help remembering Alembert's recent threats. Was this nondescript man his adversary's avenging devil?

The man removed his cap, walked to the desk, and said, "May I sit? I had a deuce of a time navigating those tunnels, and I'm no cub, if you haven't noticed."

"I'd expect a university tradesman to know those tunnels", John said.

The man waved his cigar at John dismissively. "You've already guessed I'm no tradesman."

"Then who are you?" John said, standing and looking down at the bedraggled man in his visitor's chair.

"Who I am is less important than why I'm here. Call me Drake. I had to talk to you and wanted to do it without anyone else knowing about it, especially a certain person. That's what brought me to that blasted underground maze."

Whoever this man was, John thought, he was interesting. He detected a steeliness in the man's voice and in his features.

His features . . . John had seen this man before. No, not seen him, seen pictures of him. But he hadn't looked like he looked now. The man in the chair was clean-shaven, if not clean, jowly, with piercing dark eyes and a gravelly voice. He held the cigar in his dirty hands as Richard the Lionheart might have held a broadsword. John guessed he was over fifty.

"I like this office—homey and generously provisioned with books. What's this? There's a rodent loose, my good man."

"He's my rodent", John said. "Don't fret. Only erudite quadrupeds are permitted to matriculate here."

Drake emitted a cloud of smoke and laughed. He wiped his face with the handkerchief, which contributed more grime than it removed.

"Now . . . Drake, what do you want?"

The man removed the cigar from his mouth and said, "I want to prevent your murder."

At that moment, John recognized him. His surprise must have shown because the man said in a whisper, "Let's sustain the fiction. Our adversary has eyes like an eagle." John saw the ghost of a smile on Drake's face an instant before he remembered that adler was the German word for eagle. It didn't surprise him that this man possessed facility with other languages, including German.

The professor's visitor was well known throughout Britain and in much of the world. He'd held prominent posts in several governments, but lately he had been wandering in the political wilderness, a scold to the Tory, Liberal, and Labour Parties. Why was this man, a former first minister of the navy and chancellor of the Exchequer, bothering with a university professor's troubles with Alembert?

"Have you ever traversed those tunnels? I don't suppose so. Finding your way around Paris or Moscow is a simpler matter. And nary a soul to ask for directions. I met a greaser—a pleasant chap named Hector—and a pipe fitter in the hours that I tested my wits against that maze. Thank God I had a pocketful of cigars."

John had gotten no closer to the tunnels beneath the college than once observing a tradesman as the worker descended a spiral stair.

"The stench reminds me of a South African mine", Drake said. "Do you know there's a coal furnace beneath us?

"You ought to know I have no official standing. I'm here on my own initiative. I am a loner these days. Being an iconoclast is hard and lonely work, but there's a certain mischievous satisfaction in it." Then he puffed at his cigar and said, "But that neither advances my mission nor interests you. This isn't a social call." Drake commenced pacing in front of the desk. That sent Socrates back into his hole.

"I've thought about abandoning politics for teaching," the man said, "but I fear it would bore me. My blood needs regular stirring. Even misery is preferable to ennui, and I've had my share of misery, that is."

"Teaching need not be boring", John said.

"In your case, sir, an understatement, when teaching leads to Paris, Germany, and Sweden in little more than a year. I know about that—not the details, just people and places. I don't suppose you'd care to enlighten me."

"Pardon my frankness, but I don't see that it's any of your business."

"I expected that response", Drake said. "But I am here to assure you that Alembert is our mutual business."

"How so?" John said.

"First of all, Alembert is a murderer. You may already know this, but if you don't, you should. And he's no garden-variety killer. He moves in the best circles. He has charmed the rich and the mighty. But make no mistake—men seem to fade away when that man's shadow touches them."

"I already know that", John said.

"Well then," the man said, turning toward him and ejecting a jet of smoke, "you are either a boundlessly resourceful man, or a fool."

"I'm the latter," John said, "and you aren't the first to suggest it. My wife does so regularly."

"Good", Drake rejoined, and resumed pacing. "This conversation will go more smoothly if we can be honest with ourselves, and each other."

"Do not take my candor to mean I intend to reveal my business in its entirety", John said.

"I make no assumptions. I'm stating facts and assembling evidence."

"For what purpose?"

"Would you have me reveal *my* business in its entirety?"

"You have come to me, and not vice versa", John said.

"If you knew what you were up against, it would have been vice versa. You and I may not be allies in every respect, but we're not adversaries. My mission furthers your interests, whether or not my mission corresponds to yours. I would have you tell me everything you can, or would, about this man."

"I see that you know I've met with Alembert", John said.

"At least twice in Paris, and recently in this office. Have any meetings been overlooked?"

"Your intelligence is good."

"When Alembert travels, things happen", Drake said. "We are still trying to determine why he came to Oxford. I can tell you that one of the men who was assigned to track him is dead. Alembert knows he is being watched and he is still able to murder with impunity."

"Who is the 'we' you refer to?"

"An informal 'we'—several friends who happen to work in the Foreign Office. They are the collectors of the intelligence. I am their confidante."

"And what does a confidante do?" John said, seeing Socrates' nose protruding from his hole.

"He circles the chessboard and whispers in one of the players' ears."

John was pondering how much he should confide in this man. Still, if Drake could assist John in protecting his family, how could he dismiss the man's willingness to help? Surely, E. M. would welcome this unlooked-for aid.

"What do you want?" John said.

"I want to know why you've taken an interest in Adler Alembert. I especially want to know why he's taken an interest in you."

John opened his desk and withdrew his pipe. Soon both men were smoking. The mingled cigar and pipe smoke produced a fragrance that satisfied neither. Drake was still pacing the floor, but more deliberately, stopping and starting often. Every now and then, he looked in the direction of the window. He put his hands behind his back and bit down on the cigar. It was no longer lit, but he kept rolling it over between his teeth. "I suppose one must be willing to invest capital to earn it. I've told you the most pertinent facts, if not the details. People who interest Alembert become servants or corpses." He waved his hand vigorously at John. "That isn't a threat. I told you I trade in facts. I hope to receive facts for facts.

"Let me begin with this observation: Alembert is a teacher at the Sorbonne in the same way that da Vinci was an

Italian stone carver. He can't be attached to any political movement, though he has servants in all of them. We know of a dozen of his men in Britain, which means the real number is probably ten times that."

John said, "Facts for facts—Christopher, Krieger, Agnes."

"The African goliath, we know. The other two are unfamiliar to me."

John related his meeting with Krieger in Heidelberg, including their conversation with Edith, concluding with his hasty departure from the Continent. Drake lit a fresh cigar and listened without interrupting. When John finished, Drake sat in the visitor's chair and put both hands on the desk.

"Then this Krieger is one of Alembert's Nazis. That's useful. Surveillance in Germany is complicated these days, but we have a man who might be able to learn more about him. Describe Krieger to me again."

John did so, feeling chilled all the while. Never again did he want to engage in a test of wits with that man, especially when his life was at stake. He also told Drake what little he knew about Agnes. Drake made notes in a notebook he carried.

Drake said, "You suggest that Agnes was an agent of Alembert's in the Americas and that she left his service. Alembert doesn't permit desertion. My guess is she's already dead. Christopher is rarely seen. He's too well known, and it's difficult for a seven-foot man to travel incognito. This is not to suggest he's no longer dangerous. If a person finds himself alone with that man, he would do well to make peace with his creator. By the way, why did you travel to Heidelberg?"

Drake asked the question nonchalantly, but John recognized subtlety when he encountered it. It came from many nuanced conversations with Jack, Owen, and the rest. Drake's question wasn't an aside, as he pretended; it went to the heart of what he wanted to know, and what John was determined to conceal.

"I went to Germany to meet a colleague. I wanted to consult him for a project I've undertaken."

"Stockholm too?"

"Yes."

"Why should Alembert be interested in a philologist's research project?"

"Who suggested that's why he's interested in me?" John said.

"Come now. I'm not expecting unbridled candor. If you don't want to answer, then refuse forthrightly. Subterfuge doesn't become you."

"I must decline to answer", John said.

"That's better. You have knowledge, or some thing, that Alembert wants. You will not give it to him. I pity you, Professor."

"You probably suspected as much when you entered this room", John said.

"I did so suspect. That handyman of anarchy has been collecting resources and talent wherever he can find them. We get specks of information here and there, but—make no mistake—we know next to nothing about his goals or his organization. I had hoped, dared to hope, that you might be able to help us. If I'm correct, you are able but unwilling."

"You do me an injustice. If I reserve information, it's because it doesn't bear on your interests but only my own."

"Everything that bears on that man's interests, interests me", Drake said, with a clarity that made John understand just how formidable a will this man possessed.

"His goals, as you put it, can be reduced to exercising his will and satisfying his ambition", John said. "With Alembert, they are one and the same. You called him a handyman of anarchy. There are two kinds of anarchists. One destroys from a compulsion to destroy or because it gives a sense of control. There are also those who destroy so they can grasp power from the chaos they create. Alembert is that calculating kind of anarchist. He may have compulsive anarchists working for him, but they are expendable pawns."

"A trenchant description", Drake said. "How does an academic come by that insight?"

John said, "I've learned things in France, Germany, and Sweden, and in England too for that matter."

"I daresay. You fought on the Continent. I've had my own encounters with anarchism in South Africa and India, but none of those troublemakers was in Alembert's league."

"Here", John said, opening the lowest drawer in the desk and bringing out a bottle and two glasses. "You'll join me?"

"I will", Drake said.

"A gift from the president of the college. You see that it hasn't been opened. I hope it's good."

"I see the label. It's good. Ladle it out, man. The soot in those godforsaken tunnels has parched me."

They tapped glasses. "To your good health", Drake said earnestly, then took a healthy sip.

"Let me say something", John said, feeling suddenly flushed and warm. "I have learned nothing to suggest that Alembert is a Nazi, but he apparently uses Nazis when it suits his purposes. The matter I haven't plumbed is whether the isms at the root of Nazism, and of communism for that matter—materialism, utilitarianism, relativism, determinism—are what is motivating Alembert, or if it is Alembert, his will and ambition, who is propelling these things."

"I see", Drake said. "The progeny of these isms, those belligerent political movements, form alliances of convenience, but they will be at each other's throats as often as not."

John shook his head. "Sadly, we have our own articulate advocates for eugenics and empire-building at the expense of 'lesser humans'. We aren't immune from these isms either."

"I wouldn't take it as far as that", Drake said, peering through the bottom of the glass at an emerging Socrates. "We've brought civilization to much of the world. Perhaps man can improve mankind. That can be a messy business."

"A good end justifying evil means?" John retorted.

"I'm a politician. I'm forced to see shades of gray."

John said, "You and I both know that human perfection is an impossible condition, but that fact does not seem to impede the men who will stop at nothing in trying to achieve it. We can't begin with faulty ideas and expect to arrive at good ends. It doesn't work that way, and never has. I'll concede that our enemies will eventually contest with one another. Hitler and Alembert both embrace materialism, but they're bound to be mortal enemies someday, their wills and ambitions colliding. Hitler may not realize it until it's too late, but I suspect that Alembert knows it—even now."

Drake said, "This business with the European tyrannies is too far advanced to be halted without bloodshed. Not that my colleagues in Parliament agree, but I am convinced. How I wish I was wrong, as muddled as they say I am." He was looking out the window again. John doubted they could be seen from the courtyard or from the buildings across that open space. Drake had gone to a lot of trouble to enter the building clandestinely, and he seemed determined to keep his presence there undetected.

Socrates must have been convinced that John's visitor was benign, as he was scurrying along the floorboard to the window side of the room. Every once in a while, the rodent stopped, sat on its haunches, and wrinkled its nose. It was used to smoke but this was a different concoction. His antics were not unnoticed by the visitor, who refrained from commenting but grinned between puffs on his cigar.

John got up and walked to the bookshelf, returning to his desk with the box of chocolates the student had given him months earlier. He hadn't gotten around to offering them to E. M. or bringing them to the Bird and Baby. Over the weeks, and then months, the box had faded into a background of books, photographs, and objects that weren't able to find a home anywhere else.

"Would you care for a sweet?" he asked Drake.

The man extended a hand, then withdrew it. "My doctor says I have too many vices. I'll indulge him this time by refusing your kind offer."

John set the box on the desk. "If you change your mind, help yourself."

"It is my doctor's mind that needs changing. If I have to choose between the drink and the sweets ... well, cheers." He swallowed the rest of the second glass John had poured.

"I can make you a cup of black tea."

"No thanks. It's business I came for, and it's business I'd best be at. Here are more facts. Our men in Paris suggest that Christopher has dropped out of sight. Who knows what that portends. And you, John, may not know that a man has been watching you, here and at home. He won't be bothering you anymore. We have seen to that. Problem is, Alembert has many more like him."

"Alembert is supremely surreptitious", John observed.

"Lethally surreptitious. We've had three men—good men—killed in the past two years. They were assigned to keep an eye on Alembert's organization. Two were killed with obscure poisons, and one was the recipient of a stiletto in the neck. We think the poisons came from arachnids, but we aren't sure. Of course, none of this mayhem can be traced back to the good professor."

"Is the French Secret Service a partner in your investigations?"

"Many of their agents are confused by the business, and many more are cowed. Some of them are in his employ. Those who resisted him are dead. There, I've been reasonably forthright. Are you certain there isn't more you can tell me? Let me suggest it's in your interest that we know as much as possible about that man."

John wasn't much attracted to sweets. He lifted one from its cradle before replacing it. Half of the golden liquid remained in his glass. He said, "You're correct in surmising that Alembert wants something I have, or that he thinks I have."

Drake placed the smoked cigar in the empty glass. "I won't ask if you indeed have this thing, but I wonder what an Oxford professor could have that would remotely interest a man like Alembert?"

John concluded that this man was an ally, perhaps a useful one. John would have to deliver more than he had so far, though not necessarily everything. He said, "Alembert thinks I have something connected to the Atlantean civilization."

Drake grinned and slapped his leg. "That's too outlandish a statement to be a ruse. What interest could Alembert have in that myth?"

"He doesn't believe it's a myth. He thinks knowledge from that civilization can help him achieve his ambitions."

"Are you suggesting he's a madman?"

"Not in the commonly understood sense", John said. "Madness can also be understood as a gross moral disorder. That definition fits him."

"Atlantis", Drake said softly. "He must be balmy mad if you're serious. What makes him think you have this thing?"

John had a less-than-convincing answer, but he told himself it would have to do. "I'm composing a fictional story about an ancient civilization. I approached Alembert so I could make it as historically accurate as possible."

"Then that's why you visited Hermann and Erickson."

"Yes."

"And this fictional project convinced a mental giant like Alembert that you have a valuable artifact from that civilization", Drake said, unemotionally. "That defies logic. Something doesn't ring true. From what we know of the man, he devotes his attention to those who can assist him and those who impede him. Which are you?"

"Perhaps I am both."

Drake said, "So be it. You've managed to stay alive this long. Don't count on your good fortune persisting forever. More able men than you have trusted their ingenuity in matters concerning that man and have been disappointed."

"Like Sir Richard Hope", John said.

"Well now—all right, like Sir Richard. What do you know about that business?"

"I was told by a friend that Sir Richard was killed for interfering in Alembert's affairs."

"Has Alembert mentioned Sir Richard in your meetings with him?"

"He has not, but he was in this room when my friend proposed that he was Sir Richard's murderer."

"And he permitted the accusation?"

"He wasn't happy to hear it, but as you said, I'm still alive."

"And your friend?"

"To the best of my knowledge, he's still in good health."

"May I ask that gentleman's name?"

John told Drake some of what had transpired at his first meeting with Gilbert in the pub, and when that man encountered Alembert in this office. Perhaps Drake would extend his protective wing over Gilbert too.

"We've heard your friend's theory about Sir Richard's death. It's spot on as far as I'm concerned. So that's why he was in this building the day you met with Alembert. He's a hard man to overlook. I would have liked to have seen Alembert's face when your friend expounded his theory."

"I would have forgone that experience if I'd had a choice", John said.

"If I continue to meddle in Alembert's business, I have little doubt I'll be a marked man too", Drake said. "Alembert had no reservations about targeting Hope; he won't balk at eliminating me."

"Would he dare?"

"That man would dare anything. You have been spoiled, in a macabre sense of the word, by being allowed to converse face-to-face with the man. Normally, that privilege is reserved for his elite and for those captains of government and industry he seeks to influence. Now you understand my perplexity at Alembert meeting you on three separate occasions. You are not negligible in your academic discipline, but to a man like Alembert, you're a nonentity. Perhaps the reason he's allowed you to live is that he's concluded he won't obtain this knowledge he seeks, or this thing, if you are killed."

"I've already suggested as much", John said.

"He must highly esteem this thing to allow you to frustrate him."

"A chimera is as good as the genuine article if he thinks it's so. Are you sure you wouldn't care for hot tea?"

"No. I have to be going. I suspect I've learned all I'm going to learn, but I'm not looking forward to negotiating those tunnels again."

"Where do you exit?" John said.

"If I exit where I entered—that is not a certainty—it will be three blocks north of this building, at the Biological Sciences Library, where there is another blasted ship's ladder, like the one at the end of your hallway. I'll look like a sweep by then.

"You have helped me, Professor, more than you guess. You may have chosen wisely to keep this thing secret from everyone, especially Alembert." Drake stretched out his hand, and John took it.

"I can find my own way out", he said, rising and replacing the cap on his bald pate. "Glad to be of service, Guv. It'll be the rat I'm after next time—and a crafty rat he is", he said. John was certain he wasn't speaking about the mouse in his office.

When Drake had left, John returned the candy to the shelf, cleaned the glasses, and disposed of the cigar remnants. Both Drake and Gilbert had suggested that as long as Alembert was searching for the book, he and his family might be safe. Perhaps. Drake had given John a fresh idea. He considered hiding the book in the tunnels. He would not have to travel great distances or risk exposing the box to prying eyes. His visitor had said the tunnels were lonely and replete with many corners and crevices. But hadn't the book resisted discovery where it was, in that most unlikely of repositories? Maybe that was where it was meant to be and where it ought to remain.

Still, he told himself, it wouldn't hurt to inspect the tunnels, just in case. Drake had piqued his interest. How many years had John worked above those buried passages without ever seeing them?

He had to use extreme caution descending the darkened spiral stair. By the time he reached the tunnel floor, his hands were black and his trousers were soiled. He still wasn't sure why he'd gone down. He supposed it was a combination of curiosity and the practical consideration that he might someday need an escape route.

The first thing he would need was a map. Where would he find such a thing? His visitor had one, but that man had access to resources John didn't. There were lights in the tunnel, but they were widely spaced, and the glass domes that covered and protected them were filthy with soot. The tunnel extended in two directions. From what he could tell, it was about ten feet wide and made of stone. Pipes and ducts were suspended from the walls on both sides, narrowing the corridor. At one location the pipe must have pulled the stone loose from the wall, as the wall had been repaired with concrete.

When had all this been built? He concluded from the construction of the tunnel and the age of the aboveground buildings that it might be five hundred years old. Once, these tunnels might have been a refuge in tumultuous times, or a protected pathway in foul weather. The tunnel was monotonously dim and smelled of petrol. Small stone chips and rust littered the floor. Some of the lamps needed replacement. This subterranean world was drastically different from the lecture halls and laboratories above. For a man of Drake's stature to have taken this route spoke to the gravity of that man's mission.

He might have walked a quarter mile in the direction opposite his office before he turned back and retraced his steps. After passing the spiral stair, he located the furnace Drake had described. It occupied a widened space in the tunnel. Ducts radiated from the furnace like arms from an octopus. The area around it was dirtier than anywhere else he had seen, a consequence of the coal in two big fireboxes next to the furnace, some of which had spilled on the floor. There was a third bin filled with rubbish. He figured the tradesmen must use pulleys and hoists to move the rubbish down and the ash back up. There was a room adjacent to the stair that was too small to be an office; perhaps that was where the hoist or lift was located.

A rat scurried between his feet, startling him. He didn't shout, but it was a close call. For a moment, he was in the trenches again. He took a deep breath of cold, moist, sooty air and wished he hadn't.

The furnace was cold. The door was open, but it was as black as pitch inside, and he couldn't see a thing. He wondered what trinkets might have accompanied the rubbish and what one would find if the ash was sifted.

If Alembert sought him, he reflected, that man would find him even if these tunnels extended the length and breadth of England.

By the time he ascended the stairs, he looked like he'd fallen into a dustbin. He couldn't help laughing at the sight of himself. Fortunately, none of his colleagues were in the hallway. He opened the door next to the spiral stairs. It indeed housed a small lift.

What would Alembert's next move be, for surely there would be a next move? He looked at his watch. It was time he went home to E. M. and the children. His visitor would have exited the tunnels by now and be on his way back to London.

Leaving his mouse at the guard, John locked the office door and turned out the lights.

January 19, 1932

Oxford

He was covered with snow. In the two hours since he'd left the house, the wind had increased to a howling gale. He wished he'd worn his muffler and old army hat.

John had delivered John and Christopher to friends' homes on the other side of town. In spite of the six inches of snow on the ground, they'd bundled up and walked. The boys protested, E. M. had been skeptical, but he'd had his way. Now he was frozen to the bone, and he looked, or so he told himself, more like a yeti than a man, as another two inches of snow had fallen since he left the house. The last half mile was particularly hard slogging as he was walking directly into the wind.

How glorious to pull open the door and step inside; the warmth, the still air, and the light provided immediate relief. He removed his coat, hat, gloves, and boots and slipped into his house shoes. He would have made for the kitchen and a cup of hot tea but for E. M.'s summons.

"John, may I see you?"

He followed the sound of her voice into the sitting room, melting ice dripping on the rug. He was surprised to see that she wasn't alone. Priscilla, he expected; she was seated on her mother's lap and was holding a cloth doll. But there was someone else in the room, a well-dressed woman about their own age. She was sitting in the high-backed chair with a cup of tea in her hand. A number of E. M.'s pictures were distributed around the room, and some were even on the floor, propped up by walls.

"John, I'd like you to meet Agatha. Agatha, this is my husband, John." Priscilla crawled from her mother's lap and ran to John, who lifted her and kissed her on the forehead.

"Cold", she said, tugging John's hair with one hand.

"Father is very cold", he said to her. Then he said to their guest, "How do you do?"

She was a dignified-looking woman, with beetle brows above dark, thoughtful eyes. Her face was long and narrow; so was her nose. She took her time answering. "I have heard a lot about you."

"Sit down with us", E. M. said. "Agatha arrived an hour ago. She has to leave for her train at five."

"I'm sorry you can't stay for dinner", John said. Of course, he knew the woman by reputation; who didn't these days? She was dressed tastefully in a fitted gray wool dress and pearls. Her hands were still, but her eyes never stopped moving.

"I'd expected better judgment in a man of your reputation. You might have frozen out there", she said to John mischievously.

"My better judgment comes and goes", he said, looking at E. M. and setting Priscilla down again. He pulled a wooden chair from the corner and sat. Priscilla sat on the floor at his feet and returned her attention to the doll.

Agatha said, "Do you know how daunting it is to make one's living with words and to be in the presence of an expert on the English language?"

He laughed and waved her off. "I'm a philologist, not an expert. My interests are historical. We work in different eras."

"That's some consolation", she said. "Your daughter is a lovely child."

"Thank you. She takes after her mother."

E. M. poured him a cup of tea.

"Your wife paints lovely pictures", Agatha said.

"Agatha is my secret patron", E. M. said. "I finally met her last month."

Why hadn't she told John about that meeting, or this visit? He had known there was a person who'd anonymously acquired a number of E. M.'s pictures. One evening, they'd speculated about the person's sex and age and state in life. Why hadn't she told him?

"I assure you, the pleasure is all mine", Agatha said. "So often, one meets a writer or a musician or an artist whose work one admires, and the person turns out to be a disappointment. I daresay plenty have had that experience upon making my acquaintance. As for your wife, John, I esteem her work even more highly for having met her."

"That's much too kind", E. M. said.

"It's true", Agatha said. "E. M. puts me at ease. There aren't many who are capable of that."

John hadn't read any of Agatha's stories. He was wondering how he would talk his way around that. One could hardly walk into a bookstore without being confronted by the lady's newest offering.

"I doubt you read much fiction—modern fiction, that is—so we need not pussyfoot around the subject of my books", Agatha said to John.

He would have to be careful with this woman, he concluded. Had his snow-burned face registered apprehension or was she accustomed to using that preemptive statement?

"Don't put yourself under any obligation just because we have made each other's acquaintance. Reading under the burden of obligation is drudgery and often a waste of time."

She rose from the chair. "I hope to return to London with two more pictures. It's so hard to choose."

John could hear the wind like a whistle at the window. The room was warm enough, but he could feel the air stirring. He was still chilled, in spite of the tea. "May I accompany you to the station?" he said to Agatha.

"I've hired a car, but thank you anyway. I wouldn't hear of you venturing out again. I hope this beastly weather doesn't delay the train, but when I set my mind to something—seeing your wife today—I'm not easily put off."

Though he'd known her for only a few minutes, John could see that was true. He couldn't help noticing how delighted E. M. was that Agatha had come to their home, and with the attention Agatha paid to her pictures. He was happy to see her happy. He'd noticed that E. M. was aging— gracefully, it seemed to him. She was less spontaneous than she'd once been; she now kept her fiery spirit in check most of the time. Her dark hair was flecked with gray, and she wasn't as slender as when they were younger. Nonetheless, she had grown in generosity of spirit, not to mention the enthusiasm with which she cared for their children and the zeal she applied to her pictures.

Priscilla crawled back up into her mother's lap.

"I will have to make a decision", Agatha said to E. M. "I told myself, no more than two pictures."

"John", E. M. said, and he detected a turbulent tone in her voice. "Agatha's husband has met that man."

John looked at their guest. There was no doubt who "that man" was. Had it been prudent of E. M. to reveal anything about their foe, even to someone she trusted? He was hardly prepared to say anything on this subject to a stranger.

"E. M. tells me you know him", Agatha said.

"We were collaborating on a project", John said, glancing at his wife. He was no longer thinking about the wind or the cold or E. M.'s pictures.

"But no longer?"

"No longer."

Agatha said, "I shared something with E. M. She asked me to tell you too. I'd appreciate your keeping it in confidence."

"Certainly", John said, wondering if a quid pro quo would be expected.

"My husband is an archaeologist. He's led expeditions to Iraq and Syria. Because of his facility with languages and cultures, the Foreign Office asked him to serve as an unofficial consultant. Don't misunderstand me; Max isn't an agent. He's an archaeologist who passes along information that might be useful to His Majesty's government.

"Alembert approached Max several years ago concerning a scroll he'd discovered. His questions concerned the runes, or whatever it is they're called—I think Max referred to them as glyphs. They intrigued Max. He was allowed to examine them only long enough to provide Alembert the information he sought. The Foreign Office contacted Max and asked him to pay special attention to this man—in effect, to learn as much as he could."

"Do you mind telling me what he learned?" John said.

"Not at all", Agatha said. "He learned next to nothing from Alembert himself, but Max told me that Alembert 'plays for keeps', which I believe is an American colloquialism for ruthlessness."

"He is a close man", John said.

"Your wife suggested as much. She also suggested that he has been stalking you."

"You could say that." John felt like a fish that was being reeled in by an expert angler.

"You visited him in Paris?"

"Yes. Are you assisting the Foreign Office too?" John said, wryly.

"No. I'm assisting E. M. She told me you've met Alembert's assistant—Christopher."

"I've met him. Was he traveling with Alembert when he met your husband?"

"No. You're wondering, then, how I know about Christopher. I told you that Max learned next to nothing about Alembert from the man himself, but Max's Foreign Office contact, and another man I will tell you about, were more enlightening. This Foreign Office contact told Max that Alembert was an especially dangerous man and that one should never underestimate him, in spite of the benign and cultured front he projects. He also told Max about Alembert's assistant, a Negro giant who sometimes travels with his employer but mostly resides in Paris."

She paused, as if waiting for him to speak, but John had decided to listen instead. She was a well-known personage, but so was Alembert, and John had learned to his woe that things weren't what they seemed to be with that man. Why, then, couldn't Agatha present one face to the world and be someone different behind the scenes?

As if sensing his apprehension, E. M. said, "You can trust her, John."

He wondered if Agatha was really there for the pictures. How often had she and E. M. communicated, and about what? How much did this stranger—for that was what she was—know about the business that had preoccupied him for so many years?

"Max learned that Christopher is the son of a West African chieftain. Christopher's claim to fame—rather, notoriety—is that he was once a pirate and a slaver. I was surprised to hear that those occupations still survive in the twentieth century, but Max assures me they do. That résumé apparently attracted Alembert to Christopher."

"Why are you telling me this?" John said.

"Because E. M. requested that I do so. We want to impress on you the danger of associating with that man."

"I've already informed E. M. that the relationship has been sundered."

Agatha honed in on him with a hawk's eye. "Then accept this information as reinforcement of that decision."

John watched E. M. bounce Priscilla on her knee. They might have been discussing butterflies or fairies for all that little one cared. Priscilla started laughing, and a broad smile wreathed Agatha's face too.

"Let me put both your minds at ease", John said. "I have no intention of seeing or communicating with that man ever again. I'll also say—and then I'm finished—that I'd rest easier if he felt the same way."

"What are you suggesting, John?" E. M. said, setting Priscilla on the floor. The child, who'd been enjoying the ride on her mother's knee, began to moan. Absentmindedly, John left the chair and lifted her over his head. He wanted desperately to relieve E. M.'s anxiety, but how could he do it without telling more lies?

"What would a literary detective make of Alembert?" John said to Agatha.

"My little Belgian", Agatha said, "would be very careful with that man; he would not expect a man like Alembert to make a mistake; he would learn everything he could about the man, and he would seek out the man's weakness, for every man has a weakness. Now that I've answered your question, I'll ask you one in return: What does Alembert want from you?"

329

That old chestnut, thought John. He ought to have a rote answer by now. "He believes I can help him achieve his ambition."

"And that ambition is?"

"Power. Does that surprise you?"

"Of course not," Agatha said, "but you have walked a circle around my question without answering it. You've said nothing about how a professor of philology can help a man like Alembert achieve power."

"I don't suppose I have", John said. Nor will I, he said to himself. Priscilla was running her hand through his hair. After that hike in the snow and Priscilla's ministrations, he probably looked like a scarecrow.

"Did your husband's Foreign Office contact say anything more about Alembert's lieutenants?" he said.

"No", she said. "He didn't tell Max anything else."

The tone of her voice suggested she was equivocating. Why? "Nothing about a woman named Agnes?" John said.

"Who is Agnes?" Agatha said.

"A former Alembert lieutenant who's gone AWOL, I think."

John hadn't seen Michael enter the room. He was an inquisitive twelve-year-old, growing like a weed.

"Hello, Father", the boy said.

"Hello, Michael. What have you been doing?"

"Reading." The boy was observing their guest.

"This is our son Michael", John said to Agatha.

"Glad to make your acquaintance, Michael."

"How do you do, ma'am?"

Agatha smiled at the boy.

"Have yourself some bread and jam", John said to him. Michael, even at twelve, understood that he was being invited to leave. He looked at his father as if he wanted to say something, but didn't; then he turned and left. John had been too abrupt, and he knew it. Michael was curious about this stranger, and maybe about their conversation, if he'd been listening. He was a smart boy.

"He knows more than you think", E. M. said.

"I daresay. I wish I'd never heard that man's name. I certainly didn't set out to make so powerful an enemy."

"So he is an enemy", Agatha said. "Do you know his weakness?"

"I don't believe he has a weakness."

"A man's weakness is often the mirror image of his strength. Does that make sense?"

"He's brilliant and unscrupulous. Please pardon me for saying this, but I don't know why I'm confiding in you. I barely know you", John said. He immediately regretted the words, but he was tired and frustrated, and he had the feeling he was being manipulated.

"I vouch for her", E. M. said. "I trust her."

"Thank you", Agatha said, smiling at E. M.

"That counts for something, of course", John said.

"It ought to count for more than something", E. M. said. "Have I questioned your trust in Gilbert, or the so-called colleagues you've been meeting on the Continent?"

He wondered how she so unerringly discovered his weak spot. "I don't guess you have."

"You know I haven't."

"I'm just trying to understand the purpose of this conversation. I don't mean to offend anyone." Despite these conciliatory words, he promised himself he wouldn't allow these two strong-willed women to back him into a corner.

"I'm here to look at pictures—and tell stories", Agatha said, sublimely. "Let me see them again." She rose from her chair and walked around the room, stopping at each picture. Once, she got down on her knees to inspect one more closely. The whistling at the window had abated. John was sorry for his suspicions and loss of composure. Ever since Alembert had invaded his office, for that was how he remembered it, he'd been sensitive to anything that reminded him of the man. He was frightened, and that embarrassed him.

Agatha returned to her chair. "Then there's Benedict Pfeiler", she said, pausing as if for effect. She looked at E. M. knowingly.

"I've never heard of him", John said.

"I would have been surprised if you had. Pfeiler wasn't a professional archaeologist, according to Max. He was an antiquarian who made himself into a serviceable excavator of ancient sites. There are still more of that sort in the field than there are professionals. They were having a drink in Baghdad when Pfeiler told Max a story."

"Let me guess", John said. "Our friend Alembert makes an appearance."

"Don't be gauche", E. M. said, giving John an admonitory look while combing Priscilla's hair. "I promise he won't interrupt again."

"Your husband is a delight in comparison with many I'm obligated to associate with. I would rather a man say what he means than disguise his thoughts. John's are honest questions. If he read my stories"—her eyes twinkled—"he would know that my little Belgian takes far more abuse from his skeptics. But back to the story. Max and Pfeiler were having cocktails when the tale was told about the evening that Charlemagne's Cross, the Mysterious Coin, the Peking Emerald, the Golden Scarab, Hannibal's Ring, and Bisco the Dummy disappeared."

"If I may," John said, more peevishly than he wished to sound, "items are misplaced, or lost, or stolen, or destroyed, but they don't disappear. Newton demonstrated that."

Agatha ignored him. "The count Jean-Pierre Lux de Bourbon was notorious for his high-stakes card games. His was the most expensive gaming room in Paris, if not all of France. As you can imagine, in such a setting the stakes were astronomical. Alembert was not a frequent participant, but as you might expect, when he played, he played to win. Are you interested in hearing the rest of the story, John?"

On the one hand, he ardently desired a change of subject. On the other hand, could he resist the opportunity to learn something more—something interesting, no doubt—about his mortal enemy? "I am interested", he said.

She did continue, but not immediately. She grew pensive, as if she was collecting her thoughts, even getting ready to write something down. She impressed him as needing a pen in her hand. "One night some years ago," she said, "Alembert made an appearance at the count's table. After an evening of play, Alembert suggested this same group return the following week with their most valued possessions, which would be displayed for the edification and entertainment of all present. He volunteered to bring an eleven-hundred-year-old relic, Charlemagne's Cross.

"I dislike writers who are obsessed with cartography and architecture, but it will be helpful in this case to understand the setting. Max questioned Pfeiler at some length on these points. The count's gaming room was on the fourth and top floor of his fashionable townhouse. The only other room on this floor was a vault that could be accessed by a single door. Otherwise, the entire floor was open, containing a large gaming table and an observers' table, often a station for the servants of the players. Behind the observers' table were two windows looking over the rue de Saint Louis. The only means of ingress and egress was a stair on the side of the room opposite the vault. On an imaginary north-south grid—I tell you this so you will be able to visualize the room—the vault was in the northeast corner, the windows on the north wall, the observers' table on the northwest side of the room, the players' table on the south side of the room, and the stairs on the west wall. Oh yes, there were narrow alleys separating the building from neighboring buildings to the east and west.

"Pfeiler told Max that to understand the events of that night, one must understand the psychology of the people. Everyone except Alembert was a compulsive gambler; Pfeiler admitted to being one himself. They returned the following week with their treasures. Alembert, as promised, brought Charlemagne's Cross, which had reputedly hung from the emperor's neck. Lady Clarissa Rothschild brought the Peking Emerald. Ignacio Ochoa de Castillo brought Hannibal's Royal Ring. Pfeiler brought the Golden Scarab of Alexandria, which he'd discovered in Egypt as a young man. The count displayed an ancient coin having no known origin, composed of a mysterious and unidentified alloy. In addition, a showman who'd taken Europe by storm had been invited, a ventriloquist named Hervé le Magnifique. You may have heard of him. He too brought his most valuable possession, Bisco the dummy, which had been insured, or so it was said, for a fortune."

John gently laid a blanket over Priscilla, who'd fallen asleep.

"After displaying, examining, and discussing the treasures— except for the dummy, which was to be displayed in a performance immediately before the game that evening—the participants agreed to put them in the count's vault while they played. Understand, there had been no suggestion of wagering any of these items.

"The vault, according to the count, was impregnable. It had open shelves on the north and east walls and one entrance on the south wall. A two-foot-square electrical enclosure for lights and alarms was attached to the south wall of the vault; otherwise, the room was empty except for a dozen or so closed containers of various sizes on the shelves. Upon entering, one could see everything in the vault. The walls, ceiling, and floor were reinforced with steel plates; the police later confirmed this. There were no windows. Four-inch ducts penetrating the floor circulated air. Are you beginning to understand why this story especially interested me?"

With each sentence the anticipated ending seemed more impossible. In spite of the fabulous wealth connected with these items, why would Alembert have bothered with them? Based on what John knew, that man's wealth was unlimited. He was convinced it was the coin that attracted him, a coin Alembert must have heard about, perhaps examined, and then coveted. When John heard that the alloy hadn't been identified, his heart had begun racing.

"Was anything more said to your husband about the count's coin?"

"No. I'm sorry. There was little said about any of these objects, except that they were fabulously valuable."

"Was the color of the coin mentioned—gold, silver?"

"Nothing", Agatha said. "Why does it interest you so? But where were we? Yes, this is important. In addition to the players—the count, Ignacio Ochoa de Castillo, Pfeiler, Alembert, Lady Rothschild, and Hervé, there were five others in attendance: Ochoa's male servant, Lady Rothschild's female servant, the count's male servant, a female associate of Alembert's, and Christopher. They occupied the observers' table while the principals played.

"Hervé had agreed to a performance with Bisco prior to the gaming. He removed the dummy from an ornate box, like a miniature casket, and ascended onto the observers' table. He insisted that the others assemble on the south side of the players' table. Pfeiler later learned that this was common practice with Hervé; he was obsessively possessive of the dummy, worried that a copycat would duplicate the design and art that made his act so successful. The performance was remarkable, as Pfeiler described it. The dexterity, not to say artistry, with which Hervé animated Bisco astonished the players. Pfeiler told Max he initially thought Hervé had gained admittance to the game 'cheaply' compared to the others; but after experiencing the performance and the craftsmanship that produced Bisco, he changed his mind.

"After the performance, Hervé returned the dummy to its box, which he and the count carried to the vault. They exited the safe, and then the others placed their treasures inside, one by one. All of them watched as the count went into the safe one last time, presumably to check on his own belongings, and then closed and locked the door.

"The game went on into the early hours of the morning. Wine, cocktails, and refreshments were continuously served. According to Pfeiler, Alembert, after a run of losing hands, was so bold as to suggest that he might wager the cross. Pfeiler, also losing, was tempted to wager the scarab, but nothing came of this.

"Except for the servants and Alembert's associates, no one else entered the room, and everyone was in plain sight at all times, with the exception of brief trips they all took to the water closet on the third floor. At no time was the vault opened again.

"I provide all of these details as Pfeiler provided them to Max and as Max then related them to me. Having an archaeologist's meticulous sense for minutiae is beneficial in more ways than one. Still, how I wish I could have heard the story from Pfeiler that night in Baghdad and questioned him myself. As morning approached, the game wound down, and the players prepared to depart. The count opened the vault. You may not be surprised—I am a less than compelling dramatist; I'm better with a pen at a desk—but I have no doubt the players were shocked to discover that all the treasures had vanished. Only the empty box that had contained the dummy remained. The police were immediately summoned, and a search was conducted, but without success. Interestingly, the count's other valuables—jewelry and money—that were stored on the shelves hadn't been disturbed; only his coin was missing. All the players and observers agreed to be searched. Lady Clarissa alone protested, but in the end, she acquiesced. The count removed his valuables and agreed to leave the vault open until the following day for the police forensic specialists.

"Pfeiler told Max that, to the best of his knowledge, none of the treasures were ever recovered."

"Alembert was surely behind it", John said.

"It's curious that you reached that conclusion. Pfeiler didn't suggest it to Max, nor Max to me when he related the story."

John said, "What do you think?"

"There's an epilogue", Agatha said. "The plot thickens, as those in my profession are wont to put it. Three of the six players committed suicide, and another died under mysterious circumstances. The first suicide was the count, who was suspected of orchestrating the theft.

"Hervé was said to be the most distraught. He told friends that while the others had lost treasures, he'd lost food and shelter, as without Bisco he was nothing. Bisco was a masterpiece of woodwork, one of a kind. The man who made him was dead. Hervé went from distress to despair to suicide. Ignacio Ochoa de Castillo had pledged the ring against astounding debts. He was ruined, and he jumped from a bridge into the Seine.

"Then there's Pfeiler. A month after telling Max the story, he was found murdered and naked at an excavation near the Syrian border. All these deaths have credible, if tragic, explanations, but—"

"But", John said, "where Alembert is concerned there are always alternate explanations. Do you have an alternate explanation?"

"No. Perhaps my novelist friend Mr. Carr could make something of it. He specializes in locked-room mysteries. The whole evening had the air of a performance, as Max heard Pfeiler tell it, though one often has that sense after the fact. One thing we can say: evil proceeded from this business—at least four deaths."

"Do you agree there is such a thing as evil?" he said to her.

"Of course. Evil is a conscious decision to do what one knows is wrong. That's where I begin every story I write. One cannot have a good mystery story unless someone makes a conscious decision to commit an evil act. An error in judgment or a mistake won't do."

E. M. said, "I believe evil is an act of selfishness, whether the matter is small or grave. Selfishness is what produces evil."

They were looking at John, expecting him to speak. He was still pondering the story. Was Alembert behind it, as he strongly suspected? Was it the coin he was after? As to the deaths, he had no difficulty reconciling four or four thousand deaths with the character of that man. As to the matter of evil, he had thought more about it than was healthy of late. Agatha and E. M. were both right, and eloquent in the brevity of their definitions. He said, "The relativism that the world is embracing won't permit naming evil. To the relativist, every destructive act has a motive, or perspective, that explains it. The act may be prohibited by law to maintain social order, but there's nothing that can be said to be evil in all times and places, just proscribed behavior. I wonder how your mystery stories will fare in the modern age. For my part, I believe evil is ambition that disregards the other's welfare. This ambition may be monetary, or political, or personal. Nonetheless, it seeks some end and disregards the harm it may do to another."

"Do you consider Alembert an evil man?" Agatha said.

"He would tell you that he's transcended good and evil."

"You are delightfully evasive." She stood up. "E. M., I've decided on the fox, the rabbit, and the bluebird, and have thereby violated my limit of two pictures. That will make an eclectic display in my sitting room. It's nearly five. My car will be here soon. Good-bye, E. M. It was a pleasure to meet you, John."

"The pleasure was mine", John said. "I'll fetch your wrap. I hope I wasn't too harsh."

Agatha ignored him and said, "I would like to meet that man."

"Why don't you leave that to your little Belgian", John said. "Better to give Alembert a wide berth."

"Nonsense. One collects ideas. Most of these ideas originate with people one meets, particularly those with murderous dispositions or inclinations."

The driver was waiting for her on the street. John carried the pictures out to the car and was glad to be in for the night. "I hope her train gets off on time", E. M. said when they were back in the house. "It was so good of her to come."

John gave E. M. an earnest look and said, "How much of my dealings with Alembert did you discuss with her?"

"No more than we agreed to reveal", E. M. said. "Agatha brought up his name when she talked about her husband's work in Iraq. I was so startled that before I caught myself I mentioned your association with him."

John said, "He's made me suspicious of people I don't know, until I'm sure they can be trusted."

"You can't suspect Agatha of being his agent."

"I don't suspect her, but trust is another matter."

"Well, I trust her", E. M. said. "You'll have to trust me."

"I haven't told you this, but Alembert came here last September."

"What? Here?"

"To my office at the college."

"Then he knows."

"He knows who I am. We feared as much. He doesn't know what I have—he only suspects."

"Why didn't you tell me?" Her features were so twisted that the pain might have been physical.

"I didn't want to worry you. There was nothing we could do."

"What did he say?"

"He said that he'd kill me if I didn't give it to him." John didn't say anything about Alembert's other threats.

"Did you tell the police?"

He told her about Gilbert's arrival at the office and his confrontation with Alembert, and Drake's subsequent visit.

"For a teacher, you collect quite a cast of characters. You could have told Agatha a story of your own. So did this Drake fellow say the Foreign Office is keeping an eye on us?"

"I don't think we can count on them when it comes to deterring Alembert."

"Has Alembert communicated with you since then?"

"Nary a word since I mailed the letter Gilbert suggested I write."

"He doesn't impress me as a man who would be put off by a letter", E. M. said. "He'll just change tactics."

"I've done what I can, short of giving him the book. Gilbert suggested we'd be in more danger if Alembert acquired it."

"He's probably right ... God help us. We can't change the past, no matter how much we wish we could, but if you hadn't found that book none of this would have happened."

"None of it", he said.

Priscilla had been awakened by their raised voices. John bent down and lifted her up. Then he sang a folderol from the book that he'd translated into English.

Priscilla laughed, but her mother's eyes were filled with tears.

April 10, 1932

Oxford

The hour was late, but not so late that patrons were pressing to finish their last pint. The table by the street window was occupied by three men. A white terrier lay at the feet of one of them. What was once a full plate of sardines now contained a solitary fish. A bowl of radishes sat in the center of the table. Two pints of ale and a pint of porter were partially consumed. There was the scent of tobacco in the place, but the room wasn't murky with smoke. Two of the men puffed at pipes. All of them wore jackets and ties. The dog was cleaning, or doctoring, one of his feet. The occupants of the table might have been any three Englishmen, telling stories, sharing woes, joking and needling. The window rattled, and sheets of water cascaded down the outer side. People came and went but were unnoticed by the three men at the window; the men were an island unto themselves. Their only commerce with the rest of the establishment was in the person of the pub keeper, who removed and replaced pints and sometimes stooped to scratch the dog.

"... a nice-enough chap, considering what he's been through", Jack said.

"How long has he been in England?" John said.

"One month. Hugo suggested I talk to him. He's working for a grocer under an assumed name."

"Melodrama?" John said. He crunched a radish and washed it down with ale.

"You can decide when you've heard his story", Jack retorted. "And haven't you been pawning yourself off to scholars and villains as John Hill? That's the pot calling."

Owen said, "I seem to recall a Mister Underhill cropping up in the story John has been relating to us, and I suspect that this character's name is the inspiration for our comrade's alias. If memory serves, Mister Underhill was also traveling under an alias, an irony that our friend could not pass up. His guilty smile confirms my suspicions. . . . John's predicament warrants a bit of intrigue. One doesn't discover prehistoric manuscripts every day."

"One doesn't experience what this lad has either", Jack countered.

"The suspense is palpable", John said, wryly. "We're an impatient lot."

"Why is this table so conspiratorial?" Owen said.

Jack ignored him. "The man's real name is Ulrich. He was raised in Berlin and studied psychology at the university. A promising future awaited him."

"As he's hiding in London, that promising future must have waned", Owen said. "Here, Mitchie."

"He joined the National Socialists while he was in school. He was attracted to their veneer of positivism, their approach to social organization and economic progress: growth, production, an orderly society, eugenics to improve man, the usual package of utopian pabulums. Owen, before you comment, remember that he's young, and he's not a philosopher, certainly not a moral philosopher."

Owen raised a nearly empty pint high over his head in the pub's universal signal for replenishment.

"On the way", a voice said, from the other side of the room.

"The man became a lieutenant in the movement and was assigned to one of its leaders, a brute by the name of Röhm. This promotion began his disillusionment. Over the next year, what he learned and experienced sickened him."

"It's common knowledge the Nazis are brutes", John said.

"It's not common knowledge", Jack said. "Many of our own countrymen adhere to that tired adage 'One can't make an omelet without breaking an egg.' It appeals to those who want change and care only about the ends, not the means."

"No good ends by bad means", John said, absentmindedly.

"You don't speak for the majority", Owen observed. "What was it that one of the Jacobins said? 'We despots—ah, no doubt we are, if despotism is to serve the triumph of freedom.' The Nazis have captured the popular imagination. They promise to rebuild Germany and restore its culture and pride." His ale arrived with a thud, and the empty pint vanished. The window rattled harder than it had all evening. John reached for another radish.

Jack went on. "A disillusioned disciple can be an impassioned adversary. Ulrich is such a man. I met with him at a tea shop near the grocer's. He was furtive and frightened, but he confided in me."

"What does he want?" Owen said.

"He wants someone to be his voice, someone the country will listen to."

"There are already voices in Britain opposing the Nazis", Owen said. "Men choose whom to believe, and their discernment—sadly—is often less than enlightened. Spellbinders, the Marats and Lenins and Hitlers of the world, are more attractive than honest plodders who don't promise bread and circuses. Planting the seed of authentic humanism deep within the soil of the heart is no easy thing."

"They don't know what Ulrich knows. We agreed to meet again next week. We know the Nazis are thugs, xenophobes, and nationalists. What isn't known is more chilling."

Mitchell had responded to a beckoning hand and trotted to a table near the bar that was occupied by a young couple. He was having his ears scratched and had gotten a sardine. If anyone was unreservedly at ease in the pub, it was the terrier. His perambulations were unaffected by the volume of conversations or the press of humanity. He expected the patrons to make way, and they usually did.

"It may be a moot point", John said. "What's to be done about it, except for keeping the Hun contained? England has no stomach for war, or even armament to prevent war. Memories are still fresh."

Jack relit his pipe. "Memories are short. Ulrich told me that the movement's manifesto is comically irrational. Facts are invented, and actual facts are corrupted. Its creed is a jumble of myth and passion. It echoes whatever the Führer believes and contends that whatever advances the party is good for Germany. The movement has produced an insular culture, if one can use that word to describe such a bestial cult. It's too late for Germany to turn back, according to this young man."

"How can people be so duped?" John said.

"Fear, pride, ignorance", Owen said. "There's nothing new under the sun."

"You've used up your quota of clichés", Jack said. "Ulrich told me the movement is steeped in thuggery, toadying, and a cult of adulation. If that isn't enough, the Nazis claim to be reforming Christianity, purging it of influences that have weakened and corrupted it."

John interrupted him. "There is no creed less compatible with true Christianity than that of Nazism."

345

"The grand lie is more effective than the little lie", Owen said. "Many accept the grand lie; too many reckon something that preposterous must be true."

Jack said, "Ulrich was adamant that the Nazis want to redefine Christianity as a social movement, absent the Jews, absent the historic Christ, absent the historic creed, with a gospel gutted of content. It won't dupe those who understand and practice the faith, but the Nazis hope to seduce the mass of cultural Christians. According to Ulrich, many have accepted this new definition of Christianity."

Owen said, "It seems to me that if there's a christ in the Nazi Christianity, he is an Austrian jingoist. Mitchie, quit pestering those people!" he said loudly. "You shameless beggar", he added sotto voce.

"The other troubling matter", Jack said, "is the perversion—not just the thuggery and brutality but sadism, masochism, sexual torture, and the rape of girls and boys."

"Eventually, someone will have to put a stop to it", Owen said.

"Ulrich said that Röhm is a sexual deviant. Another Nazi leader, Heines, is the worst sort of pervert. John, Ulrich said your old friend Krieger is one of the most ardent adherents of the movement."

John closed his eyes and tapped on the table. There was little color in his face.

Owen said, "The Nazis are pagans but not in the sense of the nature myths of the Greeks. They're cut from the same cloth as the worshippers of the death god Molech. This Aryan Molech may claim to be another christ, but that deity's anointed with the blood of tortured and murdered victims."

"An interesting observation", Jack said. "To borrow your cliché, 'there's nothing new under the sun.'"

"What opened Ulrich's eyes?" John said.

"I suppose good sense, reinforced when his half-brother was beaten for publicly opposing the Nazis. Ulrich had been too close to Röhm, and even the Führer, to leave the movement and remain in Germany. Men who defect from the movement don't live long."

"My friend Drake might benefit by meeting this man", John said.

"I've never heard you mention him", Jack said. "Who is he?"

"That's another story", John said. "What does Ulrich hope to accomplish?"

Jack said, "He wants to expose the lie that the National Socialists are inarticulate but well-meaning patriots."

"Be careful, Jack", John said. "I know something about getting involved in things one doesn't fully understand." John waved at the pub keeper.

"You have half a pint", Owen said, putting his hand on John's arm. "Mitchell!" he shouted again to the wandering dog. "Now that little beggar is nosing around old Mother Green. For shame."

The pub keeper himself came to the table with a box wrapped with bright green paper. He set the box on the table in front of Owen and winked.

"Happy birthday", Jack and John said.

Owen lifted the box and shook it. "It won't bite or scratch, will it?" Then he removed the paper. Inside the box was a red silk scarf.

"For festive occasions", Jack said.

Owen wrapped the scarf around his neck.

"I brought these neglected sweets in lieu of cake", John said.

"Those sweets look familiar. Have we seen them before?" Jack said. "I'm surprised your mouse hasn't discovered them."

"Socrates hasn't mastered the art of scaling shelves", John said. He removed the lid; not one had been eaten.

"I'm not inclined to pair sardines and chocolate. We've been over that before, if memory serves", Owen said.

Jack shook his head when John offered the sweets to him.

Owen said, "I have an idea." He began cutting the green wrapping paper into small squares with a tiny scissors he carried. "Where do things stand with the book?" he asked John.

"They stand still", John retorted. "I haven't heard from Alembert—that is, since I sent him the letter. Every time I set out to work on the book, I'm put off by the memory of that man's threats."

"Are you still intending to publish the story?" Jack said.

"Yes. I'll hold some things back, precisely the information Alembert most wants to obtain."

"Would he be able to use it?" Owen said.

John hesitated. How much more should he reveal to his friends? He didn't want to put them at risk. The box itself demonstrated skills and knowledge that were unknown to modern man: the alloy, and the inexplicable seal where the lid and box joined. "Alembert would be able to use the information, and abuse it. It must be protected. That's all I'm prepared to say."

"And the civilization that predates the story", Owen said. "It is Atlantis, isn't it, or the myth that's come down to us as Atlantis?"

"Yes, and it's much older than we ever imagined," John said, "even though Hermann and Erickson, the experts, scoffed at the idea."

Owen said, "What else is revealed about the civilization in the book? What morsels will you give your friends?"

"Genealogy, the names of kings and queens, descriptions of the island and its culture, where the people who lived on the island originated and how they arrived there."

"Someday, perhaps, we can hear the entire story", Jack said. "We shall not press you, John, but we can hope."

Never the whole story, John told himself; even he should never have seen portions of the manuscript. It was too late now to undo that, but he could see to it that no one else made the same mistake.

"Were they *modern* men?" Owen said. "Was that their undoing?"

John marveled at his friend's prescience. Only Owen would think to compare a thirty-thousand-year-old civilization with a modern one. John had learned that many of the Atlanteans, especially at the end, were strikingly modern, subjugating people instead of guiding them, hoarding wealth, seeking to prolong life. "They were modern", he said.

"Was it their undoing?" Owen said again.

"The evidence suggests it."

Jack said, "Could we find their ruins? We've discovered very ancient cities in the east."

"The event was so devastating that it's unlikely any trace of that civilization—building remnants, monuments—remains. Since the Atlanteans had commerce with the mainland, it's possible that relics from those encounters might have survived."

"The book survived", Owen said.

The book had survived—miraculously, it seemed to John, but he knew that it had been written subsequent to the island's destruction, though in that era. Alembert's goblet was surely a relic from the Atlantean culture. The cuneiform scroll that linked the survivors of the cataclysm and the civilizations of the mainland was created much later but still was one of the oldest artifacts ever discovered. And what about the count's coin that John suspected Alembert of coveting? Could that have been minted in the Atlantean era or by the derivative culture that produced the book?

As the window rattled so that it sounded as if a train were passing, Robert's assistant arrived at the table with two fresh pints. He shook his head at the racket but went about his business. Mitchell had returned and was nudging John, who thought about giving the dog a chocolate but decided against it. It seemed disrespectful to the student who'd given him the gift, not to mention that sardines and chocolate might not agree with terriers either. The patrons were getting livelier. The young couple that had hosted Mitchell was singing, and the adjacent table, three old men, had joined in.

"I'm going to help you with your orphaned sweets", Owen said to John, who noticed that his friend was meticulously wrapping each piece in one of the green paper squares he'd cut. "It's all in the presentation. Place these attractively packaged sweets on your office desk or in your sitting room—a nice glass bowl is required. The supply will be depleted in no time."

"An entrepreneur masquerading as a philosopher", Jack said.

"Can I interest you in one of these delicious morsels?" Owen said to Jack.

"You cannot. Begone, foul tempter."

Owen kept at his wrapping. If the appearance of the finished product wasn't up to his exacting standards, he started over. When he finished with a piece, it might have been packaged by an expert confectioner. He didn't look at John when he said, "Have you thought about a less passive response to Alembert's overtures?"

"Threats", John corrected him. "We are sticklers for precision here."

"Have you?" Owen said.

"What else can be done? I have no interest in returning to Paris. The police, if I approached them, would inform me that I'm lacking evidence; I am indeed. I'm not only David to his Goliath, I've come empty-handed—no sling or stone."

"If you gave him a portion of the book, no more than an excerpt, could he be placated?" Owen said.

"Can you placate a mad dog by throwing him a sliver of meat?" Jack said. "Once the brute discovers you have meat, there's no stopping him."

"The dog might be satiated if you throw him enough meat while retaining the choicest portion."

"Perhaps", John said.

"It depends on how certain Alembert is that John has what he wants", Jack said.

"He's convinced I have something of great value, and he's right", John said. "I've put up a bold front, but he knows that I know it's a show. He's deduced that this artifact is more than a goblet with a line of glyphs, or a ring, or a coin, but I don't think even Alembert imagines that an entire chronicle has been discovered intact. If he knew that, he'd raze half of England to acquire it."

Placing the last wrapped candy onto the table, Owen said, "Or he might try to influence you through your friends."

John knew Owen would not make that statement frivolously, or even speculatively.

"I met the man", Owen said.

"You fool!" John thundered, his splenetic outburst attracting attention from nearby patrons. Even Mitchell got to his feet and yelped.

"Reserve judgment, if you can, until you've learned what transpired", Owen said, calmly.

"That will take a Herculean effort", John said. "That villain is trying to enter by every window, chimney, and door in the house."

"Indeed," Owen said, "and the more your comrades understand the menace, the better to fend him off."

"Or worry me to distraction", John said. "Did he come to England again?"

"I traveled to Paris."

John slammed his fist on the table, causing Mitchell to yelp again.

"That's enough posturing", Jack said. "The deed is done. Let's hear the fellow out."

Owen placed the wrapped sweets on the lid of the box, now turned upside down. Then he dropped a red radish right in the middle, as a baker festoons the top of a cake. "I met Alembert in his Paris office. He invited me by letter."

John was smoking furiously.

"The man was charming and engaging, even witty. He'd pressed John for his own good, he said. Men like Erzo— you supposedly know the man—are too dangerous to cross. He was acting as something of a peacemaker."

"The peddler I told you about, the one on the trail", John said.

"Alembert referred to Erzo as the town pickpocket who bears watching. Thus, to hear him tell it, he keeps an eye on Erzo as a public service."

"Erzo is a villain and a murderer."

"You are making this chronicle more tedious than it need be", Jack said to John. "Sip your ale, smoke your pipe, and be silent until Owen's finished. There's a good fellow."

"There was no sign of Alembert's giant aide-de-camp. Alembert was attended by a young German—too young to be John's Krieger. Alembert was a gracious host. Never did I feel threatened or bullied. As I said, he claims to have pressed you so you wouldn't have to deal with men like Erzo on your own. He implied there are worse men who suspect you possess a treasure. He'd resorted to a theatrical heavy-handedness as a ploy to bring you to your senses."

"He is exceedingly clever", John said. "He would have prepared carefully for your visit, Owen."

Owen continued, "There was a large case behind Alembert's desk jammed with books. He claimed to be familiar with my work, and to esteem it."

"Did he bare his philosophical leanings?" John said. There had been no bookcase when he visited Paris—more stagecraft.

"He described himself as a humanist and a naturalist."

"Do you find that description credible?"

"It was consistent with the positions he took on the subjects we discussed", Owen said, guardedly.

"And those subjects were?"

"I can't remember everything—the evolution of human consciousness, phenomena and their significance. Did I mention his wine is very good?"

"We agree on that", John said. "And you believed what he told you?"

"I believed none of it, because I trust you, and I trust your judgment."

John put his nose into the pint of ale. Owen had deftly parried his thrust.

"Where was the matter left?" Jack said.

"He requested that I try to convince John he would be safer if the burden of this thing were shared."

The "burden of this thing" and an admonition not to bear the burden on his own; how familiar that sounded. It reminded him of that deadly object in the book ... the ring. "Was that all?" John asked.

"Certainly not. I've saved the best for last. It turns out, or so my host said, that this antiquity was secondary to the real reason he'd invited me. He overplayed his hand here, which proves he isn't intellectually invincible." Owen looked toward the window and said, "What a tempest."

"You're insufferable", Jack said. "What did the man say?"

"In recognition of his esteem for my work, he volunteered to establish an institute at the Sorbonne to advance my theories about human consciousness. There would be money and publicity. He dangled this lucre shamelessly."

Jack, reaching under the table for Mitchell's ears, said, "He pits ambition against friendship. In his universe, ambition always prevails."

John said, "For better or worse, you've met the man. What do you advise?"

"I recommend you stay out of his way", Owen said.

"It's too late for that", John said.

"Don't be hasty. I may have convinced him that I can be his Trojan horse, though I wasn't so enthusiastic as to make him suspicious. That could buy us—you—time."

"You will be a sacrificial lamb rather than a Trojan horse", John said. "I won't permit that."

"Nonsense. I'm of no use to him except for his interest in you."

John said, "You've put your foot in it, Owen. I have more to tell you. It's another incident that suggests mayhem follows in that man's wake." He related the story of the count's coin in as much detail as he could remember.

"What does that have to do with Owen?" Jack said.

John said, "If I'm correct, and Alembert's desire to acquire the coin motivated the thefts, then he's responsible for those deaths; and the moral of the story is that peripheral actors are in as much peril as the principal victim where Alembert is concerned."

Owen said, "The lady who related the story didn't offer her theory?"

"No."

"Too bad. I would have enjoyed hearing it. If it happened the way you describe it, the matter is a tour de force in logic", Owen said. "You were on the right track when you referred to Newton's Law. If we accept that the treasures went into the vault, and if we accept the competency of the police in the matter of steel cladding and the absence of hidden doors, then the objects either remained in the vault or exited via the vault door or the air ducts."

"Wouldn't the police have investigated the ducts?" Jack inquired.

"Why would the police have given the ducts much attention? None of the individuals going into the vault would have been able to dump things into them unnoticed by the others. How else could these things have exited the vault except on someone's person? On one of the people who went into the vault to leave his treasure there."

"But what about the dummy?" Jack said. "There is no way someone could have surreptitiously pocketed that."

Owen nodded enthusiastically. "Precisely. We must be suffering from a lack of information because there is no possible way for the items to have disappeared."

"I still think Alembert is to blame for the thefts and the deaths", John said.

"Logic doesn't demand the conclusion that Alembert is behind these thefts just because he's a scoundrel", Owen said. "The most likely culprit is the count. He was intimately familiar with the vault. He was the last one to exit. He committed suicide."

"Ostensibly", John said.

Owen did not reply; he was looking over John's shoulder with a changed expression. Something, or someone, had made a visible impression on him. The philosopher rose to his feet and said, "Hello, E. M."

John was taken aback. Hearing his wife's name within the confines of the Bird and Baby was an unprecedented experience. She didn't like the pub, or the people John associated with there. Jack was already fetching a chair from an adjacent table. She stood there in her jacket and rain hat. When Jack returned with the chair, the others moved their chairs to make space for her. Jack helped her be seated and then sat in his own chair to her left.

"Quite a cheery picture", E. M. said. "Owen, is the scarf a dramatic statement, or are you anticipating a frost?"

"As cheery as can be managed", Jack said. John knew him to be averse to women at these gatherings, at least to women with no literary or academic standing. Owen removed the scarf self-consciously.

"Thank you for the kind reception, Jack", she said.

They were off to a good start, John concluded.

"I couldn't help overhearing Owen's solution to Agatha's mystery."

She was there for a reason, and John wondered what it was. He knew better than to rush her, and he was prepared for anything.

"Hello, Mitchie", she said, lifting the dog onto her lap.

"We don't reserve a chair for Mitchell", Jack said.

"*We* might not, but *I* do. Mitchie, have you been consuming sardines and ale?"

Owen said, "Ale doesn't agree with him."

Sitting in E.M.'s lap apparently agreed with the dog. The assistant came to the table. E.M. told him she didn't want anything. Then she said to the three men, "I didn't come to torment you, in spite of what you may think. I came to ask Jack and Owen for something John would never ask for—their help."

"E.M.—"

"Be quiet, John. I have something to say to Owen and Jack. No doubt you know about the persecution we've been experiencing, and something of the reason for it. I fear it will soon reach a crescendo, a destructive conclusion, if something isn't done. You are John's best friends. He needs your help, your wisdom, your talents. He won't ask for it because he's afraid that your involvement will put you in danger—but I will. His survival, his family's survival, is at stake."

Her appeal was so emotionally charged that John thought she would dissolve into tears when she finished. He was surprised to see that her eyes were clear. In that moment, E.M. was less a wife and a mother than a warrior. The pints were empty, and the pipes were cold.

"We won't let you down, E.M.", Jack said. "We'll do what's necessary, and there won't be any stopping me."

"Owen's been to Paris", John said to E.M.

"What?" she said.

"He went to Paris to talk to Alembert", John said.

She turned to Owen. "You fool. I wouldn't have sent you into that snake pit, but what's done is done. What did you learn?"

"That he's formidable, as John suggests. Alembert thinks I might be useful. Rather, I think he thinks that I might be useful; who can say what that man thinks? His attention will be directed at me for a while. In that sense, my mission was a success."

Now E. M.'s eyes were moist. "I've underestimated your quality. I needn't have come here and embarrassed John."

Owen said, "You're always welcome, E. M. Any friend of Mitchell's is a friend of mine."

"I'll throw my hat into the ring with Owen", Jack said. "No sense protesting, John. Misdirection may be the best tactic. If that fails, remember that Marat had his Charlotte Corday, his bringer of doom. There may be another Corday prowling the streets of Paris. Men like Alembert, for all their power, must always be on their guard."

"I've sent a note to John's mysterious tradesman", E. M. said, "implying that you two will be brought into this business."

"Who is that blasted man?" Jack said. "Some kind of avenging angel, or harlequin?"

John told them about Drake's visit and their conversation.

E. M. said, "So far, John's told you enough so you can offer advice but not enough to put you at risk. I hope I've raised the stakes. John will have to tell you more if you're to help us. You will have to do better than talk and smoke. More than that is needed. Sometimes I wonder if you are as brilliant as you're made out to be."

"Henceforth," Owen said, lifting an empty pint, "we shall be Athos, Porthos, and Aramis, and E. M. shall be our d'Artagnan."

John shook his head. He wasn't cheered by Owen's words. "You may have met the man, but you can't comprehend what we're up against. Alembert makes Richelieu a feeble adversary by comparison." He bit into the last radish. Mitchell lifted his head and set it on the edge of the table. The window rattled, and water came down the pane in writhing sheets.

"One for all", Owen said.

"I'll have that pint", E. M. said.

"*Zut alors!*" Jack exclaimed.

May 1–2, 1932

Oxford

John closed the door to his office, sat in the familiar chair behind the familiar desk. His eyes were drawn to the crate on the top of the bookshelf on the right-hand wall. The crate was still where it had been for years. It protruded slightly from the shelf. It had weathered to a pale gray, as he'd never bothered to varnish it. Sometime that day, he would ascend the ladder, open the crate, and then the box inside the crate, to assure himself that the book and his translation were still secure. If it was an obsession, he reasoned it was justified by his adversary's machinations and threats.

Work from the previous evening littered the desk. Off to one side was a new glass bowl containing the sweets wrapped in green paper. He'd followed Owen's instructions and put them there in the hope that visitors would help themselves.

The apparent normalcy and silence notwithstanding, John sensed that something was different. He surveyed the office again. Clouds and on-and-off-again rain made the room darker than one would expect on a spring morning. The air was especially humid. Several books were on the floor. He saw the file he'd dropped on the rug the previous day. The room had needed painting for several years.

Where was Socrates?

Summer or winter, sunny or foul weather, the mouse always made an appearance. Sometimes Socrates nosed around his hole, sometimes he scampered around the room, but he could always be counted on to grace the office.

Though Socrates was accustomed to his tread, John wondered if he'd done something to frighten the creature. His eyes were acclimating to the dim light. He had yet to turn on the lamp and would not have needed it this time of day except for the gloomy weather.

He saw something out of the ordinary rather than something distinctly wrong. What was that object near the shelf? He turned on the lamp, got out of the chair, and approached it.

What it had been was a mouse. He bent down and lifted it a few inches from the floor. There was little of the animal that remained—just fur and tiny bones. Everything else seemed to have been sucked out of it.

He asked himself if this furry thing could have been Socrates. He tried to convince himself that another creature had gotten into the office or that this thing had been left in the room by another person, but the more he speculated the more he was convinced that this had been the little creature he called Socrates.

How long had it been dead, and what had killed it? He'd seen the creature, alive and hale enough, only yesterday, and in the late afternoon. What could have happened in those few hours to reduce the mouse to this desiccated object?

He sat down again. It was only a mouse, he told himself. They shared a space and accommodated each other, but it was a mouse. Mice died every day. They weren't known to be particularly long-lived, and who knew what other rooms the creature had wandered in and what poisons those rooms contained? He was apprehensive; more than that, he was troubled, as if he'd witnessed something of greater consequence than he understood.

What had the man who called himself Drake said that might explain this incident? He'd said many profound, if not distressing, things, but not about Socrates. What had he said that John ought to have remembered?

He found a paper bag in the desk and deposited the lifeless form inside it.

He was on the way to the rubbish can at the end of the hallway when the sifting of his memory produced a word, an unsettling word. John stood, staring at the bag. His conversation with Drake was coming back in bits and pieces. They'd talked about many things relating to Alembert—his ambitions, his interests, his talents. That word.

He retrieved his umbrella, locked the door, and left the building in a rush.

John hardly noticed the rain as he crossed the university grounds. Gray and dark clouds—low, tattered—were scudding from west to east. Every so often, the wind tugged at his umbrella. His grip was tight on the handle and the paper bag. His destination was the College of Natural Sciences.

He found Clyde Walters in his office. Walters was a tall man with long hair and a thick moustache; he was a pipe smoker like John and was equally at home in a lecture hall and the wilderness. The room was cluttered with everything from taxidermy to crystal goblets. With the press of all these objects, there was little room to maneuver. John removed a book from the visitor's chair but hesitated to recline.

"Sit down, John. I haven't seen you in ages. How is the family?" Walters said.

"They're well at the moment; thank you." John placed the paper bag on the desktop.

Clyde Walters frowned. "Is this a gift, or have you discovered something?"

John knew that Walters couldn't resist anything that suggested adventure or mystery. "As a matter of fact," he said, "the object inside this bag is a puzzle."

"Then let's see it", Walters said eagerly. He was one of those men who, when excited, revealed the boy he'd once been. He'd never gotten over exploring a field or a forest, and he'd found a compatible profession.

John reached inside, placed the dead mouse on the desk, and said, "A rodent, I think?"

Clyde Walters took a pencil and moved, prodded, and lifted the creature with this makeshift instrument. Then he put on his glasses, picked the mouse up by its stub of a tail and examined it, pulling and squeezing it, then putting his nose close to it. "You are correct in your taxonomic observation. It appears to be—to once have been—a rodent. Do you have any idea how long it's been dead?"

"Eighteen hours or less", John said.

"Are you sure?" he said as he drove the pencil into the inanimate creature.

John answered, "This mouse has had the run of my office. It was alive last evening."

"Less than eighteen hours", Walters said. "That's telling, along with the rest of the evidence."

"Can you guess what happened?"

"If we were in South America, I would be certain I knew how this mouse died. That we are in England complicates the matter."

"I barely recognize the creature as my mouse", John said. He realized that he'd been sitting on a leather pouch, removed it from his chair, and placed it on the corner of the desk.

"There it is. Thank you, John", Walters said. "I wondered what became of my Peruvian beetles. Now then, if

I'm correct, there's an arachnid loose in your office, probably a South American bird spider. That's a playful name for a lethal animal. They don't belong here, of course. Creatures like that make the crossing inside crates of bananas or citrus. They get loose after the ship docks and the crates are removed. Thankfully, that doesn't often happen with larger creatures—for instance, it doesn't often happen with elephants"—he was struggling to keep a straight face— "but insects, and especially arachnids, can be a nuisance."

John reflected on what Drake had told him. Two of Alembert's associates had been killed by spider toxin. "If a man were bitten by such a spider, what would be the symptoms?" he said.

"The spider uses neurotoxins and tissue-dissolving chemicals to liquefy its prey's internal organs. Then it consumes the liquefied juices while the victim is immobilized, and still alive. The bird spider, so named because its chief prey is birds, is an especially nasty creature. It hunts small rodents too. It's aggressive, and its toxin could be fatal to a full-grown man. If that creature is loose in your office, you would be wise to recruit reinforcements and bring heavy ammunition."

"Is there any other explanation?"

"If the mouse has been dead for as short a time as you suggest, then something has dissolved all of its organs. I didn't detect a scent of acid. Everything I've observed is characteristic of that eight-legged assassin."

Clyde Walters was an enthusiastic and even eccentric researcher, but no one mistook him for a sloppy scientist. It was unlikely he was mistaken. "Thank you, Walters", John said.

"Have you recently brought a box of produce into your office?"

"No."

"That's curious. The assassin that did this is too large to be concealed on one piece of fruit. And it isn't predisposed to traveling. Its modus operandi is to find a hiding place and wait for its prey. These spiders are marvelous creatures, John, if you don't mind menace."

John put Socrates' remains back inside the bag.

"John, did you hear what I said about getting help?" Walters said. He packed and lit his pipe. "These spiders aren't interested in humans as a rule, but I have heard stories of people who crossed their path coming to a bad end. Most of the time, it's a matter of someone putting his bare hands or feet somewhere they ought not to be."

Why not ask Walters for assistance? He was an experienced naturalist as well as a teacher; that's why he was so popular with students.

Walters stepped from behind his desk and came so close to John that he thought he was the creature being examined. "John, listen to me", he said. "Don't take this business lightly. I know how easily you're distracted. Even if I'm wrong, and I don't think I am, it would be wise to take every precaution—what say you?"

"I'll take precautions", John said, not knowing what he would do. "Is there anything else I should know?"

"The creature is nocturnal. If it's in your office, I'm not surprised you haven't seen it. It moves like lightning. And it's a prodigious leaper—remember that."

John decided against asking Walters for help. Walters was too observant, too perceptive, for John to allow him close to this business. John got up and put the book back on the chair. It could not be coincidence that Walters' diagnosis and Drake's suggestion that Foreign Office agents had died from spider toxin pointed to the same answer. Suddenly, he remembered that Greta had spoken about Alembert's interest in spiders. That was conclusive. John had already moved beyond the cause of Socrates' death to the matter of how to destroy this creature. Was it Alembert's plan to search his office under the auspices of exterminating the animal? That was a foolish idea, John told himself, as Alembert could get into the office any night he chose. No, this was intended to produce an altogether different effect. "Thanks for your help, Clyde", John said at the door.

Instead of returning to his office, John set off in the opposite direction. He needed time to ponder what Clyde Walters had told him and to decide what—if anything—could be done. He'd already concluded that whether Alembert's motive was inflicting terror or physical harm, the creature was in his office because someone had put it there. Fortunately for him, but not for the mouse, Socrates' demise had warned him of the danger.

He asked himself more than once what he knew about confronting a menace like this. Questions would invariably follow if he consulted professionals, questions he wasn't prepared to answer. Furthermore, he didn't want any information to get back to Alembert, for surely that man was behind it. The only way he could prevent it was to handle the matter himself, a thought that produced anxiety, bordering on panic.

By the time he reached the house, he'd made up his mind. There was no one home except for Michael, who was home from school early and in his room reading. John removed an iron poker from the fireplace. He found a large candle and a plate to place it on. Now it was a matter of acquiring one more "ingredient" and waiting.

He was sitting in the straight-backed chair in front of the window. He was in a state between consciousness and sleep when he heard a persistent knocking. Gradually, he realized that someone was at the door. He had thoughts of carrying the iron to the front room but rejected the impulse. When he opened the door, he saw a boy in a school uniform with a matching cap. The boy looked to be his son John's age, but something—he couldn't put his finger on it—wasn't right. Maybe it was the person's furtiveness, so uncharacteristic of youth. He wouldn't look John in the eye.

"The boys aren't in", he said.

"I came to see you." The visitor was already halfway inside when he said this.

The boy's voice possessed a youthful timbre, but his words seemed loaded with gravity. He made a careful examination of the front of the house and then let John lead him into the sitting room. He took a seat in the corner, where he couldn't be seen from the street or the front door.

"May I ask your name and your business?" John said, still standing.

"My name is Agnes CurLio", the boy said. "I doubt if that means anything to you. I'm an expert at pretending to be someone I'm not. If you don't mind, I won't remove the cap. I fancy myself a pretty good actress, but it took some doing to assume this role. You should have seen me six months ago."

"I've heard of you, but I never expected to meet you", John said. Then, he thought about his confrontation with Alembert and said, "You shouldn't be here."

"I've come because I learned you're in danger", she said. "You may already suspect it, even know it, but you can't imagine your peril if Adler Alembert considers you an adversary. What do you know about him?"

Should he sit? And confide in her? Was this really Agnes CurLio? It was now evident that she was a woman and not a boy, though the disguise was very good. She was small and thin, and her face, except for a crooked nose, was youthful or had been made to look so. Something told him that when she wanted to be a boy it would be difficult to penetrate the illusion unless one observed her at close quarters. That didn't prove this was Alembert's former lieutenant. This woman might be another agent, pretending to be Agnes who was pretending to be a boy. He couldn't dismiss this visit as coincidence after Socrates' destruction.

"I know something about Alembert, enough to make me wonder why I should confide in a stranger", John said.

"I don't blame you. To prove I'm genuine, I'm willing to answer your questions."

"Why should you want to help me?"

"I intend to prevent him from doing as much mischief—grave mischief—as I can. I may not be able to do much, and I may not be successful, but I have to try. Be as circumspect as you'd like, but tell me what you know about him."

John sat down in the straight-backed chair. This was something like a name in a novel acquiring form and flesh. So many mysteries. Why not test her? Why not ask a question that only a woman of Agnes CurLio's mettle—she had once enjoyed the trust and confidence of that dark mastermind—could answer?

"Are you a murderer?"

She didn't answer right away. She shrugged; her head dropped so that he could no longer see her eyes. When she spoke, he had to listen carefully to hear her. "I admit there was a time when I could have killed intellectuals or philosophers or philanthropists, or mothers and fathers, and slept like a baby."

Here was candor he hadn't expected. The iron was on the floor next to the chair. John said, "I will tell you what

I know about the man. I know that Alembert masquerades as a professor of history. I know that he commands a band of criminals."

She lifted her head and smiled, a boyish face but old eyes.

"I know that he's obsessed with a mythological civilization, that he is extremely wealthy, that his grandfather established the enterprise he now directs, that he has his fingers in many political movements, that he has a brother with whom he's at odds, and that he's an ardent naturalist."

"Very good. Few outside, and even inside, his organization know so much. No wonder you're besieged."

"I didn't say I was besieged", John said.

"I said it. Would you like me to supplement your information and correct misapprehensions?" Agnes asked.

"By all means", John said warily. She was a fascinating person, but hadn't she admitted, insouciantly at that, to being a murderer? The more they spoke, the more impressed he was with her disguise and her boldness in coming there. What she didn't know was that he had suggested to Alembert that they had already spoken.

Outside, rain was falling, and there was intermittent thunder, rumbles rather than peals. He already knew that this woman was used to inhabiting the shadows, and with no lights illuminating the room she was as much shadow as person.

"May I bring you a cup of tea? Bread and jam?"

"No, thank you. There are things I want you to know. It is essential that you know everything; who can tell when this or that fact might be helpful? Alembert's father was a curate. I heard that this man came to England to distance himself from his own father, Alembert's grandfather, and that he changed his first name to Gregory. How our adversary proceeded from Gregory Alembert is a mystery. Gregory tried to isolate the boy from his grandfather, but to no avail. If avarice and ambition skipped a generation, it returned with a vengeance in Adler Alembert. Did you know that his birth name was John Evangelist? I've surprised you, haven't I?"

"He told me his father named him Adler—"

"Lies and more lies. Adler was the name his grandfather gave him. He cast off his Christian name like a threadbare scarf. The more he gravitated to his grandfather, the more his parents tried to dissuade him. That was unfortunate. Adler's mother was eliminated. There was no subtlety in the act, no pretense that it was accidental. His father was allowed to live, but with the realization that the son had embraced his grandfather's sinister ways and that his wife had been killed trying to prevent it. Gregory Alembert died a broken man. I have no reason to believe that the boy, Adler, ever looked back.

"His grandfather established the backbone of the organization Alembert now rules. It is based on acquiring power by fostering fealty, using the lures of money and ambition, and by intimidation when necessary—blackmail or threats of violence. Adler Alembert overlaid this organization with his own creative genius. One could liken it to inheriting an already efficient coach service and then improving it by inventing trains."

Nothing in the mosaic this woman constructed was inconsistent with the picture of Alembert John had formed.

"As for the 'band of criminals' he commands," she said, "there are thousands of men and woman in his direct and indirect employ. He is adept at using a man's beliefs and sympathies; there are fascists, communists, frustrated empire builders, occultists, even Thule Society adherents, scattered about his organization."

John said, "Alembert mentioned the Thule Society in one of our conversations."

She said, "They believe in the existence of an ancient civilization—Atlantis, or something like it. Alembert didn't think much of the Thules he'd met, but he was intrigued by the idea."

"Did he ever tell you why?"

"No", she said. Then she looked at John queerly and said, "Did he tell you?"

When John didn't answer, she said, "His business includes slavery, drugs, assassination, prostitution, and wholesale slaughter. He is a czar, as Peter and Catherine were before him, or an emperor like Bonaparte, but one whose realm has no fixed borders. He has servants in government. There are three heads of state that are in thrall to him."

"Hitler?" John said.

"I don't think so, but Alembert has people close to Hitler. Alembert is a genius. That is an overused word, but not this time; no, not this time. False modesty isn't a weakness of mine. Few are my intellectual equal, but I'm a schoolgirl to his professor. Most think he possesses an intuitive gift. I came to realize that it's actually an analytical process that can't be grasped by other men. He reduces everything he sees and hears to symbols and then deciphers them, as a mathematician solves a string of equations. I don't exaggerate. If you manage to best him at something, it's only because he has underestimated you and hasn't applied his intellect and talents to their fullest degrees."

John said, "I met a woman who claims that every man has a weakness."

"Perhaps. Alembert cannot fathom goodness. He cannot fathom the weapons of goodness, if that makes any sense. They can't be reduced to variables and symbolic logic, so he dismisses them. There is nothing so banal as a self-assurance that admits no intrusion on its certainty. If Adler has a weakness, it's that. But who can say how that can be exploited?

"I felt compelled to come. I would have come sooner, but there were many impediments. This latest transformation I've undergone was ... tedious. It taxed my stamina, my will, my faith." Tears rolled down her cheeks, and she shook with anguish, though she tried to conceal it. When she'd composed herself, she said, "I don't want sympathy. I don't deserve it."

"You're safe here." Wasn't it odd that he'd spoken these words to an admitted murderer? And as soon as he said it, he realized it was at odds with his reference to Agnes in his meeting with Alembert.

"There's no safe haven for me. I'm a rabbit to his wolf, and there are no holes that will keep that wolf away. He has an uncanny ability to zero in on what he wants or needs, and to get it. Alembert possesses a da Vinci that rivals the *Mona Lisa*. He possesses Caesar's ceremonial scepter as dictator of Rome, Charlemagne's Cross, a ruby given by Marc Antony to Cleopatra, and three books rescued from the Alexandrian fire, including an unknown work by Plato. One could establish a world-class museum with those items alone."

"He showed me an artifact from Atlantis", John said.

She wiped her eyes and gave him a strange look.

"How did you learn so much about him?" John said.

"I'm his weakness, or was once. I would never have risen to such heights in his organization if we hadn't known each other as children. He made allowances for me he'd never make for anyone else. I'm not suggesting I was a witless dupe. I have intelligence, and I was ambitious. For years I did Alembert's bidding wholeheartedly. I murdered for him.

"I suspect he was fascinated by my bloodlines. For all his grandfather's power and wealth, Gorgo Alembert had been born a peasant. Adler resented it. My family name would admit me to Buckingham Palace, day or night; it used to, at least."

John could believe it. Perhaps this woman was not Alembert's intellectual equal, but she profoundly impressed him. She would be a formidable foe, even for Alembert.

"You were stationed in Argentina, weren't you?" John said.

"Alembert acquired an abandoned monastery there and made it his American headquarters. He put me in command. It was a successful operation. We continued to call it the Monastery; it was wickedly ironic, or so we thought. Business was good. Enemies were eliminated. Then one night I found a secret room, and in a niche in that room, a book. I've never been the same. I left him. I've been on the move ever since.

"I was a materialist to the core. Human lives were ledger entries, along with gold and grain. When I left Alembert, that changed. It changed sooner than that, before I finished the book. I guess you could say that words transformed me."

Hadn't words changed him too? "And now?" he said.

Another rumble and a splash of rain against the window. In the corner of the room, she looked like a boy again, but a tired boy. She was hunched over. Her hands were balled together. She displayed what could be described as a feral wariness. Here was someone, he concluded, in more peril than he. The two of them shared a doom that proceeded from Alembert's ambition.

"Do you know", she said, "that he will travel across the world to see a butterfly, and woe to the person who would do it a speck of harm, but without a second thought he will issue an order to kill hundreds of people?"

"Do you know what happened to Christopher?" he said.

"What have you been told?" She didn't try to disguise that she knew something.

John remembered Alembert's consternation when he had referred to Christopher and Agnes. "Alembert came here last September. I could tell he was worried, or angry, about Christopher—and about you. It grieves me to tell you that I suggested we had already spoken. It was an imprudent ruse. Your visit has put you in more danger than you imagined."

Agnes ignored this last comment and said, "Christopher was a valuable servant. He is dead. I killed him."

"After you left the Monastery?"

"It couldn't be helped. Alembert's brother is too head-strong for his own good. Gregory was punished for destroying his brother's precious butterflies. Suffice it to say that Alembert's punishments can be especially agonizing. I had to rescue Gregory. Christopher was an unintended casualty of that mission. He would have killed us, or worse."

"I see."

"I wonder if you do. When I served Alembert, I killed many good men without remorse. Christopher wasn't a good man—far from it—but killing him was excruciating."

"There is the taking of life with diminished culpability", John said.

"Perhaps. I'm not a philosopher or a theologian. Gregory is as safe as could be managed. As for me, that's another matter. Hordes of Alembert's faithful are searching for Agnes CurLio. I would never have come here if I didn't think it essential. I had warn you, do my part as I tried to do my part with Gregory.

"Of course, I'm curious. What do you have or know that Alembert wants so badly? Once, I would have probed, prodded, and coerced. But the days when those things consumed me are done. What you have that he wants is not my reason for being here. I have no hope of thwarting him, but perhaps by warning you, I can achieve some good before he destroys me. One could liken it to battling the devil. The best one can do is save a soul from his clutches."

"It's an excellent disguise", John said. "If you're careful—"

"There is no disguise that can deceive him, no place on earth that is beyond his reach. Survival is a matter of constantly moving and newer illusions. He is remorseless in his pursuit of enemies. And you have told me that he now connects you and his Agnes."

"Is there anything I can do?"

"Finding a kindred spirit makes me happy. I've learned to be hopeful. I may not have saved you, but perhaps I have helped. At least, you are better prepared; that's something. I ought to go."

"There's something else I'd like to ask", John said.

"I ought to go", she repeated, standing up. "I've stayed too long. It isn't safe ... for you."

John stood too. "There was an incident at the home of a man by the name of Jean-Pierre Lux de Bourbon involving the disappearance of treasures. Were you there?"

She'd taken two steps toward the door. "Yes."

"Do you know what happened?"

She smiled—the first time he had seen her smile—and it changed her appearance. Then, she led him out of the room and toward the front door. With her hand on the latch, she said, "I'll answer your question with three questions. I'll tell you more when—if—I return. You are better informed than I could have imagined."

There was a persistent rumble of thunder. She waited until it passed. She looked so vulnerable, but he knew better. With the exception of Alembert, she was probably the most dangerous person he'd ever met.

"What did all the treasures except one have in common? What object was materially different from the rest? Were there any other doors in the room?" She extended a hand, and he took it.

"Be on guard", he said.

She smiled at him. "As for me, I'm thankful the field is won—finally." Then she slipped out the door and pushed it closed behind her.

He had been with Agnes CurLio for less than an hour, but her face and voice were etched in his memory. The fact that she was still alive heartened him. He wondered what she could have meant by those parting words. They sounded familiar. He might have heard them long ago, in a different context. He wracked his brain, but nothing came of it. With the peril that dogged her, the field was hardly won. Alembert's minions were on her trail. She looked harassed and worn out with worry and fatigue. As lucid as she'd seemed, was she delusional?

And what of the questions she'd posed about the stolen treasures? Could anything be gleaned from them? He was obsessed with learning everything he could about Alembert. Perhaps some speck of information could be put to good use. The objects were all antiquities except the dummy, and the dummy was certainly different from the other objects; but John could not deduce anything from these clues. The police had confirmed that there were no other doors, if Agatha's telling of the story was accurate. But Agnes had been present, and she posed the questions as if she knew the fate of those objects.

What time was it? He must get back to the reason he'd come home and to what he intended to do. So unnerved was he that the sound of the front door startled him. "You're home early", said E. M., catching a glimpse of him from the hall, where she was unbuttoning her blue raincoat. Priscilla, in her pink rain jacket and cap, was standing next to her mother. "Are you well?"

"I'm well at the moment, thank you", he said, mechanically.

"I didn't expect you. I thought you had work to do."

John waited until Priscilla skipped down the hall before saying, "I went to see Clyde Walters. It didn't make sense to go back to the office."

"Isn't he the entomologist? Was it a social call?"

"Why are you interrogating me, E. M.?" he whispered.

"It's nothing of the sort", she said, entering the room. "When you come home in the middle of the day, there must be something brewing. I'd like to know about it."

Had she seen the iron on the floor? he wondered. And he'd left the candle on the plate in plain view.

"It's nothing."

"It's something. Are you going anywhere tonight?"

Was the woman clairvoyant? Perhaps Walters had called her, or perhaps she'd seen Agnes leaving the house.

"I have to return to the office."

"Does this have anything to do with Alembert?"

"Of course not—just work."

"I don't believe you. Something is troubling you."

"If there is, there's nothing you can do about it." He sounded harsh and abrupt, and he regretted it.

"You're impossible, John!" she said, and stormed out of the room.

He knew better than to try to deceive E. M. Hadn't he been more candid with Agnes, a person he barely knew? That was different, he told himself. E. M. would never allow him to leave the house if she suspected what he suspected.

377

And what if Walters was wrong? Didn't entomologists see spiders in every corner? He still hoped that Socrates had eaten something he shouldn't have and perished on account of it. But that didn't explain the thing the mouse had become in less than a day.

She barely said a word to him at supper. All the children were there. Priscilla had more to say with each passing week. The boys—except for Michael, who was quieter than usual—regaled them with their day's escapades. It might have been an ordinary day and an ordinary family.

An hour before sunset, John set off.

E. M. stood between him and the door. She didn't attempt to restrain him, and she didn't ask what he carried in the small wicker basket. She said, "Please be careful, John." She put her arms around him and held him urgently. "You're a special man," she said, "even if you are a liar."

"I'm a reluctant liar but a willing fool", he said, kissing her. He pushed the door open and started purposefully down the road. A light rain was still falling, which allowed him to conceal the iron inside his largest umbrella. He imagined that he made a strange sight, walking in the rain with a closed umbrella. He was frightened, and sorry that he'd left E. M. in a state of worry. By the time he reached the shop on the outskirts of campus, he was wet and his hand was stiff from gripping the umbrella handle so tightly.

He found what he was after. The proprietor even had a cloth John could use to cover the cage. He reckoned he had everything he needed, at least everything he could think to bring with him. His hands were full as he departed from the shop.

How strange it seemed to return to a place he knew so well, a place so comfortable and congenial to his needs, and feeling such dread. The building was empty, and his office was dark when he entered it. The crate on the top shelf was almost invisible. He illuminated the lamp on his desk. Everything in the room appeared to be in order. He put the umbrella, the basket, and the covered cage on the desk.

In spite of the need to focus on matters at hand and his potential peril, he couldn't get Agnes' questions out of his mind.

What did all the treasures except one have in common?

What object was materially different from the rest?

Were there any other doors in the room?

What did she know? He wanted to see her again, but she hadn't revealed where she lived or the name she was using.

He told himself that he must not be distracted. He felt his pulse quicken, felt a rush of energy. He had to focus on what Clyde Walters told him. If he couldn't tell E. M. the truth, he owed her his attention to the business at hand.

He opened the basket, removed the plate and candle, lit the candle, and placed the plate beneath it. Then he turned off the lamp. The candle produced a hazy yellow light, a subdued glow somewhere between an unlit room and the brighter lamp light. He removed the iron from inside the umbrella and placed it on the desk. In retrospect, it was a clumsy weapon, but it was the only thing he could think of, and he hardly had an arsenal from which to choose. He consoled himself with the thought that if it struck true, it would do damage. When he removed the cloth, the parakeet hopped from the floor of the cage to a hanging perch. He put the cage on the floor between his desk and the door. All was ready, he told himself. All he could do he had done.

He sat behind the desk and resolved to be as still as possible for as long as possible, or as needed. From where he sat, he could see the cage. He still expected to see Socrates make an appearance. The mouse had contributed to the charm this room had for John.

His heart continued to beat harder and faster than normal, no matter how he tried to compose himself. Soon, he could barely see the margins of the room. The sight of the door slowly opening only exacerbated these palpitations. He reached for the iron. Why hadn't he locked it? Someone entered the room, a slight figure, tentative, moving slowly. For a moment, he thought it was Agnes, but it was Michael. His hair was plastered to his head, and he was dripping. He'd worn no cap and had no umbrella.

The boy saw his father and stopped. He closed the door and took several tentative steps toward the desk.

"What are you doing here?" John whispered.

Michael came closer. He glanced at the cage but didn't say anything.

"I asked you what you are doing here."

Michael's arms hung at his sides. He didn't answer.

"Go home—immediately."

The boy still didn't answer. He wiped water from his face.

"Michael, obey me. Leave now."

"No, Father." A reply both timid and firm.

"What did you say?"

"No, Father. I won't go home", he said, with more vigor.

John stood. He was angry and, if he admitted it to himself, fearful.

"I won't go home, Father. I'm staying here—with you."

"Michael—"

"It's no use, Father. I'm staying."

"Did your mother send you?"

"No. I heard your conversations with the woman and with Mother."

Hadn't this been predictable? A boy inside a quiet house, with an open door, and possessing the inquisitiveness of youth? John pondered what more could be said or done. There was nothing else to do but go home. Shouldn't he—couldn't he—wait another day?

"I won't let them hurt you", Michael said.

"Sit down."

Michael sat across from his father. John noticed how the boy had grown. How had he missed it? Even in that feeble light, he could see the determination in his son's features. John put his head in his hands. The danger he and his family were in was his fault. He'd been warned, and now it was coming to pass. Gilbert couldn't prevent it, or E.M., or Jack and Owen, or Drake, or Agnes.

"There's something in this room", John whispered. "It killed a mouse last night. The bird will attract it. That's why I brought this iron. You will leave this room and go home, or else I will remove you."

Michael got up from his chair, walked to the bookshelf, and returned with an ornamental pewter cup that John had received as an award.

"Michael", John whispered, imploringly. The boy sat in the visitor's chair and put the cup in his lap, but he didn't release the handle. He was soaking wet and must be cold. If Michael had not obeyed his father, he had been listening to him. Often, he turned his head one way or the other to scan the room. And his eyes were as wide as saucers. In spite of himself, John was proud of his son.

The bird rustled in its cage.

"Father." So faint John almost missed it.

Michael wasn't looking at John, or the bird. His eyes were now fixed on the bookshelf. The boy's left hand came up slowly, index finger pointing at John's crate on the top shelf.

Crawling down was a shadowy shape. John figured it was six inches from end to end, brown or black, and hairy. It reminded him of the prehistoric creatures in natural history books. It moved slowly, but inexorably, toward the floor. Michael's index finger remained suspended while his other hand gripped the handle of the cup. John's own hand crept toward the iron.

When the creature reached the floor, it recoiled upon itself like a spring. Then it leaped with remarkable precision toward the cage, a distance of several feet. John couldn't help exhaling an audible gasp. The spider landed on the side of the cage and inserted one of its hairy members inside. The bird frantically flapped its wings and moved as far away from the spider's leg as it could.

The creature was intent on catching the bird, though John thought it was doubtful that it could reach the bird from outside the cage. The spider had been instinctively drawn to the bird. First one member, then another, then another, went into the cage. The spider's body rocked back and forth like a pendulum as these members groped for the bird. The bird darted frenetically from side to side. John rose slowly from his chair, iron in hand. He made toward the creature as stealthily as possible. The spider seemed oblivious to his approach. For an instant, it managed to grasp the parakeet's leg. There was a flurry of activity before the bird escaped.

Now John was very close. He raised the iron ... and struck. The spider was fast, and the blow missed its mark. It had scuttled some feet away into a shadowy corner of the room. Suddenly, it was dislodged by a moving object that nearly struck John's head. Spider and cup came to rest against the wall.

The spider was a tangle of legs. It had been stunned but not mortally wounded. It stretched out one member and then another; then it uprighted itself.

John took three steps and speared it.

The creature responded like it had been electrified. Its legs turned in toward its abdomen.

"Father", Michael said. He was pointing again.

John followed the arc of the boy's finger to another spider. This one had emerged from a stack of books on a different shelf.

The appearance of this second assassin was even more chilling than that of the first. John shuddered and reminded himself that these creatures were uninterested in him and his son as prey, that they were driven by instinct rather than will, and that any apparent malevolence derived from the person who had brought them here.

"Be still", John said. But Michael retrieved the cup and unleashed it again. His success with the first spider had emboldened him.

There was a loud bang as the cup struck the wooden case. It was a direct hit. This time the creature was more than stunned. At least two of its members were crushed by the projectile.

After John finished the creature off, they both sat down.

"I think we should stay", Michael said, as if he could read his father's mind. John had been debating with himself the choice between getting Michael away from this place and making sure that no more spiders inhabited the room.

What would E. M. say when she learned the truth? The thought caused John as much anxiety as anything he'd experienced that night. He could still drag Michael out of the office, but the boy had already dispatched two spiders. What a courageous son he and E. M. were raising.

The bird settled down, though its nervous fluttering continued. The boy put his hand into the glass bowl and grabbed a handful of sweets. Owen's packaging had finally attracted someone. Maybe Michael thought this was unseemly for a boy on a man's mission; he dropped them back into the bowl and settled into the chair, cup at the ready.

Little of the candle remained when John started. He must have fallen asleep. In his mad-cap dream, he'd been lecturing boys on butterflies and mad dogs. Michael was asleep too. The rain had stopped.

John, still half-conscious, thought he saw movement out of the corner of his eye. Then he saw it—down from the bookcase came still another spider. The thing may not have possessed intelligence, but John was convinced it had used a kind of animal sense to try to wait them out. It crept along the floor next to the bookshelf rather than leaping or darting toward the cage. It was even larger than the other two. The bird was still, asleep or something like it. John couldn't help thinking that the spider had taken sleeping prey unawares many times before.

John hadn't noticed Michael get up, so quiet were the boy's movements. The spider jumped to the side of the cage.

John knew it was too late to stop his son. Why had he allowed him to stay? Of all the idiotic things he'd done, this was the most egregious. Michael lunged forward and threw the cup, but he slipped in a puddle of rainwater and fell face down on the floor. The cup missed the spider and skidded past the cage.

John knew it was irrational, but he couldn't keep from imagining the spider making for his incapacitated son. He raced ahead and kicked at the creature, extending his leg as far as possible. He heard a pop in his knee and felt a stab of pain, but he stayed on his feet. He didn't connect with the spider but managed to make it scuttle away. He stabbed at it with the iron and missed. John wasn't frightened anymore; he was enraged. The spider darted for Socrates' hole in the wall, but as it tried to get inside, Michael—who had gotten back on his feet—dropped a book in front of the opening, preventing the spider from escaping.

John brought the iron down on the creature broadside. Though grievously wounded, it tried to crawl. Again the iron descended. The spider dodged but could only lurch to one side because of its damaged members. Back toward the shelf it crept.

The next blow killed it.

Holding Michael's hand, John hobbled to the desk. His son helped him sit. The poker clanged loudly as John dropped it on the desk. There was barely an inch of candle remaining, and the light was already flickering.

Were there more spiders in the office? There in the darkness, John pondered the fact that matters would never be the same between him and his son. John would still be Michael's father, but from now on they would also be comrades.

Sunrise found man and boy sleeping at the desk. When he opened his eyes, John saw the three spiders, now shrunken, like balloons that had lost most of their air. Standing, he tested his knee and found that it was no worse, and maybe improved. Gently, he shook his son's shoulder and said, "Let's clean up this mess."

"May I keep the spiders, Father?" Michael said, rubbing his eyes.

John thought about his imminent meeting with E. M., cringed, and said, "I think we'll spare your mother that, at least."

May 5, 1932

Oxford

She came into the sitting room and placed the newspaper in his lap. Then she walked to the sofa and sat down.

"You haven't seen the *Times*", she said.

The children were in bed. He'd opened the window, as it was a spectacular night. A full moon sought definition as the sky darkened. Only the persistent memory of the menace that had inhabited his office marred his tranquility.

Two nights ago, he'd had a dream that he fell asleep in his office and that when he woke, there were spiders everywhere. One was crawling up his arm; it had a human face: Erzo's. The door of the room had vanished; the window too. There was no way out. He reminded himself that he rarely dreamed about the trenches anymore. If he lived long enough—a problematical matter in and of itself—this new dream might also recede.

He brought the paper close to his eyes. There was still enough light from the window—barely enough—to read.

"I'm sorry", she said.

Earl of Leicester's Granddaughter Murdered

A body discovered in an flat in Soho has been identified as Miss Agnes CurLio, granddaughter of the Earl of Leicester. Scotland Yard has revealed that Miss CurLio, after death by cardiac arrest, was mutilated. Her body was found by police following receipt of an anonymous telephone call.

Doctors are uncertain as to the cause of the heart attack. Dr. Peter Henry Cooper, chief medical examiner, stated that if not for the subsequent mutilation, Miss CurLio's death might have been attributed to natural causes. Authorities have not ruled out the use of poison.

According to family members, Miss CurLio had lived abroad for several decades and rarely communicated with them. They were surprised to learn she had returned to Britain.

Neighbors in the building were under the impression that a young actor occupied the flat. They had thought Miss CurLio was a boy employed in the theater district.

One resident stated that the incident has frightened everyone in the neighborhood. "It's a bad business", the man told the *Times*. Scotland Yard has not released any information as to motive or suspects. Police are said to be investigating Miss CurLio's connections to the theater. An anonymous source at Scotland Yard suggested that considering the brutality of the crime, a madman was likely responsible.

Private funeral services are being arranged by the family. They had no further comments for the press.

John dropped the paper on the floor.

"I'm sorry", she said again.

"Agnes was a courageous woman."

"It doomed her."

John said, "You heard the story she told me. Would it have been better to remain Alembert's lieutenant? She would be rich and powerful—and alive—if she had, but at what cost?"

"I can't answer that question", E. M. said. "I'm too involved. I can't feel anything anymore. She was in this room four days ago. Do you know what that means?"

"They knew who she was."

"They knew who she was when she entered our home. They know she spoke to you. They know she revealed things they don't want anyone to know."

"That's right", he said. And I'm partly to blame, he reminded himself. "Agnes had been wise enough to realize she couldn't defeat Alembert. Her goal had been to interfere with his schemes and to do as much good as she was able to do."

John still wore his jacket, though his tie was askew. E. M. wore a white nightgown.

"He's an animal. How can someone commit such horrors?" she said.

"It's horror to us, but I wonder if there isn't a message in it."

"Don't be obtuse", E. M. snapped. "Say what you mean."

"The historic penalty for treason often involved mutilation of the body. He does everything for a reason. Even if no one else comprehends, he's compelled to be true to his genius."

"You call that genius? Don't you dare suggest it, with that poor girl cut to pieces."

"I didn't mean it that way."

"It's nothing but barbarism", she said.

"Barbarism with intent. I don't know why—yet—but it's important to glimpse his mind and motives. That's our only hope."

"Only hope for what?"

"Survival", he said. "We can't allow him to make us slaves to fear, like puppets on a string."

She was on the verge of saying something but didn't. Instead, she stared at the newspaper at John's feet and shook her head.

John said, "Do you remember what Agatha said about a man's strength also being his weakness?"

E. M. stopped shaking her head but didn't answer.

"Alembert's strength is his genius. Think about the crimes he's committed, the few we know something about: the stage-craft of Sir Richard's disappearance and probable murder, the affair with the treasures, and now this." John hadn't revealed to E. M. his war with the spiders, but that fit too. "If Alembert was behind these crimes, and I'm convinced he was, it would have been far easier to hire professional assassins or thieves. Instead, he concocts these elaborate schemes. Why? Because his genius demands it; he can't help himself."

"How can that matter to us? Sir Richard is dead, and four of the owners of those treasures are dead, and Agnes."

"If I could answer that question, we'd do more than wait for his next move. Somehow—I can't see how—it makes him vulnerable."

"I'm tired of dancing to every tune that man pipes", E. M. said. "We dare not withhold what he desires, but we dare not give it to him either."

"We can't hide from him", John said. "Agnes was eminently resourceful. He found her too in the end."

"He needn't search for us", E. M. said. "We're rabbits in his pen." John recalled that Agnes also referred to herself as a rabbit. "Where does such evil come from?" E. M. said, looking past him.

John hadn't noticed the picture on the floor next to the window. He supposed he'd gotten used to E. M.'s pictures turning up everywhere in the house. She often placed them where morning or evening or midday light illuminated them. This one was so different from her usual work that it immediately captured his attention. A thicket, a pair of red eyes—a wolf, practically invisible, lurking behind olive-gray foliage, watching, waiting. She had never before depicted menace in her work, but it oozed from this piece.

"Owen says evil is the failure to live freedom well."

"That's an odd way of putting it", E. M. said.

"I thought so too. But the more you think about it, the more sense it makes. The use of freedom—will and action—determines whether outcomes are helpful or harmful. When we use freedom poorly, harmful outcomes occur, for others and for ourselves. That isn't a bad definition of evil."

"It sounds like Owen", E. M. said. "I admit it makes sense."

"The last thing Agnes said to me was that she was grateful the field was won. Those words have haunted me; they still haunt me. What did she mean? How can a field drenched in her blood be won—unless she meant her transformation was a victory that not even death could steal from her?"

E. M. said, "Hers was an interior field, a place Alembert couldn't conquer, no matter what he did to her."

"I would like to believe that's true."

"I prefer to believe it. He hasn't conquered us, in spite of the misery he's inflicted. How narrow he is. I pity him."

"Pity? With all the malice he bears for us?"

"Yes—pity. He's empty. There's less life in him than in the pictures I draw. They have some dimension, at least. He has no dimension whatsoever. He's a mathematical point."

John visualized that point as a spider, a seething black ball, curled up in the center of a web. He remembered the spiders in his office and shuddered.

His relationship with E. M. had become complicated. In one sense, they'd never been closer: their shared mission to thwart Alembert, their fierce resolution to protect the children, a mutual recognition that they may not have long futures in front of them. On the other hand, John's secrets and his lies had built a wall of mistrust that couldn't be breached. He often weighed this against the additional burden imposed on

E. M. if he revealed everything. Good motives did not change the outcome: this wall.

"I'll make tea", she said.

"No need", he said, but she'd already left the room.

The moonlight on E. M.'s picture made it even more sinister looking. He wondered if his relationship with her would ever be what it once was. Though they'd been physically separated during the war, they'd remained emotionally united. Now, though they shared a home, there was an emotional space between them that affected every aspect of their lives.

One more time he debated with himself whether he should reveal what happened that night in the office. He reached the same conclusion every time he considered the matter, that keeping it secret was better than telling her. The revelation would have been bad enough if he had been the only one involved. The fact that Michael had participated would drive her to distraction. Still, he couldn't shake the thought that he was underestimating her. In many respects, she was stronger than he. E. M. surely suspected something, chiefly because Michael had been so close about what happened. John suspected she resented her husband's secrecy all the more because he'd recruited one of their children into his cone of silence.

The spider incident proved that Alembert was willing to eliminate him, or at least harm him. This meant that Gilbert's idea—Alembert needed to keep John alive—was no longer operative. He didn't believe that Alembert had abandoned his quest for the book. Rather, John entertained the idea that his death at Alembert's hands might convince E. M. to turn over the book out of fear that their children would be next. If John couldn't be moved—as Alembert's reasoning would proceed—E. M. could be. If this occurred, John would not be the only person who underestimated E. M.

Nonetheless, the idea of E. M. having to contend with Alembert demoralized him.

She came back into the room with a teapot, cups, and small cakes. He touched her hand when she handed him the cup. Was it his imagination, or did she withdraw?

"Are they sleeping?"

"Yes", she said.

"Michael too?"

"Michael ... why has he been having trouble sleeping?"

He sipped the hot tea. "Boys get strange ideas."

"What strange ideas does Michael have?"

"Who can say? I'm sure it will pass."

"I've given you every opportunity to tell me what happened that night."

He didn't intend to tell her, but he couldn't deceive her anymore, so he said nothing.

"I was thinking about our restaurant, our balcony", E. M. said when she realized he wasn't going to answer. "How we used to laugh. I wonder if we ever will again. I'm sorry; I'm tired of complaining. The situation won't be improved by complaining. I don't want to end up like that girl, John, but I'd gladly accept it if that would keep our family safe. Do you think your cigar-smoking tradesman will come to our aid?"

"He suggested the Foreign Office is looking over our shoulder."

"Do you believe him?"

"We haven't seen the watcher in the street for a long time."

"Do you think the Foreign Office is a match for Alembert?"

He didn't think so but said, "I imagine they can hold their own."

On so benign a night, with the moonlight and warm air penetrating the room, it was hard to believe that all was not well. Still, Agnes' death and the spiders were incontrovertible evidence that Alembert could operate in England whenever he desired.

John said, "Agnes knew what became of those treasures the night of the count's game." Though he'd related to E. M. the heart of his conversation with Agnes, he hadn't mentioned the questions she'd posed as she'd left the house.

"What do you mean?"

He repeated the questions.

"Do they make any sense?" she said.

"Not then, and not now."

E. M. said. "I'll call Agatha."

"Should we trouble her?"

"I'll trouble everyone from the prime minister to the dustman if necessary."

He got up, walked to where E. M. was sitting, took her head in his hands, and kissed her.

"I love you madly", he said.

"Do you—still?"

"Still, always, come what may. I'm not without deceit, but I'd never do anything to harm you, or the children."

"The wolf in the picture", she said. "We're riding on its back and holding its ears. We can't keep riding, but we can't turn it loose."

"No", he said. "That's the hell of it."

"We've involved so many already: the children, Owen and Jack, Gilbert. There are more than you and I at stake."

"Jack would be touched by your concern", he said, grinning.

"He needn't know. I'm certain he and Owen would do anything for us. Problem is, we need warriors in our corner, not teachers and daydreamers."

"Careful. I'm a daydreamer too."

"You used to be. You hardly mention the book anymore."

"That's Alembert's doing", John said. "When I think about the book, I can't help thinking about him too."

"Try to keep Michael and the others out of it", she said, still looking up at him.

"God knows I've tried. Michael overheard my conversation with Agnes, followed me, and defied me when I ordered him to go home. As it turned out, I wouldn't have managed without him."

E. M. bent her head and shook it. "Then I'm glad he defied you, God help me. A woman shouldn't have to choose between her lover and her children."

"You would have been proud of him. I was."

"I don't need to know any more. We'll make each decision as it comes, when it comes. It may be our fate to perish."

"That's more determinism. I won't accept a fate handed down by Alembert or any other man. We have more freedom than we think, and more friends."

"I'll trust your judgment, even if you don't trust mine", E. M. said.

He walked to the straight-backed chair and sat. "I trust your judgment more than my own, E. M."

She smiled at him. "How much time will Owen's gambit buy us?"

"No time", he said.

"Is that surmise or certainty?"

"Certainty."

"It was so bad that night with Michael?"

"If Alembert's using Owen, it won't prevent him from coming after me."

"If *I* meet him," she said, "only one of us will survive."

"Don't even consider that."

"Why not? It's better than waiting for his butchers."

And biters, John thought. "Don't ever put yourself in that man's hands, E. M., no matter what happens to me."

"It's too late for that", she said. "We're in his hands, and he's applying pressure like a vice. He's watching our every move—like that wolf."

"We're still together", John said. "We still live."

"I'm grateful for that. You're right; who knows what the future holds. He'll come when he will and how he will."

John was sure she suspected that he'd come already, but not with twenty-four legs. "The cake was good."

"Tea and cake are fortifying."

"Isn't it a beautiful night? I wish it would never end."

Though the lace curtains were drawn, they billowed inward with each warm gust. John and E. M. sat a while longer, and when something was said it was of little consequence. After midnight E. M. got up. "I'll look in on the children, and then to bed, but I hate to lose the rest of this night."

"I'll be in soon."

He sat in the chair for another hour, thinking about Agnes, E. M., the count's vault, and, especially, whether there was anything to be done that hadn't been considered. He didn't reach any conclusions, and he didn't bother to shut the window when he left the room.

May 10–11, 1932

Oxford

2:26 P.M. John read the letter a second time. "Meet me in your office at 9:00 P.M. or that meddling philosopher will be dead by dawn."

The time for withholding information from E. M., or deceiving her, had come to an end. He called her into the room and handed her the letter.

"Do you know what he wants?" she said, dropping the letter on the floor.

"Of course I do."

"You've put him off before."

"Not this time."

"What do you mean?"

"He won't be put off again, I'm afraid."

"What are you going to do?"

"There's nothing to be done. I'll have to go."

"I'm sorry, John, but that isn't encouraging."

"No."

"That's all? No?"

"That's all. He's pursued me, and now he's cornered me. If I don't go, Owen is killed. If I go, there's hope."

"There's no hope for me if you go."

He put his hands on her shoulders. She gazed at his face as if she were preparing to sketch him. Then she turned and left the room. He concluded that she was too troubled for further conversation, but she soon returned and held out her hand. Where had she gotten that shiny new pistol?

"Take it."

"No, E. M."

"For God's sake, for our sake, take it, use it, put an end to this nightmare."

"That won't put an end to it. A hundred men with guns will seek me out, and another hundred if necessary."

"A hundred men, but not that man."

"I have to do it my way."

"Your way has brought nothing but misery. I'll beg if I have to; take it with you."

"No."

Still, she held the pistol in her outstretched hand. Every feature on the map of her face was distorted with anguish. John still harbored the feeble hope that the sacrifice of his life would satisfy that dark god; he still believed that if he were to kill Alembert—an unlikely outcome even if he attempted it—or were to try to kill him, it would go worse for everyone in John's orbit.

"I can't", he said.

"Then I'll do it."

"You must think of the children."

"They need their father."

"They need to stay alive", John said. "This is the only way."

Her hand dropped to her side, and the pistol clattered onto the floor. "You and Alembert aren't as different as you think", she said, with barely contained anger. "Both of you are obsessed with that book."

How dare she say such a thing? Alembert was a tyrant and a murderer. John had a powerful urge to shout her down, to ridicule her, but as his anger waned, something, not necessarily conscious, validated her observation. He had been—was—obsessed with the book. He tried to convince himself that this obsession was noble, but he'd never been able to sustain a fiction with the headlamps of her eyes full upon him.

"The children mustn't hear us", he whispered. He remembered what Michael had done that night after overhearing John's conversations. Alembert was an even more dangerous spider. No iron poker could exterminate him.

She groaned, audibly. "You will take those principles of yours to the grave. A lot of good it will do your children."

Apprehension about his meeting with Alembert, and now this exchange with E. M., threatened to unnerve him. He tried to compose himself, but his body wouldn't cooperate. "You couldn't be more mistaken. If I thought that gun would save us, I'd use it in a minute. Get rid of it."

She slapped his face. The blow was not so hard; she held up at the last instant. She looked at him defiantly and left the room.

John stumbled to the straight-backed chair. That was an inauspicious ending to a conversation with the wife he might never see again. He reread the letter. It was an execution notice. Even E. M. recognized it.

8:21 P.M. E. M. lifted her chin and looked into his eyes. She reminded him of that Spartan mother, eschewing dismay, gathering herself for an ordeal.

"I love you, John. Remember that."

He kissed her.

"Come back to me."

He smiled, and it wasn't a forced smile. Despite what was ahead of him, he was grateful for the years with E. M., and everything that had come with them. If there were more years to come, all the better. If not, he hadn't been cheated.

He stepped outside and looked up and down the street, wondering if he would ever see that familiar landscape again. He'd made a point of seeing each of his children, telling them as much as he could about what they meant to him, but not so much that the older ones would worry or, worse, follow him. There had been days in the trenches when he and his comrades wondered if they'd see the next morning, but at least that harsh environment prepared the men for sudden death.

That evening, the setting sun bathed the street in golden light. He stopped at the bottom of the walk, well within the zone of aromatic influence of the buddleia, a magnificent arching shrub with white and purple flowers the size of small rolling pins. The scent calmed him, even stirred him. He stood there, not ignoring the somber mission on which he'd embarked, but turning a part of his mind, perhaps the better part, toward the beauty in front of him.

The sun had yet to descend below the horizon, and the bees and butterflies were numerous, especially the large black bees. Though he stood in close proximity, they were docile with a kind of inebriation produced by the nectar or the fragrance.

How could Alembert, with such a keen appreciation for natural beauty, be so dismissive of truth? He supposed he was like a man blind in one eye and with perfect vision in the other one, but he quickly dismissed this image because beauty and truth aren't separate, as two eyes are separate, but are parts of a single "eye" of the heart. He couldn't express it any other way. The matter went far deeper than vision; it went all the way to existence and will, to being itself. That was why, he told himself, his prospects would be better if he were entering a viper's den. For every move John contemplated, his adversary contemplated seven variations on that move.

A pang of imminent loss split his heart, so poignant that his determination momentarily wavered. He glanced back at the house and steeled himself. If they were to have any peace, any respite from the deep darkness that affected every aspect of their lives, he had to take this risk, even though there was little hope of success.

He decided to smoke a pipe. When would he have another opportunity? Would he ever have another opportunity? There was no wind to speak of, and the pipe began smoking right away. He inhaled and experienced the familiar calming sensation. There was time to think on his way to the office, but he didn't want to think. He wanted to remember.

8:43 P.M.   But think he did, as was his nature. Ideas stalked him. But he asked himself, what did the ideas he'd spent so much time pondering and debating, attacking and defending, matter now? Did materialism, or relativism, or utilitarianism matter, or even virtue? If he'd been more accommodating with men like Alembert, would he be marching to his death? He was wracked with what-ifs as he had never been before. As he faced his mortality, all the principles he'd held so dearly seemed a puff of smoke, like the ephemeral smoke his pipe emitted. Survival was what mattered. Was there anything at all he could say to Alembert that would prevent that man from killing him, and others he loved? Was it too late to surrender the book? Even as his mind was consumed with these questions, he knew the shame of his cowardice. Was he one of those so-called men of principle who went to their execution sniveling and begging rather than at peace? Even the fragile and fickle Louis XVI managed to die with honor and dignity; when the moment came, how would John respond?

The purest treasure mortal times afford
Is spotless reputation; that away
Men are but gilded loam or painted clay.

He knocked ash from the pipe and put it in his pocket. He turned a corner. Darkness had fallen. He could see the building, but it wasn't an object with detail and depth. How many times had he made this walk? He thought about relighting the pipe but picked up the pace instead. He knew how Louis felt in the tumbrel that day on the Paris streets. God help them both.

8:55 P.M. John stood outside the door until his watch told exactly nine. The familiar door seemed unfamiliar, even dreadful. It was locked. Not a hint of light seeped through the lines that marked the threshold.

He unlocked the door and stepped into the gloom. The shades had been pulled, something he'd never done. By memory, or instinct, he walked to the desk and turned on the lamp. Alembert was seated in the visitor's chair.

"I'm glad you are punctual", Alembert said. Then he got up from the chair and locked the door again.

"Before we begin," Alembert said, "I will describe the precautions I've taken. Not that I expect you to do anything rash, but one can't be too careful, and you have a headstrong wife."

At their previous meetings, Alembert had looked the part of the professor. There was no such pretense this time. He wore a powder-blue jacket and open-necked shirt with a pale gold silk scarf draped around his neck. His navy blue slacks were crisply pleated and cuffed. His shoes were wine colored and as polished as glass. His hands were expertly manicured, and he'd grown a moustache the width and shade of an autumn blade of grass. His thinning hair was impeccably coiffed. This was an Alembert John hadn't seen before, a regatta captain, or a prince. If he hadn't known better, he might have mistaken it for indolence.

John said, "What do you want?"

"No more questions", Alembert said, wagging his finger. "I won't be distracted. I must ask you to keep your hands in plain view. If you don't comply, it will be considered belligerence, and my response will be immediate and lethal. Not that I think it likely you brought a weapon, but the probability is greater than zero. More level-headed men than you have resorted to violence when in peril.

"You have noticed that the shades are closed. I don't want to be observed. I was disguised when I entered the building, and there are three men of irreproachable character who will swear I am dining with them in London. E. M.'s insistence that I met you in this office will fall on deaf ears.

"A dozen of my most trusted associates are guarding the building. Those who enter and exit while we are meeting will be scrutinized, and detained if necessary. I should add that, in a fight, each of these men is worth a dozen ordinary men.

"There is also this box. You aren't the only person who conceals things in unlikely packages."

John's pulse quickened.

It was teakwood, or something similar, six inches by eight inches, displaying brightly colored curvilinear designs, and with a fine varnish overlay. Alembert opened it to reveal six small darts with green, blue, and red tail feathers.

"I am an excellent dartman. These were produced by an associate, a South American native. He is an artist, but his art is functional—the best of both worlds. He taught me how to propel darts with breathtaking accuracy, if I may be so immodest as to say it. I'm not suggesting that much skill is needed to hit a target three feet away, but selecting one square inch of neck or hand adds sport to the enterprise. The tip of the dart is covered with a drug that produces effects indistinguishable from heart failure."

"I'm flattered that you consider me such a dangerous fellow", John said. "Is that how you killed Agnes?"

"She was contumacious beyond endurance. I mention these things so you aren't tempted to do anything reckless. It would be disappointing if this evening's activities were truncated. But I have not come to talk about that woman", he said, peremptorily.

A powerful sense of time and place came over John. Night had come, and with it the virtual timelessness of the period between sunset and dawn. Behind the shades was a leaky window. To his right were shelves in need of dusting and staining. Underneath the chair that Alembert sat in was the worn rug that had come from John's office at Leeds. On the desktop, next to the dart box, was the bowl of candy that Owen had so fastidiously packaged. Sadly, there was no more Socrates scampering about. The room was comfortable and familiar, down to every nook and cranny.

The man across from him would never be familiar, no matter how many times they met. How like the Traitor in the book this man was, with his mellifluous voice and hypnotically compelling reason.

"I will miss you when you are gone", Alembert said.

"I'm not contemplating travel."

"Ah, but you are, my dear fellow. And your family with you, and your friends too."

"You've threatened me often enough. I'm accustomed to it."

"I don't threaten. I state what I intend to do, and I do it. Don't deceive yourself that delay implies lack of resolve."

John closed his eyes and managed a smile. "Have you ever been sprayed from head to toe with the essence of another man, watched him disappear in half a second? Such an experience renders one impotent, or it steels him. Your worst cannot be worse than that. Your ambition is drawn in bold lines, but it has no color, no texture." He remembered E. M. comparing her pictures with Alembert. "The weakness you equate with virtue is a riot of color and texture. It's messy, I suppose, but it's endlessly creative."

"Cant and melodrama. Should I applaud?"

"You're not a young man. You will die someday—soon enough."

Alembert might have been debating a nuance of a lepidopteran chrysalis for all the emotion he displayed. "Is that intended to evoke repentance or conversion? Don't you remember that my father was a curate? I've heard that tripe before."

"What tripe?"

"Heaven and hell, ethics, virtue. Reality consists of interests, aligning and competing interests. History tells that story again and again. Your noble men are off the track of history."

When Alembert spoke, one invariably experienced the persuasive force of his argument. He did not pretend to be a virtuous man. Alembert embraced a definition of liberty that didn't recognize any restrictions.

"John", John said, using the name Agnes had revealed to him. "There's still death. Even your train comes to that tunnel."

Good. His adversary was surprised to hear that name. Alembert said, "And you, poor fool, believe that you will go around it. What do you hope to gain? And don't insult me with curate-speak. I know that creed better than you do."

"You know *about* it, but you don't *know* it", John said. How long, he wondered, would Alembert permit this repartee to continue? And what did John hope to accomplish by it? This man was the most ardent relativist John had ever encountered. There was no space whatsoever in his ethos for governing principles.

"I will concede one thing", Alembert said. "You are persistent. Is it the persistence of the man on the gallows? Are you trying to get the ear of the executioner? I'm curious. What did you think of those brown creepers I sent you?"

"We weren't compatible", John said. "We had a set-to."

"But how fruitful a gambit."

"It was a failed gambit", John said, struggling to keep his emotions in check.

"Ah, but those creatures opened the windows of two minds, yours and mine."

There was purpose in everything Alembert said and did. Where was this leading?

"You are confused", Alembert said. "Here is the explanation. If you hadn't destroyed the spiders, you wouldn't have thought to put a dead spider in a wooden box and post it to me. And if you hadn't sent me that package—a foolishly impulsive act—I wouldn't have been inspired to ponder the subject of anomalous objects in wooden boxes."

John forced himself to keep his eyes fixed on Alembert rather than glancing at the shelf. It had been a rash act, but John hadn't been able to resist the temptation to trump Alembert. Hadn't he learned his lesson, he told himself, when he had brought Agnes into his previous conversation with Alembert?

"And that idea reminded me of a wooden box on your bookshelf. In a moment of illumination, I asked myself what if, like this extraordinary spider in an ordinary box, the antiquity I was seeking was also inside an ordinary box—not a box that was hidden away but one that was visible and accessible?"

John remembered Agnes' description of Alembert's analytical reasoning, a process that seemed to be intuition. He'd just experienced how that process worked. Even after Alembert explained it, he couldn't see all the links in the process, but he knew that Agnes hadn't exaggerated. This man had been here one time, but he'd seen everything and remembered everything.

"I see I am correct. It's no use trying to disguise it." He walked to the shelf, moved the ladder, climbed it, clutched the container in both hands, descended, and walked back to the desk. No one other than John had ever handled it. Alembert placed it on top of the now-crowded desk.

"After tonight, you will never see this again."

Oddly, John felt no sense of panic or distress. As a matter of fact, he was at peace. If observed, they might have been any two colleagues engaged in a late-night conversation.

"What shall I find inside?" Alembert said, as much to himself as to John.

"Nothing that will do you any good."

"Ever the moralist. I prefer spiders to moralists. They are less pretentious. That reminds me of Agnes. Poor dear. Did you know she was a master with poisons? Did she tell you that when she visited you? I can't count the number of people she eliminated with her potions before she lost her mind."

"Was Christopher one of them?"

Alembert's nostrils flared.

"Even you, with all your money and power, can't undo death."

"How many times must I say that you are foolishly impulsive? It doesn't become you, and it displeases me."

"I'll run that risk. I found Agnes to be a delightfully intrepid woman."

"You should have seen her when my people finished with her."

"That makes you a savage, not a sage."

"You know better than that, John. Words cannot harm me, and they cannot save you—or E. M., or John, or Christopher, or Michael, or the baby—"

"Her name is Priscilla."

"—or Owen, or Gilbert. They are guilty too, by blood or association, and they will perish."

"Is that victory?"

"You ought to know me better than that. It is a reconciliation of accounts."

"You use logic to conceal brutality. You deceive yourself with the notion that you're posthuman, when there is nothing human in you."

"No one else would dare to spar with me like this. I am more accustomed to hearing pleas for mercy. I will hear them from you too before we're finished with each other."

John said, "I wonder if you will be able to manage without Agnes and Christopher. They were more than replaceable parts. Men like Krieger have their brutish uses, but one can't expect original thinking from them."

John was rewarded—or at least he thought he was—by observing an infinitesimal sign of pique before the mask descended again.

"Has Gregory been found, John?" John said.

"You attempt to rankle me. You won't succeed. Don't you realize that you're just making your family's end more excruciating?"

Alembert always held that trump. How long could John delay Alembert's playing it? He said, "Do you know that as we speak, a friend of mine—quite accomplished at this sort of thing—is removing your da Vinci from its hiding place, and quite likely other objects with it?"

"You are a shamefaced liar."

"Are you sure?"

"I am sure. If we were playing American poker, you would be all in, but you have no cards, and you know it. I do too."

"My friend left for Paris as soon as I received your letter."

"Your hypothetical associate—I no more believe in him than in an avenging angel—will be surprised when he arrives."

"Christopher will not be there to thwart him."

"Do you think one man is that important?"

"I'm beginning to wonder."

"You are desperate. You're clutching at straws and hoping to find"—he glanced at the open box of feathered projectiles on the desk—"a dart".

"May I smoke?" John said.

"By all means. We are civilized men. However, I will retrieve your pipe and tobacco." Alembert walked around the desk and reached into John's jacket pocket. He set the pipe and pouch on the desk, then returned to his chair.

"Do you keep the goblet with the da Vinci? It would be a shame to lose that too."

"I have heard enough. There is nothing new that can be said between us."

John exhaled a cloud of smoke. "You made Sir Richard into a beggar, and a beggar into a lady."

Alembert had both hands on the container. He looked up and smiled.

"How did you steal the treasure from the count's vault?" John said.

"What do you know about that? If I didn't have to kill you for withholding this treasure, I would do it for meddling in my affairs. For a teacher, you are surprisingly well informed."

"How was that accomplished?"

"You will never know the answer", Alembert said. "Insolence should not be rewarded. Now, see here. I have work to do before I leave this office. I cannot eliminate you until I no longer need you."

11:20 P.M. Alembert opened the container. He first removed John's bound translation and placed it to one side. Then he lifted the gleaming box and set it on the desk directly in front of him. There was hardly any of the working surface of the desk that was uncovered. He examined the box carefully, top and sides, but didn't touch it. He seemed so preoccupied with it that John wondered if it would be possible to reach across the desk and snatch a dart before Alembert noticed. Suddenly, John's adversary placed his thumbs on the imprints, and the lid came up in that splendid way that John never tired of observing. There was no evidence that this surprised Alembert. He lifted the book out of the box and proceeded to turn page after page in rapid succession.

12:17 A.M. When Alembert reached the back of the book, he leaned forward. "Were you able to translate these?" he said, pointing to a series of glyphs that ran down the page in columns instead of lines.

"No."

"I didn't think so. Is there explanatory text?"

Did what John say matter anymore? Eventually, Alembert would learn everything John had learned, and more. Unerringly, this man had found the part of the book that John never discussed with anyone—not Jack and Owen, not even E. M.

"There is."

"Have you translated it?"

"I have."

"Excellent. I intend to read your translation—now." He put the book back in the box and pushed it to one side, even dismissively. John was not surprised. Alembert cared nothing about the antiquity, just the content, just the information he sought.

"Did you realize that those vertical figures are descriptive equations?" Alembert said.

"So I suspected."

"Where did they come from? There is nothing else like them in the book."

Alembert had discovered all this in less than an hour. Agnes was right about his prodigious aptitude for processing information.

"They came from the realm of a person I've named the Necromancer. They were found in the desolation of his lands."

"Necromancer—how quaint."

"I chose it because there was no better word."

"What exactly was desolated?"

"Not an island, not Atlantis. A kingdom that met a bad end", John said.

"The book was discovered there?"

"Not the book; that was written a generation or two later. The particular section, or appendix, with the equations, as you called them, was discovered in the wreck of the Necromancer's kingdom. Someone appended it to the book."

"Who found it?"

"A viceroy of the king who reigned after the destruction of the Necromancer's realm."

Alembert retrieved John's translation and began to read, moving nothing but his arms and hands as he turned pages. Now and then, he tarried. For the most part, he turned page after page with such speed that John wondered how he could comprehend any of it. In the warm and silent office, John felt a powerful weariness come over him, but he warned himself of the peril of inattention, even for an instant.

"Tea?" John said, fighting the lethargy.

Alembert waved him off without lifting his eyes. As Alembert neared the end, he turned the pages more slowly. Once, he retreated several pages. When he closed the manuscript, he said to John, "I have been seeking this knowledge all my life."

What could John say that Alembert didn't already know? That John had done everything in his power to prevent him from finding what he had sought with such single-mindedness?

Alembert pushed his chair back from the desk and said, "Your so-called Necromancer was not a magician, as many supposed, but was what I choose to call a 'superscientia'. He didn't violate science but utilized the laws of the universe at a level that was unintelligible to those who inhabited his world. I doubt if the author understood this, but the person who was the story's source certainly did. Who was he?"

"I call him the Gray Pilgrim."

"Who was he?"

"A brother of sorts to the Necromancer."

"I thought so. He comprehends these elemental forces, the physical laws that constitute and sustain the world."

John said, "The Pilgrim and the Necromancer both belonged to an order of beings far more intellectually advanced than man. Does that give you pause?"

Alembert shook his head. "Than man ... what are you saying? It compels me to learn more. It compels me to decipher these equations, and then use this knowledge."

"How do you intend to use it?" John said.

Alembert ignored the question. He paged through John's translation until he arrived at the vertical characters. John had done nothing but replicate them—twelve pages in all.

"There are those who suspect that molecular encoding governs the growth and deterioration of human cells", Alembert said. "It's likely that this being you call the Necromancer had the knowledge and skills to modify this code, to accelerate or decelerate the aging process, to impart inordinate strength and vigor, to expand mental capacity, even to modify physical characteristics. Is that your understanding too?"

"In so many words", John said.

"These pages, when deciphered, will tell me how this can be accomplished."

Alembert had reached the same conclusion John had, but in minutes rather than years. True, Alembert had the benefit of the translation, but for him to have reached this conclusion in so short a period of time was breathtaking.

Alembert said, "The text that accompanies the equations—the insights of this Pilgrim—suggests that limits were imposed on the Necromancer's understanding of the universe."

"Yes."

"By whom?"

"That's a good question", John said.

"Do you have an answer?"

He had an idea, but he said, "No."

"I don't think you are being truthful."

"Are you interested in truth now?"

"In the pursuit of my ambition, of course."

John said, "Did you read the passage where the Gray Pilgrim compares the creation of the universe to a musical composition? That was the most intelligible and effective way he could explain the process of creation to that civilization."

"I saw it. It doesn't interest me. It's myth, not science."

"It interests me", John said. "There's a suggestion that there is a foundational melody, for lack of a better phrase, that governs the fabric of the universe—time and space and the most elemental forces. Using that image, musical instruments and song can be said to correspond to a derivative level of coding, the knowledge the Necromancer and Pilgrim possessed. The Necromancer and his kind participated in the melodies at this derivative level, but they didn't make the foundational melody."

Alembert said, "Who made the foundational melody? Do you have an answer?"

He did have an answer, but he said, "No."

Alembert was examining John as he might examine a beetle. "Where did they come from, these superscientiae?"

"What did you read?"

"They could assume human form, but they weren't men", Alembert said. "More myth, I suspect, to describe long-lived men of genius. The being you call the Gray Pilgrim suggests that the Necromancer was culpable for the destruction of Atlantis. Were the Gray Pilgrim and the Necromancer in competition with each other?"

"They sought competing ends. The Necromancer intended to destroy Atlantis, and he accomplished it, with the assistance of some of the Atlanteans."

"Why would they destroy their own civilization?" Alembert said.

"Why do we destroy each other? They were human. They were ambitious."

"When was this composed?" Alembert said. "The truth."

"Thirty to forty thousand years ago. Everything I've learned points to that era."

"So that is how Hermann and Erickson come into this drama. I suspected it, and I have long suspected that Atlantis is more ancient than anyone imagined. Your translation suggests that the destruction of the island preceded many of the events chronicled in this book."

"By thousands of years", John said. He could almost see the machinery of thought whirring behind Alembert's eyes.

"How is it, then, may I ask, that the Necromancer and Pilgrim were both contemporary with Atlantis and these much later events?"

"It's a question I've often pondered", John said.

"And your conclusion?"

"I believe the author recorded the truth."

"And not that there was a series of men that held titles that corresponded to 'Necromancer' and 'Pilgrim', as the pharaohs did?"

"I don't accept that explanation", John said.

"Do you think these equations contain the answer?"

"I can't say. I don't have any inkling what they mean. I'm not a scientist."

"If the Necromancer indeed lived for thousands of years—"

"Or longer", John said.

"—that would explain how so ancient a culture could have produced such marvels."

"The Necromancer was not an Atlantean", John said. "I didn't mean to suggest it."

"Nonsense. I do not accept your suggestion that the Necromancer and Pilgrim were not men. The Necromancer must have been one of that cadre of superscientiae—the Pilgrim was another, but a member of an opposing party—that formulated these equations and ruled the rest of their countrymen, and the world."

John told himself that if that was what Alembert wanted to believe, why dispute it? Still, why not keep this man talking as long as possible?

"I will decipher those equations", Alembert said. "You shouldn't have delayed me for so long."

"You're no different from those who served the Necromancer. Be careful that you don't come to the same end."

"That's unlikely. I've made provisions, and didn't I warn you against cant?"

John laughed. "Don't you think they made provisions? They were the world's overlords in their time."

"What else do you know about these equations? I have no interest in the adventures or cultures or moral conflicts."

"Nothing", John said. "My interest is in the adventures and the cultures and the moral conflicts."

Alembert loosened his scarf. He looked at John, deliberately and emotionlessly. He tapped the cover of the book. John was certain he was thinking in that ultracalculating way that portended trouble for someone—him. Alembert ran his fingers through his hair and said, "Now I will remove this treasure of treasures from your possession. You, along with your family, your philosopher friend, and that fat windbag, may expect a visit from my associates very soon. You need not worry about subtlety this time. The operation will be lethal and efficient. I can't afford to have any of you alive and at large, not with the knowledge you possess. I suppose that is plenty for one evening. I will spend the remainder of the night reading your estimable translation."

Alembert stood, reached into the glass bowl, unwrapped one of the sweets, and ate it. "I have a weakness for chocolate", he said.

That image—Alembert standing in front of the desk, the bright scarf draped around his neck, his hand touching the silvery box, those deep, dark eyes—was forever burned in John's memory. Years later, he "saw" it as clearly as he did that night.

In a matter of seconds, Alembert's expression changed from self-satisfied aplomb to confusion to distress to terror to agony. He tried to breathe, but nothing happened. Then he collapsed.

John didn't move. If Alembert had been any other man, he would have suspected a jest. Was he testing John? Why, when he already held all the cards? Finally, John got up and felt Alembert's wrist for a pulse. As unexpected, as unimaginable, as preposterous as it seemed, he was dead.

Everything had changed. Or had it? Had John's peril been eliminated, or had it heightened? There was the matter of Alembert's confederates who were stationed outside the building. What instructions had they been given?

He gazed at the dead man. That blinding intelligence was extinguished, as if the power cord from a lamp had been kicked from an electrical outlet. What had been a master of the world was now a lump of dead flesh.

John was transfixed by the body on the floor. So rapt was his attention that he might have been inspecting a favorite painting in the National Gallery.

The face was compelling, as if amazement had been etched, or a mask of amazement impressed, upon it. The eyes were excessively protuberant. The pupils were fully dilated, and hairlike veins radiated outward to the margins of the eyes. The flesh on the face had a distinctly yellow cast, with purple shading spreading around the lips and on the forehead and cheeks. The tip of the tongue slightly protruded from the closed mouth, like the tail of a snail from its shell. The ends of both ears were a bright crimson. John now saw that the eyebrows and moustache had been trimmed and artificially colored with something like theatrical precision.

As John's gaze descended from the face, he noticed that the gold scarf had cascaded on either side of the neck so that it gave the effect of butterfly wings. There was a rusty stain on the right side of the collar just below the chin that might have been chocolate or blood or both. One leg was bent with the foot tucked against the other leg. The jacket, slacks, and shoes were unaffected. The pleats in the dark blue pants, except at the knee of the bent leg, were crisp. The shiny burgundy shoes were unscuffed, and the soles, a rich sandstone hue, were like new. He could see one of the exophthalmic eyes in the mirror made by the surface of the shoe. The eye was disembodied: a wide-open, even sleepless, eye, made red by the light reflected from the polished leather. John had once looked into that eye with apprehension, or suspicion, or even fear. Now he couldn't have said what he felt.

The hands, both hands, were fixed in a rigor that reminded him of crab claws. All of the visible nails had a purple tinge.

One of the jacket buttons was in plain view. He bent to examine the insignia. It was a dragon and two swords, the same image he had seen on the letterhead on which Alembert had typed the translation of the cuneiform scroll. The image was so small that he wouldn't have been able to make it out without prior knowledge—such delicate craftsmanship.

Zeus had fallen from the heavens and been transformed into a mortal, and a pathetically insignificant man.

What had happened? Alembert wasn't a young man; had he suffered a heart attack? The box with the colorfully feathered darts still lay open on the desk. Had Alembert, without John noticing, touched one of them? He rejected that explanation. Was there another spider in the room, an outlier? It was dark enough, but John didn't believe that explanation either.

The green wrapper was within inches of Alembert's pale yellow hand. John took another sweet from the bowl, removed the wrapper, and broke the chocolate open. He took a sniff. There was a pungent odor he didn't recognize. Had something been added to the sweets? When? How? If a poison had produced these physical markers in so short a time, it would have been exceedingly potent.

His mind threatened to explode with questions and the number of mental knots he was trying to unravel. He was very tired, but he commanded himself to ignore everything except the perilous matter at hand. Had anyone else eaten the sweets since the student brought them to his office? He had tried to give them away, but there had been no takers. Not Jack, not Owen, not Gilbert, not Drake, not Michael. He shuddered when he remembered Michael reaching into the bowl. Had there been a threat more dangerous than the spiders that night in the office? Until that night in the pub when Owen repackaged them, they had been kept in the original box. Now that he considered it, he had no recollection of seeing that student before or after she gave him the gift. That wasn't unprecedented, but coupled with the fact that the only person John knew to have eaten the chocolates, Alembert, had died, it assumed momentous significance.

Had Alembert himself sent the box of chocolates, intending to kill him, or terrorize him by killing someone close to him? The spiders proved that Alembert was willing to do him harm. Alembert wasn't a careless man, but how could he have imagined that these wrapped sweets were the poisoned chocolates he'd sent so long ago? He must have concluded they'd been thrown away, since he knew that John's family and close friends were still alive. Perhaps the spiders were just act two of a lethal production.

Agatha—she insisted that a person's strength was also his weakness. Alembert could have eliminated John whenever he desired: a knife in the dark wielded by a master assassin, a bullet fired by an expert marksman. A colossal hubris fueled by colossal intelligence would not permit so pedestrian an end when it came to Richard Hope, the count, Agnes, and John. Alembert's pride demanded virtuosity. It was the demand for virtuosity that brought Alembert, personally, to John's office and to that bowl of sweets. In the end, the only person who was a match for Alembert was the man himself.

Something told John he wouldn't have to worry about subtlety when it came to Alembert's henchmen. How long would they wait before coming to find their chief? Should he call the police? That might afford him temporary safety, but he had no illusion that those men would be deterred for long. He was still a marked man.

Could anything at all be done? He'd already sat still too long for his own good. His nerves were like bow strings extended to the limits of their elasticity. He opened the desk drawer and removed the bottle of Macallan and the glass. He poured two fingers and drank. Better.

He looked at the body, and a ridiculous idea came into his head, an idea fraught with danger—the stuff of black comedy if it weren't so serious. Dare he?

1:43 A.M. John took a deep breath, got up, took hold of Alembert's wrists, and dragged him to the door. Alembert's scarf had come loose; John retied it around his neck. He unlocked the door and walked into the hallway. Only a few wall lamps were kept illuminated at night, barely enough to see. Calmed by the scotch, he walked down the hallway and went through an unlocked door. The room was even darker than the hallway. Could he be seen through the window? Not likely, as dark as it was. Gradually, his eyes got accustomed to the gloom, and he discovered that he could discern shapes by the light that came in from the courtyard. This room was used for storage, and he found what he was after, a wheeled book cart. The wheels made an awful squeaking sound in the quiet building, but there was no helping it. Any minute, he expected to encounter someone, to be questioned, or to be led against his will back to his office.

He recalled a night in the trenches when they were being shelled; walls were collapsing, and dead and wounded men were everywhere. Should they hold their ground, or should they retreat before they were killed or overrun? Afterward, he marveled at how composed he'd remained in that maelstrom. There was more anxiety after the fact than during the event. He felt that same uncanny calm now. Since he'd made up his mind, all the other mental pathways he'd been pursuing had shut down. There was only one path, and he was committed to it.

Alembert wasn't a large man, but he was bulky and heavier than John expected. John was out of practice when it came to lifting dead weight. Nonetheless, he managed to hoist the body onto the cart. One arm hung over the side, and both legs from the knees down.

The weight muffled the wheel noise as John pushed his cargo down the hallway. He had too much to do to be afraid. He opened another door, this one to the small service lift he'd found on his earlier exploration of the tunnels. It was a tight fit, but he squeezed inside with the cart. There was no light in the lift, and the machinery groaned as it descended. He contemplated what would happen if the lift were to stop midway to the tunnel level. What a surprise it would be when they found him. And what would it be like to spend hours or days in that dark space with Alembert's dead body?

The lift jerked to a stop. He'd been alert enough to keep his finger on the button that opened the door. He pressed it now, and the doors spread apart. He recognized the dimly lit tunnel. No matter the season or time of day, he imagined it would look the same. He turned right and wheeled the cart down the corridor.

His destination was not as far from the lift as he remembered. The furnace wasn't cold, but it wasn't blazing either. It had been used recently and hadn't completely cooled. John used a rag that hung on a hook to open the furnace door. Was the opening wide enough? There was an orange-pink glow inside the firebox. He saw some unburned rubbish inside, but it was mostly ash.

2:07 A.M. The enormity of his scheme momentarily arrested him, but not for long. He grabbed a coal shovel and began to stoke the furnace, hoping there was enough latent heat to support combustion. What would he do if there wasn't? He hadn't fired a furnace before; how was it done? After ten shovelfuls he waited and watched. He thought that the light was expanding. He dropped the shovel and walked to the rubbish bin that was located in the same alcove as the furnace. As he'd hoped, there were wooden crates in varying states of disassembly inside it. He retrieved a flat side section. It was rather short, but the other pieces would require a saw and more time than he could spare. He checked his watch. What if Alembert's men were to invade his office while he was away? How long would it take them to find him here?

There was no doubt that the firebox was heating up. He shoveled more coal inside; then he wondered if too much coal would overheat the furnace. He would take that risk. Better too much than too little, he told himself. The lip of the door was between two and three feet above the stone floor. Could he manage to lift the body that high?

First things first, he reflected. He set the wooden piece next to the cart. Then he pulled Alembert's body onto the floor. The sound it made when it struck the wood and stone almost unnerved him. For all he'd witnessed and experienced that night, this affected him more viscerally than anything else. He wished he'd brought the Macallan.

He told himself it was no time for wobbling. Positioning Alembert's body on the wooden pallet was akin to putting a cat in a bread box. Though the body was lifeless, muscles and tendons, not to say gravity, made it nearly impossible to shift the body's center of gravity to where he wanted it. Once, he tried to lift one end of the pallet only to discover it was too unbalanced to ascend more than a few inches before the body rolled off. Finally, he found some twine and tied the hands and feet together to keep them immobile, indignities that would have been incomprehensible an hour earlier.

By then, there was a blazing fire in the presumptive crematorium. It glowed red with a yellow aurora. Hell might be like this, he told himself. For good measure, John topped the body with a shovelful of coal dust. Then he lifted one end of the pallet and, with care and effort—the body was heavy, and the box was blisteringly hot—set that end on the lip of the opening. Once he satisfied himself that this end was stable, he went to the other end. Due to the inclination of the pallet, the body had shifted toward the lower end, an unwelcome development as the pallet was already undersized for its passenger. A full one-quarter of the body extended beyond the lower end. John decided it couldn't be helped. In spite of dangling legs, he lifted the lower end and walked the assembly toward the opening.

2:51 A.M. Nailheads in the underside of the pallet kept catching on the lip of the furnace, and he had to be careful to make sure his hands weren't impaled by the business ends of these pins. There came a moment when a third of the pallet was inside the firebox. He was unbelievably tired, tired in every sense, tired and horrified. He took a breath and charged forward, praying an errant nail wouldn't upset everything. At the last instant, he pushed with all his strength so as to launch the body as far into the furnace as possible. The last thing John saw was those unblemished soles. He stood and watched the pallet and corpse sink into a pool of fire and ash.

But the body wasn't altogether hidden or consumed—not yet. Anyone peering into the furnace could see a vaguely human form projecting above the ash line. The silk scarf caught fire and was gone. The blue jacket, now dark gray, began to shrink and shrivel. Soon it was gone too. He wondered what debris Alembert, a god among men, would leave behind.

John used the rags to close the door. There might be a time when he could reflect on what had happened and what it meant, but now was not that time. He put everything back where it had been. There was nothing more to do except hope that the furnace wouldn't be visited too soon by the tradesmen who attended it. The body would be discovered, or it wouldn't. He was filthy from the dirty environment and the work.

3:22 A.M.   He ascended in the lift and returned the cart, after swabbing it with a rag he'd brought with him. Then he spent a longer time in the lavatory than he'd intended. There was no removing all the grime, but he accomplished most of what he'd set out to do.

He reentered his office with a mixture of relief and horror. In his hurry, he'd left the door open and the lamp illuminated. The closed book was inside the open box on his desk. His translation was open to the page Alembert had been reading just before he died. The dart box was also open. The green paper Alembert had removed from the chocolate was on the floor next to the desk, where his lifeless hand had so recently been. Anyone could have entered the room and taken the box and book and translation. If Alembert's confederates had come while he was away, they would have known something was amiss.

He immediately closed and locked the door. He was grateful that Alembert had pulled the shades. John hid the box with the darts behind a book on the shelf. Then he returned the book, translation, box, and container to their accustomed place on the top shelf.

Had he ever been so weary? If so, he couldn't remember when. He knew that E. M. hadn't slept a wink; what was she thinking? She'd begged him to come back to her. He couldn't do that—not yet. There was another scene to be played, and it would take everything he had to see it through.

3:59 A.M. John retrieved three books from the shelf and placed them on the desk. He unlocked and opened the door. He lifted the shades. Not long now until morning. He sat down and began to compose the next day's lesson.

May 11, 1932

Oxford

They came in without a knock or a greeting, but John was too tired to worry about decorum. To be allowed to live would be enough, and that would largely depend on what he said and did.

There were four of them. Leading the group was a dark-skinned man of forty to fifty years old. A prematurely graying Jacob Basile was next. Naturally, John was surprised to see him, but he wasn't surprised that Basile had been drawn to Alembert. The third man was large and clean-shaven, with short reddish hair and a face that reminded John of someone, or something. The fourth man, who shut the door after they entered, was young and blond haired, handsome to dashing. John had never seen him before. They were all impeccably dressed in Savile Row suits and silk ties.

To a casual observer, this was a most ordinary office, and these men spent little time examining it. At first glance, and even upon closer inspection, there was nothing to recommend it: old furniture, books haphazardly stacked, flaking paint, and corners needing dusting. And yet John saw something different when he gazed about: there the container housing the greatest treasure in the history of the world; there an enormous spider had erupted from a niche in the shelf; there an Englishman of uncommon character and valor had sat and puffed on a cigar; there Michael had stalked one of Alembert's eight-legged assassins; there

Gilbert had burst into the room in a dire moment; there Alembert had fallen and expired; and there, and there, and there, Socrates had roamed and played.

"Do you remember me, Professor?" Basile said.

"Of course, Jacob. I'm glad to see you again." John stood and extended a hand. Basile took it cautiously. Would their past relationship make this easier or more difficult? "Jacob, are you going to introduce me to your colleagues?"

Before Basile could answer, the dark man, who John judged to have an Indian accent, said, "Where can we find another chair?"

"Professor Williams is across the hall. He's away and never locks his office. He has several."

"One will be enough", the dark man said. Then he turned and said to the blond man, "Anton, bring it here."

John sat down again. "You are welcome, of course, but I don't recall a meeting having been scheduled. It's quite possible I've forgotten, as I was up all night. Can you refresh my memory?"

"Your memory isn't faulty. We are here to learn what happened last night", the dark man said.

"May I ask what business it is of yours?" John said, determined to play the role of an innocent, even oblivious, teacher.

"You may", Basile said, preempting his colleague. "We're associates of the man you met last night. We're interested in locating him."

Anton returned with a chair and closed the door. The dark man and Basile sat, while Anton and the big man stood behind them. The latter, John was now certain, he had met before, but he could not place when or where.

Basile said, "Professor, may we ask you some questions?" These were courteous words, but there was an undercurrent that suggested questions would be asked—and better be answered—whether John minded or not.

"I'll help as I can. I hope he turns up soon."

"Of course he will", Basile said. "These are just precautions. Tell me why he came here."

If they knew everything, or close to everything, he was doomed. He would have to trust that Alembert had told these men only what they needed to know and had kept the rest to himself. That would have been in character. Thus, John would have to parse every answer with half-truths, not bold-faced lies.

"He came for an urn."

"Why did he want this urn?" the dark man asked.

"You must know that Alembert has a keen interest in antiquities. He believes this urn is connected to a civilization that interests him, a very ancient civilization."

The two seated men looked at each other knowingly.

"Do you possess this urn?" Basile said.

"My heavens, no. My stock and trade is philology. I don't have the time, the money, or the inclination for that sort of thing."

"Then you must know the person who has it", the dark man said.

"That's right."

"May we have the name?" It was a question that sounded like a command.

John said, "That's the reason he visited me, to learn the man's name. The person who has the urn is a friend. He's also someone who values privacy. I was prepared to supply the man's name to your associate, and still am, because of his longstanding interest in the antiquity. Since you have no such interest, and Alembert left before learning the man's identity, I must decline to give you his name."

"Not an entirely satisfactory answer, Professor", Basile said. "When did Professor Alembert arrive at your office?"

"I can't say. He was already here when I arrived." They knew that, of course.

"And the time of your arrival?" Basile said.

If they were among those guarding the building, they knew exactly when he arrived, and probably when he left his home. "It was a few minutes before nine."

"So it was", Basile said, giving him a sly look. "Please describe his attire."

Interrogation now, John said to himself. He'd wondered how long it would take. "He wore a blue coat and a gold scarf. I could tell you more, but that should suffice to convince you he was here."

"You have a sterling reputation", Basile said. "We don't doubt a thing you've said. It's a formality, really, standard questions—that sort of thing."

"I understand."

"Did he bring anything with him?" the dark one asked.

"Yes, a fascinating little box."

"What was inside it?"

Almost certainly, they would know what was inside the box. And why would Alembert bring it unless there might be a need for its cargo? They would also have observed that the shades were closed last night and would have known, or concluded, that it was more than a routine business meeting.

"I sensed that something of value was in the box, perhaps an antiquity. I was hoping to learn what it was. Alembert seemed to value it." John was trying to see as far ahead as possible, but there were too many interrogatory paths these men could follow.

"What was inside it?" the dark man repeated.

"I never found out. He left before its contents were revealed. I'm weary, gentlemen. Do you mind if I open the window?"

"Suit yourself", the dark man said.

He threw up the sash and glanced upon a lovely spring morning with plenty of birds on the wing and people walking on the grounds. How he wished he was out there with them.

He caught a whiff of something. Good heavens, he thought. Was it his imagination? It was ever so faint, but that cloying sweetness was something he'd never forget—the charred bodies in the war. Still, it wasn't unprecedented for pungent odors to emanate from the stack. Would this be so accepted, and who else would notice? Or was it a figment of his imagination, an apprehension or a pang of conscience, something like Poe's heart behind the wall?

"We are busy men", the dark man said.

"I'm sorry", John said, returning to his chair. He couldn't afford to be distracted, but the odor was so unexpected and startling that it was impossible to ignore. "You were saying?"

"Why did Professor Alembert leave?"

John knew that the credibility of his answer to this question would largely determine his fate, at least his immediate fate. He'd been pondering a reply, sub rosa, ever since his plan for disposing of the body was hatched. "He told me he'd seen someone he'd recognized, or thought he did, on his way to my office and that this person was probably disguised. I got the impression he didn't want to meet this person. He asked me if there was a way out, apart from the building doors."

The look of consternation on the men's faces confirmed they didn't know about the tunnels. Good. Capital.

"And is there such an exit?" Basile said.

"There is. There's a tunnel beneath the building that can be accessed by a stair down the hall. I guided him to it and told him how he could traverse the tunnel to the Biological Sciences Library. That building is blocks from here. Alembert seemed delighted to learn this."

"Did you see this mysterious person Professor Alembert was trying to avoid?" asked the dark man.

"No. Of course, I can't say for sure, but I had the impression it might have been a government man, maybe Foreign Office. That's just a guess, mind you."

"What made you conclude that?"

Careful, John warned himself. "It wasn't a conclusion so much as surmise. I don't remember everything, but I thought he used the word 'agent' in referring to this person. I realize that could mean any number of things. That's the conclusion I drew, at any rate." Too much detail and too many words, he told himself; tell them only what you must.

"Could this agent have been foreign, not British?" Basile said.

"I suppose so", John said. "I didn't actually see the man—or woman."

"German?"

"I have no reason to think it."

"Did you see any strangers in the building earlier in the day?" Basile said.

He warned himself to be precise, for surely they knew his itinerary. At length, he said, "No. It was rather quiet, but I was in the office only until noon. I went home and didn't return until nine." He wondered if they would ask about Agnes' visit to his home, and a part of his mind was pondering how he would answer.

"Did he eat or drink anything while he was here?" Basile said.

The bowl of sweets was where it had been for weeks, and had been last night. What if one of these men were to eat a chocolate? Let John try to talk his way out of that. He wasn't half as alert or crafty as he made himself out to be. First the smoke from the furnace, and now these sweets.

"No," John said.

"What time did you show Professor Alembert the tunnel?" the dark man asked.

John was still staring at the sweets. "About eleven, I'd guess."

No one spoke until the big man by the door said, "He told us—"

"Shut up", the dark man said, smartly.

At last John recognized the large man, though he'd sheared his hair and beard and traded his rustic clothing for an expensive suit. This was Gosdier Jones. So it hadn't been a chance meeting in those northern hills; the backwoods philosopher he'd met was another soldier in Alembert's army. John remembered that even on that summer day he'd been suspicious, but as time passed those suspicions receded. The delay this line of thinking produced caused the two seated men to observe John with heightened interest, like eagles watching a rabbit. Their eyes bored into John's, but intimidation had been practiced on him by a more capable man than these two. He met their gaze, though he could hardly hold his eyes open.

Basile said, "Are there any unoccupied rooms on this floor?"

John said, "There's a room used for storage. It's three doors to the right." He could not help but wonder if anything had dropped from Alembert's pockets or whether gold or blue threads might have been snagged on the cart when he loaded and unloaded the body.

"Anton", the dark man said, and the young man left the room. Then he said, "There are men on the grounds watching us. Do you know anything about that?"

"I neither know nor want to know. I'm a teacher."

"A well-traveled teacher, a teacher with an interesting cadre of friends and acquaintances."

"Perhaps Alembert saw one of those men in the building", John said.

"You have no idea who these men are?" the dark man asked.

"None. I'd expect you to know more about them than I."

"If the Professor departed at eleven, why did you remain here all night? You look exhausted. One might say preoccupied."

John said, "It seemed to be a good time to do some work I've been avoiding. Alembert's departure gave me the opportunity. As for my appearance, I'm not that young a man anymore. I haven't slept. I admit to being tired, not preoccupied."

"All very tidy", the dark man said, rising from the chair and leaning forward. His face was just inches from John's.

John knew he had to bear down despite the oppressive fatigue. "I've tried, to the best of my ability, to answer your questions. I do hope you find Alembert."

"So do we," the dark man said, "or we will be back."

"Indeed. You're always welcome. Jacob, you could use more fresh air. You look pale."

Basile responded with a smirk. At that moment, Anton returned and shook his head.

As he herded the others out of the office, the dark man said to John, "Show us the stairs to the tunnel and describe the route he took last night."

John led them down the hall to the circular stairs. He couldn't make himself go down, not so soon. "When you get to the bottom, turn left, not right. Not right," he said a second time. "If you take the primary corridor and avoid the side tunnels—they are narrower—you will arrive at the library in about ten minutes. Then you can ascend the stairs and exit from that building. That's what I directed Alembert to do last night."

Down they went, like ants into a mound of sand. John returned to his office and immediately went to the window. With the wind freshening, the scent was barely detectable.

Soon after the men left, he exited the building and began what was normally a relaxing walk home. Today, he wondered if he could accomplish it, but he found that he was modestly invigorated by the activity.

He didn't make it to the front door. He didn't even make it to the walk in front of the house when E. M. came rushing out to meet him. She held him with unaccustomed vigor. She didn't ask any questions but just clutched his arm as she led him inside the house.

Their house. He hadn't expected to see it, or her, again. Crossing the threshold exhilarated him: the cool entryway, the sound of the children's voices, the familiar rug, and E. M.'s painting on the wall.

They walked together to their bedroom and closed the door behind them. She moved the chair from the corner of the room and made him sit, while she sat on the bed. Her palpable terror broke his heart.

"You haven't slept", she said.

"No."

"It was terrible, wasn't it?"

"It was tolerable."

"It was terrible, wasn't it, John?"

"Yes."

"The children want to see you. They knew something was wrong."

"I want to see them too."

"You managed to put him off?" E. M. said, apprehensively.

How much should he reveal, and how soon, he wondered. She looked so vulnerable sitting there. If he was the only one who knew the truth, then no one else would have to lie.

John made up his mind. "He's dead."

"What?" Her hands came spasmodically to her face, as if a puppeteer had moved them.

"Dead."

"How?"

"It's not a pretty story."

"I don't care."

He told her everything, including the interrogation by Alembert's confederates. "I didn't dare call you. Someone might have been listening."

She reached out and grabbed both his hands.

"I'm all right, E. M. It's not something I'll ever forget, but it's done."

"Do they suspect?"

"Of course they do. But they knew Alembert, and they can't imagine how a teacher could kill him, dispose of the body, and withstand their inquisition. If I'm correct—and I hope I am—they think that Alembert fled the building through the tunnels or was taken by men far more capable than I."

"Let them think it", she said.

"I've cultivated those suspicions. I won't pretend we're not in peril, but even the most intelligent and most devious of Alembert's men can't hold a candle to their chief— former chief, that is."

"You're free, John", she said, with visible emotion.

"How can you say it? They're ruthless, and they're not finished with me."

"I have a sense, a feeling, that Alembert's edifice will crumble without him." She lifted his hands to her lips. "I can't explain. I've never met the man or the villains in his service, but I don't think his organization will survive."

"Why do you think that?"

"I have this feeling—a powerful feeling—that it's like a beehive that's lost its queen."

Bees and their queen—what an odd way to put it. But the more John thought about it, the more sense it made. Why shouldn't they hope? For too long hope had been denied them.

"Will someone find him?" she said.

"It was a strong fire. The more time that passes, the less likely it is he'll be discovered."

"Was he wearing jewelry?" Leave it to E. M. to take the practical view.

"I don't think so. He might have had things in his pockets. The greater threat is the discovery of bones. I can only hope they will be so charred that they'll be mistaken for debris left over from the crates and rubbish. I don't suppose the men who tend the furnaces are that particular about what they haul out of there. There's nothing to be done about it anyway. Agatha would warn me against returning to the scene of the crime. I suspect that the building will be swarming with invisible eyes and ears, for a while at least. Needless to say, every move we make will be watched. We shall let this sleeping dog lie and hope for the best."

"I agree. Stay away from those tunnels and, especially, that furnace. Promise."

"You don't have to ask me twice. Everything—here and at the university—must be perfectly normal. The story I told his men is credible, if not likely. It will stand up, I think. They didn't catch me in a lie. At least I don't think they did."

"You're famished", she said, releasing his hands and walking to the door. He followed her to the kitchen, where the children had gathered. Priscilla climbed into his lap while the boys circled him.

"Are you well, Father?" John said.

"Yes. And how are you boys?"

No one answered him. They were looking at his face and clothing. They'd never seen their father so disheveled, so dispossessed of paternal gravity. He kissed Priscilla's forehead, and the boys came closer.

"Your father's very weary", E. M. said as she prepared the food. "Don't smother him." But her admonition was cheerier than the words suggested.

"Christopher, I swear you've grown an inch since last week."

Emboldened, Christopher said, "Father, who is Alembert?"

John glanced at E. M., who pretended not to have heard. "He's a rather disagreeable Frenchman."

"He doesn't sound French", Christopher said.

"I guess not", John said.

"Is he bothering you?" John said to his father.

John and Michael looked at one another. "You can say that, but it's nothing to be concerned about." He so wished he could tell them not to worry, but even with Alembert dead that wouldn't be truthful.

E. M. had the boys set the table, and shortly the meat and loaf were set out. John had hardly eaten in several days, but he found that his appetite had abandoned him. She made

437

him eat more than he desired, which he supposed was a good thing.

When he fell asleep in the chair, sitting upright with a fork in his hand, John and Christopher, on either side, escorted him to bed in the small guest room. How quickly they were growing, he thought, in the mist of fatigue that beset him.

On one occasion, he woke to see a figure huddled next to the door, like a dwarf cloaked in a shadowy mantle. Michael was keeping vigil. John almost woke the boy and sent him to his room, but he thought better of it. Michael had earned a sentinel's respect.

The next day, when he awoke, he was famished. For the first time in a long time, there was life to be lived.

PART IV

Illuminatio

May 10, 1969

London

John wasn't rich; he was merely famous. He'd been published. He'd written a story that captured the world's imagination. But as he told Jack and Owen decades ago, the world wasn't ready for the story as history.

John wasn't young, and neither was E. M. Her health was failing, and he was worried about it. What would he do? he asked himself. How would he go on without E. M.? They spent their days together in the house in Oxford, now emptied of everyone else. Mostly, they talked about things that didn't matter much. Occasionally, they recalled the ordeal that was once a constant preoccupation but now seemed so remote, almost like it had happened in another lifetime.

When John visited the Bird and Baby, it was with the hope of having a pint of ale without being recognized and approached by aficionados of his story, and being in the company of a cheery assembly.

On a lark, he and E. M. decided to travel to their restaurant in London, the small establishment above the street where they'd spent so much time when they were young. They'd heard the restaurant had changed. It was now a rock and roll club. If they arrived and left early, or so they hoped, they might be able to dine and reminisce without too much difficulty.

John was able to get them a table on the balcony. The place was even seedier than he'd feared, with the furniture worn—and none-too-good to begin with—grime in the corners, foggy glasses, and careless waiters.

No matter, John told himself. They hadn't come for the food, or even the service. And he'd made do in shabbier and harsher conditions than this. After he seated E. M., he said to her, "How are you feeling?"

"Well enough. I'd forgotten all the steps and streets. Now that we're here, it's hard to see anything of the old place in this ... new place." Her voice trailed off.

"This wreckage? It's a nice day, the balcony still looks over the street, and the birds still make a game of going from railing to sill. That's something."

"That's something", she said.

"Will you have a bite to eat?" he said.

"Do we dare?"

"We don't, but we will have to order something if we're to stay, and we're both too tired to move."

"We are that. Let's see a menu, and we'll order something safe."

He handed her a greasy card. "They appear to specialize in drinks, American cocktails."

"Here are cheese sandwiches", she said, pointing at the card.

"That seems safe enough. And a pint of ale should be manageable. Will you join me?"

"I will—a few sips. Do you remember the last time we were here?"

"It was 1927, or thereabouts", John said. "You recognized that fellow in the street."

She squinted and said, "For a moment, that feeling of panic came back. That rarely happens anymore."

It was a Saturday, and the street was busy with people, cars, and buses. The waiter sauntered by, and John ordered for both of them. He was a short, wiry man with olive skin, an unruly mop of dark brown hair, and a patchy moustache. If he was surprised to see them in this establishment, he didn't show it; actually, he didn't exhibit interest at all.

"You're certain you're feeling well enough to eat?" he said.

"Yes; don't mind me. Michael and John are coming for dinner next Sunday. Did I already tell you that?"

"When will we see Priscilla again?" he said.

"She'll be in Thursday night. She can stay only until Friday."

When the waiter brought the ale, he tapped her glass with his and said, "Here's to us." He took a sip, but she barely wet her lips before putting it down.

"Have you heard from your publisher?" she said.

"Be ever so discreet", he said. "We are two elderly people who have lost our way, remember? As for the book, it's doing as well as ever. Seems it's the rage with collegians. They're demanding more, but I'm not up to it." Perhaps it was the idea of appending the story that prompted him to remember how he'd destroyed those twelve pages of the manuscript a week after his contretemps with Alembert. As much as John revered the book as literature and as an antiquity, he never regretted destroying the material that so interested his former adversary. Who could foretell when another Alembert might emerge?

"I guess", he said, "we could have written another book, a story featuring Gilbert and Agnes and Christopher and Alembert—even Michael, if we'd had a mind to."

"That story is better left untold", she said. "How many of that villain's confederates survive, do you think?"

Time hadn't diminished E. M.'s antipathy toward the man who had threatened her family. "I can't say, I'm sure. It may surprise you—it surprises me—to learn that I often think about Agnes."

"I wish I'd met her", E. M. said.

Plates with cheese sandwiches were placed in front of them.

"It looks edible", he said.

"Eat it, then I'll make my decision."

"That old caper", he said. "Well, here goes." He took a bite and shrugged. "It will get us back to Oxford. As for Agnes, if she'd survived for one more week, she might still be alive. You were spot on about Alembert's empire splintering, and then crumbling, when he was gone. Men like Basile and his confederates were too busy propping up their positions and trying to stay alive to bother with us."

"Drake told you that, didn't he?" she said.

"Yes. That day, a month after Alembert died, was the last time I spoke to him, except for that Downing Street fete. Are you up to traveling, E. M.?"

She was old and sick, but that wasn't what he saw when he looked at her. He saw the young girl, the devoted wife and mother, the tender lover, the artist, the fiery adversary, and the friend—mostly that.

"What do you have in mind?" She'd taken only one bite of the sandwich.

"Somewhere we can warm our bones, but not a long journey. Nice, the south of France—somewhere like that."

"I'd love it", she said.

She would love it, but they both knew she couldn't manage it. A trip to the Riviera could be no more than a reverie, wonderful to contemplate but not something that could actually occur.

"If something should happen to me, you should go, John. A long trip."

"I will not."

"You must. It would make me happy."

He might have shed tears, but that wouldn't do, not here; and E. M. wanted him to be happy, not sad. "We're going together. That's settled."

"Let's sit and watch the people and let the world go by", she said. "They're every bit as interesting as the white beach smart set."

They did, occasionally remarking on someone or something that passed. They might have been sitting in a theater gallery for how little noticed they were by the passersby. John noted the isolation, the separation one could experience inside a crowded establishment or on a busy street, the anonymity of a metropolis. He supposed that serial murderers and other sociopaths understood this phenomenon, explicitly or intuitively, and used it to their advantage.

"I don't suppose there are cubes to be had", she said.

"Ha. You become a fiend with a hexahedron at hand. And we're too old to dash out of here before they put chains on us."

"Too bad", she said.

"Too bad", he agreed.

"Dear me", she said, above the din the guitarist made as he tortured his instrument. "I almost forgot the letter I received from Agatha."

"Is she well?"

"Perfectly. She asked if I was painting."

Her pictures had brought E. M. such joy. What a shame she wasn't up to it anymore. Now and then, she made a halfhearted attempt at starting, but she hadn't finished a picture in years.

They had been fortunate to get seats on the balcony; otherwise, there wouldn't have been a chance of being heard above the cacophony of the band. The patrons who'd been on the balcony had gone inside, leaving the two of them alone. John and E.M. were a little island surrounded by a sea of revelers and another sea of people on the street.

"She invited me to visit", E.M. said loudly.

"You ought to", John said, knowing she wouldn't.

"She sent something for you." E.M. retrieved a news clipping from the envelope in her purse and handed it to him.

It was a *Times* article entitled "The Great Gismondi Dies in Venice". He didn't know a Gismondi, as best he could recall. Perhaps Agatha had confused John with someone who knew this person; Agatha wasn't young either. He spread the article out on the table. E.M. was watching him, and smiling, in spite of the racket and the ludicrous sight the two of them made in that place.

The celebrated mime Michael Gismondi died at his villa in Venice on Friday last. Mr. Gismondi was thought to be seventy years old at his death.

His star ascended in the 1930s when he performed to enthusiastic crowds on the Continent. Mr. Gismondi was a talented mime, and his size—he was less than three feet tall and weighed no more than sixty pounds—enabled him to portray nontraditional characters, including the Steadfast Tin Soldier, Tom Thumb, and Pinocchio. He often began his performances by portraying Andersen's Soldier, standing motionless in the theater while patrons went to their seats, never imagining he was anything but a statue.

His early life was shrouded in mystery. He might have been born in Venice, or Provence, or Istanbul. He told associates he'd been forced to flee Europe in the late 1920s (for unrevealed reasons) and lived in hiding in the Orient for several years. Some claim he was responsible for cultivating the rumor that he had studied the mystic arts while traveling in the East and that his performing skills were more than natural. A source told the *Times* that the deceased acquired these skills as a street performer in Turkey and as an apprentice to a French illusionist. "Mika was a gourmand in every sense of that word. His tastes were anything but mystical", the source recounted.

Mr. Gismondi performed into the 1950s, when degenerative rheumatism compelled him to retire to Venice. He married three times, once to the French actress Angelique Glacé, who was more than six feet tall.

John had no recollection of meeting the man, though he now remembered reading about him. Agatha had written a few words at the bottom of the article in cramped script. John had to put on his glasses to read it.

"That door and that room were large enough."

What nonsense, he said to himself, removing the glasses and looking up at E. M. "Did you read this?"

She nodded. While he was reading, she'd been folding and unfolding the paper napkin. "The linen leaves something to be desired", she said.

The music, the clothing, the moral ambiguity—everything about this so-called culture repelled him, but there was the matter of freedom. He believed in human freedom, even when choices were wrongheaded or silly. The mindless drivel that passed for social discourse, even among supposedly educated people, however, drove him to distraction.

A couple was preparing to occupy a table just inside the building. They were noticeable for the differences in their ages and appearances. The man couldn't have been thirty. Though the woman took pains to disguise it, she was at least sixty, if not older. The young man didn't bother to seat her. In fact, he sat before she was in her chair. The picture of the two of them evoked something John couldn't immediately identify.

"Does Agatha's note make any sense to you?" he said.

She shook her head, conserving energy.

"Is Agatha balmy?"

"I don't think so. I'm sure she isn't."

He didn't think so either. He read the article again. This time, he had the sense he'd heard the story, or a piece of it, before. The sensation was not unlike the time he'd seen Gosdier Jones in his office: familiar and unfamiliar.

"That door and that room were large enough."

What was Agatha getting at? Should he telephone her? He supposed he could, but wouldn't she have called him if she wanted to say more about it? She was a mystery writer, after all; maybe she wanted him to make the connections and draw his own conclusion.

A midget; an accomplished mime, apprenticed to an illusionist, forced to flee Europe and go into hiding; a door and a room that were large enough.

"What is rattling around in that mind of yours now?" E. M. said to him. Momentarily, the music had ceased. Their waiter took advantage of the lull to ask if they wanted anything else.

"I'll order for both of us", E. M. said. "He's too busy thinking. Two hot teas, please, with sugar cubes if you have them—lots of them."

The man was evidently disappointed by the order. His forte was pints and cocktails and hamburgers. "It'll be hot water and bags, and packets, not cubes."

"Very well", E. M. said, though her expression suggested it wasn't well at all. "See that the water's hot, if you can."

In a matter of seconds, John moved the pieces of the puzzle to make a recognizable picture. It was a startling picture. "Bisco collected the treasures after the vault was closed up and climbed into the electrical enclosure", he said to

E. M., but he was really thinking out loud. "It was large enough for a man his size, especially a mime who was accustomed to being still for long periods of time. The heist has Alembert's signature all over it; the crime is inexplicable, elegant, outlandish. Hervé was an accomplice; that was why he was eliminated. Bisco, that is, Gismondi—or is it vice versa?—would have been eliminated too if he'd remained in Europe. In the furor after the treasures went missing, it would have been unlikely for the police to have bothered with a tucked-away electrical box; how could the treasures have gotten inside it anyway? The following day, when the room was searched from stem to stern, the police would certainly have opened it up. So, after everyone left for the night and before the police returned the next day, Gismondi, a.k.a. Bisco, exited the electrical enclosure and the building; Alembert, Hervé, and Bisco certainly could have compromised the vault even if it had been resecured. The treasures were turned over to Alembert, but when Gismondi saw what happened to Hervé—who had feigned despondency over his own lost treasure, the dummy—and the count, he decided to make himself as scarce as could be managed. We know that he wasn't safe anywhere, but I guess he was lucky. Alembert's death would have signaled it was safe to return."

"How original", E. M. said, conversationally rather than expressing genuine interest. Little that involved Alembert interested her anymore. Eliminating that man had been the *denouement* she desired.

For John, it was an altogether different matter. This mystery had resisted solution for forty years. Was there anyone, except for the three of them, who even remembered it? There were many images from those times that had lost none of their vividness. He supposed these memories had

449

been permanently colored by the danger he and E. M. had experienced and by the extraordinary charisma, the magnetism, of the people they encountered. He could see Agnes standing there in that imaginative uniform and cap, with a hand on the doorknob, apprehensive, anxious to depart, and he remembered the questions she'd posed:

What did all the treasures except one have in common? Answer: All of them were inanimate objects, except Bisco.

What object was materially different from the rest? Answer: The dummy. It was flesh and blood.

Were there any other doors in the room? Answer: Yes— the door of the electrical enclosure.

Had he, and Agatha, arrived at the true solution of that affair? He doubted he would ever know for certain. He now knew that the story he'd heard so long ago, Agnes' questions, and now this article—not to mention Alembert's predisposition for dramatic gestures—all pointed in the same fantastic direction. He thought he remembered Agatha telling them that Hervé was obsessively fastidious when it came to audiences encroaching on whatever stage he used for his performance. That fit too. Even a superior mime and actor with carefully varnished features would be recognizable as human at close quarters. As Agatha told it, there was also the supernatural aura that surrounded the Hervé-Bisco act, which was hardly surprising considering that it was not comprised of a man and a dummy but of two flesh-and-blood men.

John's eyes were drawn again to that discordant couple inside the restaurant, no more than twenty feet from their table. The woman looked familiar. In spite of her best efforts, she was probably his own age and as anomalous in this place as he and E. M. Rather, he told himself, she was more anomalous because by her dress and makeup she affected to look so much younger. She didn't fool John at twenty feet, and he doubted that she fooled anyone else. It wasn't that she was unattractive; it was just absurd. Her friend was a handsome youth with shoulder-length blond hair and a trim blond beard and moustache.

She caught John's eye. It was the shape of her face that made him remember, those classic lines that age hadn't erased. Could it be? He looked at E. M., who was sipping her tea and gazing at the street.

John bent over his teacup. He lifted a spoon and stirred the liquid mechanically.

"John, is that you?"

He remembered the voice and looked up at the woman. E. M. did too, with undisguised curiosity.

"Do you remember me?"

Indeed he did. At close quarters, he could see that the measures she'd taken to look youthful were heroic: her meticulously coiffed hair; good-quality jewelry, but trendy; facial surgery too, he guessed. But it was her ensemble, something a much younger woman might wear, that most unsettled John.

"Hello, Greta."

"Is this your wife?"

How could John forget how they parted: his promise, her kiss, and then that dash to the train? The memory still shamed him, even after all these years.

"Yes. E. M., this is Greta Erickson."

"It's a pleasure to meet you", Greta said.

E. M. looked at John with bemusement, no doubt wondering where he'd encountered this woman.

"Greta and I met long ago when I was researching my book."

"Did you ever finish it?" Greta said.

So she hadn't connected his book with the man she met in Stockholm. "Yes", John said.

"I must read it", she said. He was relieved she'd said it so perfunctorily.

Her friend was watching but gave the impression of being uninterested in making the acquaintance of a tea-drinking elderly couple. In fact, the man had turned around and was talking to two girls at the next table. As Greta's back was to him, he might have concluded he had a clear field.

"I won't trouble you long", Greta said to E. M., who blanched at the remark.

"Not at all", E. M. said, mechanically. It was clear to John that she was suspicious of Greta Erickson. Perhaps her intuition told her that Greta had been more than an acquaintance.

"As you see, John, I am still an Epicurean. It is more demanding as one gets older."

He smiled at her with genuine affection. "Are you still teaching?"

"The university prefers newer ... ideas. They have pensioned me. I would never have imagined such a thing could happen. There was a time when I could have had the biology chair at any college in Europe."

"The war should have taught you that every indignity is possible", John said, with a frankness that surprised her, and E. M. "The pensioning of unwilling professors is a trifle by comparison."

"And what about you?" she said. "Are you still teaching?"

"On a much reduced schedule", he said. A young professor now occupied John's former office at Oxford.

"And you have children?" Greta asked.

"Yes," John replied, "four children, all out and about."

"I was never so inclined, but I don't suppose that surprises you." She looked over her shoulder at her companion, who had drawn his chair to the other table, and sighed. "I ought to be getting back to Paul", she said.

John stood up and took her hand. "It was good to see you, Greta. Take care of yourself."

"You have a wide circle of friends", E. M. said as Greta returned to her table. Then she whispered, "She's a brassy old vixen."

John sipped his tea. Greta was trying to get Paul's attention, but not very successfully. The waiter placed a white towel on Greta's table. For a moment, John thought the man had inadvertently dropped his wash towel there, but then he remembered. Finally, Paul turned his chair around, but not before pinching one of the girl's legs. She flashed him a smile and slapped him playfully.

Their tea was tepid, what remained of it. The street was busier than ever: people readying for Saturday night festivities, going somewhere by car or by foot, attempting to make one more purchase before the shops closed.

"We ought to leave", John said, thinking about the hired car to the station, then the train, then another hired car. He would be tired by the time they got home, and the trip would be harder on E. M.

"When you're ready. I'm not in a hurry", she said. E. M. glanced at Greta Erickson and said, "She must have been a fascinating person—once."

"Yes", he said, standing up and offering her his arm. With difficulty, she got to her feet.

"For just one of those days again", she said, looking down the street a last time. She opened her purse, removed one white cube, and pitched it over the railing.

The two of them wound their way through the restaurant, unnoticed except for one pair of wistful eyes. When they reached the street, John said, "We ought to have brought our dancing shoes. The night is young."

E. M. laughed and gripped his hand more tightly. "I'm afraid I've misplaced those shoes. Now where is that blasted car?"

March 25, 2002

Saint Hugh's Charterhouse

The round-faced man with the bald head and large ears had the bearing of a bishop, was accorded the deference due a bishop, and was well acquainted with the joys and sorrows of his office, but when he looked in the mirror he saw an inquisitive and energetic porter. Sometimes he found it difficult to believe that he—*he*—had traversed the path from the Charterhouse to the chancery. He smiled at the idea that this evening he was making the reverse trip.

In recent days, he could not help remembering that long-ago night when he had escorted the old man into the abbot's office. Now it seemed that something that happened that night was the reason he was on his way to the Charterhouse.

"Are you comfortable, Your Reverence?" the driver said, intruding on these reflections.

"Very well, thank you, Benjamin."

"I understand, Your Reverence, that you were once a monk at the Charterhouse."

"Indeed I was. I look back on those days with affection." He'd lived in the cloister for seven years, until the abbot assigned him to the former bishop's staff. He fondly recalled Brother Leo, Brother Richard, Brother Lawrence, and, of course, the abbot, his spiritual father and the reason he was now a bishop. While he embraced his role as bishop wholeheartedly, there were plenty of days when he yearned for the contemplative serenity of the Charterhouse.

The car began to swerve, first a modest sweep, and then uncontrollably. It lurched to the left, then plunged down an incline before coming to an abrupt and violent halt. No glass shattered, but unsecured items rocketed about. The bishop's empty coffee cup glanced off his shoulder on its way to a collision with the dashboard.

"Damn that hedgehog", the voice from the front seat said, or moaned. "I ought to have snuffed the bloody bugger—begging your pardon, sir."

Perhaps he ought to have, the bishop reflected, rubbing an elbow that had tried unsuccessfully to pierce the door frame. "Are you in one piece, Benjamin?"

"I guess I am. We're at the bottom of a ditch. Lucky we haven't had storms. I can't swim."

The bishop wasn't thinking about swimming. Actually, he was relieved that both of them seemed to be undamaged.

"The bloody bugger! Beg your pardon, again, Your Reverence."

"Let the creature be. It's done now, and there's no permanent harm."

"I'll be canned on account of it; you can bet on it, Your Reverence."

"I'll see you're not. This too shall pass." That sounded preachy, something the bishop despised in others, and especially in himself.

"How far are we from assistance?" the bishop said.

"We passed through Horsham twenty miles back. They'll have to come from there."

"And how far to the Charterhouse?"

"That's the blasted sorrow of it all. We can't be more than two miles away."

"Please telephone someone to assist us, Benjamin. I will get out of the car and walk up to the road."

"Let me help you, Your Reverence", Benjamin said.

"Nonsense. If I need help, I'll call out." The bishop couldn't open the right-hand door, but the left was sound. He stepped out, glad the ground was merely moist. The depression was several yards deep. He was grateful that the vehicle hadn't turned over.

He had to use all four limbs to climb the incline, like a crab—an undignified posture for a bishop but good spiritual exercise, he told himself.

He reached the road. It would be dark soon. There was a band of orange-yellow sky to the west, topped by the invading gloom.

"Are you all right, Your Reverence?"

"Very well." The bishop looked up and down the road. He thought he detected a glow to the east and soon recognized the lights of an approaching vehicle. It was a late-model BMW, and it halted next to him, windows descending with a purr.

"Trouble?" a voice said.

"We've put our automobile in the drain", the bishop said.

A voice from below cursed and said, "It was a hedgehog what done it." The bishop hoped Benjamin's cursing wouldn't scare the man off.

Perhaps the driver saw the bishop's pectoral cross and collar. He said, "Can I take you somewhere?"

"That would be kind of you. As it turns out, I'm not going far."

"Is there someone in the car? Is he hurt?"

"Just his pride. Benjamin, here's a lift to the Charterhouse."

"If you don't mind, Your Reverence", the voice erupted like an oracle from the underworld, "I'll stay with this lame horse until help comes."

The bishop opened the door of the man's car and sat in the leather seat. He shook hands with the driver, a cadaverous man with an incongruous broad grin and blond hair.

"My name's Farthing—Bob Farthing", the man said.

"You're an American", the bishop said.

"Figure a man named Farthing from America."

"Let me guess", the bishop said. "I've made a hobby of American dialects. Midwest."

"Right. Now guess the state."

"I doubt if I can. Illinois?"

"Nope. Guess again."

"You'll see a great wall with a castled entrance on your left. You seem to be driving on the wrong side of the road."

"Well, there I go again. All the excitement about your car in the ditch turned my head. I haven't made that mistake in two days."

"I won't disturb you. Just remember the wall and castle", the bishop said. "It's hard to miss."

"I'll be OK. Guess again."

"How about Michigan?"

"Bingo. Ann Arbor, University of Michigan. There it is. Bless Pat, what a piece of stonework."

There they were. He felt as if he'd left yesterday.

"Are you some kind of parson?" Farthing said.

"Some kind. It was good of you to bring me here. Can I give you something for your trouble?"

"How about a farthing? Got you. It was no trouble. Is that castle yonder your destination?"

"That's just the entryway. Beyond it is the Charterhouse. You'd call it a monastery", the bishop said.

"It's kind of creepy, if you ask me. Indoor plumbing?"

"Yes. Ovens and refrigerators too."

"Well, what do you know. I'm in real estate, by the way. What a chore to list that old barn. Here we are. Want me to drive you up the lane? I might be able to squeeze through."

The bishop said, "I'm grateful for your kindness. I'll walk the rest of the way." At that moment, neither Benjamin nor Farthing inspired much confidence.

"It's no bother. There's no mucking it up on a one-lane road, Your Holiness." He laughed exuberantly.

In the space of ten minutes, he'd been elevated to the papacy. "I'd rather walk. I've been in the car a long time— from London."

"Well, Padre, nice to meet you." Farthing shook the bishop's hand.

"Safe travels", the bishop said, closing the door. He was thinking about the drivers who'd be sharing the road with Bob Farthing.

The bishop waited for the car to drive away before he started down the lane. It was gravel, well kept, with neatly trimmed edges—an efficient abbot, he thought. He wasn't in a hurry. It would be there when he arrived. His schedule had been cleared for this day and the next.

The one-quarter mile walk to the Charterhouse entrance was as pleasant as could be imagined. With the exception of a sore elbow, he felt good for a sedentary man of fifty-eight. The cut grass was like an expansive green carpet, now graying in the twilight. It was dotted with hares, seemingly oblivious to his presence. The pond midway between the road and the Charterhouse was unchanged from when he'd tidied it up. There was a big turtle on a log with its head extended but all four legs retracted.

He remembered the night John Hill rang the Charterhouse bell. What an ordinary man he appeared to be. He could see the old man standing in the portico with that wooden container in his arms, fagged from the long walk. At first, he thought the visitor might be a vagrant. They occasionally made their way to the Charterhouse, knowing the rule concerning charity to strangers. Not this man. He was neat and alert, in spite of his evident fatigue. John Hill was admitted, he broke silence, and the rest followed as eggs follow hens.

He remembered Abbot informing him that John Hill had died, hardly a year after the man's visit to the Charterhouse. It was only after the bishop went to the chancery that he learned who this visitor really was, a university professor and a famous author. He didn't give that enigmatic man another thought until the letter arrived on his desk announcing the old abbot's death and bearing another letter inside—a message from the abbot himself—to be opened by the bishop upon the abbot's death; that was seven days ago.

The abbot's letter recounted the strange story the man the bishop had known as John Hill told that night and the abbot's custodial role for the past three decades. He was placing the responsibility before the bishop. The bishop couldn't wait to examine the contents of the box.

They must have been waiting for him. He was a few minutes late, what with hedgehogs and farthings. The abbot and another brother were standing in the portico, characteristically patient. He took his time too, wondering when, or if, he would ever see these grounds again.

"Welcome, Your Reverence", the abbot said, as the bishop approached. The bishop shook hands with the two brothers and followed them inside. Who said one couldn't relive an experience?

"This is Brother Linus," the abbot said, "our porter."

Of course, the bishop said to himself. Every piece had to fit.

He enjoyed a simple but hearty meal with the abbot and three brothers, including the ale master, who provided a delightful draught. The abbot knew why he'd come. Nothing more needed to be said about it.

"You know your way, I believe", the abbot said when the plates were cleared and the others had departed.

"Yes."

"Don't forget the lantern. It would be wise to carry your own light, but you know that." The abbot made a little bow and exited.

The bishop was all alone. He walked down a long, windowless corridor, one of the Charterhouse's many interior passages. He could see, though the passage wasn't well illuminated. Oil lamps on the walls radiated a golden glow, as they had for centuries. At the end of the passage were branches to the right and left. The right-hand branch was another long corridor, but the left-hand passage was only ten paces long; despite the gloom, he could see the obstructing wall. He chose that path. When he reached the wall, he counted stones from the floor and from the right-hand wall. He pushed the selected stone. Nothing happened. Then he pushed harder with his undamaged arm; this time the wall turned in, complaining as it inched inward.

He stepped into the chamber and elevated the wick in the lantern to provide more light, as there were no lamps in the room. He immediately pushed the door closed, noticing that it was stone clad on the outside and wood paneled inside. He heard the closing mechanism engage and wondered what would happen if he couldn't open the door. Years or decades might pass without the door being exercised. Hadn't the old abbot written that he hadn't entered the room since 1979?

Over the centuries, this chamber had been used to hide sacred objects from the Vikings, followers of King Stephen and his rival Maud, and Henry VIII's vandals, not to mention the rogue gangs that achieved territorial hegemony from time to time. How many others had stood where he stood, and what had been their motivation and emotions? The gamut, he imagined: honorable, dishonorable, conflicted, terrified.

There was a niche in the wall, reminding him of a votive recess, and there was the wooden container he'd glimpsed thirty years ago, the same nondescript object the old man had borne. Ever since he had read the abbot's chronicle of what he'd learned from the old man, the bishop had desired to see this thing. The idea of something so ancient and so alien entranced him. He'd convinced himself it was time this historical, cultural, even metaphysical treasure saw the light of day. But before that, he must see it for himself, examine it, hold it, turn its pages. It belonged to him now. In fact, he harbored a sliver of resentment toward the old abbot for keeping it from him. He was the bishop, wasn't he? The decision whether to keep these antiquities hidden or to reveal them ought to have been his.

Yet the abbot had been his father, and later his friend. What had possessed the bishop to display so critical a spirit? This chagrin, however, didn't mean he'd reconsidered his decision. He still intended to convey these antiquities to London and announce their existence with some fanfare.

He lifted the lantern to eye level. The container was dusty. Even in this feeble light, he could see fine debris on the end that projected beyond the recess. The container would be bulky, but he thought he could manage it under one arm, as the old man had, and carry the lantern in the other.

Why did he hesitate? There'd been no hesitation when he read the abbot's letter and made the decision to come here. There'd been no hesitation on the trip from London. There'd been no hesitation when he entered the grounds and supped with the brothers. Even that unfortunate encounter with the drain hadn't deterred him. But now that it came down to it ...

The old man—John, his name had been John—had decided that these objects belonged here. John had sacrificed to bring them here, and if the abbot's chronicle was accurate, John had risked everything to protect them. But who was to say the whole business hadn't been exaggerated? Self-importance was a common-enough temptation. The story seemed to possess the aroma of truth, but could the bishop be sure? The abbot apparently agreed with John Hill. He'd had thirty years to reveal the existence of these things, and he'd chosen to honor the old man's wishes. Did that mean those wishes had to be honored in perpetuity? the bishop argued with himself. He wasn't subject, he told himself—and caught himself bristling again—to personal pledges or promises the abbot had made. It wasn't as if that man were the pope.

Not three feet from him and at eye level, a rather large brown spider was suspended from a single strand of silk. It was an ugly little beast, and the bishop automatically stepped back. How did the creature survive in this chamber? There were ways in and out, he supposed, if a thing was small enough. It wouldn't do to be bitten; it wouldn't do at all.

Better keep an eye on the lantern, he warned himself. If it exhausted its fuel, he would be in a bad way. There was the chain pull on the wall, but how long would it take him to find it in an environment absolutely devoid of light? And there was that spider to be considered.

The old abbot hadn't said anything about John demanding these things be kept here for any length of time, only that the old man had entrusted them to the brothers. Could it be that the abbot came to agree with John that these things belonged here—until a favorable day arrived? Well, perhaps that day was now. He set the lantern on the floor, stretched out his hands, and touched the container.

What you must do, do quickly. The words leaped into his mind. His hands retracted. This isn't a moral matter, he told himself. Why was he framing it that way? This was his property.

His property. Was that the problem? All things considered—not the least his own lust to see the treasures and announce them to the world—shouldn't he defer to those two wise men? He could do worse, he admitted.

He picked up the lantern. He knew that if he left this chamber, he might never return, that someday he might be composing a letter to his successor. He reached for the chain, but he was still looking at the wooden container. Would it do any harm to open it and see something that may have been seen by only a handful of people in thousands of years? Would it do any harm to examine the book, to see those ancient runes and images?

Later, he knew this to have been the most powerful temptation of all. He could honor John Hill and the old abbot while indulging his curiosity. But all the while that he was gazing at the box, he knew that if he were to open it, the antiquities would return to London with him and, ultimately, be revealed.

What a test it proved to be. Never before or after did he experience such a battle. He might be counted among the great. His name might be inked in books around the world—the greatest discovery ever made. In that chamber where the temperature never varied more than a few degrees, he felt uncomfortably warm.

He clutched the chain and pulled, the door ground open, and he stepped outside.

The abbot was waiting for him at the entrance.

"You have come back empty-handed", the abbot said.

"But enriched", said the bishop.

"By what you've seen?"

"By what I haven't seen."

"Then I am a caretaker still."

"With your concurrence."

"Of course", the abbot said. "I expected it."

"How could you have? I had every intention of carrying those things off."

"I expected it", the abbot said again. "Your man is waiting."

"Already? Thank you for the delicious supper." He stepped toward the open door, then turned around and said, "Would you ask the ale master to send me a few bottles of that nectar he brews?"

"Of course. Good night, Your Reverence."

It was dark now. There were two small lamps outside the door and two more on the interior walls of the castle at the end of the gravel lane. He thought he saw headlamps, though they were pointed down the road rather than toward him.

The bishop had no regrets as he walked down the path. He was at peace with his decision. Indeed, he hadn't returned empty-handed.

Benjamin was standing next to a Mini. Could the two of them fit inside that machine? the bishop wondered.

"I'm sorry about this clown car, Your Reverence," Benjamin said, "but ours is indisposed. This was the best they could do on short notice." He stepped aside to open the door. The lamps high on the walls of the castle illuminated the message on the side of the car:

Courtesy of Alembert Towing

A cold wind had started blowing, and the bishop decided that the inside of the car, no matter how cramped, would be more comfortable than the night air.

Benjamin muttered as he got behind the wheel. "Beggars ain't choosers. That's what the lad told me when I gave this machine the queer eye. He was a nice enough fellow, cheerful, and helpful too. What was the lad's name?" The car started with a rumble and a bang, then settled on a whiny equilibrium. "Gregory—that's it. Four generations of Gregorys. Granddad had a spot of trouble on the Continent and made his way to Horsham. The lad gives the brothers a hand when they need something mechanical done."

"He's a Catholic?" the bishop said.

"Not hardly", Benjamin said, with self-satisfied vindication, as he wasn't Catholic either. "The boy's granddad had a warm spot for the brothers, told the lad that the Monks in France did him a good turn once when he was in mortal peril."

The bishop couldn't help thinking about the chamber, the wooden container, the box within the container, and the book. It was just as well, he told himself. They would never have fit in this glorified golf cart.

They were rattling down the road. There was no question of sleep. They might as well have been in a lifeboat with this infernal pitching about. It would be a miracle, the bishop reflected, if they made it all the way to London.

Benjamin seemed to have accommodated himself to everything that had occurred that day. There'd been nary a word about hedgehogs since the bishop met him at the Charterhouse.

"I guess it's a mercy," Benjamin said, "when you consider everything that's happened."

The bishop smiled. He could not help but smile. "Yes, Benjamin. It's mercy."